"Go," he urged, even as he limped along as fast as he could muster. "Get yourself inside. I'll be with you shortly."

"I'm not leaving you, you silly man," she declared.

There went that warmth in his chest again. And he realized as they trudged along, getting more soaked by the second, that he was beginning to care for this woman.

The realization stunned him nearly senseless. But he had no time to process it. They reached the side door just then and ducked inside. And he found himself in a small, dark sitting room. And much too close to Margery for any coherent thoughts to take shape.

He stared down at her in the gloom, his eyes drinking her in as she removed her bedraggled bonnet.

"Goodness me," she said, laughter and surprise lighting up her face. "We're soaked through, aren't we? That was quite...unexpected..." Her voice trailed off as her gaze rose to meet his. Eyes widening, she licked her lips.

His entire body pulled tight as a bow. Ah, God, if she only knew what that small action did to him.

But perhaps she did. In the next instant her hands came up, resting like nervous birds on his shoulders. Before he quite knew what to make of it, she rose up on her toes and pressed her lips to his.

Praise for
Christina Britton

"First-rate Regency fun!"
—Grace Burrowes, *New York Times* bestselling author

"Moving and heartfelt."
—*Kirkus Reviews* on *Someday My Duke Will Come*

"Swoonworthy romance."
—*Publishers Weekly* on *Someday My Duke Will Come*

"Christina Britton proves she has mastered the craft of engaging Regency romance."
—*Shelf Awareness* on *Someday My Duke Will Come*

"Readers will be hooked."
—*Publishers Weekly*, starred review, on *A Good Duke Is Hard to Find*

"This was my first book by Christina Britton. It won't be my last."
—TheRomanceDish.com on *A Good Duke Is Hard to Find*

A Duke Worth Fighting For

CHRISTINA BRITTON

FOREVER

NEW YORK BOSTON

Forever
Hachette Book Group
1290 Avenue of the Americas, New York, NY 10104
read-forever.com
twitter.com/readforeverpub

First Edition: August 2021

Forever is an imprint of Grand Central Publishing. The Forever name and logo are trademarks of Hachette Book Group, Inc.

The publisher is not responsible for websites (or their content) that are not owned by the publisher.

The Hachette Speakers Bureau provides a wide range of authors for speaking events. To find out more, go to www.hachettespeakersbureau.com or call (866) 376-6591.

ISBNs: 978-1-5387-1755-4 (mass market), 978-1-5387-1753-0 (ebook)

Printed in the United States of America

CW

10 9 8 7 6 5 4 3 2 1

To my amazing daughter, who is
strong and passionate and
beautiful inside and out.
I'm so proud to be your mom.
I love you, baby girl.

Acknowledgments

A HUGE thank you to my readers. I am absolutely honored that you've embraced my Isle of Synne and its romantic misfits. Your support and enthusiasm mean everything to me.

Thank you to my awesome agent, Kim Lionetti. I'm so blessed to be working with you.

Thank you to my wonderful editor, Madeleine Colavita, and to Jodi, Estelle, Leah, and the entire Grand Central/Forever team. It's an absolute dream come true to work with you.

Thank you to the friends and family who continue to show me unwavering support and love, especially Hannah, Julie, Jayci, and Cathy. Through texts and e-mails and video calls, you've helped me so much this past year.

A special thank you to my late grandmother, who inspired Lady Tesh's "You'll all miss me when I'm gone." You were right, Nani; we do miss you, so much.

And, as always, thank you to my incredible husband and children. You have shown me in everything you do just how much you love and support me, even helping me create my very own writer's shed to work in peace (despite STILL not adding a sword with a hidden compartment in the hilt to my books—sorry, hunny). I love you so much.

Author's Note

A DUKE WORTH FIGHTING FOR is a story of overcoming the tragedies of the past to find happiness and love. However, it also contains content that may distress some readers. For content warnings, please visit my website:

http://christinabritton.com/bookshelf/content-warnings/

Affectionately Yours,
Christina Britton

A Duke Worth Fighting For

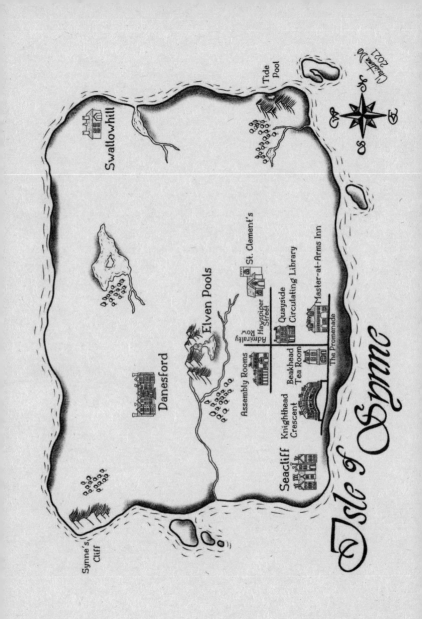

Chapter 1

Mrs. Aaron Kitteridge,

Your husband was not the hero you believe him to be. I was witness to his cowardice at Waterloo, how he ran just before his death, leaving his fellow men to die, turning traitor to his country. If you wish to keep this fact silent—as I'm sure you must, related as you are to a viscount and not one, but two dukes—you will pay to do so. I require the sum of one hundred pounds to make certain I don't send off letters to every major paper in the country detailing your husband's cowardly retreat. I shall give you a full month, until the first of October, to secure the amount; I shall write to you when the date approaches to instruct you where to leave the funds.

 Don't fail me in this.

Where in God's name was she going to get one hundred pounds?

The question had been burning through Mrs. Margery Kitteridge's mind ever since the arrival of the blackmail letter two days ago. It had devastated her, that letter. Not that she had believed for a moment that her Aaron had been capable of turning his back on his fellow soldiers. He had been the most honorable, the most courageous man she had ever known. It was one of the reasons she had loved him so.

But who could possibly wish to cast such a dark cloud on him? Who could possibly hate him enough to commit such a heinous act?

Had the person known him? Had he served in the same regiment as Aaron, sat at meals with him, perhaps talked and laughed with him? Her mind drifted to the veterans who had come to settle on the Isle of Synne after the war, to make a new home here. She thought of their kindness, their friendship and support. And, not for the first time in the past two days, she considered the possibility of one of those men committing such a horrible crime.

Her mind recoiled from the very idea. No, it could not have been anyone who had known him. To have known Aaron was to see how innately good he had been.

Regardless of who the blackmailer was, however, she could not let this villain lie and besmirch her husband's good name. No, she would fight to preserve his memory until her dying day.

But, though she tried to focus on the gaiety surrounding her—with so much of her family back on the Isle, this should be a time of celebration and joy, after all—there was no escaping the fact that she did not have the funds needed to pay off the blackmailer.

She could go to a number of family members for the money, of course. They would be only too happy to help her financially. But an image of her father rose up in her mind, his fury a palpable thing as he'd attempted to dissuade her from marrying Aaron.

"He will ruin you," he'd railed, his face red, his steps growing more agitated by the second as he'd paced the floor of his study. "He's nothing but a poor blacksmith's son, a simple soldier. You are the daughter of a viscount, the great-granddaughter of a duke. You would sink so low as to marry some *nobody*?"

Margery had grasped tight to Aaron's hand and smiled firmly up at him. His beloved face had been drawn with worry, pain etched in his gentle eyes. "He's not a nobody to me, Father," she'd replied with quiet pride. "Aaron is a good man, an honorable man. And I love him, with my whole heart. I'm going to marry him, even if I have to elope to do it."

"Then you are cut off," her father had snarled. "I disown you."

The words had cut Margery to the quick. Instead of crying and begging her father's forgiveness, as he no doubt expected, however, Margery had raised her chin, and with a shaky voice, said, "Very well. Goodbye, Father."

As she'd left with Aaron, however, her father had called after her, "You'll be back. If not to me for funds, then your grandmother, or your cousin the duke. This soldier of yours will break your heart and ruin you, mark my words."

Despite her father's proclamations, however, and despite the heartache the split from him had caused,

Margery had never regretted her decision to marry
Aaron. And they'd been happy, for what little time they'd
had together. When he'd died at Waterloo, she'd nearly
been destroyed from the grief of it. It was as if half her
soul had died along with him. In the four years since that
devastating day, she'd healed. For the most part. She'd
found meaning and purpose with the rest of her family,
those that had given her support and love through all
the joys and sorrows that had followed her elopement.
And though she missed her dear Aaron every day, she'd
found happiness in her place in the world.

Until the letter had arrived...

She shook her head sharply. No, she would not think
of that now. There would be plenty of time, after all,
to find a way to secure the funds. The portion she'd
received from her mother upon her death some years
ago, while enough to live modestly on, could never cover
the amount needed, but surely there was something she
could do, mayhap something she could sell.

Again her father's cruel words flashed through her
mind. Whatever solution she found, however, she would
do it on her own. She would not give her father the
satisfaction of seeing her crawl to any of her family
for funds.

Her grandmother's strident voice broke into her
thoughts then, blessedly distracting her from her miserable musings.

"And when will I be able to visit Swallowhill and see
the changes you've made, I ask you?"

Margery's cousin Clara, now Duchess of Reigate,
gave her husband an amused glance, her hand drifting
over her swollen belly. "Soon, Aunt Olivia. Lenora is

finishing up the mural in the nursery and we want it just so before we unveil it to you."

"Poppycock," Gran grumbled. "I've waited long enough. It's been over a year since you had the work started on the house, after all. And all that time while it was being done, with you traipsing about the globe and refusing to allow me near the place until your return, I've been patient."

"And we appreciate your impressive patience, dear aunt," Clara's husband, Quincy, Duke of Reigate, drawled with his easy grin.

"Flirt," Gran muttered, though her heavily lined cheeks pinkened. "Don't think to charm me, m'boy."

"I would never," Quincy declared with impressive solemnity, before ruining the effect with a wink.

Margery, her troubles forgotten for the time being, smiled fondly at the exchange and glanced about her grandmother's sitting room. Clara and Quincy, who had returned to Synne some weeks ago for the birth of their first child, were not the only ones present. Clara's sister, Phoebe, had just arrived that afternoon with her husband, Lord Oswin, as support for the soon-to-be parents. Margery's cousin Peter, Duke of Dane, and his wife, Lenora—who also happened to be Margery's closest friend—were there as well, their infant daughter, Charlotte, slumbering peacefully in her father's massive arms. And, of course, Margery's grandmother, the dowager Lady Tesh, was seated amid them all, her darling pup, Freya, resting on a cushion beside her. Miss Katrina Denby, Lady Tesh's new companion, was ever attentive at her side, as was Miss Denby's dog, somehow named Mouse, though the creature was nearly as large as a horse. Gran looked as pleased as any one person should. No wonder, for there was no doubt in Margery's mind that Gran had something to do with each happy union present.

Margery was thrilled for them. She adored them all, and knowing they were all so happily matched gave her the greatest joy. Yet for a haunting moment, as she glanced about the room and took in these couples who were so very much in love, Margery felt her loneliness like a suffocating cloak about her. Not that she was alone, of course. Not with so many of her loved ones surrounding her. Yet she was lonely just the same. She missed her dear Aaron every single day. At times like these, however, his loss was felt all the more, their stolen future almost too painful to bear. And now with the added grief of someone trying to soil his name? She clenched her teeth tight, her fingers finding the thin gold band that cradled her fourth finger. She would do anything to prevent that from happening, to keep these people who had supported her in her marriage in open defiance of her father from thinking even one unkind thought about Aaron.

"I do hope you're not planning on leaving again right after that baby of yours is born," her grandmother said, shooting Quincy and Clara a disgruntled look. "I vow, a year is too long to be off running wild while we're stuck here on Synne."

"Stuck?" Peter queried with a raised golden brow, looking up from his daughter's peaceful features. "I thought you loved it here, Aunt."

"I do, I do," she grumbled, waving a heavily beringed hand in dismissal. "But that does not mean I don't like to travel now and again. Not that any of you care a bit what I like." She sniffed, her offense palpable.

Peter, as expected, rolled his eyes. The two were ever at one another's throats—a pastime that seemed dear to them if the wicked joy they each took in taunting one another was any indication. He kept his voice low and pleasing when he spoke, however, the better to keep his daughter slumbering. A far cry from the gruff grumbling he usually adopted with the dowager. "We have only just returned from London."

Gran rolled her eyes right back at him. "That was well over a year ago, and you know it. And at my advanced years, goodness knows how much time I might have left…"

Phoebe exchanged amused glances with her sister before turning to the older woman. "Oswin and I will be heading to London for the return to Parliament in November, Aunt Olivia. We would be happy to take you with us."

"As if I would want to return to that dirty, smelly place," she scoffed. "And in winter, of all times."

That sharp pronouncement was met with faint amusement by most of them. The only one seemingly affected at all by it was Miss Denby, who bit her lip in worry while simultaneously shooing her beast of a dog away from Freya. Mouse had been enamored of the smaller pup from the moment he'd stepped foot—er, paw—in Seacliff, and that adoration had not ceased, but instead it only grew stronger. It was a comical thing, indeed, as Freya was approximately the size of Mouse's head, and seemed to view him as nothing more than an annoying gnat buzzing about her.

But while most in society thought of Miss Denby

as a stunning if flighty thing with nothing of any sub-
stance between her ears, she had shown over the past
weeks since taking her position that she was not stupid.
Having learned to take her cues from the rest of the
family regarding her irascible employer, she took stock
of the room and settled back in her seat with a relieved
sigh, her hand firmly on Mouse's collar, once it became
apparent that there was no danger.

"Besides," the older woman continued, her expression
turning suddenly sly, "I'm expecting a guest and won't
have time for traveling willy-nilly all over England."

There was a moment of stunned silence. And then
Peter's voice, overloud in the sudden quiet of the room:
"Who would be visiting you?" Wee Charlotte opened
pale blue eyes the same hue as her father's and scrunched
up her face in preparation of a squall, seemingly more
than happy to jump in at the dowager's defense.

"Peter," Lenora scolded gently, taking up her daughter
with a smile. "Don't tease your aunt so."

"Now, now, Lenora," Quincy said, leaving off whispering with his blushing wife to jump into the fray, "the
man has every right to be surprised. I know I am." He
grunted, grinning, as Clara elbowed him in the side.
"That is," he amended, trying and failing spectacularly at
looking contrite, "Lady Tesh doesn't seem like the type
to entertain." Doing a poor job of holding in his laughter
as his wife attempted to place a silencing hand over his
mouth, he continued louder, "Besides housing Peter and
me that fateful summer two years ago, I've not known
her to have any guests for a lengthy stay."

Gran glared at him. "I shall not miss your impertinence
one bit when you go sailing off again, young man."

"Yes you will," he quipped, giving the older woman another broad wink.

Clara spoke up then. "Quincy, darling, do stop antagonizing her. Of course Aunt Olivia has entertained guests besides you."

"Oh, really? Name one." He looked down at his wife with smug expectance.

"Well, there's..." She paused, blinking in befuddlement. "That is, there was that one time..." Clara frowned, looking to her sister. "Goodness, I can't recall a one, can you?"

Gran let loose a low growl that had her pup raising her head in confusion. "Oh, you all vex me so. Well, you may as well go right ahead and continue to make me the brunt of your jokes, but I know you'll all miss me when I'm gone."

It had been a common enough refrain in the past that it roused only the weakest responses from those around her. In an effort to redirect the quickly spiraling conversation, Margery spoke up. "But you were telling us of your guest, Gran? I vow, I'm waiting on tenterhooks to learn who might be visiting."

The others took the hint, thank goodness, and added their rousing curiosity. Mollified by what she must deem as appropriate interest, Gran's outrage melted away. That did not mean, however, that she had forgotten the effrontery of the past minutes. "Well, now," she said, raising her nose high in the air, "I'm not sure I want to tell you all after that display."

Margery knew her grandmother well enough to recognize that her ire had passed, and she now only held on to the remnants of it because of an excess of pride.

"Of course, it's your right not to say a thing," she said in a seemingly offhand manner.

Gran glared at her. "Oh no you don't. You won't get out of it that easy." She took stock of the room, no doubt verifying she had everyone's undivided attention. "You all, of course, know of my very great friendship with the Duchess of Carlisle."

Margery, of course, did not. She recalled vaguely that the viscountess and the duchess had exchanged letters sporadically over the years. The relationship between the two, however, never seemed particularly close. But she nodded and smiled all the same, as did everyone else.

Gran ran her fingers through the white mop of fur that topped Freya's head. "She wrote not long ago telling me of her poor health and a need for sea air. I, being the caring woman I am, insisted she visit for a time."

How Margery did not snort at that, she would never know. Peter and Quincy, of course, were not so circumspect. Blessedly their wives knew them well, and soon the two men were coughing to cover up their less-than-complimentary reactions.

"How wonderful to have your friend for a stay," Clara said.

"Yes," the older woman mused, eyeing the two men with a stern glare but blessedly refraining from commenting on their rudeness. "It will be a refreshing change. I do grow lonely at times."

Margery kept her expression serene, though she wanted nothing more than to sigh in exasperation. "You're hardly alone, Gran," she said. "I'm staying here with you, after all. And now you have dear Miss Denby and Mouse to keep you company. And with Phoebe and Clara and their spouses on the Isle, and dear little Charlotte beginning to visit as well, I'd say you're kept quite busy with company."

"That's all well and good," Gran said, "except everyone has their own concerns and responsibilities to keep them busy, and I'm merely an afterthought. Except with Katrina, of course," she grumbled, giving the young woman an arch look. "But I pay her to be here."

"Oh, Lady Tesh," Miss Denby exclaimed in her exuberant way, her pixie face alight with emotion. "I assure you, I would not want to be anywhere else. And neither would Mouse." She finished with a fond smile for her dog, who had wormed his way free of Miss Denby's grip and was prostrate once more before Freya, his eyes glazed with adoration. Freya, for her part, merely sniffed imperiously and turned away.

As Miss Denby continued to fuss over Gran—and Mouse continued to sigh in raptures over Freya—Margery tried and failed to stem her hurt from her grandmother's speech. The irascible Lady Tesh was deemed "irascible" for a reason, after all. She was outspoken on anything that vexed her. And there was plenty that vexed her.

Yet Margery could not seem to let it go. Though she had vehemently refused any monetary help—her pride would not allow her to do any less—Gran had given her unfailing emotional support. And not only during the falling-out with her father and throughout her short marriage, but also when she'd been left heartbroken and in reduced circumstances, as Lord Tesh had predicted. Margery had always tried to make certain Gran knew how much she was loved and appreciated. But mayhap, in

the chaos of the past months with Charlotte's birth and
Clara and Quincy's arrival—and, more recently, with the
arrival of the blackmail letter—the dowager viscountess
had become something of an afterthought for her.

As Miss Denby hurried away on some errand, pulling
Mouse along with her to prevent the beast from smoth-
ering Freya, Margery leaned toward her grandmother
and laid a hand over hers. "I'm sorry for deserting you,
Gran," she said quietly.

The older woman sighed and patted Margery's hand.
"I know you've been kept busy. And I would not have
you any other way than the kind, generous person
you are."

A sudden sting of tears had Margery blinking. Gran
was brusque and blunt, and quite the most opinion-
ated person Margery knew, speaking her thoughts often
without regard for the feelings of others. Though she
loved her family fiercely, affectionate words were not
often offered up. Which made that little speech all the
more dear.

She gave her grandmother a watery smile. "Thank
you, Gran."

For a shining moment the viscountess appeared completely overcome, her brown eyes, so like Margery's in
color if not in temperament, shining bright with tears.
But she was not one for the softer emotions. She
straightened, clearing her throat, and the moment was
gone, the stern lady back in place.

"That does not mean I am not vexed with you."

"Of course," Margery murmured contritely, fighting a
fond smile. "And I shall endeavor to make myself indispensable to you now that Phoebe is here for Clara."

A sudden crafty expression came over the older woman's lined features. "Is that a promise, my girl?"

Why, Margery thought in sudden panic, did she feel like a chicken being stalked by a fox? She cast a desperate, confused glance Lenora's way. Her friend stared back in a kind of surprised dread but could only shrug, seeming as bewildered and taken aback as Margery.

"Well?" her grandmother demanded.

"Er, very well, Gran," Margery said. "I promise."

The older woman grinned and thumped her cane on the ground. "Splendid."

As Margery managed a sickly smile, wondering just what she had inadvertently entangled herself in, Phoebe asked, "When is Her Grace expected to arrive, Aunt Olivia?"

Gran opened her mouth to answer. Just then, however, the front bell rang, echoing its sonorous tones through the house. Her face broke into a smug smile that seemed to hold a wealth of knowledge. "They're set to arrive now."

They all turned their attention to the sitting room door like a flock of...sheep? Truly, she was getting tired of feeling like a barnyard animal. Not one of them made a sound, their curiosity over this unknown friend of the viscountess a potent thing. Even wee Charlotte, who had continued to fuss despite her mother's rocking, fell silent. A low murmur of voices sounded, followed by several sets of footsteps coming closer, one with—an uneven gait?

Curiosity was palpable in the air. But for Margery it was more, a strange anticipation sizzling along her nerves. She clenched her hands tightly in her lap, trying to understand her baffling reaction. It could only be because of her grandmother's peculiar demand for a promise that Margery make herself indispensable to her. It had thrown her off completely. Though it must surely be innocent, merely the older woman wanting to make certain she was not abandoned. As if Margery could ever abandon her, as dear as she was to her.

That did not lessen the sudden unease in Margery's gut, however. It increased as the footsteps grew closer and she felt a churning in her belly. And then the butler was entering the room, a painfully thin, pale woman at his heels.

But Margery hardly saw her. Her entire attention had been snagged by the behemoth of a man that followed.

Tall and stocky, with harsh features that appeared chiseled from stone, his eyes swept over them all as if taking stock of a battlefield before a charge. He stood ramrod straight, his broad shoulders a tense line under the snug fit of his stark black jacket. There was nothing remotely soft or welcoming about him.

Yet, for the life of her, she could not tear her eyes from him.

Just then his gaze shifted to her. If Margery had looked up to see the ceiling opened to the sky and storm clouds raining electric jolts of lightning down on her she would not have been the least surprised.

"Goodness," she whispered, quite without meaning to.

Blessedly Gran didn't hear her. She was too busy rising to her feet. Flustered, Margery sprang up and assisted her.

"My dear Helen," Gran said with a broad smile. "I vow, you look just as you did all those years ago when you took London by storm and snagged yourself a duke."

"Olivia," the duchess said with a trembling smile,

rushing forward to embrace the dowager viscountess. "I've missed you these past years. How is it that time flies so swiftly?"

"I wish I knew." Gran's eyes shifted to the large man who had accompanied the duchess, still standing in the doorway. "And this must be your son. I vow, Helen, I did not expect such a giant. Well, then, my boy, come here so I might have a better look at you."

Margery, trying her best not to look at the man in question, gaped at her grandmother. She was just about to quietly berate her for her rudeness—truly, the woman had no boundaries when it came to speaking her mind— when she heard it again, an uneven thumping. Quite against her will her gaze shifted back to the man, only now noticing his limping gait and the heavy way he leaned on his cane as he walked.

How in the world had she missed the cane?

Now that she had noticed it, however, she began to see other things as well. Such as the deep scar that ran from his left ear, across his cheek, and curved down to his chin, just missing the corner of his mouth. There were other paler scars across the left side of his face as well. One dissected his eyebrow, another reached into his hairline, yet another along the line of his jaw. The man was a walking battlefield.

He cleared his throat, and she realized that he had been silently watching her reaction to him. He redirected his attention to the dowager, but not before Margery saw the wry acceptance in his eyes—eyes the very color of a stormy sky.

"So, you are the Duke of Carlisle," her grandmother said, craning her neck to better see the man.

"I am," he intoned. "And you are the dowager

Viscountess Tesh." His voice was dark, and deep, with a delicious timbre that was as rich and mouthwatering as the chocolate Margery drank in the morning.

"I am at that." Gran looked the man up and down, finally coming to rest on his cane. "Though we have something in common, don't we?" she said, tapping it with her own.

The entire room froze. Margery, stunned to her very bones, didn't have the ability to do more than gasp. Surely the man would not take such effrontery.

To her everlasting shock, however, his lips lifted in a small smile. "That we do." He held up the plainly carved bit of wood for her grandmother's inspection, and pointed out a bit of dull metal just below the curved handle. "Though I doubt yours has the bullet that lamed you embedded in it."

The dowager viscountess grinned and turned back to the duchess. "Oh, I like him, Helen. Yes, he'll do nicely."

As Gran turned to the room at large to make the necessary introductions, Margery was much too busy marveling at the change that came over his countenance to wonder at her grandmother's strange comment. His smile was warm, and open, and with the endearing crookedness his scar lent it, it had her stomach fluttering in the most peculiar way. She felt light-headed and warm, as if she had imbibed too much champagne.

"And this is my granddaughter, Mrs. Margery Kitteridge."

Margery flushed as the duke shifted his guarded gaze to her. She dipped into a deep curtsy. "Your Grace, it's a pleasure."

"Mrs. Kitteridge," he said with an awkward bow.

"I hear you're working up the nerve to take on London," Gran said with her typical bluntness. She quirked a thumb in Margery's direction. "My granddaughter will help you."

As the duke's eyes flared wide in shock, Margery gaped at her grandmother. "I'm sorry, what?" she blurted.

"Don't say *what*, Margery, say *pardon*. Goodness, one would think you have no manners at all."

Which did not help Margery's frame of mind one bit. She frowned. "Gran, what is this about helping His Grace?"

"Oh, but didn't I tell you?"

Which never boded well, Margery thought, feeling faintly nauseated as her grandmother looked innocently at her—or, at least, as innocent as she was capable of. Which wasn't much.

"No," Margery replied with a tight smile. "You did not." And a quick glance at the duke was proof that she hadn't bothered to tell him, either.

"I'm certain I said something about it," Gran said in an offhand manner.

The duke spoke up then, sending an apologetic nod Margery's way, a ruddy hue staining his cheeks, his discomfort palpable. "I assure you, I'm more than capable of making my own way."

"Nonsense," Gran said with a dismissive wave of her hand. "You need an entrance into Synne society, and I certainly cannot provide it, dedicated as I am to making certain your mother gets the rest and relaxation she requires. No, Margery is the only one available to help you. Besides, she has promised to be indispensable to me, and, by extension, you."

And there it was—the bit of slyness Margery had suspected was hidden beneath her grandmother's request. She very nearly groaned.

But Gran was not done driving the nail into the coffin. "It really is the ideal plan, for you both have so much in common. Margery's husband was killed at Waterloo, you know."

If her grandmother had slapped her, Margery would not have been more stunned. "Gran," she mumbled. "I'm sure His Grace doesn't wish to hear such things."

"And why not?" her grandmother demanded. "He was at Waterloo as well, and might have known Aaron."

Margery sucked in a sharp breath, her gaze snagging once more on the man's cane, seeing it in a new light. But she could not meet his eyes. It was not owing to any pity she feared might be present in his stormy gaze. What if this man had known Aaron? What if he had seen what the blackmailer claimed to have seen, thereby proving that the stories about her husband being a coward and a traitor were true?

But no, she told herself fiercely, desperately. Aaron was not a coward. It was a lie.

Even so, she was horrified to realize that the blackmailer had planted a seed of doubt in her. Her eyes burned with unshed tears. She would not let it take root.

The room seemed caught in amber, every person still and silent. Even Peter, who was usually quick to point out the dowager's shortcomings, was without words.

Suddenly the duke's deep voice rumbled through the thick tension.

"I am very sorry for your loss, madam. I wish I could say I knew an Aaron Kitteridge. Unfortunately, I did not. There were too many men on that battlefield, and far too many lost."

Margery merely nodded as relief flooded her. She should, perhaps, say something kind to the man to relieve what must be a highly uncomfortable, if not outright painful, situation. But in that moment, she was beyond words.

Blessedly Clara spoke then, her gentle voice like a soothing balm. "Have you ever had a chance to visit the Isle, Your Grace?"

"Er, no," the duke said. "If my mother had not needed this trip, I would not have come. That is," he continued, coloring, no doubt realizing just how rude he must have sounded, "I would not have thought of visiting. Rather," he stumbled along, "Lady Tesh has extolled the Isle's glories over the years, and a more detailed accounting these past months as she attempted to entice us to visit. It sounds like a lovely place."

As the rest of them jumped in, no doubt just as eager to see the conversation steered to safer waters, Margery took the chance to excuse herself under the pretense of checking with the housekeeper on the state of the rooms that were no doubt being readied. She was to assist the duke in getting about in society, was she? The very idea of being in such forced proximity with him made her nerves feel like tangled threads.

These next weeks would be interesting, indeed.

Chapter 2

*D*aniel Hayle, Duke of Carlisle, ran a hand over his weary eyes and stared morosely at his reflection. He'd been a fool to think this would work. It had seemed an ideal plan back at Brackley Court. He could accompany his mother to the Isle and see two things accomplished: making sure she began to heal from his brother Nathaniel's untimely passing three years ago, and to prepare himself for the necessary search for a wife, something he had put off for as long as possible but could ignore no longer. Unfortunately, his long-standing social ineptitude had increased exponentially since his injuries, and so a bit of practice at a less populous locale before tackling London for the first time had seemed ideal.

Now, however...

Blessedly a knock sounded at the door, stopping whatever self-flagellating thoughts had been about to fill his head. Wilkins, his valet, answered it, stepping aside as Daniel's mother was revealed. She greeted the valet warmly before making her way across the room to Daniel's side.

"Oh, don't you look splendid, darling. But I'm about to head down early with the viscountess. She's told me to inform you she'll send a maid up to show you the way to the drawing room. You will be fine, won't you?"

Damnation, she looked exhausted. These past years had been hard on her, first with losing her husband, then with Daniel's near-death at Waterloo and the months of painful recovery, and finally—and most devastatingly—with Nathaniel's death a mere year after Daniel's return home. Surely this trip would be just what she needed.

Yet the pale cast to her skin, the dark shadows beneath her eyes, the way her clothing—still the black of mourning—fairly hung off her small frame from the weight she'd lost made him fear that the road to recovery would be a long one, if even feasible. It was quite possible that, given the devastation she'd endured, she might not ever come back from the dark place her mind had sunk to.

But he would not consider that now. He forced a smile as she reached him, trying not to flinch when she kissed his cheek—his good cheek. She knew better than to get near his ruined cheek.

"Of course, I'll be fine," he replied, before frowning. "Though are you certain you're up for a dinner party on your first night here? Mayhap it would be best to take dinner in your room, to rest—"

"You dear thing," she said with a fond smile. "To worry so for me. But it's hardly a dinner party. Only the same people we met this morning, each and every one of them Olivia's relations. But Olivia is waiting on me. I'll see you downstairs." Patting his arm, she made her way from the room, closing the door quietly behind her.

Daniel pressed his lips tight as he watched her go. If she had thought to reassure him with the fact that only Lady Tesh's family would be present, she was sorely mistaken. Especially as he was not thrilled about seeing again one particular member of that woman's family.

He exhaled sharply, the image of Mrs. Kitteridge's stricken face when she'd first laid eyes on him searing through his brain. That moment, standing before such a lovely woman and seeing just how he affected her, had been torture.

And it had not been only her. Though everyone present in that blasted sitting room had been incredibly polite and welcoming, no matter his awkward blunders, they had nevertheless betrayed their unease with him in small ways, either by openly staring at him or pointedly not looking his way. The very idea of how much worse London would be had him breaking into a cold sweat.

Which was laughable, really. He was a hardened soldier who had never balked at battle. And yet the thought of walking into a London ballroom had him wanting to turn tail and flee. Perhaps if he had been more socially gifted before his injuries he might have been able to pass himself off as dashing in his battle scars, or might have been able to deflect attention from his appearance with a happy, open spirit. But no, he had never been that. And never would be.

He frowned and absently rubbed his thigh, wincing as his fingers found a particularly tender spot in the twisted flesh. The ache in the once-shredded muscles and shattered bone was much worse tonight after the three days' travel from Brackley Court. And a constant reminder that navigating society and finding a wife who was not put off by his awkwardness, much less disgusted by his appearance, would be no easy feat.

He was luckier than so many others, of course. A quick flash of that young man who'd stepped in front of Daniel's gun, inadvertently taking a bullet not meant for him and losing his life in the process. He let out a harsh breath, pain flaring in his chest at the memory, the echo of that boy's death rattle, his cries for his sweetheart, as clear as it had been four short years ago. No, Daniel could not possibly complain about the minor inconvenience of having to find a wife.

"Do you not like any of the pins, Your Grace?"

Wilkins, his valet, peered up at him anxiously, a tray of stickpins held aloft for Daniel's perusal. Having been valet to Daniel's older brother, Wilkins had been passed on to Daniel along with the rest of the Carlisle holdings upon Nathaniel's death.

Daniel would give every bit of it up if he could have his brother back.

He cleared his throat against a sudden thickness. His brother should be here now, looking over the selection of brilliant stones, preparing to descend below and charm everyone with his sparkling humor and devilish good looks. Instead it was Daniel forced to do these things, his too-large form poured into stylish clothes that he abhorred, steeling himself for an evening of stress and strain as he attempted to hide the glaring fact that he had no wish to be here.

He cleared his throat and forced his attention to the tray in the valet's hands.

"The sapphire will do, I think," he murmured. "Thank you, Wilkins."

As the man nodded, turning away to place the tray down, Daniel took the chance to move out of view of his image in the glass. Further perusal of himself would only hinder his ability to calm his nerves. Yet his leg didn't appreciate the sudden movement; it gave another protesting twinge of pain. Quite without meaning to, Daniel grunted.

Wilkins, having turned back to Daniel with pin in hand in precisely that moment, caught sight of his employer's unguarded reaction. He paused, holding the jewel to his narrow chest, emotions at war in his angular face. And then, the words bursting from him in a jumble, he said, "Are you certain you don't wish me to massage the muscle, Your Grace? It may help—"

"No." Mortification boiled up, making the word come out more sharply than he'd intended. Silently cursing himself as Wilkins drew back, Daniel gentled his tone. "That is, it isn't that bad, truly. I merely stepped on it wrong."

"If you're certain."

"I am," Daniel replied with a firm smile, hoping the man didn't hear the lie in the words.

The valet, however, didn't look as if he believed Daniel one bit. If anything, it seemed that hurt was now mixed liberally with the nervous worry that strained Wilkins's features. But he merely nodded and quickly went back to work.

Daniel, for his part, wanted to feel relief that their relationship, beginning to tilt dangerously into a more personal one, had been quickly righted. But only a regretful ache rose up in him. He knew Nathaniel and Wilkins had shared a close bond, and Daniel had seen signs the man would be only too happy to be a friend to Daniel. But he couldn't. He just couldn't. Letting someone in was just too damn hard.

Just as Wilkins was putting the finishing touches to Daniel's ensemble there was a quiet knock on the door. The valet once more answered it with alacrity. A young maid stood in the hallway.

"I've been sent to guide His Grace to the drawing room," she said, scanning the room with an air of anticipation. Her gaze widened when she saw Daniel, her jaw dropping open as she took stock of him, from carefully brushed hair to highly polished shoes.

Gritting his teeth, Daniel accepted his cane from Wilkins. Still refusing to look at his reflection—the young maid was gaping at his scars enough for the both of them—he set his shoulders and made for the door. "I thank you for your escort," he murmured.

Face flaming, no doubt at being caught staring, she dipped into a deep curtsy and spun about. Instead of walking at a normal pace, however, she moved almost comically slow, like some demented bride, shuffling one foot forward, then bringing the other up to meet it before moving that one on. Daniel tortured himself for a moment, wondering what stories the servants had passed among them to prompt such a reaction. Had they talked of him in pitying tones, the lamed duke who so ill fit his new position? The Ugly Dukeling.

He frowned. Such musings weren't doing him a bit of good and would make the coming evening, not to mention the impending months of torture as he attempted to secure a duchess, much worse than they had to be. Heaving an imperceptible sigh, Daniel attempted to focus on the positive aspect of the situation; the girl was giving him extra time to traverse the long halls, after all, and he should be grateful he didn't have to push his leg. But frustration had already laid claim to him, made even worse when he considered just who would eventually take over the dukedom should he fail to find a wife and produce an heir.

His cousin's face flashed through his thoughts, souring his stomach. Gregory had always been a wastrel and a bounder. Taken in by Daniel's parents when his own had created a scandal so horrendous it had resulted in the death of one and a flight to the Continent of the other, he had grown up alongside Daniel and Nathaniel, raised as if he were the duke's own son.

But that had not stopped Gregory's bitterness at his lot in life from poisoning his heart with anger, no matter that he was loved by his extended family. As he'd grown, that anger had manifested itself in cruelty toward Daniel, fights with the duke and duchess, and a bitter rivalry with Nathaniel that had lasted well into adulthood, resulting in Gregory returning to Brackley Court only when he needed something of the dukedom. Like a vulture looking for scraps. If their father had not forced a promise from them to watch out for Gregory, Daniel rather thought he and Nathaniel would have been all too happy to never have to deal with their cousin again.

Since Nathaniel's death, however, Gregory had begun to tighten his circle on Daniel, visiting their country seat in Cheshire County much more often, eroding what little remaining confidence Daniel had with well-placed comments aimed to do the maximum amount of damage. It was a painful reiteration of the abuse he'd heaped on Daniel when they were children, before Daniel had finally escaped by going off to war. Ironically, the effects of that decision were what now fueled his cousin's increased, though much more slyly executed, maltreatment.

Gregory's last visit, however, had completely undermined Daniel's brittle self-worth, and in the worst possible way.

"I saw Erica recently. She's fairly glowing these days. But then, that's no surprise, seeing as she's expecting Thrushton's heir."

Daniel had frozen, pain slamming into him, nearly as potent as the bullet that had ripped into his leg. Erica was expecting?

It shouldn't have hurt as much as it had. But he had still been able to recall the time not so very long past when he'd dreamt of Erica expecting a child—his child.

"Oh! But do forgive me," Gregory had said with a horrified look that did nothing to hide the slyness behind it. "Of course you wouldn't know of it. I hope I haven't given you too much grief. I know how difficult it was when she broke things off with you upon your return from the Continent."

It had been glaringly obvious what his cousin had been about, of course. But that did not ease the sting of it, nor quiet the voices in Daniel's head that said if a woman who had claimed to love him could not stand the sight of him, then surely no one would.

But no, she had never loved him, he reminded himself brutally. She'd made certain he was aware of that fact upon his return home, that her father had forced her into pursuing him. And that she could no longer pretend even for his sake now that Daniel had returned as less of a man.

But he would not think of her now. For, quite the opposite of what his cousin had no doubt intended, his gleeful flaunting of Erica's impending motherhood had only fueled Daniel's determination to finally cede to his mother's increasingly anxious entreaties that he find a wife. He could not see a man such as Gregory, someone who so clearly reveled in the pain and discomfort of others, become duke.

He and the maid had just reached the bottom of the grand staircase—at this pace they would be lucky to reach the drawing room by Christmas—when he spied a woman heading toward them at a swift pace. And not just any woman, but Mrs. Kitteridge. He fought back a groan. Of all the people in this house, he was looking forward to dealing with her the least. An inconvenience, for certain, as Lady Tesh—and his mother, too, as he'd learned from the quiet conversation he'd had with her on the way to their rooms—had decreed they were to spend a good portion of their time together.

Instead of her wide-eyed gaping upon meeting him, however, she wore a bright, if slightly strained, smile now.

"Lillian, thank you so much for guiding His Grace down. I'm afraid, though, that Mrs. Hortenson needs you quite urgently in the kitchen. I shall show His Grace to the drawing room."

The girl dipped into a deep curtsy, with a long look at him no doubt meant to catalogue every awkward inch to regale the servants below stairs with, before she scampered off.

And Daniel and Mrs. Kitteridge were left quite thoroughly alone. Or as alone as any two people could be in a house with so many servants about.

He cleared his throat, turning to face the woman, half-prepared for the same shock in her eyes as before. But though there was a decided strain in her round face, her eyes were somber with regret. "I must apologize, Your Grace, for the way I treated you upon our initial meeting."

Whatever he had expected from her, it certainly hadn't been that. "Please," he said, wanting nothing more than to reach the drawing room and escape this woman's unnerving presence, "think nothing of it." He made to start off again in his painfully awkward way. But the woman, it seemed, wasn't done with him, for she remained firmly planted in his path.

"You are most kind. I, however, acted unpardonably. Please, I do hope you'll forgive and forget, and we may begin anew." She held out her hand.

He stared down at it, noticing the faintest tremor in her fingers. And then, knowing he could do little else, he reached out and gripped her fingers in his own.

Heat, and energy, and a jolt of something inexplicable and undeniable swirled deep in his belly at that innocent touch. It was a much more potent attraction than what he'd experienced upon his initial sight of her in her grandmother's sitting room. Her open shock had quickly eclipsed the temptation of her. Now, however, it all came roaring back, and he recalled with stunning clarity what he had seen in her when he'd first entered that room, in the split second before reality had come crashing back down again: large brown eyes with dark, curling lashes;

rosy cheeks that framed a sweet, round face; softly curling brown hair that surrounded her head in a veritable halo; a full figure that fairly made his mouth water despite the chaste cut of her violet gown.

She sucked in a sharp breath, her fingers tightening on his. His face heated and he hastily dropped her hand, clearing his throat several times to unstick the words that needed to be said. "There is nothing to forgive."

"But there is," she said. Her hands came together before her, her fingers working at the gold band on her fourth finger. "I know what you must be thinking of me."

He let loose a surprised bark of laughter. "I doubt it," he muttered. And thank goodness for it.

She gave him an arch look. "You think my reaction was owing to your scars, did you not?"

Well, he certainly hadn't expected such forthrightness. Most people pointedly refused to acknowledge his appearance at all. Which, of course, only brought it more sharply into focus, their determined dancing about and fumbling making him feel as if he were the maypole in some bizarre dance, getting more tangled by the minute in ribbons of social politeness.

This, however, was something completely new. Though perhaps it should not have been such a surprise, seeing who her grandmother was. He had immediately liked the old woman; she was a blunt one, and he got on best with people like her. Despite the unease her forthrightness had brought about, he would much rather deal with a person who spoke their mind than one who danced about trying to pretend things were well when they so clearly weren't.

"I assure you," Mrs. Kitteridge continued with a raised chin when he only stared at her, "your wounds were the last thing I noticed about you."

He laughed again, but it was bitter this time. Speaking of people dancing about ignoring the obvious. He might have accepted what she said to save further uncomfortableness as he typically did. But suddenly the weariness and strain and pain of the past three days came to a head and he found himself saying, "You needn't lie to me, madam."

"But I'm not lying."

Her expression was so earnest, so sincere, he almost believed her. A dangerous thing, surely. He did not trust easily. In truth, he did not trust at all. Too many people he had respected and revered had betrayed his once-staunch sense of right and wrong. War, he had soon learned after purchasing his commission, did not allow one to follow one's conscience. There had been too many gray areas, too many lines crossed for king and country.

"It doesn't matter," he said, shaking his head and offering her a smile though his demons would insist on breathing down his neck. "I assure you, my looking glass doesn't lie. Nor does this leg of mine. But I have had four years to learn to live with it. With luck I shall have many more ahead of me. I'm luckier than many men I served with—" He closed his mouth with a snap of teeth a moment too late, mortification filling him. And here was proof of just how hopeless he was in dealing with other people.

"I am so sorry," he rasped as Mrs. Kitteridge's face leached of color.

"No need for apologies," she managed. "What did you

speak but the truth?" The trembling smile she attempted died before it could find purchase. She heaved a sigh. "War is not fair, is it, Your Grace?"

An understatement if there ever was one. But he saw from the muted grief in her eyes that she knew as much as anyone just how unfair war could be. "You have the right of it," he murmured.

She didn't seem to hear him, the distant look in her eyes proof that her thoughts were elsewhere. Suddenly she shook her head sharply, as if to dislodge whatever held her in thrall. "But there is one more thing I must address before we join the others. My grandmother, I'm afraid, is quite outspoken. I'm so sorry if she pained you by bringing up the war. And I must apologize in advance for anything more she might say to upset you. Which," she said with a grimace, "I'm afraid will be much more often than you might like."

"You mustn't apologize for her, truly. For then I will apologize for something, and then you shall add on, and we'll never pull ourselves out of the quicksand of our politeness."

That, finally, alleviated the morose look that strained her features. She smiled fully at him, the sparkle of humor in her warm brown eyes, her cheeks taking on the lovely bloom of summer roses.

Once, when Daniel was a boy, he'd gotten too close to the back end of a particularly ill-tempered horse. The beast had kicked out, catching Daniel in the chest. The force of it had thrown Daniel back. He'd landed on the ground, the wind knocked out of him, not knowing who or where he was for some seconds.

Mrs. Kitteridge's smile, an expression that turned her

from a mildly pretty woman to a stunning creature, had nearly the same effect on him as those horse hooves. He could only stare down at her mutely, unable to form a coherent thought.

"You're right, of course," she said in her sweet voice. "And, as we have already determined to begin anew, remaining in the past is not doing either of us any good. That, and we'll be in close company the next several weeks; it will no doubt grow tiresome if we don't nip it in the bud now." She let loose a light laugh that reverberated through his chest in a pleasant way.

But her words reminded him just how neatly her grandmother had trapped him into being an unwelcome burden to Mrs. Kitteridge over the coming month. "I've no need of assistance in Synne society," he lied.

She frowned. "I assure you, Your Grace, it will be my pleasure."

"Truly, you've no need to."

Her cheeks colored. "If I gave the impression that it was in any way distasteful—"

"Not at all. I just have...other plans is all."

Again that little dip between her brows, this time one of confusion. "Other plans? You have someone else you're meeting with?"

"What? Oh, no. That's not it."

"What then—Oh." She bit her lip, guilt flaring in her cinnamon-brown eyes. "I assure you, I'm not normally so rude as I've made myself out to be."

"No!" Ah, God, why could he never get through an interaction without mucking things up? "It has nothing at all to do with you, and everything to do with me."

"I see," she said, though from the hurt tone of her

voice and the shuttered look in her eyes it was obvious she didn't.

"It's just," he stammered, desperate to climb out of whatever ditch he'd dug himself into, "I wouldn't want to put an unnecessary burden on you."

"You've no need to explain, Your Grace." Her voice was stiff, her smile stiffer, holding not an ounce of the warmth it had just minutes ago.

"Mrs. Kitteridge, you misunderstand. Ah, God, this is embarrassing." He groaned, running a hand over his face. "As you can see, I'm not the most articulate fellow. I more often than not botch even the most casual interactions. Which," he murmured wryly, "this one right here proves."

She worried at her wedding ring once more. "I'm sorry, Your Grace. I shouldn't have reacted as I did."

He chuckled. "Are we to start another round of apologies, Mrs. Kitteridge?"

Her relieved laugh was like bells. "Goodness, I hope not."

But the moment of lightness was short-lived. Silence descended between them, fraught with uncertainty. And no wonder; she must be unsure of how to deal with someone so lacking in social graces. She motioned down the hall, no doubt in the direction of the drawing room, and as one they began their slow way there.

"You mentioned you're headed to London after your trip to Synne," she said quietly. At his tight nod, she continued. "Forgive me for being blunt, but is your purpose in town purely parliamentary, or is it also...matrimonial?"

His cheeks flared with heat. "Are you applying for

the position, Mrs. Kitteridge?" he blurted, hoping to alleviate the tense moment with a bit of humor.

The second the words were out of his mouth, however, he knew it had been the wrong thing to say. She stumbled, thankfully quickly righting herself. What the hell was wrong with him? He'd known the woman mere hours, and he joked about marrying her?

"Ah, no," she managed with impressive poise. "That is, I'm not applying for a wifely position with anyone, now or ever."

"Of course. My apologies." He cleared his throat. "But to answer your question, yes, I am planning on looking for a wife. Though," he muttered, more to himself, "if I could manage that without having to go to London I'd be a sight happier."

But, of course, she overheard him. "You hope to find a wife on Synne?"

Well, he hadn't until now. But the idea jolted something in him, latching onto his brain, refusing to let go. Why not find a bride on Synne? If he were to find someone to marry, he could avoid London for good. There would be no need for him to attend crushing balls, or to be forced to sit in a theater box while everyone gaped at him, or make conversation with slews of young women all the while praying he didn't send them running for the hills.

"Yes, Mrs. Kitteridge," he said slowly. "That is exactly what I hope to do."

She nodded, then fell silent once more. He thought that was the end of it, was just about to breathe a sigh of relief that they would soon be with the others.

Suddenly, though the drawing room was just steps

away, she stopped and looked at him. "Your Grace, I have a proposition for you."

Shock and a molten heat shot through him. A proposition?

Her next words erased whatever erotic fantasies had decided to play out in his mind at those thoroughly charged words. "You need a bride in the next weeks," she said, "I assume to prevent you from having to go to London. Or, at least, to prevent you from going with the purpose of finding a bride." She bit her lip, suddenly unsure of herself. And then, in a rush, "I can help you find a bride. For a price."

He blinked. "A price?"

"Yes." She nodded with impressive confidence, though there was the sheen of uncertainty lingering in her eyes. "I'm in need of funds, which you seem to have. You're in need of a wife, and I know every eligible woman on Synne. I propose an exchange: I will introduce you to the single women on Synne, and help you secure the hand of the woman of your choosing by the last day of the month, and you shall pay me."

He gaped at her. "Mrs. Kitteridge, are you proposing I hire you on as my...matchmaker?"

Her lips twisted. "Matchmaker sounds so unprofessional. It's something my grandmother does to alleviate her boredom."

Humor flared in his chest. "Unprofessional? Are you taking this on as a profession, then?"

She raised her chin mutinously. "And if I am?"

He held up his hand. "I'm in no way disparaging your chosen occupation, madam. But what should I call you if not *matchmaker*?"

She thought on that for a minute, her deliciously full lips forming a plump bow. Suddenly her eyes lit with a spark of mischief. "I do think I prefer the term 'conjugality coordinator.'"

He nodded, trying to keep a straight face though he had the mad desire to laugh as he hadn't for years. "That's very professional. And what is your fee?"

Once more uncertainty seemed to take hold of her. Though this time she actually blanched. "Ah, yes. The fee."

He raised a brow. "I assume you have a number in mind?"

"I do." She nodded rapidly, muttering almost to herself, "Oh, I certainly have a number in mind." And then, as if building up the courage to say it, she straightened her back and raised her chin, looking him full in the face. "I think one hundred pounds would suffice. And I would have this agreement kept between the two of us."

Somehow he managed to keep his expression impassive. Though he would gladly pay ten times that amount to keep from having to go to London, he hadn't expected her to require such a sum.

She'd mentioned needing funds. But why would she require such a sum? Why didn't she go to her family for the money if she was in such dire straits? And why keep it quiet? Was she in trouble?

But it was none of his business, he told himself firmly. In truth, he would be a fool to refuse, for it would solve all of his problems. Well, he conceded wryly, most of his problems.

"Of course," he replied. "Whatever you need."

Shock and relief flared in her eyes before she quickly

brought it under control. "You will hire me on then, Your Grace? As your conjugality coordinator?" She held out her hand.

This was ridiculous, a mad scheme straight out of a sensational novel. People did not do such things in this day and age.

And he knew in a moment he would be the greatest fool to refuse.

He took her hand in a strong grip, ignoring the zing that shot from her palm into his. "You're hired, Mrs. Kitteridge."

Chapter 3

Margery watched the duke later that night from under her lashes. She should be relieved she had found a way to pay the blackmailer. The duke and his problems were a blessing dropped right in her lap, after all.

Yet she was still amazed at her daring. *Conjugality coordinator?* It was madness.

More surprising than her own daring in offering her services, however, had been his accepting her proposal so quickly. But as the evening had progressed, her disbelief had quickly disappeared.

The man truly was awkward in company. All night long he'd stumbled and blushed and sat in glaring silence. Even now, with dinner over and everyone settled once again in the drawing room, he could not seem to relax. As Margery watched, he reached for a glass of wine from a footman, then promptly spilled a good portion of it down the front of the man's uniform. Effusive apologies ensued, the duke retrieving a handkerchief from his pocket, hurriedly wiping the man's coat. A slight tussle occurred, with the footman aghast, attempting to extricate himself. In short order the mess was cleared up, a fresh glass in the duke's hand. But the damage had been done, for His Grace, quickly retreating to an empty corner of the room, appeared more miserable than he had all evening.

She bit her lip. This was no mere unease with his appearance. No, this appeared to go much deeper, an awkwardness that seemed part and parcel with the man himself. It had mayhap worsened with the addition of his scars and his perception of how others viewed him, but she had a feeling that was merely the tip of the proverbial iceberg.

Suddenly the couch dipped beside her. Startled, she turned her head to see Lenora happily smiling at her.

"I vow," her friend said, tucking an arm through Margery's and giving it a squeeze, "though I miss my dear little Charlotte, it is lovely to get out for an evening. Especially now that both our Clara and Phoebe are back on the Isle. I've missed them dreadfully."

Margery was glad for the distraction from the duke. She was only beginning to comprehend just how difficult finding him a bride in just under four weeks was going to be, no matter his station. Would that she had more time. But no, she reminded herself, four weeks it must be, allowing her to secure the funds from His Grace just before the blackmail money came due.

Her stomach lurched at the reminder of just why she was embarking on this scheme in the first place. *Aaron*, she told herself. She was doing this for Aaron and his good name. And she would ignore the difficulty of the job ahead…as well as her peculiar physical reactions to the duke. Something she might need to work at controlling, if his effect on her in the hall was any indication.

"I've missed them as well," Margery said, looking to her cousins and their spouses, refusing to even think on her unwelcome attraction to the duke a moment longer. "But it does my heart good to see how very happy they are."

"I've never seen them so radiant." Lenora's smile turned mischievous. "Your grandmother must be over the moon, with the spoils of her matchmaking surrounding her on all sides. And with His Grace here, she must have another conquest planned. He is her preferred specimen, after all: a young, single duke."

Matchmaking. Margery's smile turned sickly, wondering what her friend would think of her own newly acquired profession of *conjugality coordinator*.

Though perhaps Gran's obsession—and talent—for matching couples might work in her favor. Perhaps if she could deduce who the older woman was planning on matching the man with, she could utilize the information to her benefit.

She schooled her features into mild curiosity. "Who do you suppose she's thinking of for the duke's love interest?"

Lenora merely pursed her lips and arched one brow.

It took Margery some seconds to understand the very pointed look her friend was giving her. "Me?" Margery squeaked, even as her heart beat out a disturbingly rapid rhythm at such a suggestion. She cleared her throat, praying her face didn't appear as hot as it felt. "Please, that couldn't possibly be true. If there's anyone she's planning on matching him with, it would be Miss Denby." An idea that should not have sat so very wrong with Margery. She was fully planning on finding someone to wed the man, after all, and Miss Denby would make a fine candidate for the position. In fact, it would be a positively brilliant match, as the woman was not only the sister of a baronet, but was also staying in the same household and would, therefore, provide Margery with a veritable live-in option. As the sour taste in her mouth persisted, she determined that Miss Denby would be the first candidate on her list of prospective brides.

"Though I don't doubt that Miss Denby will one day become the recipient, willing or not, of Lady Tesh's matchmaking prowess," Lenora said with a smile, "you know your grandmother better than anyone, and so should fully comprehend that there may be something behind her suggestion that you assist His Grace in getting about in Synne society, such as it is this time of year."

Which Margery had not considered at all until that moment. "But that's ridiculous," she sputtered, more than a little flustered at the idea.

"It's not ridiculous in the least. You have to admit, it does sound like something she would do."

"Well, yes," Margery conceded grudgingly. "And I might think you were onto something, if you were not including *me* in this equation."

"And why ever not?" Lenora demanded. "Though we all know how deeply you loved Aaron, and how difficult it was for you after his death, you're still young. And she loves you and wants to see you happy."

But Margery had heard enough. She pulled her arm

from Lenora's and, pressing her lips tight, worked the gold band on her fourth finger in agitated circles. "You know where I stand on this, Lenora. As does my grand-mother."

"Yes, we know." Lenora's expression turned sad. "I was the one with you when you received word of Aaron's death. I know the struggles you faced day in and day out to keep your head above water when the grief threatened to drown you completely."

Pain tore through Margery. She had a sudden flash of that long-ago day: the quiet afternoon she and Lenora had spent together in the small house Margery had shared with Aaron in London, the tension so thick they could fairly taste the bitterness of it, a strange premoni-tion having settled deep in her bones. Then a knock on the door, the trembling in her limbs as she'd exchanged a fearful glance with Lenora, the somber look on the messenger's face as he handed over the sealed letter. And then the chaos and confusion of the next days, her wails mingling with Lenora's tearful words of comfort, curling in a ball in her friend's arms on the bed she'd shared with Aaron, each hour bleeding into the next until she didn't know night from day.

She shook her head to dispel the unending grief of that memory. "Yes," she whispered, reaching for her wine-glass. Her hands, she noticed as if from a distance, were shaking as she took a deep swallow. "And so you also know I'll never marry again. I will never love another as I loved him, will never replace him in my heart. Ever."

"Of course, dear," Lenora soothed. She rubbed a hand over Margery's back in gentle circles, just as she'd done the day Margery's life had split apart into a million pieces, jagged fragments that she had not been able to fully mend back together. "Forgive me. I never meant to cause you pain."

"I know," Margery said. And she did know. Lenora was her dearest friend in the world. They had been there for one another through so many of life's tragedies. Hurting one another was the last thing either of them wanted.

"But," Margery continued, straightening and turning to smile bracingly at her friend, "though I'll agree that my grandmother most likely has matchmaking on her mind, I cannot agree with you that I'm the recipient. If we exercise patience, I'm sure she'll show her hand soon enough."

Lenora returned the smile, her eyes shining with relief. "I do hope I won't have to say 'I told you so' in a month's time," she teased.

Margery laughed. "You won't have to." Her smile slipped as her friend turned away. *You can depend upon it.*

* * *

After a fitful night's sleep, Daniel woke at dawn to a sky teeming with gray clouds. It seemed the inclement, unseasonable weather they had been battered with in Cheshire had followed them to the Isle. To most people it would be an unfortunate start to a holiday.

Not so to Daniel.

He was all too aware that sunny skies and warm weather would mean there would be no stalling his entry into Synne society. And though he needed to begin working with Mrs. Kitteridge on the search for a bride with all haste if he was to avoid the marriage mart in

London—as limited as it would be in autumn—after the strain of the evening before, he was in no mood to converse and smile with strangers.

He had never been easy in company, of course. But in his youth he'd at least had the protection of being a second son. No one had paid him the least mind, especially when Nathaniel had been present, and most had even indulged his propensity for preferring solitude to company. Now, however, he didn't have Nathaniel to hide behind.

He exhaled a heavy breath and peered out his borrowed bedroom window to the rose garden below, hardly seeing the late-summer blooms that gave a cheery cast to the landscape despite the thick clouds that loomed over it all. He may not have ever wanted this life, but he had gotten it regardless. And he would do the best he could with it. With luck he would succeed, at least in finding a wife. Especially as he now apparently had Mrs. Kitteridge in his corner.

If, of course, she still wanted to assist him after the disaster that was last night.

He blanched as the memories came flooding back. Between spilling the wine on the footman, to fumbling through every question put his way, to dealing with a dog that was much too interested in sniffing his . . . delicate areas, every minute had been rife with embarrassment. If Mrs. Kitteridge wanted to renege on her offer, he would not be the least bit surprised.

He sighed, his fingers tightening on the plain curved head of his cane, his finger finding and rubbing anxiously at the bit of bullet embedded in the wood. But he would never know if he didn't leave his room. Gathering his courage—sadly lacking this morning—he headed to the ground floor.

The descent was slightly easier than the night before. Even so, his ruined muscles made their outrage known, and he took a moment to lean against the banister once at the bottom, surreptitiously using the last riser to stretch his leg.

"Your Grace, do you require assistance?"

Apparently not surreptitious enough. Daniel straightened and turned to face the butler. "Perhaps you might point me the way to the breakfast room?" he inquired with a polite smile.

The man's face fell. "Ah, I am sorry, Your Grace, but breakfast is not yet ready. I'll hurry down to the kitchen to speed things along."

Daniel's face flamed. And there went his hopes to remain unobtrusive and no bother. He was so used to rising with the sun, he quite forgot that wasn't how things were done in the majority of the homes of the British nobility. "No, please," he said when the butler made to turn away. "That is, I'm not at all hungry just yet. Though if you could let me know where I might find the duchess?"

"Her Grace has not yet descended for the day. Would you like me to show you the way to her rooms?"

Oh, *God*, no. The very idea of climbing those stairs again had him feeling vaguely ill. Though he could only be grateful that she was resting. More often than not, over the past few years his mother had woken well before him—if she even slept at all. He hoped this was a sign that the Isle would be able to work its magic on her and return her to good health. And to give her contentment, if not happiness. Goodness knew being surrounded by reminders of Nathaniel and all they had lost with his passing had done the opposite of that.

"No, thank you," he said to the butler. "I do believe I'll take a bit of a walk."

"As Your Grace wishes," the man murmured. Quick as a wink he retrieved Daniel's hat and cloak, and handing them over, he opened the front doors wide.

Well, hell.

Truly, the man should be commended for his ability to react so swiftly, Daniel thought as he gave a sickly smile and strode—or at least a close approximation of a stride—from the house. The moment he stepped foot out the front doors, however, and the brisk sea air hit him full in the face, everything else was forgotten for one blessed moment. The salty flavor and cool sting of it jolted his senses in the most invigorating way. He stopped for a moment on the front step and closed his eyes, taking a deep, cleansing breath as the cobwebs of the morning cleared from his brain. Glorious life, all green and briny and heavy with moisture. And the faintest sound of waves crashing against rock, Seacliff being exactly what its name implied, the grand manor house inhabiting the cliff top above an unforgiving sea. He felt an instant invigoration in his limbs. Ah, yes, now he could see it, the draw of a place like this. There was something strangely comforting in being so close to the edge of the land, to let the vast ocean into your very soul.

But, though he considered crossing the drive to the cliffs beyond so he might better see the churning waves and feel the wind bathe his scars, something turned his steps to the side of the house, down the path, into the rose garden he had spied from his window.

In a moment he understood why. It was peaceful here, the sounds of the ocean fading to a dull hush.

For once he didn't mind his slow pace. Able to relax for the first time since leaving Cheshire, he breathed in deeply, filling his lungs with the myriad scents carried on the breeze, combined in a kaleidoscope of impressions: the delicate petals of the roses, the rolling white-tipped waves, and the heady smell of rich earth. His vision, too, was filled with all the details he might have missed had he been in possession of a hale and hearty body: the flitting of a small bird in the dark dirt beneath a bush, a whimsical statue of a satyr hidden in the bare bramble.

A pale purple skirt peeking out from behind an art-fully trimmed hedge.

He stopped hard in the path, his boots kicking up gravel. Damnation, he had thought no one was up. Who could possibly be out of doors at such an early hour? But the question had not whispered through his mind before the answer popped into his head with stark certainty: Mrs. Kitteridge.

For one insane moment he was caught in a kind of purgatory as he tried to decide between forging forward and greeting her as a proper person would or escaping back to the house.

She peered around the hedge, however, making the decision for him.

"Your Grace," she said. "I heard a noise but thought it was a gardener."

"I apologize if I've startled you." He moved forward until he stood in front of her. She was seated on a stone bench tucked back within the hedge, bundled up in a dark gray cloak, a simple bonnet perched on her head and a sketchbook balanced on her knees. "I didn't know anyone was up at this hour," he continued. "I'm afraid I'm quite the early riser, something I picked up during the war and haven't been able to break myself of."

"I'm an early riser myself." Her expression darkened for a moment before she smiled brightly. "I hope you slept well."

"I did, thank you," he lied. What good would the truth do, anyway?

"That's wonderful to hear. But won't you have a seat beside me?" She slid over to one side of the wide stone bench and adjusted her skirts.

But the idea of sitting so close to her dredged up a vague panic in him; no matter that they were in full view of the house and could not be construed as doing anything untoward, her proximity would no doubt affect him just as it had last night. "Ah, no, thank you. You're busy, and I would not want to impose upon your private time."

"Nonsense," she said. "And besides, I was feeling lonely and would love the company. Please sit."

What could he say to that kind speech? And so, gritting his teeth, he moved forward and sank his bulk to the bench. But being this close to her, with her skirts brushing his leg and her warmth traversing the small space between them, was affecting him in wholly base ways. He was embarrassingly lacking in knowledge of the physical arts—his awkwardness had assured his experience with the fairer sex was limited—but his imagination was alive and well, and that imagination was dreaming up all manner of things where Mrs. Kitteridge was concerned.

Aghast that he would think of her in such a manner, he cast about for something, anything, to say. Finally his desperate eyes lit on her sketchbook. "What's that you're drawing?" he managed, praying she didn't hear the hoarseness in his voice.

In answer she held the sketch out to him. He took it with only the barest hesitation, being careful not to touch her as he did so. A detailed drawing of Freya, Lady Tesh's pup, graced the page. He studied it a moment in silence, as much to take in the simple beauty of it as to compose himself. The lines were delicate, with several sections scrubbed out and redrawn. Yet with the too-large ears perked up, the head tilt, the large eyes that held a surprising amount of humanity, the image was lovely.

"You have captured her perfectly," he said.

"Do you think so?" She leaned in closer to peer at it, and her scent wafted to him on the chill morning air: a delicate fragrance that was deliciously akin to sugared violets.

"I admit," she continued, blessedly unaware of the turmoil within him, "I had trouble capturing her expression. For a canine, she is incredibly demonstrative."

"I think you have done a beautiful job," he said. Then, hoping to put much-needed distance between them, he handed the sketch back and, under the pretense of rearranging his leg, shifted farther from her on the stone bench. "You're quite talented."

"You're very kind," she murmured. "Though I know my talent is merely average, I do hope my grandmother appreciates my attempt when I'm through." She held up a hand when he would have spoken and denounced her claim. "That is not my way of fishing for further compliments, I assure you." She gave a small laugh. "If you could see Lenora's drawings you would think mine the mere scribblings of a child."

He frowned. "Lenora?"

"The Duchess of Dane," she corrected.

"She is talented?"

"Incredibly so. One might even say she's gifted. She sells her paintings, and gives lessons during the summer months to visitors of the Isle. She is quite sought after." She paused then, and when he remained silent, not quite knowing what to say to that, she continued in a quieter voice that held an undercurrent of steel to it, "You might think a woman in her position should not pursue such things, however."

"No," he was quick to assure her, appalled that his silence might be construed as disapproval. "I think it commendable." He paused. "As I think your own newly acquired profession of *conjugality coordinator* is commendable as well. Though, after last night, you may have changed your mind about me."

She blinked in surprise. "Why ever would I do that?"

His lips quirked in a wry smile. "I think you saw first-hand just how hopeless I can be in social situations."

"I wouldn't call you hopeless," she hedged.

"Mrs. Kitteridge, you needn't lie. I have been a passenger in this head of mine for nine and twenty years; I know what I'm capable of—and not capable of. Which is a startling amount."

She let out an exasperated breath. "Very well, you're not what one would call a charming swain." She grabbed his sleeve when he made to rise and held him in place with impressive strength. "But I daresay someone with smooth, easy manners wouldn't have need of my services, would they?"

"I suppose not," he grumbled.

"There now," she said, her tone bright, her smile wide, "you see? I'm not ready to abandon our agreement, not in the least."

Relief flared in his chest. "Thank you," he managed.

"There's no need to thank me, Your Grace. I assure you, you're doing just as much of a favor for me as I am for you."

Once again questions flitted through his mind on why she might need funds. But even he, as clueless as he was in social niceties, knew better than to question her on her finances. No doubt she had her reasons. She was a war widow, after all; too many families had been left destitute after the dust of battle had cleared.

"We may as well discuss what kind of lady you're looking for in a wife while we're on the subject," she said. She flipped the page in her sketchbook and held her pencil aloft over the blank page, then looked at him in anticipation. "Do you have any preferences? Status? Manners? Looks? Do you require an heiress?"

He barked out a sharp laugh, startled—and, to be truthful, a bit intimidated—by her sudden air of intense competence. "I assure you, I have no preferences at all, save that she is of child-bearing years. As vulgar as that may sound."

She nodded, jotting the pertinent information down. "You're a duke; you require an heir. There is nothing vulgar about it. Or, rather," she corrected, with an arch smile his way, "it's an accepted vulgarity in our society."

He was struck mute, the humor changing her features from cool and collected to mischievous in a moment. Goodness, she truly was lovely.

"What of temperament or manners?" she continued, all business once again. Thank goodness. "Family connections? Are you opposed to a commoner?"

"Truly, Mrs. Kitteridge," he said, his head beginning to spin, "I don't care if she is highborn or the daughter of a farmer, if she has fine manners or burps and swears like a sailor. As long as she can stomach bedding me, I'll be happy."

She stilled, her eyes widening in shock. He groaned. "I'm very sorry for being so crass."

She flapped her hands in dismissal. "I assure you, such talk doesn't bother me in the least. Why, my cousin Peter, the Duke of Dane, has been known to blurt out inappropriate things himself, especially when going to battle with my grandmother. But I'll not have you disparaging yourself in such a way, sir. You will make someone a wonderful husband."

He found his gaze dropping from her piercing one, overcome by her sudden defense of him. "I thank you for your optimism, Mrs. Kitteridge," he murmured, studying the plain handle of his cane with much more interest than it warranted, rubbing his finger over the embedded bullet, buffed to a sheen after years of such nervous actions. "I, however, don't see it as disparaging myself; I'm merely being realistic."

There was a charged moment of silence. Suddenly she stood. He looked up at her in surprise.

"I'll not have you talking in such a way in my presence," she declared with a bright smile. "It will do no one, most especially yourself, any good at all. Now, shall we head inside? Breakfast should be ready, and I'm famished, as I'm sure you are as well after a morning of exercise. A full stomach will perhaps help us to decide where to begin."

He rose with the help of his cane and fell into step beside her as they headed back to the house. As they walked in companionable silence, however, he realized that already things did not seem so dark. Was it owing to her presence? He should, perhaps, find her effect on him a cause for concern. Theirs was to be a business arrangement, after all, and even if it weren't, he had no wish to develop a close relationship with her. But in that moment, able to breathe a bit more freely than he had in too long, he found he could not regret it. Nothing would come of it, he reminded himself. He would find a bride in just under four weeks' time, and would leave Synne. And he need never worry about his troubling reaction to Mrs. Kitteridge again.

Chapter 4

Daniel rather thought that if the rest of his interactions with the unmarried women on Synne
went as horribly as his time with Miss Katrina Denby
was going, however, he was in trouble, indeed.

"I am so sorry," the young lady mumbled, face red
as a beet as she tugged futilely on Mouse's collar. The
black-and-white-spotted beast of a dog—it was as large
as a pony, and Miss Denby could easily ride it about the
Isle if she had a mind to—once more had its nose buried
in Daniel's... nether regions. "Are you quite certain you
didn't drop a bit of sausage on your breeches this morning at breakfast? Mouse does love sausage, you know,
and it would certainly explain his interest in... ahem,
well..."

Daniel, who rather thought he must be as red as
Miss Denby at the moment if the heat in his face
was any indication, would have been more than happy
to melt right into the flagstones. Instead he forced a
smile and did his best to push the dog away—and keep

Miss Denby's nervous hands from brushing the most sensitive aspects of his person. "No, I'm quite certain. But perhaps, if we continue walking, he might find something to distract him?"

Miss Denby sent a concerned glance to his leg and worried at her lip with her teeth. "Are you certain we should continue walking, Your Grace?" she asked with a small grunt as she yanked again on her dog's collar. "Would you like me to secure a footman to assist you back to the house?"

Daniel glanced back at the manor in some disbelief, doing his best to rein in his annoyance. They had not even left the balcony. "I assure you," he replied in as pleasant a manner as he was able, "that I am more than capable of accompanying you."

"But the stairs," she said, looking to the stone steps leading down to the back lawn, then glancing back to his cane. "Are you certain you can maneuver them?"

"Seeing as how I have managed to maneuver the stairs from my room several times now, I would say that I'll be just fine."

But Miss Denby did not seem to see just how annoyed he was becoming. "My brother was left without a leg, you know," she blathered on. "He was wounded in a duel. Though you must have heard about it. Everyone has heard about it. It's why I'm here on the Isle, after all. He took to drinking after, and gambling, and our family was left in dire straits. I would have married to save us, had anyone wanted me. But no one wants me. I'm quite scandalous, it seems, though I certainly didn't do anything to warrant it. Truly, is it my fault Lord Ludlow became obsessed with me? I certainly didn't encourage him. Though my brother would tell me otherwise. I'm apparently *too friendly* with men, whatever that means. But I have a natural openness. It's not a failing. Would you think it's a failing, Your Grace?"

All the while she was speaking, with a quickness and candor that had his head spinning, Daniel could do little more than gape at her. Even the dog and his offensive sniffing was forgotten. "Your brother was in a duel?"

Why that was the first thing that popped out of his mouth, he would never know. Blessedly Miss Denby didn't seem to think there was anything odd in it.

"Oh, yes," she said, apparently giving up tugging her dog away entirely as she warmed to her story. "It was silly for him to enter into it, and so I told him when he found Lord Ludlow in my room. It must have been a mistake, I told him. Surely Lord Ludlow had entered the wrong window. There was no sense in getting himself killed over it. Which only seemed to enrage him the more, now that I think on it. I did not learn until later, of course, that Lord Ludlow truly had meant to climb into my window. But how was I to know, I ask you?"

Which she actually seemed to be doing, as she finally paused to take breath and looked at him expectantly. He managed a sickly smile—blessedly the dog had lost interest in him and was now bounding across the back lawn in a kind of uncoordinated canine abandon, and so he was able to focus solely on Miss Denby—and managed a weak "I'm sure I don't know."

She threw her hands up—as if to say, *Exactly!*—then drew in a deep breath. He watched her in fatalistic horror, certain she was going to start off again on another long-winded monologue, when a frantic barking sounded.

Her attention was diverted in an instant. "Mouse," she cried, "leave that poor squirrel alone." Then, with barely a glance his way, she bolted after the creature. He watched, mouth agape, as she grabbed up her skirts in both hands and sprinted down the stone steps and across the back lawn.

"Holy hell," he mumbled.

A sudden laugh sounded behind him. He turned to see Mrs. Kitteridge striding across the balcony toward him.

She placed a hand over her mouth. "I am so sorry for finding any amusement in the situation," she said through her fingers—a useless endeavor in hiding her laugh, as her eyes fairly danced with her mirth. "But you really can't blame me, can you?"

"I suppose not," he grumbled. "Is she always like that?"

"Exuberant, you mean?" she queried with impressive innocence, before ruining the effect and laughing again, this time outright. "Ah, yes, I'm afraid so. Though this was not her most exuberant conversation by far."

He felt himself go green. She gave him a commiserating smile. "Shall I take her off the list of prospectives, then?"

It was on the tip of his tongue to declare that, yes, that would be the wisest course of action. He glanced at Miss Denby then, and watched as she laughingly flung a stick for her dog to chase. She wasn't a horrible person. She had already proven to be kind, and friendly—or *too friendly*, as her brother had apparently termed her. And besides, he had only known her a day. No one could truly know a person after such a short time. It would be ridiculous at this early stage to discount anyone, especially as he'd been informed that Synne was not exactly flush in marital prospects this late in the summer season.

"No," he said. "Not entirely. Though"—he sent a wry smile Mrs. Kitteridge's way—"perhaps we'd best focus our attentions elsewhere for now? At least until I've grown a bit more used to Miss Denby's particular brand of high spirits."

She chuckled. "A wise course of action, indeed. And duly noted. If the weather clears by tomorrow we'll head into town, and we shall see if there isn't someone else that suits you better."

As he watched her retreat back inside, he rather thought that, if he was looking for someone who suited him, Mrs. Kitteridge would be it.

But no, he told himself fiercely, turning his attention back to Miss Denby galloping across the lawn after her dog, he was not looking for someone who might call to his heart, not after the heartbreak of daring to love before. And Mrs. Kitteridge, he knew instinctively, would do just that if he gave her the chance.

* * *

After the debacle with Miss Denby—who seemed blessedly unaware that the attempts to get her alone with the duke the previous day had been anything other than mere politeness—Margery refused to lose even a modicum of hope that she could match His Grace with someone on Synne. Miss Denby had a very energetic personality, after all, and though she had been popular in London before the scandal that had taken her brother's leg, Margery was forced to admit that her volubleness was not to everyone's taste. Most especially not to a quiet, awkward duke who seemed to dread going about in society so much that he had hired a *conjugality coordinator* to find him a bride.

Taking advantage of the blue skies and warmer weather that had visited them overnight, she thought a stroll in town would surely be the perfect place to start the duke's indoctrination into Synne society. She would be able to see how he might truly interact with the young, single—and decidedly calmer—women on the Isle. It was one thing to be subjected to a forced evening with a group of strangers, or to converse alone with a woman who was the very opposite of himself; it was quite another to take a casual walk with Gran and the duke's mother, mayhap meeting new acquaintances along the way yet able to extricate himself in a moment. Perhaps he would be more relaxed in such a setting. And there was no time to waste, after all, with the clock ticking ever closer to the date that the blackmail funds were due...

As soon as Margery stepped foot from the carriage, however, any hope she might have had that her job of finding him a wife would be easier than she'd first assumed—something that had taken a significant beating after his walk with Miss Denby—was dashed to pieces. She bit her lip as she watched him from under her lashes, anxiety rising up in her. Though the foot traffic on Admiralty Row was light, the duke showed no signs of relaxing. If anything, the farther down the wide avenue they traversed, the starker and more guarded his expression became.

And, the crux of it was, she understood only too well why.

Margery winced as yet another young woman—a Miss Abigail Swan, the painfully thin, colorless daughter to the town's physician—hastily extricated herself from conversation with Gran, her eyes sliding anxiously to the duke as she did so. It was not the first time that morning that a young woman had shown a less-than-complimentary reaction to the man. She peered at him from under her lashes, any hope she might have had that he hadn't witnessed Miss Swan's nervous exit quickly snuffed as she spied the ruddy hue staining his cheeks.

She blew out a frustrated breath as they continued on their way down the avenue, her worries put aside as aggravation reared. What was wrong with the women on this Isle? So the man had some scars? They certainly did not detract from his attractiveness. In fact, he was one of the most magnetic, striking, desirable men she had ever seen.

For a moment she entertained herself with musings on where else he might have scars. Which transformed into wondering what he might look like unclothed, if he were as powerful beneath his fine wardrobe as he appeared, what his skin might feel like, taste like...

She blanched. Goodness, was she such a letch as that? To pant after a man who was in essence her client? Of course, she'd been incredibly lonely these past years without Aaron. And her body had begun aching for physical affection. But that was no excuse. No excuse at all.

Though surely if she were this attracted to the man, someone else on this blasted Isle would be as well. Or at least not so intimidated by his appearance that they might remain in his company for more than a few minutes.

Just then she spied Mr. and Mrs. Pickering and their daughter across the street. The couple caught sight of Gran and, waving and calling out energetically, dragged their protesting daughter into the light early-afternoon traffic, earning them more than one loud curse as drivers were forced to pull their horses up.

The Pickerings paid the drivers no mind, their slick society smiles already firmly in place. As they ever were where Gran was concerned. As one of the wealthy families who had come to the Isle for health reasons and remained once it came into fashion, they liked to present themselves as benign benefactors to all who visited Synne. They were also horribly vain, outspoken, and always trying to ingratiate themselves into society. They made no secret that they wanted a title for their only daughter, a girl who, thankfully, had more sense than both of her parents combined. A fact that might just work in Margery's favor where the duke was concerned.

If, that was, the girl's parents didn't botch any attempts at matching their daughter with the man within the first minute. Which they were in danger of doing, if the way they stopped in the middle of the walkway and stared at His Grace was any indication.

Mr. Pickering was the first to recover. "My dear Lady Tesh, Mrs. Kitteridge," he effused, all the while eyeing the duke askance. "How lovely to see you both out and about on this fine day. But who are your companions? I don't recall seeing them on Synne before."

Gran, rolling her eyes in blatant disgust at the man's fishing for information, nevertheless made the necessary introductions. After which an immediate change came over the couple, their caution replaced with a disturbing cunning.

"Your Graces," Mr. Pickering said, with a bow so deep Margery was certain he'd eventually be kissing his own posterior if his daughter hadn't yanked on his sleeve. "It is a pleasure to make your acquaintance. A pleasure, indeed. You're for London after your visit, you say? We have longed to bring my darling daughter for a proper season, but my dear Mrs. Pickering's health has thus far prevented us from making the trip."

It was doubtful that was the true reason why. Margery eyed the girl. More than likely it had been Miss Bron-wyn Pickering who had been the one to put a stop to any such trips. Unlike her parents, the girl had never seemed particularly interested in toadying up to society. No doubt bored—or embarrassed—by her father's fawning attentions to the duke and his mother, Miss Pickering stepped away from their group and became thoroughly engrossed in the stationer's window display.

The girl hadn't shown the least interest in the duke upon meeting him. Which, Margery hated to admit, was an improvement over any other young woman they'd met with today. Biting her lip, she moved to her side.

"That stationery is quite lovely," Margery said, peering at the selection of fine vellum within. "It would be perfect for writing letters to a dear friend or relation."

"Yes," Miss Pickering murmured, adjusting her spectacles. "Though I've no one to write to, and so it would be wasted on me."

Margery blinked. Well, she certainly hadn't expected that.

"Though," the girl continued, pursing her lips, "I daresay it would give the proper gravitas to my correspondence with the Entomological Society of London."

Margery smiled. "I see you are still interested in insects."

"Entomology, Mrs. Kitteridge. From the Latin word *entomon*, which means 'notched,' and therefore refers to the segmented body of the insect."

"Er, yes. Of course," Margery said. She cleared her throat. "One wonders you don't wish to visit London and the Entomological Society yourself."

The other woman's expression fell at that and she returned her attention to the window. "Yes, well, I'm afraid since Waterloo, the Society has met only occasionally. And there is no sense in my hying off to the capital until a proper society is founded. Besides, I have ever so much work to do on the Isle."

"I see," Margery said. Though, of course, she didn't.

But she had approached the girl with a purpose. "His Grace is from Cheshire County. I daresay there are some interesting specimens there you would not find on the Isle."

"Hmm, yes. I suppose."

"You should ask His Grace about them."

"Yes. Later. For now, I really must purchase that notebook; it will be perfect for recording my specimens. If you'll excuse me?" And with that she was off, disappearing into the shop.

Margery stared after her for a time, not quite sure what had just happened. The young woman, while incredibly smart and sensible, was prone to changing the track of a conversation without warning. While it could be unnerving, it in no way removed her from consideration for the duke. Truly, the only thing working against the girl was her parents.

Which, she realized with dawning horror as she turned and spied Mr. Pickering sidled up close to the duke's scarred side, was considerable, indeed.

"Waterloo, eh?" the man was saying. He peered closer at His Grace's scars, his lip curling in a kind of fascinated disgust. Suddenly he grinned and waggled his brows. "I bet you killed a good number of Frogs in your day. Big fellow like you—pardon my bluntness, Your Grace—must have been a sight to behold in that glorious battle."

A flash of something—annoyance or pain or anger—was quickly smoothed from the duke's brow. "I would hardly call it glorious."

"Yes, yes," the man said, obviously not put off in the least by the duke's attempts to halt the distasteful conversation in its tracks. "But those French had it coming. Backing an upstart, marching on innocent people, killing and raping."

"Mr. Pickering"—the duke's expression darkened—"I hardly think this is the place for such a conversation."

Mr. Pickering cast a glance at the females present. "Too right. Of course, Your Grace. How noble of you."

He stood perturbed for a time, staring at the duke's cane. Margery, who had been about to intervene, took a relieved breath. Mayhap the man would finally see sense.

Suddenly, however, Mr. Pickering leaned in close and said in a loud whisper that did nothing at all to hide the curiosity in his voice, "Saw your share of men killed, eh? What was that like?"

And that was enough of that. Margery stepped forward as the duke's face turned ashen. "Your Grace," she exclaimed, forcing a bright smile though she longed to tell Mr. Pickering exactly where he could stick his curiosity, "you were telling me just yesterday that you were a great lover of timepieces, were you not? The jeweler across the way has the most cunning display set up in the window if you've a mind to see it." Before he had time to answer her, she turned to Mr. Pickering. "If you'll excuse me for stealing His Grace away."

"What? Oh! Of course." He peered across the street to the shop in question. "Why, I like a good watch myself," he mused. "Mayhap I'll join you."

Damn and blast. But she was a master at handling difficult people; hadn't all her years visiting her grandmother and all her time spent in London taught her something of that? "But we could not possibly take you away from the other ladies," she said with mock dismay. "Why, I was certain the viscountess had something important to ask you, though for the life of me I cannot recall what it was."

The man, greedy eagerness lighting his eyes, turned toward the dowager. No doubt he would pester Gran until she came up with something to placate him. But Margery could not feel an ounce of guilt. Her sole concern in that moment was to get the duke as far away from Mr. Pickering as possible.

"Your Grace, if you've a mind to view the watches in question?"

The poor man looked positively ill. But he nodded and followed her across the street. They stepped around some young men loitering on the walkway and moved up to the window. The next minutes were spent in blessed silence, each of them buried under their own thoughts.

Margery surreptitiously gazed at the duke's reflection in the glass. Was encountering men like Mr. Pickering and his tactless questions a common occurrence for him? No wonder he was so on guard all the time.

He spoke then, his voice quiet but gruff. "I must thank you, Mrs. Kitteridge, for your intervention."

"Think nothing of it, Your Grace."

"You will perhaps think me rude when I insist on thinking a great deal of it." He turned to her then, and though his eyes still held ghosts, he smiled at her. "You have already proven to be my guardian angel, and here we are not two days into my stay."

She flushed at the sight of that smile, the scar near the corner of his mouth making it endearingly lopsided. "I do hope I didn't offend Your Grace by interfering."

"Not at all. You were only being kind." His smile faltered then. "I think I'm prepared for such questions," he murmured, looking over his shoulder, presumably to make certain Mr. Pickering was still on the other side of the street. "But then something like that occurs and I'm completely caught off guard."

"You deal with such horrid questions often?"

"More than you know." He gave a humorless chuckle. "There's something about the 'glory' of war that gives men the idea that it's all trumpets playing while you march forward in sparkling clean uniforms and cut down the opposing army like a farmer scything wheat."

Such was the way Aaron had thought of it. Margery recalled the grin on his face when he'd kissed her good-bye. His certainty when he'd told her he would return before she could even miss him.

Her heart gave a pitiful lurch at the memory. How

very wrong he had been. Before she knew it, she had placed a hand on the duke's dark wool sleeve. Though she wasn't certain if it was to give comfort or to receive it. "I'm sorry you're forced to deal with such unfeeling behavior."

His features softened, his gaze dropping to her fingers. Then his large hand covered hers, the warmth in it sinking down into her very bones. "You've nothing to apologize for."

She looked down to their joined hands, fascinated by his scarred fingers, the blunt nails. How had she not realized until just that moment that he had not put on gloves? She suddenly wished she were not wearing gloves, either. How long had it been since a man had touched her?

A vision rose up in her mind then, of this powerful man lowering his head to hers, taking her lips in a kiss . . .

She pulled her hand back, as if burned. And perhaps she had been, for she felt ridiculously hot just then, in every part of her.

Blessedly he didn't quiz her on her reaction. Yet he stepped closer, his voice lowering to an intimate rumble.

"I believe you have much to teach me, Mrs. Kitteridge."

Such words only fueled the lingering ache of desire in her. Oh, yes, there were all manner of things she could teach him. Her gaze snagged on the harsh line of his lips. And quite a few he could no doubt instruct her on, as well. She swallowed hard. "Teach you?" she managed weakly.

"How to navigate in society. While searching for a bride."

It took her some seconds to understand what he was saying. And just as many seconds to overcome her embarrassment enough to answer him. "Yes, of course. Your bride." She gave a laugh at that, the sound almost manic to her ears. "What else would it be?"

He gave her a curious look but seemed to shake it off quickly enough. "Thank you again, by the way, for taking me on. I had my doubts at the outset, as I'm sure you're aware. But now I find I'm quite grateful to have you in my corner. I can use all the help I can get, apparently."

Her heart twisted at the self-disgust just barely visible in his gaze. "I will help you in any way I can," she said quietly.

His expression shifted again, like the sand after the tide, revealing something that had been hidden until then, an intensity that drew her like a moth to a flame.

What the devil was wrong with her?

She cleared her throat. "Miss Pickering, though unconventional, would make a fine wife, I think. Are you opposed to me adding her to the list of prospectives? If, that is, her parents haven't frightened you off."

He appeared lost for several seconds until, with a small shake of his head, he answered. "Ah, Miss Pickering. I'm afraid I didn't have any time with her, but if you think she might make a fine wife, then I am not opposed. I'm certain any in-laws I might obtain will not affect my life much, after all."

She gave a small laugh at that. "You obviously do not know how marriage works. I assure you, any family attached to your future wife will have an impact on you. Especially the Pickerings, who have been anxious to see their daughter marry a title. You're a duke; I'm sure they will happily make themselves regular visitors to your estate."

He cocked his head. "Are you trying to frighten me off of Miss Pickering, Mrs. Kitteridge?"

She stilled. Heavens, was she? There were few candidates on Synne as it was; she'd be a fool to discourage him from any of them.

Why, then, had she pressed the negatives of this particular match? Surely it had nothing to do with her attraction to him.

"No," she answered firmly, as much to center her emotions as it was to answer him. "Certainly not. Miss Pickering would make a fine wife, after all. She's intelligent, and sensible, and would no doubt be happy to rusticate in the country. The better to focus on her passion."

"Which is?"

"Insects."

He blinked. "Insects." At Margery's nod he let out a small laugh. "Well, we certainly have insects in abundance at Brackley Court."

Margery smiled. "Shall we find the lady in question? I guarantee, if you are at all interested in insects—or, rather, in listening to Miss Pickering wax poetic about them—you shall have an admirer for life."

His lips twisted in that endearingly lopsided smile of his and he nodded. As they made their way back across the street and to the stationer's, in search of Miss Pickering, however, Margery found her resolve to be professional slipping. Though she knew Miss Pickering to be a perfectly fine candidate, she wanted nothing more than to yank on the duke's arm and drag him in the other direction.

Why? Surely she didn't want the duke for herself. She didn't want anyone, after all; she would not replace Aaron in her heart.

But desire wasn't love, her mind whispered. And she was so lonely.

No. She clenched her jaw and pushed into the shop, making a beeline for the young lady in question, His Grace following close behind. *Think of Aaron*, she told herself sternly. For, as horrifying as it was, it seemed she needed the reminder of why she was taking on this job of finding a bride for the duke. And she *would* find a wife for him before the blackmail funds were due. Even if it killed her.

Which, she thought as she guided the duke into a conversation about insects with Miss Pickering—and the sourness of jealousy filled her mouth—it just might.

Chapter 5

*T*hree days later and Daniel had met just about every eligible woman on Synne.

Truly, he felt a bit like the prince, traveling about looking for his Cinderella, visiting every house with an unmarried female and hoping for a perfect fit. Or, rather, he thought with a frown, like the Beast, looking for a woman who would see beyond his appearance and take him as he was.

But this was no fairy tale, he told himself fiercely. There would be no happily-ever-after at the end of his story.

Even so, it was hard not to hope for more with Mrs. Kitteridge manning the helm of his future marriage.

Truly, the woman was a marvel, he mused as he accompanied her into the Assembly Rooms. She was like a whirlwind of positivity, all wrapped up in alluring curves and soft brown curls.

But the crowd was larger than he'd assumed it would be, no doubt due to the improving weather. Several of the people present were ones he had met in the past days on his excursions with Mrs. Kitteridge. And yet there were many he hadn't. Too many perhaps. He stepped back from a group of young women blindly headed his way, nearly falling over a young man with overlarge ears and a high collar in the process. Face hot, he mumbled an apology before, trying to tamp down on his growing panic, he gripped his cane tight and looked about for where Mrs. Kitteridge might have disappeared to.

But she was already beside him, tucking her arm in his, steadying him. In more ways than just physically, he thought dazedly. He took a deep breath, aware of a deep easing of the tension within him. But he refused to look too closely at why he might react so strongly to her mere touch. He could only be grateful right then that he had a port in the storm at all.

"I admit," she murmured as they made their way through the anteroom and into the long Ball Room, "that I underestimated how the improving weather would affect the turnout for tonight's performance."

He eyed the people askance as he maneuvered through the room beside her. "Are you certain this is wise?" he mumbled in her ear as they passed a group of matrons, who stared openly at him while whispering behind their fans. Thus far they'd confined themselves to afternoon visits and small gatherings of her close friends. They had certainly never tackled anything of this size. Not even remotely.

"Mayhap we should collect my mother and your grand-mother and take our leave," he continued a bit hoarsely, scanning the milling crowd for any sign of the two women. But no, those ladies had separated themselves from him and Mrs. Kitteridge the moment they'd alighted from the carriage and were now nowhere to be seen. No doubt they had already taken possession of the two seats specially reserved for the dowager viscountess in the front row on such occasions and he would not see them again until the performance was at an end.

"That is the last thing we should do," Mrs. Kitteridge said with a bracing smile. "You admitted yourself that any of the vicar's daughters or nieces would make a fine wife. As they're performing tonight this will be the perfect opportunity to ingratiate yourself with them. Miss Emmeline Gadfeld is particularly enamored of music, and will no doubt look with favor on anyone who shows interest in her passion."

"Much like Miss Pickering and her insects?"

She laughed softly. "And Miss Athwart and her parrot. And Miss Peacham and her baking."

He found himself chuckling along with her. How did she do it? How did she put him at ease when by all rights he should be riddled with anxiety?

And yet she managed it. Just as she managed everyone around her, using the buoyant mood of the gathering to her advantage. She didn't allow one person to linger overlong. There was no time for anyone to question him, as Mr. Pickering had, no chance for gawking and gaping. She was always smiling, resting her hand on his arm to show her ease with him, taking any undue attention away from him by asking each person a question that seemed highly catered toward them. And then, once that was done, she would spot another acquaintance and sweetly excuse them. As they walked away, she would lean in close to him and whisper some fact or other about the person in his ear, thereby cementing them in his memory.

"Mr. Juniper is quite the purveyor of fanciful teapots," she murmured as they left that man behind. "He has an impressive collection of them displayed at his inn, the Master-at-Arms on The Promenade, if you've ever a mind to view them."

"Do you suppose me to have an interest in teapots then, Mrs. Kitteridge?" he asked, his lips quirking in a teasing smile. "I thought my interest lay in watches."

She laughed, a delightful sound. "Oh, you are horrible to throw that back in my face. Though I don't recall you calling me out on my small fib."

"Well, now, why on earth would I have? It extricated me from Mr. Pickering, after all."

She grinned up at him, and he was struck again by the extraordinary prettiness of her features. Tonight she wore her hair in intricate braids, interwoven with seed pearls to match the single pearl nestled in the hollow of her throat. Her dress was a deep amethyst, a simple but elegant creation that hugged her full bosom and fell in gentle folds to the ground.

He realized in that moment that he had never seen her in anything but varying shades of purple and gray. Both were the colors of half-mourning; she must have loved her husband deeply to be grieving his loss still, so long after his passing.

It was a sobering thought, and one that must have showed on his face if the sudden worry in her eyes was any indication.

"Are you well, Your Grace? Goodness, perhaps you're right and this was too much for you in such a short time." She frowned, seeming to look over the crowd with new eyes, then eyeing the door as if weighing the possibility of an early escape.

He gave her a wry smile. "You seemed much more confident a half hour ago."

To her credit, she blushed. "Yes, well. Mayhap I was a tad optimistic."

"A tad?"

She grinned. "Very well, a bit more than a tad. But we don't have a terribly forgiving amount of time. We have just over three weeks, after all."

"I'm certain we can extend the deadline if it means finding a bride," he said.

But he didn't expect the look of strain to appear on her face. "No," she declared with a finality that brooked no argument, "it will have to be in the time we agreed upon and no more."

Before he could quiz her on such a surprisingly stringent rule, however, her expression shifted. "However, though we're working under a fixed deadline, you truly must let me know if my suggestions make you at all uncomfortable. I'm afraid I can get quite enthusiastic, and I wouldn't want you to feel I'm running rampant over you."

The mention of her enthusiasm had his brain veering off into wholly improper avenues. Namely, where else she might show that enthusiasm, especially if that place had anything to do with a bed...

Forcefully burying such thoughts—there was no way he was going to think of this woman in such a way—he considered returning to the matter at hand and questioning her on her timeline. But one look at her face and he thought better of it. She obviously had her reasons. And after all, the quicker he found a wife the better he would be.

"I admit I was nervous," he said instead. "But I am surprisingly comfortable. Or, at least, as comfortable as one can be amid staring strangers. Though after your expert managing, I'm not sure how I'll navigate London without you."

He had meant it as a joke. Yet a strange melancholy entered her eyes, one that he felt mirrored deep in his soul. Before he could make heads or tails of her reaction—and what exactly it meant—a pleasant voice sounded close by.

"Mrs. Kitteridge, how nice to see you here. Oh! And you as well, Your Grace."

"Miss Peacham, good evening. This is a pleasure," Mrs. Kitteridge said with a smile. When the woman, the young proprietress of the Beakhead Tea Room, would have passed them by with a nod, however, Mrs. Kitteridge spoke. "His Grace was just telling me how much he enjoyed the ices we sampled at your establishment yesterday."

The woman stopped her hasty exit and blushed, nodding her thanks to Daniel. "I'm so glad you enjoyed them. And which was your favorite?"

Daniel, caught off guard—for they most certainly hadn't been discussing ices before the young woman's arrival—felt his face heat. "Er—I think—that is—"

"It was the barberry, wasn't it, Your Grace?" Mrs. Kitteridge interjected smoothly. "I do think I recall you declaring that the superior flavor."

"Yes!" he exclaimed. With much more force than the

subject warranted, if the startled look on Miss Peacham's face was any indication. He cleared his throat. "That is, yes, I did enjoy the barberry very much. Thank you."

"I'm glad to hear it. It's my favorite as well. Though I should probably not admit as much, for it would be like choosing a favorite child." When Daniel, at a loss for what to say to that, merely gave her a sickly smile, she looked to Mrs. Kitteridge. "But where is your grandmother? Is she not here this evening?"

"She was of a mind to stay in this evening with Her Grace," Mrs. Kitteridge replied. "Apparently they wished to have an evening without, as my grandmother so subtly said, 'you interfering young people rationing my good liquor.' But I managed to talk her into accompanying us. She is in her customary place at the front of the room."

Miss Peacham laughed. "That does sound like your grandmother. But I'm so glad you were able to persuade her. I was looking forward to her scathing comments, and now I may indulge myself in them when I see her."

"Ah, yes," Mrs. Kitteridge said with a wry twist to her lips. "Gran does add spice to an evening. But shall we find a seat together? I do believe the concert is about to begin."

They were soon seated, Daniel somehow maneuvered between the two. Which did nothing at all for his comfort. He wasn't a small man, after all, and in an effort to keep his bulk from spilling over into the ladies' spaces, he tucked his arms as tight as he could against his sides and held himself as still as possible. He had dealt with long marches and biting cold and all manner of inhumane conditions during his time in the army; surely he could manage an evening seated between two women listening to an amateur musicale.

As the rest of the attendees moved to their seats, however, creating a cacophony of conversation and laughter and shifting of chairs, Daniel was painfully aware of the silence between himself and the two women. Mayhap, he thought a bit wildly, he had been a bit optimistic that this type of situation would be at all comfortable for him.

Suddenly an elbow rammed into his side. He turned, surprised, to see Mrs. Kitteridge motion with her eyes to Miss Peacham on his other side.

"Talk to her," she whispered out of the corner of her mouth.

"Ah. Yes." Face flaming, he pivoted to Miss Peacham. She blinked, glancing at him in surprise. He opened his mouth to speak.

But nothing came out. What the devil was he supposed to say to this woman? He knew nothing about her, after all.

Suddenly he heard Mrs. Kitteridge's voice in his head: *Miss Peacham and her baking.* Of course.

He cleared his throat. "You like to bake."

Miss Peacham blinked. "Er, yes. I suppose I do."

He nodded. And she nodded. And his mind went blank. Had he exhausted the subject of her baking already? Damnation, he was hopeless.

But Miss Peacham continued to look at him, as if she fully expected him to continue his line of questioning. Beginning to panic, Daniel looked over his shoulder at Mrs. Kitteridge, as if to ask *now what?*

She let out a nearly imperceptible sigh but smiled

brightly and looked across him to Miss Peacham. "His Grace has voiced his particular interest in the history of Synne. He was quite fascinated to hear of your dear aunt's part in it all, and how she financed the Beakhead Tea Room by baking for the king himself. He has the utmost respect for independent women of business, you know, and mentioned his dear wish to learn more about your aunt."

Mrs. Kitteridge seemed adept at not only making up stories on the spot that were not the least bit true, but she did it in a way that even he was almost convinced. To his surprise, Miss Peacham turned glowing eyes on him.

"You truly wish to know more about my dear Aunt Bea?"

After only a moment's stunned pause, he said with what he thought was impressive gravity, "Yes, I certainly would."

Which, it seemed, was all it took for the woman to launch into an energetic monologue on her aunt and the history of the Beakhead. He listened as raptly as he was able, trying to ignore the small relieved sigh and chuckle on his other side.

Just as Miss Peacham was explaining how her aunt had taken her in when she was a child and immediately began her indoctrination into becoming a baker, the musicians took their places at the front of the room. Miss Peacham, whose manner was decidedly warmer toward him now, smiled brightly.

"Perhaps we might continue our conversation later in the evening."

"Er, yes. Yes, that would be lovely," he managed.

As the woman began reading over her program, Mrs. Kitteridge leaned in close. "Well done, Your Grace."

He stared at her. "But I didn't do anything."

"You listened," she explained. "Sometimes that is all it takes."

"Listening I can do," he mumbled. "It's the questioning in order to get to the listening that I'm sadly lacking in."

She laughed softly, her brown eyes twinkling at him. "Just as well you hired me on, then."

The effect on his body from the loveliness of her expression and the intimate murmuring of her sweet voice was total and immediate. Heat flooded him, making certain aspects of his person uncomfortable in the extreme. He flushed hot, shifted…

And immediately regretted the abrupt movement as his thigh protested mightily. He winced, rubbing the thing, all the while silently cursing it.

"Are you in pain, Your Grace?"

He grimaced. Of course, Mrs. Kitteridge would have seen. "I'm fine, madam," he managed, praying she would let the subject go.

She nodded, turning her attention to the front of the room as the musicians began tuning their instruments, and it seemed his prayers would be answered. Unfortunately, he had left Miss Peacham out of that particular heavenly request. Having noticed his and Mrs. Kitteridge's exchange, she spoke up.

"Have you gone sea-bathing yet? The cold is invigorating and helps with injuries."

"Ah, no," Daniel mumbled as mortification washed over him. "I'm not certain I would be at all comfortable wading out in such a public place."

"Oh, well, if that is your concern." She shifted to look around Daniel. "Mrs. Kitteridge, you must direct His Grace to the small inlet on the far northeastern tip of the Isle. You know of it?"

"What an inspired idea," Margery proclaimed with a smile. "Indeed, I know it well." She looked at Daniel. He must have looked dubious at best, for an understanding light brightened her eyes and she dropped her voice to a whisper as she leaned closer. "Truly, it would help more than you could ever guess. I have seen the positive effects myself. One of my cousins was injured as a boy in a riding accident, and his groom had him exercise in the swimming pond near his home. The buoyancy eased his efforts and quickened his healing."

Her delicate scent of sugared violets wrapped around him, made all the more potent as the gentle swells of music began to fill the room, and he found it difficult to concentrate on her words. He should perhaps quickly agree and put the conversation behind them, and then spend the rest of the evening charming Miss Peacham— as dubious as it was that he had any talent in that particular area. After the initial unease between them, she had finally managed to be comfortable in his presence, and seemed a sensible and kind woman.

Instead he cleared his throat and said to Mrs. Kitteridge under the cover of the music, "I won't ever heal further. It would be wasted on me."

"Nonsense, Your Grace," she declared with a firmness and utter lack of pity that amused—and delighted— him more than it should. "While it may not miraculously heal you, it can only help in providing you some relief."

"Very well," he muttered. "I will go. But only if you accompany me and show me what I should do."

She blushed scarlet, and he knew with a horrified certainty that he should have never suggested such a thing. Though she was a widow, it would still be highly improper for her to join him in such an endeavor. Before he could recall the words, however, she raised her chin and nodded.

"Very well, Your Grace. I will. Low tide for tomorrow should be just after luncheon, blessedly when the day is at its warmest. We can visit with the Gadfelds, where you can exclaim over their uncommon talent in tonight's performance, and head to the inlet after."

She turned resolutely back to the front of the room as the music swelled louder, putting an end to their whispered conversation. But as he followed suit and redirected his gaze to the musicians on their raised dais he found himself utterly distracted by Mrs. Kitteridge at his side—as well as the surge of anticipation for what the morrow might bring. An anticipation that had nothing at all to do with visiting the Gadfelds and, possibly, his future bride, and everything to do with Mrs. Kitteridge herself.

Chapter 6

As much as Margery might have wished it, the weather of the following day did not miraculously bring in chill winds and storm clouds. No, it dawned bright and warm, a last gasp of summer, exploding in all its splendor.

Damnation.

Casting one last dark look at the cheerful puffs of white clouds that hung about in the endless blue sky, Margery turned away from her window, and grabbing up the basket she'd prepared for today's outing, she hurried from her room to her grandmother's suites. Why had she agreed to accompany His Grace to the tide pool? It would have been an easy thing to refuse. He no doubt would have understood; already there had been a dawning horror in his eyes at the impropriety of his suggestion.

Yet the hint of challenge in his words had drawn a surprising amount of stubbornness from her. Why? For what purpose? Surely she only wished for his well-being and was assuring he followed through with the proper way to swim to better relieve the pain in his leg. It was certainly not because, for one shining moment, she had *wanted* to swim with him...

But no, she thought harshly, frowning as she reached her grandmother's room and knocked sharply on the door, she was merely doing him a kindness, nothing more. Besides, it wouldn't do to leave the man to his own devices. Why, he could harm himself, slipping on the rocks. He could get a stitch in his side and find himself in distress. Yes, she thought with some relief at her reasoning, this was the best thing all around.

A slight scuffle on the other side of the door distracted her from these thoughts. A large black nose peeked under the door for a moment, then a sharp exhale, followed by a great deal of grunting and scrabbling and canine nails on the polished wood floor. Then the door was flung wide, and a flushed Miss Denby stood in the entrance, one hand firmly on Mouse's collar as he attempted to show Margery just how very happy he was to see her.

"Ah, Mrs. Kitteridge," Miss Denby said breathlessly. "Good morning to you. Please excuse Mouse; I do think he's due for a walk—"

It was the wrong word to say, it seemed. Before it had left Miss Denby's lips the beast let out a joyful woof and lunged out the door, tearing his collar free from her fingers, pushing past Margery in his unbridled joy at the coming treat. Miss Denby stood staring after him in dismay for a moment before turning her gaze back to Gran, who was currently seated at the desk in the corner.

The viscountess rolled her eyes. "Oh, go after the creature," she said, using one hand to shoo the girl on her way. With a quick bob and thanks Miss Denby was out the door and after her pet, the pink ribbons of her gown trailing her like banners.

Bemused, Margery chuckled and moved into the room. "It was good of you to allow Miss Denby to bring Mouse with her when you took her on. Not many employers would have."

"Hmm." Gran frowned and looked to the doorway, as if she could see Miss Denby from where she sat. "I dare-say if I had been able to see into the future and witness just how that beast would upend my life, I would not have been so quick to do so."

Highly doubtful. Margery hid a smile. Gran never said as much, but Margery could see how she'd come to care for the young woman. And Gran would do just about anything for those she cared for, no matter her bluster.

"But where are you off to today?" the dowager vis-countess queried, pointing at the basket in Margery's hand with her quill. "Got something planned for His Grace, have you?"

And there went Margery's good mood right out the window. "Er, yes. I have." She cleared her throat. She had yet to tell anyone where they were headed after their visit to the Gadfelds; she did not want anyone construing something improper from it, after all. But nothing was ever hidden indefinitely from Gran. She had the sharpest mind of anyone Margery knew, after all.

Another clearing of the throat. "Which brings me to why I'm here," she continued.

Gran, who had been in the process of returning her attention to the missive she'd penned, cast an arch look up at Margery. "So you didn't come here because of your undying affection for me?" she drawled.

"Of course I did," Margery said soothingly. "But I also have need of a maid to accompany His Grace and myself, and was wondering if I could steal one away for a time."

"A maid? Whyever for? It's not as if you haven't gone about with the duke these past days in a completely proper manner."

Indeed, they had. Every trip had been conducted in an open carriage, visiting friends and acquaintances. Her face heated as she shifted from foot to foot. But then, they had never traveled to such a secluded locale.

"Yes, I'm aware of that," she said. "But today requires a bit of chaperonage."

"Chaperonage?" Gran scoffed. "At your age and station? You've no need of a maid." She turned back to her letter, an indication she was done with the conversation.

But she did not understand. Margery blew out a frustrated breath. "I require a maid, as I'm bringing His Grace to the tide pool on the opposite side of the Isle."

Finally a reaction from Gran. She stilled, then looked up at Margery with an arched brow. "Are you now?"

Margery's face flamed hotter. "Yes. And so which maid might I bring with me? Or should I ask Mrs. Hortenson which of her girls she can part with?"

"You shall do no such thing," Gran said, her voice sharp. "You're being missish. And those girls have enough to do without having to accompany you all over the Isle. Now run along, I've things to do." Once more Gran turned back to her letter.

Margery's frustration grew as she stared at the back of the viscountess's bent head, but Lenora's voice suddenly whispered through her mind: *You know your grandmother better than anyone, and so should fully comprehend that there may be something behind her suggestion that you assist His Grace in getting about in Synne society...*

Could it possibly be true? Margery had dismissed it, but perhaps she shouldn't have. She narrowed her eyes, suspicion rearing in her. And then, before she could think better of it, she blurted, "Are you attempting to match me with His Grace?"

There were any number of reactions Margery expected from her grandmother, from anger to outrage to outright dismissal. What she did not expect, however, was for Gran to throw her head back and laugh.

Margery blinked, quite unable to comprehend what she was witnessing. The viscountess laughed as she hadn't in years, large guffaws escaping her lips, tears forming at the corners of her eyes, her heavily beringed hands pressed to her stomach.

Finally her mirth subsided to mere chuckles, and Gran looked up at her with a wide smile. "Goodness, thank you," she said, wiping her eyes. "I needed that."

Margery could only gape at her. When she found her voice, she demanded, "And so you're denying it?"

"Of course I'm denying it, you silly thing," Gran scoffed. "Haven't you told me these past four years that you shall never replace Aaron? Haven't you proclaimed to all and sundry that you will never remarry?"

"Well, yes," Margery managed when her grandmother stopped and looked expectantly at her.

"I assure you," Gran continued with a decisive nod, "there is not one person on Synne who believes you could be in any danger from the duke. After such loud proclamations on your part, no one in their right mind would think anything scandalous could occur between you and His Grace. Why, the very idea is preposterous. You may as well have joined a nunnery, for all you're seen as a possible marital prospect."

Margery rode out her grandmother's tirade mutely, feeling lower by the second and not having the foggiest idea why. It was what she had always wanted, after all, for people to understand that the love she'd shared with Aaron could never be replaced, and to finally leave off on expecting her to make another match of it.

Why, then, did she suddenly have the urge to cry?

"You can be certain," Gran continued, blessedly unaware of Margery's dismay, "that even if you were found naked with His Grace, not one person would think anything untoward had happened."

Margery had officially heard enough. "Thank you, Gran," she squeaked, mortified down to her toes at her grandmother's crass speech. "You have quite made your point. I'll be off then."

Without waiting for her grandmother to reply, Margery fled the room, praying with all her might she never had to have a conversation of that sort ever again.

* * *

"My dear Honoria," Margery said as they took a stroll in the vicarage's rose garden a short time later, "you've done a beautiful job caring for your mother's plants. Why, I've never seen such an abundance of glorious blooms."

Miss Honoria Gadfeld, eldest daughter of Mr. Gadfeld, the Isle's widowed vicar, smiled and blushed and launched into an energetic explanation of soil and weather and proper methods of trimming to promote the most growth. Margery, however, hardly heard her. The majority of her focus was on the duke, who was currently standing with the vicar's youngest, Emmeline, and her cousins Felicity and Coralie, who had come to live with the vicar and his daughters after their parents' deaths several years before. The group was watching the antics of Emmeline's chickens as they scrabbled after a butterfly, their laughter carrying on the air.

Well, she rectified, the Gadfeld girls were laughing. The duke looked as if he were being roasted alive over hot coals.

But though he could not appear more uncomfortable, he was at least attempting to make conversation. As they'd discussed, he'd complimented all the Gadfelds on their exemplary musical performances from the evening before, making certain as she'd warned him not to pay particular attention to any of the young ladies to prevent any talk should he decide to look elsewhere for a wife.

Thus far none of the Gadfelds were showing even a modicum of romantic interest in the duke. But then, they weren't snubbing the man, either. Which she would think would help to alleviate the duke's discomfort. But from the way he pulled at his collar and held his cane in front of him like a shield, it was obvious the man was nowhere near relaxed.

Just then Emmeline leaned in closer to him to speak. The duke started, stumbling back a step, nearly toppling in his attempt to keep himself from trampling one of her chickens. Emmeline grabbed his arm, steadying him, her light laughter carrying to Margery as the duke blushed crimson. Was it Margery or was there a small spark of interest in the girl's eyes?

A chill swept over Margery. She frowned, pulling her pelisse more firmly about her. The day was unseasonably warm, with nary a breeze. Why on earth would she feel chilled? Surely it wasn't owing to Emmeline's possible interest in the duke. That was why they were here, after all, to see if any of the young women might welcome His Grace's attentions, whether he might secure one of them as his bride. And the quicker he secured someone's hand on the Isle, the sooner she could alleviate her increasing anxieties over taking possession of the funds needed to pay the blackmailer for his silence.

But no matter her internal reassurances, the chill in her bones remained. *Think of Aaron*, she told herself firmly. His beloved face swam before her mind's eye, his eyes unfailingly kind, that shock of pale blond hair curling over his forehead in that rebellious way it had.

But, to her horror, another image was quickly supplanting that: her husband running in terror, deserting his men in the chaos of the battlefield.

She blanched. No, that wasn't what happened at all. She was letting the blackmailer rewrite her memories. Aaron would have never done something so heinous.

Her eyes found the duke again, forcing the poisonous, creeping thoughts of Aaron down to the very pit of her soul. Right now she would focus on the duke, and finding him a wife, and securing the funds she needed to keep the blackmailer quiet. Only when that was all behind her would she deal with these false accusations. And, hopefully, not find her memories altered in the process.

"And what is your opinion, Margery?"

Margery started, flushing guiltily as she turned to find Honoria looking at her expectantly. "I'm so very sorry, I'm afraid my mind was elsewhere."

Instead of repeating her question, however, the other woman pursed her lips, her gaze drifting to the other group. "You and I have known one another for some time, have we not?"

"We have," Margery agreed carefully, not sure where this was going, nor if she wanted to know.

"I like to think you and I are friends."

"We are," Margery agreed again, her trepidation growing.

Suddenly Honoria leaned in close to her, excitement shining in her hazel eyes as she dropped her voice to a whisper. "Is the duke looking for a bride?"

Margery should not have been taken off guard by the question. Honoria was one of the most forthright women she knew, after all. And really, her friend bringing this up was an ideal situation—and perhaps proof that what Gran had said was only too true, and no one saw her as a possible match for His Grace. She pushed aside the sudden lowering of her spirits at that and focused on the positives of this new development. Honoria's interest, whether it be for herself or the younger Gadfeld girls, could only be a boon to their endeavors. And if the people of Synne became aware that the duke was actively searching for a bride, it would make her job all the easier, luring every eligible woman who had an interest in becoming his duchess. In fact, she was surprised she hadn't considered such an action sooner.

And yet all Margery could seem to do was stare

dumbly at her friend, bafflingly loath to confirm her suspicions.

Honoria, no doubt interpreting Margery's silence as offense, grinned sheepishly. "That wasn't well done of me, I suppose. Father is always going on about the sins of curiosity. Of which I'm horribly guilty of. All the time." She chuckled, showing not a bit of concern for her immortal soul. As if one could go to hell for being curious.

And apparently she had no intention of curbing that particular sin anytime soon, for she leaned in close again, eyes bright. "But is His Grace looking for a wife?"

This time, at least, Margery was ready for the question. That did not make it much easier to control her reaction, however. But control it she did, with impressive willpower. There was no reason to keep silent on the matter, after all, not when it would benefit them to let the truth out.

And so it was time to plant the seed. "I would never gossip, you know," she proclaimed with an innocent expression. Then, after giving a pause for effect, to which Honoria seemed to hold her breath in anticipation, she continued, "But I'm certain His Grace will make some lucky young woman a fine husband."

Honoria appeared as if Margery had just presented her with the Crown Jewels, her entire expression lighting with barely suppressed excitement. She looked at the duke standing beside her sister and cousins with bright eyes, and Margery could almost see the wheels begin to turn in her friend's agile mind.

"Now," Margery continued, smiling brightly though it felt brittle on her face, "you simply must give me the recipe of those delectable biscuits you served at tea. My grandmother is quite put out with Miss Peacham for refusing to share her own, and I do think yours would be just the thing to mollify her."

As Honoria, distracted now from her matrimonial musings, guided her back inside the house to provide the necessary recipe, Margery bit her lip and worried at her wedding ring. What was the matter with her? Honoria had practically dropped a gift in her lap with her question, yet Margery had faltered in providing the very information necessary to assist herself in endeavoring to see His Grace engaged with all haste. Yes, she desired the man. She thought him attractive and magnetic, had dreams about him at night, found herself transfixed by the strength of him, even imagining his large hands on her...

She cleared her throat and fanned herself with her hand as heat suffused her. She obviously could not control her thoughts about the man. But what on earth could she do about it? She had no fears that she would fall in love with him. She could not possibly love anyone as she'd loved her Aaron, after all. But desire, as she had seen from her time in London while witnessing the majority of the *ton* chasing pleasure without the benefit of affection, was a different beast entirely. Wasn't it...?

She blanched. What, did she think she might jump into bed with the man? That maybe her interest in him lay in her loneliness these past four years? That if they were to become lovers she might rid herself of this unwelcome attraction and finally be able to think around him again?

Well, she hadn't until now. She bit her lip, trying to

focus on Honoria as she copied the recipe, chattering all the while. Only too aware that quite another set of wheels had been put into motion.

* * *

As much as Daniel had dreaded the visit to the vicar's, he'd dreaded the trip after to the inlet even more. What fresh hell was this, after all, that had him preparing to swim alone with Mrs. Kitteridge, who was quite possibly the most alluring woman he'd ever met?

No, not quite possibly. She was definitely the most alluring woman he'd ever met.

He had hoped that something might prevent the trip. Surely the ocean could stir up a good frigid breeze, the clouds might come in drunk from a night of carousing over the vast ocean, and a heavy downpour would commence as they relieved themselves of their excess. Was he asking so much, really?

But the truth could not be further from reality. There were nothing but blue skies and wisps of clouds, and the glorious sun shining down on it all.

It was as if even Mother Nature herself was conspiring against him, he thought grimly, glaring at the clear horizon as they traveled along the coastline.

"The Gadfeld women were all looking exceptionally pretty today."

Mrs. Kitteridge's voice was cheerful, carrying on the warm breeze. He cleared his throat, dragging his gaze away from the offensively lovely vista to look her way. "Er, yes. Yes, they were."

"And Miss Emmeline seemed quite taken with you,"

she said. Her brown eyes were large in her face, her expression encouraging.

He blanched. "I'm not sure *taken* is the appropriate word. I nearly crushed one of her beloved chickens, after all."

She pursed her lips as she studied him. "You, of course, did not see the way she looked at you after the chicken fiasco. I daresay she found you adorable."

He let out a surprised laugh. It was on the tip of his tongue to state that she required spectacles. But he halted the words before they could find purchase; Mrs. Kitteridge had proved herself to be quite staunch in her defense of him, most especially when he talked badly of himself.

Which should not have warmed him so.

"I daresay," she continued, not daunted in the least by his silence, "one of them would make a fine wife. They are all amiable girls. Do you see yourself able to care for any of them?"

"I am not looking to care for anyone, Mrs. Kitteridge," he mumbled. He gripped the handle of his cane, rubbing his finger anxiously over the small bit of metal there, forcing himself to recall just why he insisted on sticking to that particular rule. As if he needed the reminder.

She blinked. "But surely it's possible that you and your future wife might develop feelings for one another."

"No." The word came out harsh and sharp. Her jaw dropped and she drew back against the plush squabs. He silently cursed himself for his handling of the subject. But she must understand if they were to continue with this agreement that he was not searching for affection. In fact, he was actively hoping to avoid any chance of it.

When he continued, his voice was a great deal gentler, though no less firm. "I will happily consider any of the girls as a wife. Just as I happily consider Miss Pickering, or Miss Peacham, or Miss Denby, or any of the other young ladies I've met over the course of my short time here. But under no circumstance am I looking for love."

She nodded, as if she understood all too well. There was too much knowing in her gaze, and panic reared in him, that she might see to the heart of the matter.

Desperate to distract her, he blurted, "You seem to know everyone on the Isle. Did you grow up here then?"

She blinked, no doubt surprised at his abrupt change in subject. But she quickly recovered. "Er, no. That is, the bulk of my time was spent at my father's estate, just outside of Ampleforth. But after my grandfather passed, I spent my summers here, to be a comfort to Gran. She was despondent after he died. They were quite in love."

It was an image he could not seem to come to terms with, the confident, gruff Lady Tesh as a young woman in love. His lips quirked. But then, she had not been born as she appeared now, like Athena, who sprang full grown from the forehead of Zeus.

His humor must have shown on his face, for she smiled. "I assure you, she and my grandfather were quite thoroughly in love. Why, the times I came across him whispering in her ear, making her blush something fierce."

Suddenly her expression fell. "She missed him terribly when he passed. And, as my father had recently remarried, and my brother had just arrived, my father thought it best if I spent time with Gran."

There seemed so much behind such a simple retelling, some hidden heartache buried deep. The ghost of it lurked in her soft brown eyes. "Tell me about your time here," he said, hoping to direct her thoughts to happier ones.

He was rewarded with her soft smile. "It was like a dream. Gran refused to allow a moment of sadness to darken our time together. She made certain each day was filled with adventures and outings. And so our every waking moment was spent walking along the beach and hiking to the Elven Pools and drinking tea at the Beakhead. And then Lenora began to spend her summers here as well, after her own mother's death, and she became my dearest friend. And, of course, there were my cousins, close to our age." She laughed. "The mischief we got up to. Why, we fairly ran wild on the Isle."

He was transfixed by the change in her. The way her face glowed with happiness as she told him about her childhood touched something deep inside him. He felt something loosen in his chest, like a pebble worked free of its rocky bed.

Just then the carriage rocked to a halt. He blinked, and the strange moment was gone. Thank goodness, he told himself firmly, ignoring the ache of loss deep in his chest.

The groom came around the side of the carriage and threw the door open wide. Mrs. Kitteridge smiled brightly at Daniel. "Here we are!" she chirped. Gathering her skirts, she moved toward the door. And nearly lost her balance as she tried to maneuver around his legs and cane.

Daniel reached out and gripped her arm to steady

her. There was a jolt of heat, sizzling and sparking between them. He thought that if he looked at his hand, it must surely be aflame. They were so close he could smell the sweetness of the biscuits she had eaten at tea on her breath as it fanned his face, could see the faint gold flecks in her brown eyes as they widened. For one glorious moment he thought he saw a reflection of his own potent desire for her mirrored in her eyes.

Surely not, he thought as shock coursed through him. She could not possibly want him.

The groom held a hand out for her. Mrs. Kitteridge started and tore her gaze from his to look at the groom. "Thank you so much, Henry," she murmured. Then, gently extricating her arm from Daniel's grip, she placed her hand in the other man's and descended the carriage step. Seeming to leave a great, gaping hole where she had been.

Chapter 7

Daniel took a moment to compose himself, closing his eyes and drawing in a shaky breath. For one mad moment he considered settling deeper into his seat and refusing to descend. Surely he could hide away in here for a good long while. Why, if he utilized his cane as a makeshift sword, he could fend off everyone indefinitely.

It was a tempting fantasy, to say the least. But not at all possible. And so, heaving a sigh, he descended from the carriage in his awkward, slow way. Taking the hamper of supplies from the groom, he turned and followed Mrs. Kitteridge. Both of them walked in silence, traversing a small path that dipped in a gentle slope toward the sea. The sound of waves was loud here, the sheer cliff on one side providing a bowl that trapped the sound. Suddenly the path curved a sharp left. And a flat terrain of rock and damp sand lay before them, a pool of water in its midst.

It was an oasis; that was the only word for it. Hugged

by soaring cliffs on three sides, with hardy trees and brush clinging to it all like an evergreen tapestry, it was as private as one could imagine any natural space to be. Mrs. Kitteridge stopped where the path ended and stared up at it all, a look of dismay crossing her gentle features.

Mayhap she would suggest they turn back, he thought a bit desperately, determinedly ignoring the surge of disappointment in his chest. Clearing his throat, he queried quietly, "Is something amiss?"

"What?" She started, looking at him with wide eyes. "Ah, no, forgive me, Your Grace. It's just that I haven't visited this place for some time and had forgotten how…isolated it is." A tremulous smile moved across her lips like a wave, coming in with a hush and quickly retreating. "But that is the point, isn't it?" she asked, her voice gaining strength as she turned and made her way to the pool of water.

Pressing his lips tight, that same damn anticipation pounding through him as he eyed the full flare of her hips swaying beneath the violet of her gown, Daniel made his careful way behind her. A path of sorts had been created, though whether from centuries of feet pounding it flat or purposely carved he couldn't tell. Regardless, it was an easy walk and quickly brought him to where Mrs. Kitteridge stood at the cliff face.

"You may change first," she said, a riotous blush staining her cheeks, her eyes determinedly glued to his cravat. With a trembling finger she pointed to the cliff behind her.

He turned with grim determination, spying what he had not been able to see before: a small opening in the cliff face, a convenient dressing room created by Nature herself. Squaring his shoulders, he retrieved his bundle from the hamper and ducked inside.

It was larger than he had first assumed, with more than enough room to stand and maneuver. Daniel clumsily divested himself of the majority of his clothes; he had chosen simple, no-fuss pieces for today, but that did not mean they were at all easy to remove. Eventually he stood in nothing but his smalls and a loose linen shirt in the chill space. He would not look down at himself, he told himself fiercely. The worst of his scars were hidden, after all. Even so he could not help remembering the one time a female had seen his unclothed body.

He shuddered at the memory. It had been shortly after Nathaniel's unexpected death. He had been stunned, reeling. And yet his mind had clearly understood one devastating fact: he was responsible for the dukedom now. Which meant he must marry and produce an heir.

But Erica's disgust of him was still fresh, an open cut doused liberally with salt on an almost daily basis. He had healed some, in body if not in mind, since that devastating day. Surely, he had told himself stoutly, determined to do right by his family, he was not as bad as all that. And so he had gone to the local pub, had gotten himself stinking drunk. And had accepted one of the barmaid's invitations up to her room.

She had been willing enough to start. He could still recall the pleasure of her hands on his body as she began to undress him, the ache for a physical touch he had never experienced.

But, more than that, he remembered the pain that had surged in him as she'd uncovered scar after scar, soft gasps of dismay escaping her though she had hidden it as well as she had been able to. She had soldiered on, though, and he'd had a pitiful hope sputter to life that it could be done.

Until she'd come to his leg.

At the sight of his mangled flesh she had drawn back from him, a horrified sound escaping her lips, muffled behind a hastily placed hand. She had quickly recovered, of course. But he had not remained to hear her apologies, instead grabbing up his clothes and cane and hobbling from the room as fast as he was able.

"Your Grace, are you well?"

Mrs. Kitteridge's voice trailed to him, banishing the vivid memory. He blinked in incomprehension for a moment, looking about at the rough walls and filtered sunlight coming in through the cave opening. Ah, yes, he was on the Isle of Synne, he recalled with a grim twist of his lips. And about to swim with a gentle young woman who would no doubt run screaming back to her grandmother's house should she actually catch sight of the battlefield that was his body, no matter how she might defend him.

But it was much too late to back out now, wasn't it? "I'm quite well, Mrs. Kitteridge," he managed, his voice rough even to his own ears. And with that he took up his cane and made his way from the cave.

The sun blinded him for one brief moment, and so he did not immediately see Mrs. Kitteridge's reaction to his appearance. But her breathy "Oh" was quite unmistakable.

He had never in all his time in battle felt the urge to flee, not even when the outlook appeared dire. Now, however, standing before this attractive woman, half-clothed, he had the mad desire to turn tail and run. "This was a mistake," he mumbled, turning to retreat back into the cave.

"No!" And then her small hand was on his arm. He froze, caught between pleasure and pain at that light touch, and squeezed his eyes tight as the burn in them threatened to transform into tears.

"I know my appearance must disturb you, madam." He gritted his teeth. "If you'll allow me to dress, we can return to Seacliff and forget this ever happened."

"You mistake me," she said, her voice soft. "I am not disgusted by your appearance. Quite the opposite, in fact."

He glanced sharply at her, unable to comprehend the meaning behind the unmistakably husky quality of her words. Only to find her staring with fascination at her hand on his arm.

Again that question burned through his mind: Did she want him? The very idea was incomprehensible. If someone who had vowed to marry him didn't want him, if someone who charged for her services had been unable to take him to her bed, how could this lovely, gentle woman desire him?

Suddenly she blinked and, flushing bright red, stepped away from him. He felt the loss of her touch down to his soul.

"Ah, forgive me," she said, the words sounding strangled in her throat. "That was inexcusably bold of me." She stood still for a moment in utter confusion before, with a wild kind of laugh, she ducked around him and into the cave.

Daniel blinked. What the devil had that been about? But he wasn't about to wait around and find out. Straightening his shoulders, he made his way to the water, taking care with where he placed his cane, prodding for the firmness of solid stone beneath soft sand.

The tide pool was large, and much deeper on one side than he'd first surmised, the pale green of the shallower area quickly darkening to hidden depths. The water at the surface, however, hinted at the life within. Small fish darted about, algae clung to the walls. He eyed it with trepidation for a moment. No matter the warmth of the day, it looked blasted cold.

But a sudden sound from her direction put a stop to any delay he might have been attempting. Dropping to the ground as quickly as he was able, he swung his legs over the edge and, sucking in a sharp breath, let himself sink feet first into the pool.

Ice. It was like pure ice needling his skin. He gasped, his limbs—among other things—instinctively drawing inward. "Shit!" he yelped. "What the ever-loving hell!"

Laughter reached him. He cast disbelieving eyes to where Mrs. Kitteridge stood before the cave entrance. She was dressed in a modest gray flannel shift secured clear up to her throat. And yet, though there was nothing seductive about it, desire pumped hard and fast through his veins. Her bare toes peeked enticingly pink from the edge of the garment, her hair a rich, thick plait over her shoulder. She was full-figured, and the simple garment was no match for her enticing curves. It hugged her breasts and flirted with the flare of her hips as she approached.

His mouth went dry, his mind going blank. Though he didn't know if it was owing to the cold shutting down his bodily functions or the alluring sight of Mrs. Kitteridge.

"In my defense," she said, stopping near him, "I didn't think I would have to tell you it would be cold."

He blanched. "Forgive my language, madam."

She waved an unconcerned hand in the air. "As I've said, I'm not missish when it comes to such things. Now then, shall we get started?"

And with that she walked to the deeper end of the pool and dove in headfirst.

She disappeared under the water's surface, then quickly shot up, gasping for air. Her head was thrown back, the shift clinging to the curve of her back. His heart pounded at the fleeting sight of it; despite the fact that it was undoubtedly a modest swimming garment, it left little to the imagination.

He watched, transfixed, as she turned about and swam toward him. Her shift drifted behind her like a bride's veil, each kick of her legs sure and strong, her arms cutting through the water. She stopped in front of him, grinning.

"Goodness," she said as she found her feet on the sandy bottom and sloughed water from her face, "so much for being prepared. But we'll quickly grow used to the chill, as long as we keep moving."

He set his jaw and nodded, trying his damnedest not to look at her breasts just beneath the surface. Thank God she was small in stature. As it was, the water played about her shoulders, lapped at her neck. *As he wished to do. With his tongue.* The thought careened through his mind, making his mouth water. He swallowed hard and forced himself to focus on her words.

"This area is quite even," she was saying, "and is the perfect location for the particular exercises we'll be performing today. The water will give you a buoyancy that you don't possess on land, so you might work the muscles of your leg without the resistance of gravity."

"I see," he said. Though he really didn't.

She smiled wryly at him. "You are a horrible liar. But you're showing an impressive trust in my judgment, and so I shan't hold it against you."

A laugh rose up in him, wholly unexpected. And with it the band of tension across his chest eased.

The exercises started off slowly. It was unnerving, taking those first steps without his cane, feeling the sand shift beneath his bare feet. But he quickly came to the conclusion that she had been right, that without the added weight of his body his leg was able to move more freely and with little pain.

And he also learned that the more he focused on his movements, the less he focused on her. Which was a necessity just then. He had pointedly refused any offer of physical help from her in getting started—if he would not allow Wilkins to massage his leg, he sure as hell wasn't going to allow this tempting woman to offer herself as some kind of living crutch. But that did not lessen the impact of her soft voice in his ear, or the faint drifting of her shift against him. Or, even worse, the occasional brush of her full breasts against his arm.

Thank God the water was cold.

At the end of nearly half an hour she peered up at the sky, shielding her eyes with her hand. Daniel swallowed hard as, for one dazzling moment, he saw the wet flannel of her shift outline her breasts in glorious detail.

"We'd best leave soon, or that sun will make our skin as red as tomatoes. But first," she said, with a wicked grin his way. In the next moment she'd disappeared beneath the surface.

He watched, transfixed, as she swam the length of the tide pool, pushing through the water just beneath the surface. Her hair, which had come loose from the thick plait she'd secured it in, flowed behind her. She looked like some water sprite. And, God help him, he had the insane urge to follow wherever she might lead.

She finally resurfaced, grinning, at the far end of the pool. "Goodness, but that felt glorious," she called to him. "Do you know how to swim, Your Grace?"

"Of course," he scoffed. In truth he wasn't certain, not even a bit; he hadn't swum since he was a child and had no idea if he was capable of it any longer. But after an afternoon of putting the focus on how broken he was, he suddenly wanted nothing more than to have this amazing woman see him as whole.

"Well, then?" she prompted.

In answer he set his jaw and, calling on knowledge he had ignored for the better part of two decades, he started off toward her. And was almost overcome with emotion.

His legs moved easily, his injury no hindrance to his ability to propel himself forward. It was as if there was no injury, nothing holding him back. He felt strong, truly strong, for the first time in years.

A smile stretched his cheeks, overwhelming happiness flooding him. He did not realize he was crying, however, until he reached Mrs. Kitteridge. Her grin slipped away, and she reached out with chill fingers to wipe the moisture from his cheek.

"I am so sorry, I shouldn't have pushed you. Does your leg pain you?"

"You misunderstand me," he managed, his voice gruff. "It is exhilarating."

The smile she gifted him was breathtaking to behold. So much so that he reacted without thinking, snaking an arm about her waist, hauling her against his chest, his mouth finding hers.

She went rigid in his arms. Ah, God, what the hell was he doing? He released her, retreating, letting the cold water swirl in that aching space between them, though he knew there was nothing on this earth that would cool his ardor. "I'm so very sorry," he mumbled, gripping the rocky edge of the pool, the words coming in a rush of mortification. "That was unforgiveable of me—"

She reached out and gripped his shoulders, stalling the awkward apology in his throat. And then she drifted against him. He stared, uncomprehending, as the shock in her face was replaced with a nervous kind of determination. And then she did the last thing he ever thought she would do: she wound her arms about his neck and pressed her lips to his.

* * *

Kissing the duke was one of the boldest things Margery had ever done in her life. And for one horrified moment she feared she had mis-stepped. Yes, the man had kissed her. But he had only been caught up in the moment. He was on the lookout for a bride, not an affair.

But then he groaned, and his free arm came about her, hauling her tight to his chest. And all her doubts and fears melted away under the fire from his kiss.

Ah, God, how good this felt. To be held, to be
kissed, when for so many lonely years she had thought
to never experience this again. Her breasts, unhampered
by either corset or layers of clothing, pressed against
the broad width of his chest. The water swirled and
eddied about them, adding another layer to the exquisite
pleasure of it all.

But though he gripped at her wet shift, pressing
desperate fingers into her lower back, his kiss was surprisingly chaste. Wanting to deepen the kiss more than
she wanted air to breathe, she tilted her head, opening her mouth, and pressed her tongue to the seam
of his lips.

He shuddered under her hands, his lips opening in a
gasp. She took full advantage of it, thrusting her tongue
into the hot recesses of his mouth, touching it to his own.

It was as if something was unlocked in him. He
twisted, pressing her back against the wall of the pool.
His body was as hard as the surf-worn rocks at her back,
though infinitely warmer. She arched into him, her fingers diving into his damp hair even as his tongue sparred
with her own. There was nothing smooth or practiced
about it. Rather, it seemed to be the raw reactions of
his body. And she reveled in it, in the barely leashed
power in his arms and the strength of his muscles as her
hands drifted down to grip his shoulders. She let loose a
low moan.

Then he was gone, nothing but icy water swirling
around her.

She blinked, staring uncomprehendingly at him. He
was treading water several feet from her, his expression
aghast.

Only then did she realize what had occurred. The full ramifications crashed down on her head. Never mind that she had never kissed another man besides Aaron in her life. The duke was paying her to find him a wife; if she failed she was looking at Aaron's good name forever tarnished, as well as ruination and scandal, not only for herself but also for her entire family. Her actions were reckless and unthinking, and totally went against her character.

But did they really? The question whispered through her mind, making her remember who she had been before Aaron's death. She was a passionate creature despite her typically calm exterior, and always had been. When she had been younger, that passionate side had led her to do the unimaginable—for her love of Aaron she had stood up to her father and walked away from his house and his support for her. And so, in reacting to the duke's kiss as she had, it seemed the more daring aspect of her personality was still alive and well.

That, however, was no excuse for her actions where this man was concerned.

"I'm sorry," she whispered, holding tight to the pool's edge. Knowing if she let go her trembling legs wouldn't be able to keep her afloat.

"*You're* sorry?" There was ripe disbelief in his voice.

She nodded miserably. "I shouldn't have kissed you."

"*I* kissed *you*. I should be the one who's sorry."

"That may be true, but I continued it when you would have stopped."

"Yes, but you wouldn't have done so if I hadn't started it in the first place."

She tried for a smile. "Are we to compete once more for who was most at fault?"

There was no answering spark of humor in his eyes as she'd hoped. Instead his expression became more stark. "We should return to Seacliff," he mumbled. "They'll be wondering where we are." With that he turned and began swimming toward the far side of the pool.

After several long seconds Margery followed. No doubt the trip back to Seacliff would be the longest in her life.

Chapter 8

"My dear Miss Athwart," Lady Tesh said with a wide smile as their party entered the Quayside Circulating Library. "I do hope the duchess and I are not late."

Daniel might have smiled at the viscountess's abrupt about-face; after all, just seconds ago she had been simultaneously berating the driver for taking too long to reach town, ordering Miss Denby in the proper handling of Freya—Mouse had been banned from the excursion, poor, heartbroken thing, a fact that Daniel could only be grateful for, as the beast had not lost his interest in Daniel's ... nether regions—and snapping at some young gentlemen loitering on the walkway.

But after the debacle at the tide pool yesterday with Margery—naturally she was Margery to him now, and could be nothing else—he was having difficulty in focusing on anything else. Why the hell had he kissed her?

Miss Athwart's approach blessedly distracted him from further distressing reminiscence. He had met the three

Athwart sisters, proprietresses of the circulating library, during his first visit the week before. All were highly eligible, if odd, young ladies. Miss Seraphina Athwart, the eldest, was the sternest of the trio. Her equally stern pet, a green-and-red parrot, was perched on her shoulder, giving her the faint air of a pirate captain.

Pushing her overlarge spectacles up her nose and bringing her piercing gaze into focus, she nodded to the dowager viscountess and his mother. "Of course you're not late, my lady." She greeted them all in turn, then turned back to Lady Tesh, her brusque greetings completed before anyone had a chance to reply in kind. "My sisters have just set up tea in preparation of our discussion."

"Discussion?" Margery frowned at her grandmother. "What discussion is Miss Athwart referring to, Gran?"

Lady Tesh gave the proprietress a fond smile. "Why, Miss Athwart had the most cunning idea for a pamphlet extolling the glories of the Isle. Our previous booklet is sadly out-of-date, and she thought it was time to modernize it. I have agreed to finance her endeavor. The duchess and I are set to discuss the details now."

Margery shot Daniel a guarded look before turning back to smile at Miss Athwart. "Perhaps you might postpone for a few minutes? His Grace was quite interested in talking with you on the merits of owning a parrot such as your dear Phineas."

Instead of gaining the woman's interest, as Margery had no doubt intended, however, Miss Athwart shot him a condescending look. The bird, too, eyed Daniel with a certain amount of sharpness. "Parrots are not for the hobbyist, Your Grace," the woman said. "They are much more than a mere pet, or a decoration or oddity you wish to lay claim to, to be brought out when the amusement strikes you. I will, of course, be quite happy to talk to you another time. Though I daresay anything I might have to impart would dissuade you quite thoroughly. For now, this pamphlet is of utmost importance. It is imperative we showcase Synne's superior features. I will never understand," she continued, shooting a frustrated glare out the shop window to Admiralty Row beyond, "why Brighton is so popular. We've a much more pleasant position, in my opinion. Just because some rotund Regent has decided to build his Pavilion there?" She made an aggravated little sound. Her parrot puffed up its feathers and mimicked the sound, as if in agreement with its mistress.

"Too true," Lady Tesh chimed in, her perturbed expression a mirror of the young lady's. And the parrot's as well, if Daniel was being honest.

He saw in that moment just why the two women, from such different ages and backgrounds, seemed to share such a camaraderie. For, as frightening as it was, they were alike as any two people he had ever seen.

"Shall we, my lady, Your Grace?" Miss Athwart said in her no-nonsense way, motioning to a rich blue brocade curtain at the back of the shop.

They all started off together, Margery and Daniel bringing up the rear. Suddenly Lady Tesh stopped and turned to her granddaughter.

"Where are you going?"

Margery blinked. "Accompanying you, Gran."

The dowager viscountess frowned. "Why?"

Before Margery could react—truly, Daniel didn't have a clue how to react, either—his mother intervened.

"Olivia, dear, perhaps Mrs. Kitteridge did not hear your plans when you were talking of them in the carriage."

Lady Tesh pursed her lips and speared her grand-daughter with a stern glare. "Let your mind wander again, did you? And you?" she demanded of Daniel, turning sharp eyes on him. "I suppose you didn't hear me, either?"

How was it, he thought, panic setting in as she glared up at him, that one frail-looking elderly dowager viscountess could instill such terror in him? "Er—"

"Daniel, I thought I taught you to listen to your elders," his mother reproached gently, though the faint humor in her eyes took away any sting that her words might have caused.

"Hmmph." Lady Tesh turned back to her grand-daughter, her disgust palpable. "Very well, since the two of you could not bother to listen to me the first time I mentioned it I shall repeat myself. I have sent word ahead to Miss Peacham at the Beakhead Tea Room to inform her that you will both be by this afternoon. Neither of you can possibly have any interest in what we're about to discuss; no doubt you'll be bored to tears. Now, go and have some refreshments, and take in some sea air after you're done. Unless," she continued with a sly look, "you've a mind to join us after our meeting with the Misses Athwarts for our excursion to the modiste's. I could buy you some lovely pink gowns, Margery. Or mayhap green?"

Margery held up her hands before her grandmother had even stopped talking. "No, Gran, I'm fine with my wardrobe as it is."

"Well, then," Lady Tesh said, her frown back in place

as she shooed her granddaughter off, "don't keep us. Off with you both." And with that she turned about and trailed after Miss Athwart.

For a moment Daniel and Margery stood staring in befuddlement after them. As one they turned to look at one another. And he nearly drowned in her eyes. It came flooding back to him then, the feel of her in his arms, her eager mouth opening under his, her tongue . . .

He nearly groaned at the memory. Holding his cane in front of himself, he motioned to the door with his free hand. "Shall we?" he muttered.

Seemingly flustered—had she been remembering yesterday as well?—she nodded in agreement and they exited the shop into the bright early-afternoon sunshine. It was an assault on his senses after the dim quiet of the circulating library, and he determinedly welcomed it, lifting his face to the sun, breathing in deeply of the fresh sea air. Anything to erase the remembrance of Margery at the tide pool. To his consternation, however, it only managed to re-create some of that setting, cementing the memory all the more.

Heaving a frustrated breath, he started off beside Margery down the long street that was Admiralty Row, to The Promenade and the Beakhead Tea Room.

Miss Peacham was there to welcome them, her face wreathed in smiles, her thick black hair wound about her head like a crown.

"Mrs. Kitteridge, Your Grace. How wonderful to see you again. Lady Tesh informed me of your intended arrival, and so I have saved you our best table."

They were directed through the establishment, between small round tables topped with all manner of lace and fine linen and delicate porcelain pieces, straight to the table that the viscountess typically secured for herself. Larger than the others, accompanied by large chairs topped with plush blue and yellow cushions that matched the curtains in the bow window, it possessed an unencumbered view of The Promenade and the beach beyond, and the wide sea beyond all that.

"You would like the barberry ice, would you not, Your Grace?" Miss Peacham asked with a smile, her eyes dancing.

It was the perfect opening, he told himself, to expand on their conversation from the night of the musicale. The young proprietress would be a fine choice as his wife, after all, with her friendly, elegant manners.

And yet he could do no more than dredge up a weak smile and nod. Looking faintly confused, Miss Peacham nevertheless took their order and sailed off.

Leaving Daniel alone with Margery.

He frowned. *Alone* may be overreaching; while the shop wasn't empty, it still had a respectable showing of patrons happily sampling the delicious wares. Low conversation hummed and laughter rang out, the clink of silverware on porcelain joining in, the delectable scents of baked goods filling the air.

And yet, seated at this private table beside Margery, he felt as if they had been wrapped in a bubble. A tense, anxiety-ridden bubble, but a bubble all the same.

Margery must have felt it, too, for she cleared her throat and shifted in her seat. "I'm sorry for having been so distracted this morning. Here we had chances for you to get to know both Miss Athwart and Miss Peacham better and I failed spectacularly."

He started. Was she really going to pretend everything had gone back to normal? Which, he supposed, they should if they were at all wise. They had only shared a kiss, after all. It had not been life-altering—or so he would continue to tell himself. Nor did it change the very real fact that he needed to marry, and preferably before the dreaded trip to London.

And yet he couldn't help but resent that she had so quickly turned her back on it and fallen back into the details of their agreement.

"I don't wish to know either of them better," he growled before he could stop himself.

She glanced at him, startled. "You wish to take Miss Athwart and Miss Peacham from our list of prospective wives?"

He shook his head in agitation and blew out a frustrated breath. "I don't wish to talk about the damn list at all right now."

"But we have less than three weeks to find your duchess."

"I can delay my trip to London."

"But I cannot delay," she cried. Her sudden gasp, the hasty hand she clapped over her mouth, reminded him that she was in dire need of the funds she would get from assisting him, apparently in a very specific amount of time. And he as yet didn't know why she was so desperate for them.

He narrowed his eyes. "Are you in trouble?"

She paled, her typically rosy complexion turning a sickly green as her gaze slid from his. "I can find you a wife within the time we agreed upon" was all she said. And then, in a bright tone that had a brittleness to it, "Oh, how lovely; our order is here."

He ached to know what the devil was wrong. It was both a blessing and a curse, really, that they had been interrupted. While he wanted to help her in any way he could, he knew that asking her to confide in him would open up an emotional intimacy between them that he was not looking to have.

Damn Erica for hurting him. Damn *himself* for allowing her to hurt him so. He should have known that a woman as beautiful and polished as her, a woman who had been made for the glittering London scene, would never love someone as awkward as he. But he had been fooled by her attempts to get him alone, by her shy proclamations of affection, by her kisses. When all along she had been playing him as expertly as her pianoforte.

But he would not allow himself to be fooled again, and would most certainly not allow himself to be hurt again. Which was exactly why this cold advancement to matrimony was so very necessary.

As they ate she chattered with an almost manic busyness that fairly made his head ache. And every bit of her one-sided conversation was centered on the damn list of prospective brides. The Gadfelds, she said, would surely agree to an invitation to tea at Seacliff, where he could show Miss Emmeline the rose garden. And did he have chickens back at Brackley Court that he could discuss with her? Miss Denby, while constantly made busy by Lady Tesh, would surely enjoy his company in the morning again when she took her private time to walk Mouse. And perhaps on this occasion Margery might accompany them, the better to get Mouse away from his...ahem, person...so he might better secure the young lady's focus on him. There was a ball, too, in just a few days; mayhap he might secure Miss Peacham for a set. And while she knew he did not dance, he could sit with the young lady and talk, surely. Miss Pickering's parents had invited them on a picnic; while the young lady would no doubt be ever watchful for her beloved insects, mayhap he might assist her. She was certain they could get Miss Athwart away from her beloved circulating library, though she doubted they would be as lucky to separate her from her parrot. And did he mind the creature? It could be rude at times, but she was certain it didn't bite. At least, not unduly hard.

Daniel ate, and drank, and sat in increasingly morose silence. Because the more she spoke, the more he realized that no matter which of the young ladies he pictured himself with, he could not see himself kissing them as he'd kissed Margery.

Why not marry her, then?

The thought came with a suddenness that left him breathless. Marry Margery? No, she had declared she would never remarry. Yet now that the idea had taken hold it would not let him go. And he realized it made perfect sense. He desired her. And she had kissed him, with a surprising enthusiasm. She had mentioned more than once that she didn't mind his scars.

Really, he was surprised it hadn't come to him sooner.

Just then she took a sip of her tea—no doubt she was parched from the constant stream of words that had poured from her mouth over the past half hour. Knowing there would not be a better time, and that he might lose his nerve if he thought on it any longer, he blurted, "Why don't *you* marry me?"

Chapter 9

Margery blinked. A ringing started up in her ears, her mind going blank. Surely she'd heard him wrong. "Pardon?"

His face fell, seemingly as shocked as she was by his question. "Which, I suppose, is not the most romantic proposal," he mumbled to himself. But a look of determination entering his blue-gray eyes, he asked, "So what do you think? Will you marry me?"

She could not have held back the sharp bark of laughter that exploded from her if she'd tried. "You're jesting." He had to be jesting. It was all a cruel joke. He could not have possibly suggested that *she* be the one to marry him.

He proved her wrong in the next moment. "Not a bit."

But Margery's shock was beginning to wear off, and was quickly being replaced with a hurt so profound it made her hands shake—made so much worse by the disturbing longing that filled her. "I thought you understood," she managed through lips that felt stiff, ignoring any emotion but for the pain caused by his suggestion. "I won't remarry. Ever."

Uncertainty flickered in his eyes. "I know you said as much," he said, his large, blunt-tipped fingers demolishing a biscuit. "But I thought—"

"What, that because I had kissed you, I might have changed my mind?"

"No—"

"Because I assure you, women are allowed to have desires. And I've seen enough of the world, as limited as my view has been, to know that one does not have to have deeper emotions to feel desire. Why, as a widow I could have a discreet affair and no one would bat an eye."

Her voice was climbing in volume along with her agitation. Flushing, belatedly realizing that this was no place for such a conversation—and that she seemed to be attempting to convince not only him but herself as well that it was natural to have desires—she closed her mouth with a snap and glanced about them. Blessedly, however, not a soul seemed to be paying them the least attention.

"Though you are the only man I have kissed besides Aaron," she continued in a low, strained voice, her eyes fixed on the empty teacup before her, "that in no way means I wish to remarry. Why, it would be the grossest betrayal to his memory. I could never replace him. Not ever—"

Her voice broke off on a sob. She clamped her lips shut, fingers working at her wedding band in agitation. The silence stretched on between them, the duke unmoving beside her.

Suddenly his voice, achingly gentle. "I'm sorry."

She raised her eyes to him and took in the sorrow that seemed to fill his craggy face. For what, her broken heart? Or was it something else?

But what did it matter? "Please," she said in a mere whisper, "don't mention such a thing again."

"I won't," he said.

But as he turned away, she wondered at the regret that filled her. He was a distraction, she knew. Her desires for him were not going away anytime soon. If she was to find him a bride and collect the money necessary in paying off the blackmailer, she had to quench this physical need for him. But how?

* * *

"My goodness," Margery cooed later that night as she lay on her side on the floor of her goddaughter's nursery, one hand propping up her head and the other tickling Charlotte's toes, "aren't you the sweetest angel in all of creation. I could just eat you up, you darling thing."

Lenora, seated cross-legged on the floor beside her, looked up from the sketch she was making of her daughter and chuckled. "Though I am biased, I agree with you completely. Why, these rolls look like the most succulent sausages." With that she took her daughter's pudgy arm and planted a wet kiss on it.

Charlotte gurgled merrily at the attention, her wide blue eyes swinging back and forth between the two women as she kicked her feet.

Margery laughed. This was what she needed to distract herself from her troubles. To spend an evening away from Seacliff and Daniel, to forget the horrible debacle at the Beakhead Tea Room and pretend, for even a few hours, that she was back in those halcyon days before Daniel had arrived and turned her world on its head.

But no, her life had not been ideal before his arrival. In fact, with the delivery of the blackmail letter her life had begun to unravel completely.

Would that she could get out of her deal with Daniel. How was she going to find him a wife when she wanted him for her own?

And there was the crux of the problem, the reason she had reacted so strongly to his offhand suggestion that they marry. Because she knew now what that longing in her had been when he'd made his hasty proposal: for a split second, she had wanted to say yes.

"Margery."

Lenora's voice startled her, so much so that her hand slipped from under her head and she nearly toppled over. "Pardon? Oh! Sorry, dear heart. I'm afraid my mind was elsewhere."

"Yes, I'd noticed," her friend replied dryly.

Margery chuckled. "I have been a bit distracted this evening, haven't I? But is it any wonder, with such a dear, sweet creature to do the distracting?" She took up a rattle that lay nearby and shook it. Charlotte blew bubbles and kicked her legs, her pudgy arms flailing in excitement.

Margery went back to talking in silly singsong tones to the baby. All the while, however, she was sharply aware that her friend was watching her with a peculiar intensity. They knew one another better than anyone; Lenora could not have failed to see that, no matter how much Margery might deny it, there was something very wrong, indeed.

As the seconds passed Lenora seemed to go back

to her sketch. Just as Margery was beginning to relax a bit and think she might come away from this visit unscathed, however, Lenora went in for the kill.

"How is His Grace, Margery?"

From anyone else it would have been mere polite curiosity. But Margery knew that Lenora's seemingly casual question was anything but.

She cleared her throat. "He seems to be doing well."

"Is that so?"

"Yes."

Again, a beat of silence, broken only by Charlotte's loud smacks as she gnawed on her fist and the faint scratch of pencil on paper.

Finally Lenora spoke again. "I've heard quite a bit of talk regarding the duke."

"Have you?"

"Yes. It seems he's all anyone can talk about. Miss Gadfeld was particularly vocal when she came to visit just two days ago."

"Was she?"

"Mmmm."

Margery, done with this game of cat and mouse, rolled her eyes and looked at her friend. Lenora was watching her closely, her pale green eyes shrewd. "I suppose you learned that His Grace is searching for a bride."

"I have."

"And I suppose you have come to the conclusion that I'm assisting him in his endeavors."

"You are astute."

Margery fought the urge to stick her tongue out, as she used to do when they were children. "And...?" she demanded.

Lenora shrugged. "It just surprises me, is all, that you would look elsewhere when there is a perfectly obvious choice staring at you in the mirror every morning."

"Lenora," Margery growled. Again that flare of hurt and longing from yesterday. Though now that she understood it for what it was, wasn't the longing so much more potent?

"You cannot tell me, after our conversation just after His Grace arrived, that it has not crossed your mind."

"Not in the least," Margery lied.

But her friend must have heard the falsehood. She narrowed her eyes. "So there is nothing at all between you?"

No. The word bubbled up in her chest. But her throat, traitorous thing, would not let it out. She flushed hot.

She feared for a moment that her friend would gloat. Lenora had predicted, after all, that something might happen between herself and Daniel, and that she would be only too happy to claim victory when she was proven right.

Instead she placed her sketch pad aside and sidled close to Margery. "What's happened?"

Her voice was soft and quiet, and undermined Margery's determination to keep to herself what had occurred. With the kiss, at least, as well as the messy proposal—if one could even call it that. The blackmail, however, and the horrible things said about her Aaron were another matter entirely. No, she would make certain no one learned of that, ever. No matter if it destroyed her in doing so.

She let out an exhausted breath, and stroked Charlotte's downy gold curls. The baby opened her mouth in a yawn.

"I kissed the duke."

"Oh."

That one soft sound was all that escaped Lenora's lips. But it carried a wealth of meaning.

Margery's lips twisted. Though she ached to look at her friend, to see her reaction, she nevertheless kept her gaze firmly on Charlotte. Her goddaughter's eyelids were drooping now over her clear blue eyes, her bow mouth working silently.

Suddenly the child's nurse appeared. "I'll put Lady Charlotte to bed, shall I, Your Grace?"

"Henrietta, you are wonderful, thank you," Lenora murmured. Margery gave Charlotte a soft kiss on her brow, and Lenora took her daughter up, passing her to the nurse. And Margery and Lenora were alone.

Margery expected her friend to suggest they go to her sitting room to talk. Instead Lenora sank back to the floor beside her. Her pale yellow skirts billowed about her as she settled herself on the rug.

"Tell me what happened," she said softly.

Margery sighed and sat up, hugging her knees to her chest. "What is there to say? I kissed the duke. Well, actually, he kissed me. But when he would have stopped, I continued it. Quite enthusiastically." She groaned and pressed her eyes into her knees. "What was I thinking, Lenora?"

Suddenly Lenora's hand was rubbing comforting circles on her back. "I daresay you were lonely."

"Yes," she whispered. "But that is no reason to kiss the man." She raised her head and looked at her friend. "After our...kiss...he suggested I marry him."

Lenora's eyes flared wide in shock, but she stayed quiet, patiently waiting.

Margery nodded wryly. "I refused, of course. Though I rather think you're going to tell me I was a fool for doing so."

"No, my dear," Lenora said. "In truth, I think that's the wisest thing you could have done."

Now it was Margery's turn to be surprised. "Truly?"

"Yes." She smiled sadly. "You didn't settle for anything less than a strong love with Aaron. As much as I tease you, if you're to remarry, it should be for the same reasons."

Tears burned in Margery's throat. "I don't think that could possibly happen. How can anyone be blessed so twice in their lives?"

"I do believe," Lenora whispered, "that if anyone deserves to be blessed in such a way again, it would be you."

"Nonsense," Margery managed, fighting back tears.

They stayed that way for a time, Lenora with her arms about Margery, the faint crackle of the nursery fire and the soft lullaby of the nurse in the next room the only sounds.

Suddenly Lenora stilled. "That doesn't mean," she said slowly, "that you need to remain alone all your life, you know."

Margery frowned, turning her head to look at her friend. "I assure you, I don't plan on getting myself a parrot like Miss Athwart. I've already been informed that such creatures are not for hobbyists."

"Silly thing. I certainly don't mean a parrot, or a dog, or even a gaggle of chickens like Miss Emmeline. I just mean," she continued with an intent look in her eyes, "that you might find companionship. *Physical* companionship."

Margery gaped at her. "Are you suggesting I take a lover?"

Lenora shrugged. "And why not? You are a widow, after all. And there is no crime in a woman finding pleasure, is there?"

"But...a lover?...Lenora..."

Her friend laughed. "You act as if I've told you to go out this very night and find someone to take to your bed. But I'm much too selfish for that; now that I have you here for an evening, I'm not about to let you get away so easily."

She rose, holding out a hand for Margery, who took it, allowing herself to be hauled to her feet. But as they left the nursery arm in arm, she learned that Lenora wasn't quite through with her mad plan.

"You can find a lover tomorrow," she quipped with a wink.

* * *

If Daniel could have stayed holed up at Seacliff all the next day he would have, and gladly.

But when one was so pointedly reminded of one's promise to join the rest of the household on a long-awaited excursion by a certain dowager viscountess, there really was no getting out of it, save for something life-threatening. Which, unfortunately, major embarrassment did not fall under.

And so, doing his best to act like everything was normal—though in reality it was the furthest thing from it—he hauled himself into Lady Tesh's carriage, seated as usual beside Margery, and tried his best to ignore her thigh so very close to his own. The trip was long, quite possibly the longest of his life, figuratively speaking. He held himself as still as possible, the better to keep from touching her. But every bump and turn had him in danger of leaning into her. By the time they reached their destination, his thigh was not the only thing aching; every muscle in his body screamed at his attempt to hold himself as far away from Margery as was possible. Finally, however, it was time to alight, and the women descended from the carriage. Stretching his stiff neck from side to side, he heaved a sigh and lurched from the conveyance, looking up at the building before them.

Swallowhill, belonging to the Duke and Duchess of Reigate, was a compact, square house, seemingly plucked from a fairy tale. With its pale gray stone exterior, mullioned windows that sparkled in the sun, bright white-painted sills, and delicate roses climbing up its face, it was simple, and yet exceedingly lovely.

Just then Reigate himself flung the front door open and bounded down the steps.

"Hallo," he greeted them cheerfully, grinning as he approached. "Clara will be tickled pink you're here. As am I, for even my sparkling wit and Phoebe's loving attentions haven't been enough to distract my wife these past days."

Daniel frowned. There seemed something decidedly off about Reigate. He appeared happy enough, as no doubt he should be, with his wife due to birth their first child soon. But the man appeared almost brittle, the tight lines that radiated from the corners of his mouth and his faintly mussed, harried air speaking of a hidden strain.

As Lord Oswin appeared and greeted the other women, Margery sidled up to Reigate, her face tight with worry. "And how are you holding up, my friend?"

Daniel didn't hear the man's answer, for his mother approached then and tucked her hand in the crook of his arm.

"Darling, you remember Lord Oswin, of course."

Ah, yes. It was time for the social niceties he was trying his damnedest to master—truly, he regretted more than ever dodging his lessons on manners and comportment as a child, as well as the countless times he'd huddled in corners during social engagements. Dredging up a smile, he moved forward and held out his hand. "Certainly. My lord, I hope you're well?"

Which must have been the correct thing to say, for the man grinned and shook his hand heartily. "I am. Phoebe and I have not been back to Synne since our marriage, and I had forgotten how invigorating the sea air could be. And you, Your Grace? Are you enjoying your stay?"

Thus began a polite back-and-forth that, though simple and easy enough, nevertheless had Daniel feeling drained by the time the other man turned away. But he had done it, hadn't he? He had made it through an innocuous conversation unaided. Feeling strangely exuberant at this small victory, he turned to look for Margery—only to find she had disappeared along with Reigate into the house.

The disappointment and loss that coursed through him was disturbing in its intensity. It was not as if he needed her approval, he told himself fiercely. He was not doing it for her. Rather, he was utilizing the skills she had shown him to manage himself alone.

Alone. Suddenly that word, which had given him such comfort in past years, didn't seem so comforting any longer.

"Let's head inside, shall we?" Lady Tesh said then. "I grow overwarm." She glared up at the bright sun as if it had offended her in some way. Which, even with what little he knew of the woman, Daniel had no doubt it somehow had.

Miss Denby was there in an instant. She set Freya down on the ground, opening the parasol she had brought along for just such a purpose, nearly clipping Lady Tesh's nose in the process. Lady Tesh watched her, her expression stony, as the mauve and lace concoction was held aloft above her snow-white head.

"Thank you, Katrina," she muttered before turning back to Lord Oswin. "Well, then?"

He grinned and offered his arm to the dowager. "Of course, my lady."

They made their way into the house. In her awkward, bouncing way, Miss Denby followed Lady Tesh and Lord Oswin, trying to manage the parasol even as she called brightly to Freya, who was studiously sniffing a flower, as if taking stock of its merit. Daniel and his mother followed, keeping well clear of Miss Denby as, within seconds, she went to work wrestling the parasol closed in order to enter the house.

Daniel winced as she got the thing stuck on the doorjamb. "Do you require assistance, Miss Denby?"

"Pardon? Oh! No, not at all, Your Grace." She smiled brightly before, her pixie face scrunching in concentration, she forced the thing closed and swung it in a triumphant arc. Which perhaps was not the brightest thing to do, as it bumped Freya in the backside. The dog let loose a yip of outrage and went careening inside the house to hide under her mistress's skirts. Chaos ensued as Lady Tesh simultaneously tried to extract her dog from her skirts, comfort the creature, and berate her companion for injuring her beloved pet. All the while Miss Denby fluttered about them like an anxious butterfly, the parasol swinging from her arm and further enraging Freya, who peered from her bower of bright pink silk, her dark eyes almost human-like in their contempt.

Daniel and his mother stood on the front step, gaping at the scene. Finally Lady Oswin appeared, bringing immediate calm and reason as she effortlessly managed everyone, directing the lone maid in the removal of outer garments—he had been told the duke and his bride kept few servants at Swallowhill—soothing her great-aunt, and comforting Miss Denby.

"Well," Daniel said as he watched the small group disappear from view, "I suppose we must count our blessings that Mouse was not allowed to accompany us."

There was a moment of silence. Suddenly an unexpected chuckle had him peering down at his mother. And his breath stalled in his chest. Her face was alight with humor, her eyes sparkling. When she looked up at him, he thought for a powerful moment he might cry. She wore an easy, happy expression he had not seen on her face since before his going off to war.

"Goodness, it's like a comedy of errors, isn't it?" She laughed. Then, patting his arm, she released him and walked inside.

He watched her for a moment, overcome. While his mother had insisted that he visit Synne to learn the social skills he would need in London—if with not total confidence, then at least a passable semblance thereof— it had been his mother's peace of mind that had been the determining factor in his finally agreeing to her mad scheme. And this was proof positive that it had all been worth it.

His heart lighter, he followed her, stepping into the front hall. The interior of the house was small but welcoming, the intricate inlaid floor buffed to a sheen, the great curving staircase that swept up the back wall in a graceful arc polished and gleaming. He followed the sound of voices into a bright sitting room off the side of the hall, its wide windows and plush floral carpets as welcoming and cheerful as the moss-green furniture and collection of lovingly framed watercolors that graced its soft yellow walls.

But he hardly saw it at all, for his attention was immediately fixed on Margery. She was seated beside the Duchess of Reigate on a wide couch, their arms about one another, their heads bent close in whispered conversation. But that was not the thing that froze him in his tracks. No, the thing that struck him was Margery's hand on the duchess's swollen stomach. He suddenly had a vivid image of Margery herself heavy with his child...

He stumbled, just catching himself with his cane. "Ah, my apologies," he muttered when every eye swung his way. Face hot, he greeted the duchess and Lady Oswin before sinking down into an overlarge chair as far from the others as he could manage without appearing rude.

What the devil was wrong with him? He was not going to marry Margery. She had quite emphatically refused, after all. And the plan was still for her to help him locate a bride before it was time for him to travel to London; fantasizing about her expecting his child was not conducive to succeeding in that particular endeavor.

Even so, as he watched Reigate sink beside his duchess and kiss her temple, as he watched her smile slightly and lean into his side—and as he caught the small, wistful smile that flitted across Margery's face at the act of affection—he grew aware of a dull ache in his chest. He rubbed the ache, frowning, and forced his attention away from the scene. Perhaps the Isle was doing something to him, undermining all those rules he had set out for himself when the plan to take a wife had first formed.

Or perhaps it was Margery.

No, certainly not. He gripped the handle of his cane tight and straightened his spine. Regardless of the reason, he was a man of strength and determination, and knew what had to be done. He would take every precaution to ensure he did his duty with the least amount of emotional entanglement possible.

Suddenly the Duchess of Reigate stood. Or, rather, she did a kind of roll, her stomach leading the way as she lurched to her feet. Her husband was at her side in an instant, offering his arm as support.

"But Aunt Olivia and dear Miss Denby and Their Graces have yet to see the nursery," she said brightly. "Lenora has painted the most cunning mural on the wall; I simply must show you."

With that she was off. The rest of them dutifully followed in a kind of slow-moving procession, out into the hall, up the sweeping staircase, down the long upper hallway to the room at the far end.

It was surprisingly spacious for the size of the house,

with large windows thrown wide to let in the ocean breeze. Soft colors lent a magical air to it all, from the delicate violet drapes fluttering in the gently shifting air to the small cradle with its hand-stitched blanket to the vines and flowers in the rug at their feet. And dominating the space was the most breathtaking image he had ever beheld.

It was as if he were staring straight into a sun-dappled forest. The mural was incredibly detailed, each leaf captured in a single moment, each branch delicate and reaching for the heavens. Here was the faint blue of a bird flitting in the branches, there the spotted back of a fawn as it rested in the brush.

The breath left Daniel in a soft exhale of disbelief. As the others spoke and exclaimed over the piece, he found he could only stare in wonder. He felt certain in that moment that if he stared long enough, the whole thing would come to life before his very eyes.

"I told you she was talented."

The soft voice murmured in his ear, startling him back to the present. He turned to see Margery beside him. It was the first time she had looked directly at him since yesterday afternoon, and he felt the power of it clear to his toes.

But he saw, too, that there was uncertainty lurking in her gaze. A feeling he could understand only too well. Something had shifted between them, first with his kiss, then with his ill-conceived proposal. And for the life of him he didn't have the faintest clue how to navigate these dangerous shoals.

Though he supposed a bit of normalcy could only help. "The duchess truly painted this?" he asked.

"She did."

"I've never seen anything like it." He returned his gaze back to the mural. There were more hidden wonders the more he looked. Was that a hedgehog beneath a fallen branch? And a...fairy?

He let loose a small laugh. "I vow, if I'd had anything like this when I was growing up, I would have remained in the nursery until they removed me by force."

She chuckled. "I daresay it would have been the same for me."

But the beat of camaraderie was quickly gone, and they were left standing in awkward silence. The others talked and laughed and exclaimed over every little detail of the nursery. Finally the duchess said something about a greenhouse, and they all filed out. He was about to follow them when Margery's hand on his arm stopped him. He glanced down at her in surprise.

Her gentle brown eyes were solemn. "I must apologize for my reaction to your...suggestion...yesterday."

He gaped at her. "What the devil are you sorry for?"

"I shouldn't have snapped at you as I did. It was a perfectly logical line of thinking, after all."

"You had every right to be surprised. Hell," he quipped, hoping his light tone might ease her discomfort, "I surprised myself."

The smile she gave him was sickly at best. His gaze drifted down to her hand. As he'd expected, she was once more working anxiously at the thin gold band on her finger. "You loved your husband greatly," he murmured.

She flinched and clenched her fingers into fists. "Yes, I did," she managed.

"Won't you tell me of him?"

She blinked owlishly at him. "You wish me to tell you of Aaron?"

"If you'd like."

She frowned, her expression suddenly guarded. "What would you know?"

A strange reaction, that. From the tense line of her shoulders she appeared ready to go to battle.

"Erm, whatever you wish to speak of. How did you meet?"

"Oh." Her face relaxed some at that, her gaze going hazy, as if she were suddenly transported elsewhere. "I met him when I was quite young. He was the son of the town blacksmith, near my father's property, Epping Manor. We grew up together, and were close friends." A small smile flitted about her mouth. "And then, one day, we were more than friends. Truthfully, it happened so gradually, I was completely in love with him before I even knew I had begun."

He thought, for a moment, he could see clear to her soul. "It must have been very romantic."

"It was." She gave a small sigh. Then, suddenly, her smile slipped, pain dulling her eyes. "My father wasn't happy with the union, of course. He was quite adamant that I not marry a person of such low birth. And so we eloped, to Gretna Green. And then went on to live in London for a short time."

"And he enlisted."

She swallowed hard, looking toward the mural. But her expression was so haunted he didn't think she saw the mural at all. "My grandmother tried to insist on buying him a commission. I thought for a moment he might take her up on her offer. But I saw, though he considered it, that he wasn't happy. When I pressed him, he admitted he would not be comfortable having his way paid, that he wanted to go up in ranks by his own merit. I had not realized until just that moment that he was just as prideful as I—" Her voice cracked, the rawness of it tearing at his heart. "I imagine he would not have been...welcome...buying his way into a higher rank, considering his origins. He only considered my grandmother's suggestion to please me."

Daniel could imagine what young Aaron Kitteridge would have gone through had he taken Lady Tesh up on her offer. There was a strict hierarchy in the military. No doubt both nobles and commoners would have taken exception to his position. They would have made the man's life miserable.

Mrs. Kitteridge closed her eyes for a moment, breathing slow and deep. Finally she opened her eyes, and though the ghost of grief was present, it was under control. "He would have gone through all that and more for me. But I supported his choice so he might be happy. And he was, so very happy. His eyes were so bright when he left, so full of excitement—"

Again, she broke off. This time, however, she remained silent, her gaze focused on her wedding ring, shining against the violet of her half-mourning gown.

"I'm sorry."

The words were so inconsequential. And yet, it was all he could think to say.

She gave a small, strained laugh. "It's the same story told by so many war widows. I'm hardly anything special."

"Yes, you are."

The words surprised him. And her, if the shock in her eyes when she looked up at him was any indication. Thank goodness she was faster to recover than he was.

"And what of you? Did you leave behind any sweethearts?"

She would touch on the one subject he had no wish to discuss. But there was still something infinitely brittle in her gaze. She had confided in him, though it had taken much out of her. It was only right that he reveal something of his past to her. It was common knowledge, after all, that he'd been engaged before buying his commission; he could confine his own story to the bare facts and nothing more.

He dragged in a deep breath. "I did. Lady Erica Harcourt, daughter of the Earl of Gadby. She accepted my proposal, but wished to wait until my return from the Continent to marry."

He fell silent. She watched him with solemn eyes, waiting patiently. Finally he let out a huff of a laugh. "I think, seeing as why I've hired you, you can guess what happened upon my return."

"She broke it off with you because of your injuries?"

He shrugged. "It was to be expected, I suppose. She was gently born. And though you may not believe it"— he attempted a smile, though feared it must resemble more of a grimace—"my injuries were even more unpleasant back then."

To his surprise, anger flared in her typically mild brown eyes. "Your appearance is not unpleasant. And the addition of a few scars is no reason to abandon someone. Why, it's absolutely despicable what she did."

Once more her staunch defense of him warmed something deep inside him. And not only was she defending him, but she was also quickly working herself up into a fury. He smiled, a true one this time. "You are a rarity," he murmured.

That seemed to stop her ranting in its tracks. "I'm only stating the obvious."

"The obvious perhaps to you. Unfortunately, most people aren't as kind as you."

"Well," she said, her embarrassment palpable. She looked about the nursery for a moment, as if lost, before motioning to the door with an odd flapping motion. "Shall we join the others?"

As they made their way from the room Daniel felt the lightening of a weight that had been pressing down on him. It had felt surprisingly cathartic to talk about Erica. Not that he was planning on making it a common occurrence, of course.

But as they made their way into the side garden and he gazed down at her sweet profile, he thought that maybe, just maybe, it would be nice to have a friend for a short while. His gaze shifted to her lips. And surely, he thought with a hard swallow as he tried not to remember the feel of them beneath his own, he could ignore his desire for her. It was only a few weeks, after all. What could possibly happen in that time?

Chapter 10

$\mathcal{M}$argery reached into her desk drawer with shaking fingers, lifting out the small plain wooden box from within. When she had hidden the blackmail letter there nearly a fortnight ago, she had not wanted to touch the thing again. She felt soiled just looking at it; to pick the thing up was like branding those damning words into her flesh.

But over the past two days, since their trip to Swallowhill, she had found she was rapidly losing sight of her purpose in finding Daniel a wife.

She was still working hard at securing scenarios where he might finally make his choice of which lady on the Isle he might like to marry, of course. Not an afternoon passed that didn't see them in town on some pretext or other, no evening where they weren't at a dinner party or card party.

Nor was there a moment when she didn't think about that kiss and her conversation with Lenora.

Take a lover? Certainly not. She still openly mourned

her husband, after all. It would be the grossest betrayal to take another man to her bed.

Each day that passed, however, made that argument weaker and weaker. It was only physical, after all. Her heart would not be involved.

And perhaps, with her increasingly vivid thoughts of what it might feel like to have him trail his hands over her body, how it might be to have him slide between her legs, easing the ache deep inside her, which was growing stronger by the day, she could finally focus on finding him a wife. Because whether she liked it or not, the deadline to pay the blackmailer was marching closer. And Daniel was no more decided on which of the young women he wanted to marry. And if she did not stop mooning over the man and start focusing all her efforts on securing that bride for him—thereby making certain she received her fee and was able to keep Aaron's memory protected—she would fail. She bit her lip, tension strumming through her veins as she recalled the neat black checks on the calendar in her desk, bringing her closer to October first and her day of reckoning. And she could not fail; she just couldn't.

Before she went down the path of diving into an affair with the duke to quiet the urges inside her, however—goodness knew if she did, there would be no returning to the person she was now—she was determined to utilize every defense in her arsenal against the pull of him. Even if that meant reading once more that most disturbing, vile letter.

Dragging in a deep breath, she unfolded the parchment. It was common stock; no expensive vellum here, but neither was it rough paper. The words glared up at her, sharp and bold in their construction, the ink harsh against the white background. Disgust and fear shuddered through her, but she fought the urge to crumple the hated thing and hurl it into the fire, instead focusing on the message. Fragments of it stood out:

> *Your husband was not the hero you believe him to be...*
>   *...traitor to his country...*
>   *...keep this fact silent...*
>   *...one hundred pounds...*
>   *...Don't fail me in this.*

Nauseated, she felt bile rising up in her throat. She fought it back, forcing herself to read the letter again and again. She could obtain the means to pay off the evil creature who had sent it. She need only get through these last weeks and secure a wife for Daniel. Surely, she thought as she hid the letter back in its box and left her room to join the others for their trip to the Assembly Rooms and the ball that was to take place, she could manage the rest of their time together with little trouble.

As she caught sight of Daniel in the front hall with his mother and Gran, resplendent in his stark black evening wear, dread—and a kind of anticipation—churned inside her as her gaze met his and she knew, she would be lucky if she could manage an evening.

* * *

"And what is your opinion, Your Grace?"

Daniel started, dragging his gaze away from Margery.

She looked exceedingly pretty tonight, the soft light from the glittering chandeliers catching in her upswept curls, highlighting the myriad hues within the seemingly plain brown locks. He'd been doing that with disturbing regularity this evening, finding his mind and his eyes wandering to her when he should be paying attention to whatever young woman he was supposed to be conversing with. Which, in that particular moment, was Miss Peacham. Who was waiting in patient expectation for him to answer her on whatever it was she'd been talking about.

He gave her a sickly smile. "I'm sorry, what was that?"

Annoyance flared in her eyes, there and gone in a moment. And no wonder, for it was not the first time in the past ten minutes he had lost track of the conversation. "Now that you have swum at the tide pool, what is your opinion on the effects of saltwater therapy?"

Which was the very last thing he wanted to think about just then, for it brought to mind that kiss, something he had been thinking about with disturbing frequency ever since it happened. "Ah, it was quite invigorating. That is," he hurried to say, his face going hot, "I do believe it helped. My leg, I mean."

"I'm glad to hear it, Your Grace," Miss Peacham said. "And will you be returning to the tide pool?"

"No!"

She drew back, no doubt startled by his overly forceful refusal. "I . . . see," she managed, though it was obvious from her tone and the way her gaze flitted to the orchestra—no doubt praying they might finish their set with all haste—that she didn't.

As if taking pity on her, the music ended just then.

Miss Peacham, a look of abject relief plastered to her face, fairly leapt to her feet. Before he could so much as begin to rise she dipped into a quick curtsy, said a pretty, if rapid, farewell, and hurried off.

Margery, in the process of heading his way, stared after the proprietress in surprise. "And how did your set with Miss Peacham go?" she asked with impressive neutrality when she reached him, sinking into the seat vacated with such expediency by the lady in question.

"About as well as it appeared, I fear," he mumbled. He cast a cautious glance her way. "Who is the next poor soul who will be forced to sit and talk to me?"

"Actually," she said, "you're free for this set."

"Thank God." He groaned.

Her lips twisted in commiseration. "Was it really that bad?"

He gave her a miserable look. "You witnessed for yourself the young lady's relieved exit. I leave you to your own conclusions."

She pressed her lips tightly together into a nearly nonexistent line. That did not stop the laughter from dancing in her eyes, however.

He narrowed his eyes. "It is not a cause for humor." Nevertheless, he felt an answering smile tug on his lips. They stared at one another for several seconds before simultaneously bursting into laughter.

"You're right, of course," she managed between chuckles. "It's not remotely funny. But did you see that woman's face?"

Which made him laugh all the harder. "She could not get away fast enough," he wheezed. "Truly, if you can manage to get me engaged to one of these ladies in two weeks you deserve much more than a paltry one hundred pounds."

Her laughter cut off as quickly as it had begun. When he glanced her way, her expression was stark.

"Of course," she mumbled. "We've just over a fortnight before the money is due."

That sobered him as nothing could. "Due to whom?"

Fear flashed through her eyes before she quickly shuttered them. "Why, due to me, of course," she said. She gave a strained laugh. "Though I suppose we must now cross Miss Peacham off our list of possibilities. Unless you think there's a chance?"

She was hiding something. He was certain of it. Though, of course, he admitted morosely to himself, weren't they all?

"No," he answered quietly, "there's no chance."

She nodded, as if checking off some invisible list. Her gaze scanned the crowd, presumably to search for the remaining candidates. Or was it to keep him from seeing something in her eyes?

He mentally shook himself. It was no business of his if she was hiding something. And he'd best remember that.

"You must have some preference in a wife by now," she said.

Yes, but you've refused. The words nearly escaped his lips. By some miracle he held them back. What the devil was wrong with him? By turning him down, she was saving him from what would have surely turned out to be a highly ill-conceived idea. She affected him too much for his heart to remain safe from her indefinitely, after all.

"N-no," he managed. He cleared his throat. "Any one of them will do, really." *And the quicker the better.* Though how he was supposed to court any of them while his every waking thought was spent on Margery he didn't have a clue.

She must feel the same frustrations he did—or, at least, the same level of frustration. But there was no way on earth she could possibly be frustrated for the same reasons he was, he thought as she blew out an aggravated breath. "You should choose soon. We don't have much time, after all. Before the month is up, I mean."

Again that note of latent panic quickly muted. He frowned.

Before he could be tempted to question her on something that was no doubt a private matter, however, she pursed her lips, and it took all his willpower not to focus on the lusciousness of them. "I do believe you should decide by tomorrow morning, before breakfast. That way you might have the entirety of a fortnight to court her and secure her hand. Ah! But it's nearly time for your set, such as it is, with Miss Emmeline. Let's go find her, shall we?"

As he followed Margery down the length of the ballroom to where Miss Emmeline conversed with her cousins, he tried his damnedest to focus on his goal. By selecting a woman to court and, with luck, convince to marry him, he would not have to worry about such a thing when he arrived in London.

If, that was, he could rein in his desire for Margery in order to succeed.

Chapter 11

*T*he weather turned overnight, a thick cloud cover coming in from the sea, the air taking on a decided chill. Nevertheless, Daniel made his way to the side rose garden just as he and Margery had agreed on the night before. The conversation they were to have this morning was to mark the beginning of his earnest courting of one of the young women on the Isle, after all. And if there was anything he needed just then, it was to focus on one woman and one woman only. And preferably one who was not Margery.

The moment she appeared from a side door and began moving through the garden toward him, however, he could think of little else. How was it, he thought helplessly, that she could mesmerize him without even trying. There was nothing remotely seductive in the way she moved just then, after all. Her head was down, her step quick and efficient. Yet he could not tear his eyes away from the sway of her hips beneath her gown, or the determined set of her luscious mouth, or the way her curls bounced against that delicious curve where neck met shoulder.

Despite the briskness of the air, his body warmed considerably. Even more so when she raised her gaze to his and he found himself held captive by those incredible brown eyes of hers.

"Your Grace," she said a bit breathlessly when she reached him.

"Mrs. Kitteridge. I hope you slept well?"

"I did, thank you." She looked to the sky. "It looks as if it might rain."

"Does it?" he managed, unable to look away from the sweep of her lashes, so dark against her porcelain skin, so long they nearly reached the gentle arch of her brows.

"Yes." She cleared her throat, flushed again, the pink in her cheeks darkening and spreading down her neck. "We'd best get to it, before those clouds open up."

Ah, yes. The wife thing. "I agree," he said, though, for some insane reason he could not comprehend, discussing the topic of choosing someone he might make his duchess was the very last thing he wanted just then. He motioned to the small stone bench nestled back in the hedges, that same bench they had shared his first morning on Synne. A veritable lifetime ago. "Shall we?"

She looked to the bench like it was a beast about to leap at her. "Ah, no, thank you. I think I'd rather stand."

Which, now that he thought of it, was probably the wisest course of action. He had no wish to be in such forced proximity with her, after all.

"But let's get to it, shall we?" She attempted a smile, but it was a weak thing. "Have you had time to decide who you would like to court?"

He blinked. Damnation, he hadn't. Which was ridiculous, really, as that was the whole point of this meeting. But he had been so focused on Margery—again—that he had quite forgotten there was a decision to make.

But as she stared at him with a kind of guarded expectation, and he wracked his brain going over his options, he realized with horrible certainty that, though each young woman was wonderful in her own way, to him they all paled in comparison to Margery.

Which would not do. After all, she had stated clearly—very clearly—that she would not ever consider remarrying.

Yet his mind remained blank. Finally, desperate, he decided he would blurt out the very first name that came to him. "I choose—"

A bright flash, followed quickly by a loud crack, drowned out whatever it was he might have said. In the next instant the sky opened up, pouring a sheet of icy rain down on them.

They both gasped and started off for the house. But when Margery might have rushed to cover, she instead slowed her steps to stay by his side.

"Go," he urged, even as he limped along as fast as he could muster. "Get yourself inside. I'll be with you shortly."

"I'm not leaving you, you silly man," she declared.

There went that warmth in his chest again. And he realized as they trudged along, getting more soaked by the second, that he was beginning to care for this woman.

The realization stunned him nearly senseless. But he had no time to process it. They reached the side door just then and ducked inside. And he found himself in a small, dark sitting room. And much too close to Margery for any coherent thoughts to take shape.

He stared down at her in the gloom, his eyes drinking her in as she removed her bedraggled bonnet.

"Goodness me," she said, laughter and surprise lighting up her face. "We're soaked through, aren't we? That was quite...unexpected..." Her voice trailed off as her gaze rose to meet his. Eyes widening, she licked her lips.

His entire body pulled tight as a bow. Ah, God, if she only knew what that small action did to him.

But perhaps she did. In the next instant her hands came up, resting like nervous birds on his shoulders. Before he quite knew what to make of it, she rose up on her toes and pressed her lips to his.

The effect was instantaneous. His body, which should have been chilled to the bone from their drenching, exploded in heat. He groaned, wrapping his arms about her, crushing her to him. She gasped, and he took advantage, twining his tongue with hers. The taste of her was heady and all-consuming, driving him wild with need. He pressed his hand to the small of her back, reveling in the graceful arch of her spine beneath the dampened layers of clothing, bringing her even closer until he could feel every soft curve of her pressed against him.

But it wasn't enough. He needed to taste more of her. Tearing his mouth away, he trailed his lips along her smooth cheek, down the long line of her neck, until he found that delicate spot just beneath her ear. She let her head fall back, and a low moan escaped her. She was so damn beautiful. How the hell was he supposed to think of who to marry when she took up his every thought?

Suddenly she stilled. And he realized in that horrifying moment that he had spoken aloud.

"You're right, of course," she muttered as she disentangled herself from his arms. She patted her hair with nervous hands. Which was pointless, as it was plastered to her head in a wet mass. "I've been distracted by you as well. Which will *not do*. Lenora was right; I should have taken care of this days ago."

Lenora? He frowned. What the devil did the Duchess of Dane have to do with anything?

She blew out a sharp breath, as if building up to something unpleasant. Or terrifying. And then, her features rearranging into a kind of determination, she looked him full in the eye and raised her chin. "There's only one thing to do, of course. As we cannot avoid it, we must meet it head-on."

He blinked. "Pardon?"

She cleared her throat, as if to unstick the words there. "I'm a widow," she explained, her voice warbling slightly. "And there are certain…liberties…a widow may take, as long as she is discreet."

"Liberties," he repeated blankly. An idea had begun to form in his mind of what she could be trying to say. But, holy hell, it was so far-fetched as to be laughable, the mere fantasy of his lust-fogged mind.

Her cheeks bloomed with violent color, and she closed her eyes, as if in pain. "Do I truly need to be more explicit than that?"

Oh, God, yes. "Please do."

She blew out a breath. "Very well," she muttered, almost to herself. "I may as well make my embarrassment complete." Squaring her shoulders, she opened her eyes and blurted, "I wish to take you to my bed."

He gaped at her; though it was as he'd guessed, it was still so utterly unbelievable that he could not make sense of it. "You mean you wish to have an affair? With me?"

"Yes." Again she cleared her throat. Her gaze wavered but she kept her eyes on him, as if by sheer will. "Mayhap it would be for the best. There seems to be some physical attraction between us, after all. I do think—nay, I'm certain—that if we were to release those…desires…we might be able to put the whole mess behind us and focus on the pertinent goal of finding you a wife."

Still, he couldn't seem to react in any way that allowed him to respond. She wanted him? And so much so that she was having trouble concentrating? It seemed impossible.

But he was taking too long to answer. She turned from him, making a hasty exit for the hall door, her nervous laugh trailing behind her like the churning wake after a ship.

"Goodness, please forgive me," she called over her shoulder. "That was horribly forward. I don't know what I was thinking. I assure you, I've never done anything like this in my life."

"Wait!" Blessedly she stopped, though she didn't turn to face him. He didn't know what the hell he would have done if he'd had to chase her through the damn house.

He hurried to her side as quick as he was able and spun her about to face him, hooking a finger under her chin, dragging her gaze up to his.

"You wish to have an affair with me?"

She tried looking away but he kept his finger in place, holding her gaze to his. She swallowed hard. And then, in a voice barely above a whisper, she said, "Yes."

One quiet word. Yet it unlocked something in him. He cradled her face, his breath leaving him in a rush. "Oh." Which was not the most articulate of responses. But as he had never in his life been propositioned before, his brain was quite incapable of forming anything even remotely coherent.

She swallowed hard, her hands balling into fists, where they rested on his waist. "It would be merely physical," she said, the words coming in a rush. "A one-time thing. A single night with no expectations beside mutual pleasure. And so you've no need to worry about my emotions getting involved. I still have no intention of marrying again, of course. It's just been many, many— goodness, so many—years since I've been with some-one. And we seem to have an attraction, you and I. Which, unfortunately, seems to be distracting us from the—ahem—matter at hand. Unless, of course, you've no wish to—"

His lips cut off the rest of what she had been about to say. She gave a soft little sigh into his mouth, melting against him, her arms coming about his waist. And he thought he might combust from the fire that sparked to life within him.

He lifted his head, but just enough to look down into her eyes. "Yes," he whispered against her lips.

She blinked. "Truly?"

He smiled. "Yes. When?"

She laughed, a happy sound he felt clear to his toes. That laugh turned into a gasp as he ran his tongue along her full lower lip. She shivered in his arms, her eyes flut-tering closed. "T—tonight?" she managed on a breath.

"Yes," he murmured before finding her lips again.

Chapter 12

What was I thinking?

It was not the first time that question had ricocheted about in Margery's mind throughout that exceptionally long day. More than once she'd been ready to tell Daniel to forget the whole thing. She did not have the time for this detour. She had a deadline to meet and she could not fail.

But then she would look his way, and see the heat in his eyes, and remember the kiss they'd shared that morning. Which promptly shut that more cautious side of her right up. Her physical reactions to the man were too much of a distraction. She needed to relieve this ache in her body, to get past this so she could forge ahead and finish what needed to be done.

Now that the time was here, however...

She bit her lip, checking her reflection for what must have been the hundredth time since they'd retired. It was like looking at a stranger. Not that she looked exceptionally different. After her initial uncertainty regarding her wardrobe for such a liaison—she didn't own anything remotely alluring, after all, and wasn't about to lounge around in nothing at all—she had quickly readied herself for bed as she normally did, donning a plain cotton nightgown and soft robe, brushing her hair until it shimmered in the firelight, washing her face with trembling hands, praying the cool water would help soothe her anxiety.

Yes, her external appearance was the same as ever. But something inside her had changed. It was there in her eyes, a new knowledge of herself. It startled her, that difference, so much so that she hastily looked down. And immediately caught sight of the glint of her gold wedding ring, shining bright and bold on her finger.

Gasping, she tore at it with a fumbling hand. It caught on her knuckle, wholly unused to being removed, and tears burned in her eyes as she tugged harder. Finally, however, it slid free. She hurried to her desk in the corner, opened a drawer, and hastily dropped the ring inside. Aaron's miniature followed, and she shut the drawer with a resounding snap.

There, she thought as she smoothed shaking hands down the front of her nightgown, ignoring the strange emptiness on her finger. Yet, though she expected to feel relief, there was only an increase in tension. It was as if she were being pulled taut and were ready to snap in two. Two different people, the woman she was used to being, and this new, bold creature she had become.

She paced the carpet, certain her feet would burn a path in the fine wool, so swiftly did her steps eat up the space. This was a mistake. A horrible mistake. Surely she could control her reactions to the man long enough to find him a wife, secure the necessary funds, and pay off the blackmailer. She needn't jump into bed with him to ensure that happened.

Yet she knew her reasons for lying with Daniel were mere excuses, and flimsy ones at that. She did not want to bed Daniel because she was distracted from her goals. No, she was certain, deep in her bones, that she would have wanted him regardless of the ticking clock that was growing louder each day that passed. Which was a far more troubling truth.

As that disturbing realization took form, the knock sounded. She jumped, a yelp escaping her lips even as her heart pounded in anticipation. For a moment she couldn't move, her wide eyes going to the door, her shaking fingers gripping her robe closed at her throat. Then, before she could think better of it, she hurried on bare feet to the door and swung it wide.

Any doubts she might have had at the wisdom of her plan melted away in an instant. She may not love Daniel. But she certainly liked him. And she wanted him. Oh goodness, how she wanted him. As she looked on him now, dressed in a soft pair of breeches and a loosely tucked lawn shirt open at the throat that did nothing to hide the magnetic strength of him, her knees grew weak. She gripped tight to the door to keep her legs from buckling.

"Daniel," she managed on a whisper.

"Margery." His voice was deep, and dark, the delicious timbre of it vibrating through her already-sensitive body. It was the first time he had spoken her name, and to her hungry ears it sounded like a benediction.

Wordlessly she stepped back. With only the barest hesitation he stepped over the threshold. And then she closed the door, giving the key in the lock a twist.

The sound of it grated on the air, bringing reality with it. She stood stock-still, facing the door, unable to dredge up the nerve to turn around and face him. Perhaps, she thought wildly, squeezing her eyes shut, she was asleep and would wake up and this whole awkward debacle would be a mere dream brought on by the fever of pent-up desires.

But she realized a sharp truth that could not be denied—she didn't want that. Not at all. Despite the dismay and embarrassment—and, if she was being completely honest, the fear—she wanted him here, more than anything.

He spoke then, his voice rough in the quiet of the room.

"Have you changed your mind?"

"No!" She paused, her teeth digging into her lower lip to bite back anything further. That one word had been bad enough, as fraught with need as it had been. Drawing in a deep breath to steady herself, she asked the one question that must be voiced, though she dreaded his answer more than she expected to. "Have you?"

"No." The word came out on an exhale, without the least hesitation. She spun about to face him. And immediately lost her breath. His gaze was molten heat, traveling down her body, scorching her wherever it landed.

"You're beautiful," he whispered, his voice ragged. "So damn beautiful."

His unguarded words broke through the last barricade within her. She went to him, wanting—no, needing—to close the space between them. His arms opened to her immediately, drawing her against the hard length of his body, the clatter of his cane as it hit the ground a distant echo in her passion-hazed mind. And then his lips claimed hers, and there was nothing that existed for her in that moment but him.

How was it, she thought dazedly with the one small part of her mind that could still form coherent thought, that this could feel so very right? Her body molded against his, her generous curves giving with ease to the hard planes of his. She could feel in her arms his barely leashed strength. The muscles of his shoulders bunched under her fingers, his hands roaming over her back with hungry intent. And his manhood...Ah goodness, her knees went weak. It pressed into her stomach, hard and insistent. Bringing to mind just where this was all leading.

She broke their kiss with a gasp but didn't release him. If the ceiling opened up just then she wouldn't have been able to let him go. "We need to talk," she managed.

His lips found the sensitive curve where her neck met her shoulder. "Mmm hmm."

Margery could fairly hear her eyes roll back in her head as his lips did wicked things to her skin. What had she been about to say? Ah, yes. "Th-there are things we need to"—she gasped as his teeth scraped up her neck to that wondrous place just beneath her ear—"discuss," she finally finished.

"Discuss," he murmured against her skin, the vibration of his deep voice nearly sending her mind off once more to parts unknown.

But this was too important to overlook in the heat of the moment. With incredible will—for there was nothing she wanted more just then than to lose herself in his embrace—she planted her hands on his shoulders and pushed.

He backed away with surprising quickness, releasing her, stepping away. The space between their bodies fairly thrummed with desire, the proof of his passion straining against his breeches, his eyes pure flames. There was no doubt in her mind he wanted her.

And yet he had given her space the instant she'd asked for it. Her heart lurched in her chest.

"I'm sorry." Hurriedly retrieving his cane from the floor, he held it in front of him with both hands, a kind of shield, his fingers white where they gripped it. "I went too fast."

"No," she said. Her own fingers were busy as well, though for her it was the bodice of her nightgown she held. "No, you didn't go too fast. But there are certain aspects of our...affair...we need to discuss before we go any further."

And suddenly he was all business. He swept an arm out, indicating the chairs facing the hearth. She went to them on trembling legs, gratefully sinking down into the plush seat. He sat facing her, his attention fixed on her as he patiently waited.

For a single, torturous moment worry surged that he had been able to so completely turn off his desires. Mayhap he didn't want her as desperately as she wanted him. But one look at his face and those doubts vanished. His eyes fairly devoured her. The heat in his eyes, barely leashed, so much hotter than the blaze in the hearth, made her shiver with longing.

Desperate to rein in her quickly spiraling thoughts, she cleared her throat and straightened. "As I said, there are some things we need to discuss."

He nodded.

Once more she cleared her throat. "I mentioned this morning, of course, that this is to be merely physical."

"Physical," he murmured in agreement. Yet the way his tongue worked at the single word made it sound positively indecent. Once more she shivered, but with a burning heat that had her shifting in her chair.

But she had to keep her head if they were to get through this. She nearly cleared her throat again, then thought better of it. The man would think her growing ill if she kept this up. "Yes, physical, and nothing further. As I also stated, this will be a onetime affair, based on mutual respect."

"I respect you, Margery."

Which she should have expected, of course. Any man in the position he was in, forced to listen to a person rambling on and on with demands before they were able to do the deed, would promise to all sorts of things to get on with it.

Yet she felt the sincerity of his words down to the very marrow of her bones.

Once more her heart lurched in her chest, though this time with a softening that should have had alarm bells pealing through her. But in that moment she didn't care for caution. "And I respect you, Daniel."

His gaze gentled. "Then we are in agreement. There will be nothing expected from either of us. This is a union of purely physical desires."

Oh, so many physical desires, Margery thought hazily, her gaze fastening on his full bottom lip. Needing to clear her head, she shook it sharply, then quickly said, lest he think she was disagreeing with him, "Precisely."

But there was still something more they must be in accord on. "As well, I would like to take every precaution against a child being conceived." When he merely stared at her in silence, she expelled a sharp breath and continued. "Which would, of course, require you to—ahem—not come to... completion. Inside me."

For a moment he appeared utterly confused. Had she not been clear enough? She really didn't know how she could have been any clearer, save for spouting a lengthy description of the deed itself.

Finally, however, understanding dawned in his face. "Ah, yes. I see. You may be assured, I will do everything in my power to prevent a child."

Relief flooded her, and she just stopped herself from thanking him profusely. She nodded instead. Then, not knowing what else to say, she made to rise. "Shall we?"

Ah, God, if the floor had opened up in that moment she would have jumped in headfirst. *Shall we?* That's how she wished to start this, as if they were at a garden party?

He must think her mad as well, for his expression suddenly altered, turning to a sharp uncertainty. Face flaming, she opened her mouth to mend the breach. He spoke, however, before the words—whatever they might have been—could leave her lips.

"I have my own requirements."

She blinked. Well, she hadn't expected that. But she should not have been surprised, she supposed. She nodded and eased herself back in her seat, her eyes on his face the whole while. Was this how things were done with affairs then? For while this whole situation was uncomfortable in the extreme, and seemed incredibly odd, he did not seem even a bit surprised by how things were proceeding. Mentally shrugging, she waited for him to begin.

However, it took him much longer to start than she had expected. As the seconds ticked by, every one of her insecurities came roaring back to horrible life, a deafening barrage of uncertainty parading through her mind: she was deluded to think this would work; he could not want her as she wanted him; she was not at all alluring. Finally, blessedly, he continued.

"We have already talked of our respect for one another, of course," he said, his eyes seeming to fix somewhere over her left shoulder, "and that we'll mutually end this affair after tonight, with no expectations. But I would have your promise that, should you grow even the least bit uncomfortable tonight, you will tell me immediately."

She blinked, for there was something incredibly intense about him in that moment. "Of course," she said, thinking that would be the end of it. But he frowned and shook his head.

"You don't understand, Margery." He let out a sharp breath, looking down to his lap. His hand, she noticed, had fisted and was pressed into his thigh.

And suddenly she knew. She knew just what he was trying to say. She leaned forward, ducking her head, trying to catch his eye. "You needn't worry about your injury, Daniel."

His gaze shot up and snagged on hers then. And her breath stalled in her chest at the agony in his eyes.

"It's not pretty, Margery," he rasped. "The other scars are not, either, of course. And there are many. My leg, however..."

His voice trailed off, and he swallowed, hard. Her

heart twisted, for she understood the truth hidden in his words: that he had been hurt, and deeply, because of the appearance of his leg.

She had guessed as much earlier. But it was only now, with the specters of a very specific tragedy haunting the beautiful rich blue-gray of his eyes, that she knew her premonitions had been correct. Was this pain due to his ex-fiancée? Or was it something—or someone—else?

To her shock, outrage flared deep in her stomach. She didn't anger easily, after all. But there it was, hot and bitter and impossible to ignore. She ached to invite his confidence—not only to offer him comfort, but also to secretly curse the person responsible, much to her chagrin—and though she knew instinctively he would refuse, she said, "You can tell me anything you wish, you know. I'm a very good listener."

She kept her tone light and easy. Yet his reaction was almost violent. He drew back, a sound close to a hiss escaping his lips. "No. That is," he amended when she unconsciously shrunk into herself, "I would not soil your ears. But I do hope you understand the importance of complete honesty in this matter. I need to know that you will tell me immediately should you become offended by my appearance."

She could see that there was no amount of placating that would ease his mind on this. And so instead she slid from her seat and sank to her knees before him.

His eyes flared wide with shock, desire once more replacing the guarded hurt there. His hand was still fisted over his thigh and she laid hers over it. "I don't see a need for it, for I know I shan't change my mind about wanting you. But I swear I will tell you should I experience any distress."

He sagged with relief. Leaning forward, he cupped her cheek with his free hand. "Margery."

Anticipation rose up in her again. He was going to kiss her. And then there would be no turning back, for there was nothing she wanted more in that moment than to lose herself in him. Her eyes fluttered closed and she raised her face for his kiss.

But it never came. Confused, she opened her eyes and looked up at him once more. Again, uncertainty clouded his face. But this time it was not a painful one. Rather, he appeared utterly sheepish.

"Daniel?"

He smiled, though there was no humor in it. "There is one very important thing I think you should know before we continue. And I really don't know how to say it in a delicate way."

She blinked in confusion. "Yes?"

He laughed, a harsh sound. "Ah, God. All right then. I need you to know... I've never done this before."

Relief filled her. "You've never had an affair? I haven't either."

But already he was shaking his head. "No, that's not it. Well, it is it, but it goes beyond—far beyond—that."

And then he did the very last thing she expected him to do: he colored. And not just a faint blush, but a raging red that stained his cheeks. "I've never done *this* before," he managed.

A ghost of an idea formed in her fog-enshrouded brain. She frowned. But no, surely he didn't mean—

In the next minute he dashed that faint thought to pieces.

"I'm a virgin."

Chapter 13

A virgin."

He winced. It sounded even more ludicrous when she said it. "Yes."

She settled back to sit on the floor. Rather, it was more of a jarring drop, her bottom hitting the rug with a muffled thud. Regardless of how you framed it, however, she moved beyond his reach. For a horrible moment his hand hung suspended like a leaf caught on the thinnest spiderweb before dropping awkwardly to his lap.

Damn it, he should have kept his mouth shut. He needn't have told her. Surely he could have faked knowledge enough to make her believe he wasn't completely without experience. He had seen enough with the engravings in the books his brother had secreted into the house when they'd been young, after all; had heard enough ribald comments from schoolmates and fellow soldiers to be able to be quite creative should the need arise.

But no, he told himself a moment later. He had

promised respect and honesty with this woman. He was not going to disregard that vow before they'd even begun.

"Yes," he replied.

"I see."

But she made no move to rise. Her gaze went unfocused, flitting about the room, as if it didn't know where to settle.

Ah, God, this had been a colossal mistake. Gathering his cane with stiff fingers, he braced himself to rise, praying he would be able to maneuver about her without falling flat on his face. Truly, the evening only needed that embarrassment.

"I can see I've distressed you," he mumbled. "I'll leave you now."

"No!"

Her answer was swift and unexpected. More unexpected, however, was her body as she lurched toward him. He reared back, losing what little ground he had made in rising. And then she settled between his thighs, her full hips pushing into that sensitive space with aching intimacy. His breath left him on a harsh, ragged exhale.

She planted her hands on his chest, no doubt determined to hold him in place by physical strength if need be.

As if he could leave just then.

"I'm sorry for my reaction," she said, her voice low. "I was merely surprised. But it makes no difference to me."

He quirked one eyebrow. "Doesn't it?"

Her lips kicked up at one corner, a faint humor

lighting her eyes. "Well, mayhap a small bit. But not in any negative way."

And then, because he was a masochist, he asked, "In what way, then?"

Once more, however, Margery surprised him. Her lids went heavy, enhancing the firelight in her eyes until he thought it would scorch him on the spot. Her hands, which had remained planted on his chest, drifted down over his torso to his hips.

His mouth went dry.

"Would you think any less of me if I told you it was...arousing?"

Well, he certainly hadn't expected that. And neither had his...nether region...if the way it suddenly came back to life was any indication. "God, no. I think you being aroused is...arousing."

She smiled. But it was no simple smile. No, this one held all the mysteries of the universe in it.

"Margery."

Her name escaped him on a breath of sound, and he was powerless to rein in the need that laced it. But he needn't have worried that he was showing his hand to her. Her response to it was more than he could ever have imagined. Her full lips opened in a small gasp, the fire seeming to have jumped from the hearth to her eyes. She leaned into him, her full breasts pressing into his chest, her stomach rubbing against his manhood. And then her mouth was on his.

If he had thought he'd wanted her before, this made it seem laughable by comparison. He was consumed, reduced to smoldering cinders under her. His cane clattered to the floor but he hardly heard it for the roaring in his ears. He cupped her face with both hands, the rich fall of her hair cascading over his fingers as he tilted her head, the better to drink of the aching sweetness that was her mouth. She opened her lips to him readily, her tongue touching his, sweeping into his mouth with a heady boldness.

But the kiss was all too short. He nearly cried out from the loss of her. It was then, however, that he felt the wet heat of her mouth on his neck. He shuddered under her, tilting his head, welcoming the exquisite torture. Her teeth dragged down the cords of his throat, working him like the finest instrument, wringing a low moan from his lips. She worked at the open neckline of his shirt, and soon her mouth trailed lower, across his collarbone, to the place just over his galloping heart.

She made a small noise deep in her throat when she could go no farther. "Well, this certainly needs to go," she murmured. And then her small hands were on the hem of his shirt.

Instinct kicked in then. Quite without meaning to, he gripped her hands in his, stalling the removal of his shirt. She gasped, her gaze flying to his, and he fought to focus on the dazed desire glowing in her eyes. A desire that was quickly being replaced by confusion, and that would extinguish completely if he didn't get ahold of himself. *This needs to happen*, he told himself firmly. *Release her, and let her do what she wishes*. If he was going to take a wife he needed to grow used to a woman looking at his body, after all.

But no amount of reasoning could lessen the panic in him. Instead it grew until he could no longer ignore it.

"The firelight," he gasped, shame rearing up that his fear was so beyond his control.

Margery blinked, looking in hazy bewilderment from his still-clothed chest to his hands gently but firmly holding her own, and finally back to his face. She must have seen something in his carefully smoothed expression, however, for her gaze cleared in an instant, a look of understanding taking its place. "If you're certain."

He wasn't; while she would not be able to see him well, it also meant he would be denied the glory of her unclothed. And it would be glorious. He softened—and hardened at the same time. To see Margery in all her splendor, each delectable inch of her bared to his gaze, would bring him untold pleasure.

But he couldn't chance it. He just couldn't.

"I'm certain," he managed.

She nodded, immediately moving away to bank the fire. Regret crashed down on him at the loss of her, further compounded as the light dimmed to such a degree that he could barely make her out. But then she stood, and turned to face him. And the sight of her backlit by the faint orange glow of what was left of the once-roaring blaze effectively doused whatever portions of his brain were still in working order.

He lurched to his feet and strode the few feet to her, not caring if the sudden movement would bring him pain in the morning, knowing only he needed her more than breath in his lungs in that moment. Before she could react he caught her in his arms.

There was no holding back now. Their mouths clashed, teeth scraping, hands fumbling. He should perhaps worry that all intentions he might have had to be smooth and gentle had flown out the proverbial window. But all he could think of in that moment was how wondrous she felt under his hands. Her simple cotton nightgown left nothing to his imagination. And yet it was not enough.

An encroaching thought slunk into his addled mind in that moment that he would never have enough of her. Before it could take hold, however, she yanked her lips free and gasped, "The bed."

There was much stumbling and lurching as they made their way across the room. But he would be damned if he would fetch his cane in that moment. It was bad enough he couldn't sweep his arms beneath her and carry her in chivalrous fashion to the bed as he truly wished to. Regardless of how they got there, however, they finally did and collapsed onto the plush mattress in a heap of tangled limbs.

It was even darker here so far from the hearth, only the faintest light reaching them. Even so, pure instinct had him tensing as she once more reached for the hem of his shirt. But he didn't stop her this time as she lifted it up and over his head. As her slender, quick fingers brushed against his lower belly to find the fall of his breeches, however, he couldn't ignore the panic building in him. Once more he stayed her hand.

She paused. And then, her lips at his ear, she kissed his temple and whispered, "Trust me, Daniel."

He shuddered, and not just from the exquisite sensation of her lips, or the sweet sound of her saying his name—something he did not think he could ever get enough of—but also from the truth that shined deep in his chest in that moment: he did trust her. More than he had ever wanted to trust anyone ever again.

He let loose a ragged breath and nodded, loosening her fingers. All too soon she undid the fastenings, releasing his member to the cool night air, and was pushing his breeches down over his hips and off his legs.

He lay there in shock, waiting for the panic to set in. He did not have time, however, for after a faint rustling she was back with him, stretching over him. And his shock was compounded as her silky skin, warm and utterly bare, dragged against his own.

Heaven. Ah, God, it was utter heaven. He groaned at the sensation, and it mingled with her faint gasp until he could not tell where one sound ended and the other began. How was this exquisite torture even possible? How did people ever leave their beds? But he also knew they were far from done. And he was suddenly eager to experience everything.

Just then her hand found his straining member, and he nearly bucked right off the bed. Not that they would have time tonight to experience everything. He would be lucky if he didn't spend himself in her hand right in that very moment.

"No," he gasped, pulling her hand from him though all he wanted was to pump himself into her fingers and into oblivion. "Too close."

She chuckled, a low, throaty sound he felt clear to his toes. After a moment's shock he found a smile lifting his lips. Was this part of it, then, this wonderful camaraderie that enhanced pure physicality?

Feeling suddenly and inexplicably playful, he nipped her shoulder gently with his teeth. "Minx," he growled. "You would laugh at my lack of control?"

Which only made her laugh harder. There was something incredibly joyous in the sound, as if she'd been freed from captivity and had seen the sun for the first time.

Which was a feeling he could relate to. What else was she to him but the sun, lighting everything that had, up until then, been dreary and dark and hopeless?

Grinning, he said in as menacing a voice as he was able, "You wound my manhood, madam."

Once again her hand found him, brushing with the lightest touch against the hard length of him. "I have only the deepest respect for your manhood."

His breath stalled in his chest as he was caught between delight at her teasing and a raging need for her. But the latter quickly took precedence until it was all he was. Gripping her hips, ignoring the pain in his thigh, he rolled her beneath him.

Her laughter died as quickly as it had started. "Daniel," she moaned, her fingers diving into his hair. Trembling, he trailed kisses over her cheek, down the long length of her neck, across her chest, just as she had done to him. But there was nothing to hinder his progress. Lower and lower he went, the taste of her skin filling him, the sugared violet scent of her driving him mad with need. When he reached the softness of her breasts he thought he would lose his mind entirely. And then his questing lips found her nipple, and he drew her deep into his mouth.

She cried out, arching up for more. The very idea that he could bring her pleasure sent him completely over the edge. He filled his palms with her breasts, plumping them in his hand even as his mouth devoured her. He could have kissed her there forever, so glorious was the feel of her, soft and supple and gloriously delicious, under his lips.

Until Margery took hold of one of his hands and

pulled it away from her breast. He did not have time to worry that she wished him to stop, however, for he quickly realized where she was guiding his hand: down, over the fullness of her stomach, her hips, to the downy mound of hair covering that most sacred place.

He had heard of women becoming wet from loving. But he had never dreamed of the glorious heat and slickness he found at the center of her. He rubbed a finger against her folds, transfixed. To his shock a low cry escaped her. And then she was pressing up into his hand.

"Daniel, now," she begged, tugging on his shoulders.

He went willingly. With an ancient instinct he settled between her trembling thighs. And then her legs wrapped about his hips and she guided him within her.

"Margery," he groaned against her shoulder as her heat enveloped him. She was tight, so gloriously tight around him, and he could not imagine there could be anything better than this. He took a long moment just to feel her, to make certain he never forgot this moment and how she felt wrapped around him. Then he began to move.

How wrong he had been.

* * *

Fullness, such glorious fullness and stretching, with Daniel deep inside her. Margery's breath left her on a long exhale. How she had missed this, the connection to another through lovemaking, the physical intimacy of such an act. But as wonderful as it felt, having him inside her, having his strong body pressing into her with a welcome weight, she wanted more. So much more.

But would he know what to do? Did the fact that he was a virgin—or rather, had been, for he certainly wasn't one now—also mean that he would not know how to proceed? A silly thought, perhaps. There was such a thing as instinct, after all.

The longer he lay still, however, his arms trembling on each side of her as he held himself above her, his breath ragged against her neck, the more doubt crept in. But perhaps it wasn't his lack of knowledge that had him pausing. Mayhap it was his injury. Was he in pain? Should she say something? Or would it shatter the moment?

Before she could decide how to proceed, however, he began to move. And all coherent thought vanished.

Her low moan as he slowly pulled out, only to push back within her with the same exquisite slowness, was echoed by his own deep groan. "My God." He repeated the action, his voice hitching on a breath, "Margery. You feel—you're—"

"Yes," she whispered against his temple, her hands diving into his hair. She pressed her heels into the soft mattress, angling her hips to take him more deeply within her, and he shuddered.

"Heaven," he managed, his lips brushing against her shoulder with that one word, his hot breath bathing her skin.

And it was heaven, in every way. His body was pure bliss in her arms, the feel of his member, large and throbbing within her, quickly bringing her aching body to heights that her hands and fingers had only hinted at over the years. His movements became frantic, each pump of his hips bringing them both closer to the precipice. She soared, higher, faster. Until, with all the force of a wave in a storm-raged sea, the pleasure crashed over her head, drowning her in exquisite completion.

With the tremors still wracking her sated body, he groaned and pulled himself free. But, as mindless with pleasure as she was, she could not think of him finding release alone just then. Immediately she was there, pushing him onto his back, replacing his hand with her own. She worked her fingers over his slick member, squeezing the thick shaft, dragging her fingers over the head.

"Margery," he moaned. And she suddenly wished she could see him finding his release, for it would have been a beautiful sight. Instead she strained to see him in the shadows, watching with hungry eyes as he threw his head back against the pillows, his hands gripping the sheets beneath him. Suddenly he covered his mouth with a hand, his muffled shout nevertheless ringing through the dark room as he found completion.

Grabbing a towel, she cleaned them both before curling against his chest. His arms came around her, his grip on her tight.

"Margery," he managed, his breathing ragged. "My God, Margery—that was—my God—"

She smiled, listening to his heart galloping beneath her ear, a perfect accompaniment to her own. Despite the racing of her heart, a wonderful lethargy had taken over her. Her body felt sated as it had not in too long. "Yes it was," she murmured with feeling.

"I've never—that is, I never imagined—"

Suddenly he stilled, then shifted, pulling back to look down at her. His eyes glittered in the faint orange glow from the banked fire. "Did you—that is, are you—?"

Her smile widened. Of course he was concerned for her own pleasure, being the utterly wonderful man he was. "Oh, yes, Daniel."

He released a relieved breath, relaxing beneath her. They lay in silence for some time, as their breathing returned to normal, as their hearts slowed. Exhaustion dragged down on Margery then. Her eyes grew heavy, the peace of such a moment, with Daniel's strong arm secure about her and the steady rise and fall of his chest beneath her head, lulling her closer to slumber. Just as she was about to drift over the edge, however, his hesitant voice rumbled in her ear.

"I don't suppose you would wish to repeat that, would you?"

And suddenly she was wide awake, desire—somehow even more potent than before—coursing through her. In answer she rose over him, taking his lips in a kiss. And there was no room for talk, only sensation, and pleasure, long into the night.

Chapter 14

Margery wasn't certain what she'd expected to happen the following morning. Whatever possibilities might have been swirling about in her mind, however, she certainly didn't expect to receive an urgent missive from Swallowhill before she'd even had her morning chocolate.

She rushed to her grandmother's room, the letter held tight in her hand, fear and joy and anticipation making her heart gallop like mad in her chest. "Gran," she said as she burst through the door. "I've been called to Swallowhill."

Gran, already sitting up in bed and accepting a plate of toast from Miss Denby, promptly dropped it. Perfect points of browned and buttered bread fell to the sheets, but she didn't pay it the least mind. One hand flew to her neck. "Clara?"

Margery rushed forward to hand the letter over with trembling fingers. "Not yet," she managed. "But soon. Quincy is asking for me to be there for her. Though I rather think he'll need the distraction more than Clara will need my help. She has Phoebe and the midwife and the physician, after all. And Lenora has been summoned as well."

"Pish," Gran said, scowling at Miss Denby as she attempted to clean up the mess of toast and crumbs, all the while fending off Mouse as he tried to reach the treat. "Quincy will have Peter and Oswin on hand. You go help that cousin of yours birth her child." She grinned, her excitement plain to see. "And give it a kiss from me."

Margery couldn't help but grin back. "I will, Gran." She kissed the older woman on the cheek before spinning about and rushing down the hall. So immersed was she in what had to be done, however, that she didn't immediately see the very large figure emerging from a room just ahead of her.

"Mrs. Kitteridge."

There wasn't much that could have stopped her just then. Daniel's voice, however, was one of them. She skidded to a halt, her breath leaving her as she took him in. His hair was carefully brushed, his clothes just so. He looked no different from how he had yesterday.

Yet there was something different all the same. She felt it deep in her belly, this new knowledge of him. And he felt it, too, if the quiet way he sucked in his breath when their eyes met was any indication.

"Your Grace," she whispered. "Good morning."

"It is," he whispered back, then swallowed hard. "That is, good morning to you as well."

"Did you sleep well?" It was inane, really, to ask him that. She knew very well he hadn't. At least not before he'd left her bed just a few short hours ago. Yet she found she was loath to leave him just then.

A small, lopsided smile played about his lips. "I did not. And yet I'm surprisingly rested."

Her gaze snagged on that smile, tracing the contours of his lips. Remembering them on her skin last night. "Are you?" she murmured.

"Oh, yes." His voice was deep and vibrated through her in a delicious way.

Suddenly a commotion behind her. And then Miss Denby was at her side. "Lady Tesh bid me to give you these," she said, pressing something wrapped in a snowy handkerchief into Margery's hands. "Scones from her breakfast tray, for the journey. Said you could eat them in the carriage. Your Grace," she quipped with a bright smile, dipping into a curtsy before hurrying back to her employer's room.

But Daniel appeared not to acknowledge her departure. "Journey?"

"Goodness, yes. Please forgive me. My cousin Clara has need of me; it's most urgent." Her mind blessedly back on track, she made to dart around him. His voice, however, stopped her again.

"Shall I wait up for you if you're not back by this evening?"

She knew what he was asking: Did she wish him to come to her again? *It was to have been a onetime thing*, her mind cautioned. She was to have put her desire for him behind her now that her body's urges had been sated, to get on with the very important business of finding him a wife. As well as to secure the money she required.

Her body, however, had other ideas. He had re-awakened something in her that she was reluctant to put back in its neat little box again. She could not very well assist him today, she reasoned. Not with her being called to Swallowhill. And, as she could not resume her efforts until tomorrow at the earliest, there was no reason not to have one more night together. To make certain her need for him was well and truly behind her.

"Yes," she whispered before, with a smile, she hurried away.

* * *

Daniel had not planned on dozing off. He'd purposely sat up in one of the chairs before the hearth in Margery's room, had even brought a book to read.

But the lack of sleep the night before finally caught up to him. One minute he was trying to focus on the words in his hands, the next, there was the softest of caresses on his scarred cheek.

He froze, confusion momentarily scattering his wits, and instinctively he grabbed at the trailing fingers. It took him some seconds to make sense of what was happening, but when he finally did the breath left him entirely.

Margery knelt before him, just as she had last night. Though now she was fully dressed, hair up but several bedraggled curls having escaped her coiffure. There were dark shadows beneath her eyes, proof of a difficult day, though a small smile played about her lips.

He had never seen anything so beautiful in his life.

"I'm sorry to startle you," she murmured.

In answer he leaned forward and caught her lips in

a kiss. She sighed into his mouth, melting against him, then just as quickly pulled away to yawn into her hand.

"You're exhausted," he said. "Let's get you to bed."

She didn't fight as he took her elbow, guiding her to standing before lurching to his feet. Once more he was struck with the potent desire to sweep her up in his arms and carry her to the bed. Though this time the feelings were decidedly more tender, a wish to care for her. He fought down his bitterness at not being able to do so—so much stronger tonight than it had been last night—instead propelling her with a hand to the small of her back to the bed.

"Sit," he ordered her.

She gave a huff of a laugh but did as she was bid, hiding another yawn behind her hand as she sank onto the mattress. "Truly, I'm fine."

"So fine you can barely stand without swaying," he muttered. As she gave another small laugh he went to work, removing her shoes, peeling down her stockings. When that was done, he helped her back to her feet and assisted her in removing her clothes. They were service-able, securing where she could easily reach, worn but cared for. He frowned as he guided her back down to the bed and settled her against the pillows. Again the ques-tions swirled about in his brain: Why did a viscount's daughter and cousin of not one but two dukes wear such clothes? Why did she so desperately need money that she was willing to help him find a wife to get it?

But now was not the time, he told himself firmly as he carefully removed pins from her hair and gently spread it out over her pillow. Throughout his ministrations she lay quiet, not fighting him as he fussed. He thought for a moment she had fallen asleep. But as he turned away preparing to leave her to her rest, her soft voice called out to him.

"Don't go, Daniel."

There was nothing on earth that could have prevented him from returning to her. She gazed sleepily up at him, her eyes shining in the faint firelight. She held out a hand. "Lie with me."

Heat shot through him as he remembered the previous night. He hastily doused it. "You need to sleep, Margery."

"I will," she promised, her hand still suspended in the air. "I just want you to hold me."

He couldn't have refused if he'd tried. Which he did not remotely wish to do. Sitting on the edge of her bed, he removed his boots, then slid in next to her. She curled against his side, as if she had always belonged there.

"Mmm, you feel wonderful," she whispered, her cheek rubbing against his chest.

He tightened his arm about her, dropping a kiss into her mussed curls. "Everything went well?"

"Yes." He could fairly hear the smile in her voice. "My dear cousin has a healthy baby boy. He's so very beautiful, Daniel. I'm so happy for Clara and Quincy."

"I'm glad," he said. "Now, sleep. Your work is done; you need rest."

She heaved a sigh. "My mind is too full to sleep. Won't you talk to me?"

Stubborn minx. He smiled into the crown of her hair. "What would you have me talk about?"

"Anything. Everything. Tell me about what you were like as a child."

He laughed in surprise. "I was not very interesting as a child, I'm afraid."

"A lie, I'm certain," she teased sleepily, her hand playing lazily over his stomach.

"Oh no. It's the truth. Nathaniel, on the other hand, was the exact opposite."

"You loved your brother very much, didn't you?"

He cleared the sudden, inexplicable thickness from his throat. "I did," he answered.

She nodded, her hair rubbing against his chin, as if he had verified something she had guessed all along. Then, "Tell me about him."

He blinked, his hand tightening on her arm. "You wish to hear about Nathaniel?"

"I do," she murmured.

Though the words were slurred with exhaustion, he could hear the sincerity in them. It had been so long since he'd talked about Nathaniel with anyone besides his mother. Even then, she didn't speak of him with any regularity, her pain over his passing still achingly deep, an endless chasm that he feared would never be scaled.

When he spoke again he was hesitant, carefully prodding those memories he'd purposely repressed, testing the flavor of the words on his tongue. "My brother was...vibrant. He was all light and color. There was a natural exuberance to him, a passion for life. And people flocked to him because of it."

"You admired him."

"Yes." He smiled, something he had not thought to do again when speaking of Nathaniel. His chest lightened as he continued. "How could I not? He was everything I ever thought a person should be: kind and compassionate, talented and cheerful and giving. But more than that, I knew he loved me. He never left me in any doubt of it. It was in everything he did."

"He sounds incredible."

"He was. Now, go to sleep."

She shifted more fully against him, her arm stealing about his waist, her leg draping over his own. "I've no wish to sleep yet," she grumbled. "Tell me a story of the two of you as children."

He chuckled, rubbing his hand along her arm. "Has anyone ever told you that you can be stubborn?"

He felt her cheeks lift in a grin. "Oh, certainly."

He laughed again, wracking his mind for a memory that might pacify her. Finally he lit upon something.

"I was not the most eager pupil. I could not focus enough to retain anything my tutors tried to teach me. I wanted to be out and about, playing at being a soldier, riding hell-bent for leather over the countryside. My tutors were forever at their wits' end with trying to keep me contained.

"My father was constantly on me to be more like Nathaniel, who was an ideal pupil. He excelled at everything, was quick and smart, never missed a lesson. You would think I would have resented my brother. On the contrary, it only made me love him more, even while I was painfully aware that I could never live up to his example.

"Nathaniel was kinder to me than I was to myself. He knew that what I needed was more time out of doors, not less. And so, unbeknownst to me, he used his never-ending charm to convince my father to allow him to take over my lessons for one day. If I came away from it having learned something previously beyond me, my father must promise to implement this new method of learning there on out.

"And so, the following day, Nathaniel woke me at dawn, declaring it a holiday for us both. He then proceeded to take me about the grounds of our estate for a day of fresh air and exercise. I didn't think to question the game he made up of playing catch while reciting sums, or of the fun we had spinning our father's globe and pretending we were visiting whatever country our finger happened to land on, or of writing letters in the dirt with sticks, pretending we were leaving notes for explorers to find.

"At the end of the day, my father took me before him and quizzed me. And I was able to recite things I hadn't been able to before. And my father changed my lesson plans the very next day."

He laughed softly. Damnation, he hadn't thought of that in years. He could still remember his father's astonishment and the bold wink Nathaniel had given him when Daniel had finally understood what he had been about all that wonderful day. It warmed him, that memory, reminding him of happier times before he had gone off to war, and found his childhood ideals crushed. Before Nathaniel had lost his life in a horrible accident.

But Margery was quiet. She must have fallen asleep. It made him inexplicably sad, for some reason. He realized then he wanted her to know these things about him, about his brother. In sharing his memories, it was as if he had not lost Nathaniel; not completely, anyway.

Heaving a sigh, he settled more fully into the mattress,

knowing he must leave soon though he ached to stay. Suddenly her voice drifted to him, quiet and gentle in the still night air.

"Thank you for telling me about your brother."

He smiled into her hair as he felt her drift off to sleep in his arms. "Thank you for listening." *And thank you for healing my heart a bit.*

Chapter 15

When Margery finally awoke the following day, the sun was already at its zenith. And yet the loss of half a day was not the most surprising thing. Nor was the fact that Gran had actually allowed her to sleep, especially considering how anxious she must be for information regarding Clara and Quincy's child. No, the bulk of her surprise lay in her disappointment that Daniel wasn't in her bed when she opened her eyes.

But she would not allow anything to disturb the happy glow that enveloped her, even if that meant purposely ignoring the very troubling realization that she still wanted Daniel and, in fact, wanted him more than ever. But the day was halfway to being done, she reasoned as she began to dress, and so surely one more day enjoying this small affair they had entered into wouldn't hurt. She pulled on a clean shift and corset, securing the latter with quick fingers. One more day—and night—to lose herself in Daniel, before she returned to her life.

Which suddenly didn't seem as perfect as she had

believed it was. She bit her lip as she fastened her gown. She had thought it noble to spend the rest of her days mourning Aaron, to preserve their love instead of embracing life's possibilities. To live in the past instead of looking forward to the future. Now, however, that life didn't seem as brave as it had at first. Instead it seemed based in fear, and no way to live at all.

Before she quite knew what she was about, she strode to her wardrobe, flung it open, and dropped to the floor. Rooting around, pushing aside violet and purple and gray skirts, she located the large chest hidden in the very depths. It was what was left of her life before, when times had been happy and new and full of hope. She opened it now, revealing colorful gowns wrapped in tissue, shawls in bright hues, long lengths of ribbon, dancing slippers and fans and all the accoutrements of a debutante. Biting her lip, she lifted out a shimmering soft pink ribbon. Then, before she could think twice about it, she rose and hurried to her dressing table, working the silk through her hair. It seemed so small, the merest hint of color. And yet, to Margery, it was as loud as a scream. The beginnings of maybe, just maybe, moving forward.

It was with trepidation that she made her way to her grandmother's sitting room. She fully expected her to comment on the ribbon; after all, hadn't she spent the last several years trying to get Margery to wear colors again?

But beyond a slight double-take, the older woman didn't remark on it at all, instead diving right into the important subject of the day.

"I've heard from Lenora, of course, and she was even kind enough to send over a quick sketch of Clara's child." Here she gave Margery a withering look that spoke volumes about Margery's own lack of supplying information up until then, no matter that she had been sleeping. "But now that you're awake I would have the whole story from you. And don't think to skimp on details," she continued, her voice stern, as Margery sat beside her. "I wish to hear everything. We shall have plenty of time; Katrina blessedly has taken the afternoon off to run some errands in town, dragging Mouse along with her, and so we have all the peace and quiet we shall need."

Suppressing an amused smile, Margery launched into a retelling of the events of the previous day. The birth had been long, but Clara had been brave throughout the ordeal, listening intently to the midwife, pacing herself so she didn't tire easily. And when dear Frederick—named for Clara's father, the previous Duke of Dane—had been born, and had let out his first lusty cry, there had not been a dry eye in the entire house.

Gran hung on Margery's every word. And, though she tried to pretend otherwise, she was not immune to a tear or two herself. She surreptitiously dabbed at her eyes when Margery was through, clearing her throat several times.

"Well, then," she said, her voice gruff, "that's wonderful news. Just wonderful. I cannot wait to meet the child. And Quincy? He did not make a pest of himself, did he?"

Margery, knowing what was to come when the truth came out, pressed her lips tight and busied herself with smoothing her skirts.

Gran stilled and speared her with suspicious eyes. "I do

hope," she said with a frown, "that Peter and Oswin were wise enough to keep Quincy away from the birth."

"Oh, you know Quincy," she said, purposely vague.

"Yes," her grandmother said slowly, "I do." When Margery remained silent, Gran let out a huff of frustration. "He was there, wasn't he? In the room for the birth?"

Margery couldn't help but grin. "You know how dearly Quincy loves Clara, Gran. He wouldn't hear of staying away, and insisted on remaining by her side through the entire ordeal."

As expected, Gran's reaction was not pleasant. She rolled her eyes and threw her hands up in the air, letting loose a low curse. Freya, curled up until then in her lap, jerked awake and glared up at her mistress.

"And here I thought the boy was smarter than that," she raged. "To put that strain on Clara, so she had to worry about him as well as herself and the child? When I see him next, I'll tell him exactly what I think of his actions."

Gran was quickly working herself up into a frenzy. Margery, laughing, placed a hand on her arm.

"Truly, he was wonderful, Gran," she said. "If anything, he made the situation easier on Clara. He was supportive, and gentle, and was so very helpful. The rest of us were nearly rendered superfluous."

That seemed to deflate some of Gran's ire. "Well," she grumbled, "if that's the case. But it's still not natural, I say. Men are too squeamish, too weak, for the horrors of childbirth."

Margery laughed outright. At that moment Daniel and his mother arrived.

The laugh died in her throat at the sight of him. Goodness, he looked wonderful, so tall and strong and capable. As she knew he could be from firsthand experience. Her body went liquid at the thought of it. He caught her eye, an answering simmer in his gaze. And then he looked up toward her hair, and stilled.

She had forgotten about the ribbon. And, even if she had not, she wouldn't have expected anyone else beyond Gran to understand the meaning behind it. But he seemed to. His face lit up with an endearingly lopsided smile that told her he knew exactly what that simple ribbon meant.

It should perhaps worry her that he might misconstrue what the ribbon meant, that he might think she was reconsidering his suggestion that they marry. But the happiness bubbling up inside her overwhelmed everything else, even common sense.

Conversation was light and easy as tea and a small repast was ordered up. They ate, and drank, and talked of Clara and the babe. When the meal was over and Margery brought up what the rest of the day's schedule would bring, however, Gran interjected with customary firmness.

"You exhausted yourself yesterday," she declared, spearing Margery with a firm look. "You shall take the rest of the day off and do something enjoyable and relaxing. Take a walk on the beach perhaps." She pursed her lips and gave Margery an innocent look that did nothing to detract from the slyness behind it. "And take His Grace with you."

Margery might have been surprised and annoyed at such a blatant attempt at throwing her and Daniel together—especially as it contradicted Gran's previous denial of any intention to match them—if she wasn't so blasted happy at the chance for some time with the man. *What was wrong with her?* She should be concerned that she wanted to spend time with him outside of the agreement they had made. Yes, they had entered into a short-term affair. But that was physical. An afternoon at the shore decidedly was not.

But her concerns lost whatever ground they had made when Daniel stood and, looking down at her, held out his hand. She fairly melted under the regard in his eyes as she placed her hand in his and rose. Reality could intrude later, she determined as they exited the sitting room in order to prepare for their outing. For now, she thought with a small smile as she walked alongside him, she would focus on the here and now. And enjoy every moment of it.

* * *

Daniel could not recall the last time he'd been so content.

He rested back on his elbow on the large flat rock Margery had found for them. Farther down the stretch of sand bright yellow bathing machines were being pulled out into the water, white tents shaded groups from the late-afternoon sun, children teased the waves, and several couples strolled arm in arm. Yet Daniel was hard-pressed to look away from Margery, who sat beside him.

She was positively radiant. That was the only word for it. Her face fairly glowed from within as she gave a happy sigh and smiled at the gentle surf—could one feel jealousy for the sea? And that ribbon...

Ah, that ribbon, the faintest pink blush against the rich brown of her hair. Yet it was like a beacon to him. Did it signify something? Had she perhaps changed her mind about his suggestion that they make a match of it?

And why did that thought make him so deliriously happy?

But no, this was temporary. She had said as much, had been most adamant about it. He'd do his best to remember that.

Which, unfortunately, did not lessen the tiny spark of hope that nevertheless lit his insides up like a lantern.

"Do you think," she said, her voice quiet and slow, "that Gran would know if I removed my bonnet and raised my face to the sun for ten minutes?"

He chuckled. "I rather think your grandmother would know that you're even considering it. Though whether her frightening knowledge would be from paid spies or the supernatural, I really couldn't say."

She turned her head to look at him, her warm brown eyes dancing with humor. "Why, one would think you're afraid of her."

"Oh, I am," he admitted readily enough. "I like her more than most people, of course. She's refreshingly honest and candid. But she terrifies me."

She laughed, a light, joyous thing he felt clear to his soul.

Suddenly several shadows fell over them.

"Why, hello, Mrs. Kitteridge. Imagine seeing you here."

Daniel glanced up, more than a little dazed after having witnessed Margery's unbridled happiness. The sun shone behind the newcomers, casting their features in shadows.

"Oh!" Margery exclaimed, rising. "How lovely to see you all. But please allow me to introduce my companion, the Duke of Carlisle. Your Grace, Mr. Newton, Mr. Emmett, and Mr. McTavish," she said, pointing to each in turn. "These gentlemen were friends of my late husband's. They served in the same regiment together."

Daniel lurched to his feet and faced the men. Only then, as he smiled politely and held out his hand—trying not to curse Margery's acquaintances for disturbing them—could he ascertain their features and understand her words.

The beach was gone in an instant. He was in the midst of a field. Mud, mixed liberally with blood, sucked at his boots. Screams and shouts and the constant roar of muskets and cannons rent the air. The acrid stench mixed with blood and excrement, filling his nose. A panicked boy pushed past, face spattered with mud and blood, horror etching deep grooves for the mud to cling to.

"Daniel?"

Margery's voice seemed to come from far away, the faintest of sounds. Yet still vivid, still devastating, was the death and horror all about him, as if he were back in that cursed field. And in his arms, that dead boy, pale blue eyes staring up at a smoke-choked sky—

"Daniel!"

Margery's alarmed tone, her hand on his arm, dragged him back to the present. He breathed in deeply through his nose, dragging in the fresh, briny air, forcing the memories back to hell where they belonged.

"Pardon." His voice was a mere croak. Clearing his throat, he tried again. "Please, forgive me."

Margery's brows were pulled together in the middle,

worry stark on her lovely face. "Are you well?" she asked quietly.

Before he could summon an answer—he didn't have the faintest idea how to respond anyway—a deep voice broke into the moment.

"But you're Captain Lord Daniel Hayle."

Daniel flinched. That name seemed to call from a veritable lifetime ago, a haunting echo of the idealistic boy he had been. Taking a deep breath, he turned to face Margery's acquaintances.

Again, that shock of memory that tried so violently to make itself known. This time, however, his defenses were firmly in place, and it blessedly slipped away, leaving numbness in its wake.

"By God, McTavish, you're right." The tallest of the three, a Mr. Newton, gaped at him.

"My word," the one with the light brown skin, Mr. Emmett, breathed. "We saw you that day. On the battlefield."

Daniel cleared his throat. "I was Captain Lord Daniel Hayle. Now I am the Duke of Carlisle."

"Ah." The man flushed, bowed. "My apologies, Your Grace. And my condolences."

Daniel inclined his head in thanks.

Mr. Newton looked to Margery in confusion. "But how do you know one another?"

"His Grace is the son of my grandmother's dear friend. They are visiting until the end of the month."

"Why, that's splendid." The man smiled broadly.

Mr. Emmett reached for Daniel's hand, shaking it heartily. "It's an honor to meet you, sir. Er, Your Grace. I do hope you're enjoying the Isle."

Daniel, wanting nothing more than to be done with this conversation—and every conversation hereafter that even brushed with mention of the war—nevertheless could not be rude to these men, who had seen the same hells he himself had. Clearing his throat, he said, "Er, I am, thank you. And you all live on the Isle?" The words sounded normal to his own ears, yet far off, as if another had said them.

"We do," Mr. McTavish said, his broad chest puffing up. "Came here just after the war. Aaron extolled the beauty of Synne so eloquently that, when I found myself looking for a place to settle, I wasted no time coming here. And apparently these two had the very same brilliant idea." He jerked a thumb in his friends' direction, chuckling.

"There are quite a few veterans, soldiers and sailors alike, who have taken lodgings here," Mr. Newton explained. "Mrs. Kitteridge visits us from time to time. She's most kind."

"Nonsense," Margery said with a gentle smile. "It is all of you who are being kind, letting me talk on about my husband. But where are you all off to?"

"We're to meet several of the boys at the Master-at-Arms," McTavish said. His eyes lit up and he turned to Daniel. "Say, why don't you join us, Your Grace? It would be our honor to buy you a drink. And I know the others would love to meet you."

Daniel nearly blanched. Oh, God, that was the last thing he wanted to do. He managed a smile, however sickly as it might be, and replied, "I'm unable to just now. Perhaps another time."

"Of course," the man said jovially.

The three took their leave then, with hearty hand-shakes and boisterous farewells.

As they walked off, Daniel felt the pull of the memory again. He gripped tightly to the head of his cane as the unwelcome recollection slipped back into the murky depths of his mind.

Margery stepped in front of him, filling his vision, her warm brown eyes filled with concern. "Daniel, are you well?"

He dredged up a smile, achingly aware of the tightness of the scar on his cheek as he did so. "Certainly. But we'd best be returning to Seacliff before your grand-mother misses us."

She didn't believe that nothing was wrong. He saw it in the small line that dipped between her brows, in the tight press of her lips. But she merely inclined her head in acknowledgment and started off toward the flat path that led to The Promenade and the carriage.

As he followed, however, he knew that, to keep those memories at bay, he could not be so unguarded again.

* * *

Let it go. The refrain bounced about in Margery's head for the next half hour as they made their way back to Sea-cliff. It was none of her business. Whatever had affected Daniel—no doubt Aaron's friends had reminded him of the war; though that, of course, was mere conjecture on her part—he did not want to reveal it. She should respect the man's unspoken wishes and leave him in peace.

By the time they traversed the upstairs hallway, how-ever, making their way back to their rooms so they might dress for dinner, Margery had nearly lost the battle with herself to remain silent. No doubt she would have blurted something out before disappearing into her room.

If Daniel, after taking a quick glance about to make certain the hallway was clear of servants, hadn't followed her within.

His mouth was on hers before she could take a breath. The shock of it was rapidly replaced with a desire so fierce, so consuming, she forgot everything but the feel of his lips. She wound her arms about his neck, diving her fingers into his thick chestnut hair, arching her body up into his. He groaned, the sound filling her up until she thought she'd go mad with it.

"Margery," he rasped. "What you do to me."

A shiver of pure pleasure worked over her as his lips found the side of her throat. "The feeling is mutual," she managed. A gasp escaped her as his teeth scraped the sensitive spot just beneath her ear.

She felt his lips turn up in a smile against her skin. "Is it?" he murmured huskily before placing a hot, open-mouthed kiss to that same spot.

"Oh, yes." Her breath quickened. His hands found the curve of her bottom then and he drew her tight against him. The hard length of him pressed into her belly and a dewy heat bloomed in that most sensitive place of her. If she melted into a liquid puddle right then she would not have been the least surprised. "We have time," she whispered, desperate to ease the ache within her, needing him more than air just then. "They won't expect us for dinner for another hour."

The mood shifted in an instant. To her bewilderment he tensed under her hands. Before she could make sense of it he pulled back. "Ah, no," he said, his voice hoarse, his breathing heavy. He quickly—much more quickly than she liked—gained control of himself and straightened, smoothing his hair and adjusting his cravat, picking up his cane where he'd dropped it. He sent a small smile her way. "I wouldn't chance infuriating your grandmother."

Margery gave an answering smile, for it seemed a necessary return to normalcy just then. But she did not fail to see the sidelong glance he slid to the wide windows, where the sun was shining through in golden beams that illuminated the rich floral rug gracing the floor. She recalled with an aching heart then his fear two evenings before, his need for total darkness before he felt he could lose himself in her.

He made his way to the door. Before he opened it, however, he turned to look at her. Once more, the heat was back in his gaze. "Shall I come to you tonight?" he asked, his voice husky and low and utterly delicious.

Her bones fairly melted. "Yes," she whispered, lost once more in her need for him. With a small smile, he let himself out into the hall. And she was left alone with only her thoughts for company.

His refusal to allow her to see him unclothed shouldn't bother her as it did. She made her way to her armoire, determined to put the whole episode from her mind. She was to find him a wife in less than a fortnight, after all. Their relationship was purely physical on both their parts; neither of them was here to fix the other.

And yet...

No, she told herself firmly as she rifled through her wardrobe for an appropriate gown. No "and yet." This was temporary.

Temporary.

And mayhap, she told herself as her gaze drifted from the dull dresses to the chest she had removed the pink ribbon from earlier, if she repeated that word to herself enough times she would believe it.

* * *

It was the thrashing that woke her.

Daniel had come to her bed again that evening, and they had spent the night in one another's arms. She had drifted off with her head on his chest and his strong arm about her, his heartbeat in her ears. Just as she had the past two nights.

But there was no gradual waking to the rising sun and an empty bed. No, the room was still pitch-black, the night air chill on her uncovered body. And the bed fairly vibrating from Daniel as he trembled and twitched beside her.

Shaking the confused fog from her brain, she reached for him in the dark, laid a hand on his chest. His skin was clammy to the touch, sweat dripping from him. "Daniel," she whispered. "Wake up, Daniel."

He didn't seem to hear her. Strange sounds were bubbling up from his throat, shouts strangled before they could find purchase.

She shook his shoulder hard. "Daniel!"

He gasped, lurching upright. "Wh-where—"

"You're with me, Daniel," she murmured. Heart pounding, not certain how he would react, she gingerly touched his arm.

"Margery?"

"Yes."

Immediately she was in his arms. She gripped him tight, relief replacing her shock, despite the faint trembling in her limbs.

But when he would have kissed her she pushed him back against the pillows, reaching out blindly to find the covers, untangling them with fumbling fingers from his legs and pulling them up and over them both. Only then did she return back to him, curling up against his side.

His heart beat fiercely beneath her hand. "Are you well?" she asked.

"Yes." He let loose a shuddering breath that stirred the hair at her temple. "Damnation, it's been over a year since I've fallen prey to that. I'm sorry."

"Don't apologize, please."

He seemed not to have heard her. "It's just so damn real. I can see everything, hear everything. And that boy—"

She could hear the faint click of his teeth as he closed his jaw. Why? To stop from telling her about his nightmare? But she couldn't stand the idea of him bottling it up, suffering with it alone.

"You can tell me about it if you'd like."

Already his head was shaking his denial. "It's not fit for a lady's ears."

"And when have I ever given the indication that I cannot handle it?" She caressed his chest to take away the faint sting of the words. "It might help, Daniel." And then when he remained quiet, "What happened to the boy?"

His exhale was hot and ragged. "He was so damn young. And it was my fault he died. It was chaos. You couldn't see for the smoke. And the mud. It had rained the day before, and the ground was sodden. I'd been jostled, slipped in the stuff, thought I'd be trampled. When I gained my feet again I took aim, pulled the trigger. Suddenly this boy was there, in front of me, one of ours. He was running from the battle. I would have let him go; God knows what horrible hell that moment was. No one deserved to live through it. But I couldn't stop the damn ball. For a second I thought the gun had misfired; it was coated in mud, soaked through. But when the smoke cleared he was gripping his chest. Blood was seeping from between his fingers..."

Daniel shuddered beneath her. She moved her hand over his chest in soothing, gentle circles. "It wasn't your fault."

Again, he seemed incapable of hearing her. "I dropped the gun, ran to him. But it was too late. Too damn late. Blood was bubbling from his lips. He was calling for his sweetheart. And then he was gone. He was gone, Margery."

She didn't realize she was crying until she felt the wetness of her tears pool under her temple. Ah, God, what he must have suffered. "It wasn't your fault," she whispered. "It was a horrible accident, and nothing more. It wasn't your fault."

He didn't answer her, but eventually he began to relax under her hand, then to breathe deep and slow in sleep. She kissed his chest, snuggling closer into his embrace. But sleep didn't come for her all that long night.

Chapter 16

*I*f meeting Margery's veteran friends the day before, the subsequent return of those horrifying nightmares, and his shame in then burdening Margery with the truth of that most devastating history had shaken Daniel, the visitor to Seacliff the following day completely undermined what little confidence he had managed to build these past weeks on Synne.

"Mr. Gregory Hayle is here to see you, Your Grace."

Daniel gaped at the butler. Surely he'd misheard. "I beg your pardon?"

"Mr. Gregory Hayle. Shall I show him to the drawing room, Your Grace?"

Still, he couldn't manage to comprehend what the butler was telling him. Gregory, here?

Wilkins, who had been putting the finishing touches to Daniel's cravat, leaned in closer. "You can turn him away, you know."

Daniel blinked down at him. The valet hadn't attempted to cross the line between them into familiarity since that first night on Synne. Now, however, he gazed up at Daniel with a ferocious fire. "What was that?"

"Mr. Hayle. You needn't see him."

Daniel gaped at him. "But he's my cousin, and came all this way."

The valet mumbled something that sounded suspiciously like, "To cause mischief, no doubt." When Daniel would have questioned Wilkins on it, however, the butler spoke again.

"Your Grace?"

Daniel started. "Er, yes, please have him shown to the drawing room."

"Very good, Your Grace."

With the butler gone, Daniel turned back to Wilkins to question him on his reaction to Gregory's arrival. It had been so out of character for the valet. But the man had already turned away and was hurrying into the adjacent room. Sighing, Daniel faced the mirror.

Everything was in order. And yet he suddenly felt every bit of his awkwardness. The scars that ravaged his cheek and temple made his already-rough features even more so. The elegant clothes, the best that money could buy, could not fail to hide the stocky, inelegant form beneath. He had managed to forget for a time who he really was, that he was a sham, that he didn't belong. Margery had helped him begin to overcome that, he knew.

But no matter how she'd made him feel, he was still the same man he'd always been.

Nevertheless, he straightened his shoulders and, taking up his cane, made his way from the room.

Gregory turned from his position at the window when Daniel entered the drawing room. He grinned, striding forward, hand extended. "Ah, Cousin. You're looking...decent."

Daniel pressed his lips tight as he took the man's hand. Trying and failing not to notice that *decent* was the least accurate description he would use for his cousin. The man was devilishly handsome as always, his long, lean form draped in clothes of the finest fit, the most expensive material. His features looked as if they'd been swiped from an ancient statue, his hair thick and wavy and combed just so.

Heading for a seat, Daniel indicated a chair some distance away. "Won't you have a seat?"

Instead of taking the suggested chair, however, Gregory settled himself beside Daniel, exhaling a satisfied breath as he did so. "I vow, it was quite the journey to get here from London. I must look a veritable mess; I shouldn't be seen in public." He laughed heartily.

Daniel gave him a sickly smile. "What brings you to Synne, Gregory?"

"Why, to see you, of course. And my dear aunt. Where is she, by the way?"

"Taking a walk with Lady Tesh, I assume."

"This healthful sea air doing her some good, I hope?"

Daniel merely nodded. His nerves were strung tight as a nocked bow, his mind whirling. What the devil did the man want?

"Good," Gregory said with a wide smile, looking to his cuff and adjusting it. "Glad to hear it. But what is this I hear about you heading to London after?" He re-arranged his features into a semblance of great concern. "Surely you don't intend on dragging my aunt to the capital when she's so frail."

Daniel felt the blood leave his face. How had he forgotten the planned trip to London, as well as the most nerve-wracking part of it should he fail to find a bride while still on Synne?

But he knew in an instant: Margery. She had so bewitched him the last few days that he had not been able to think straight. Or, rather, he had willingly lost himself in her. And had completely lost sight of what he needed to do, which was to marry quickly.

As if Gregory heard Daniel's troubled thoughts, he leaned forward in his seat and dropped his voice to a nearly believable concern. "Erica is still in London, you know. I'd expected them to travel to Thrushton's country seat for the rest of her confinement, thereby saving you the pain of seeing them while you're in town. But he's of a mind to stay on for the opening of Parliament, and so they'll remain for the birth as well. I thought it wise to forewarn you, so you are not caught unaware."

"There was no reason for you to warn me; their presence in London will not affect me at all," Daniel managed, wholly unsure if it was a lie or not. If anything, he felt numb.

"Oh, well, that's a relief." Gregory smiled widely, clapping a hand on Daniel's shoulder. Daniel flinched, an instinctual reaction where his cousin was concerned. He sent up a quick prayer that Gregory had not seen. The man thrived on people's vulnerabilities, and used them to his advantage.

But those prayers were ignored. His cousin let out a bark of laughter. "Never tell me you still fear my fist, Danny."

He should not. He was larger than Gregory now, after all, a man grown, a veteran of the war, a bloody *duke*.

And yet inside he still felt that same debilitating fear that he used to. There had not been a corner he had not rounded where he had not tensed for the possibility of Gregory being in the room. There had not been a single moment while in his presence that he had not held his breath, waiting for the swiftly wielded words that would cut as deftly as an assassin's blade, leaving deep wounds, yet done under cover of politeness so that no one saw them for what they were. And there had not been a moment while alone in his presence that Daniel had not expected a heavy hand to descend. Punches carefully placed, so the bruising would not show.

Gregory seemed blessedly unaware of Daniel's tortured memories. He rambled on, extolling the glories of London, even though mere moments ago he had been attempting to dissuade Daniel from visiting that same city. But wasn't this a much slyer way of seeing that Daniel did not visit the capital? He made certain to touch upon every one of the things that would cause Daniel to turn tail and run: routs and balls, musicales and the theater, meeting so-and-so in Hyde Park, which was apparently the place to see and be seen. The man could be lying through his damn teeth, for all Daniel knew. He didn't have a clue what London was like, after all, and most especially not in the off-season.

But that didn't matter. His cousin's words were dredging up a wild panic in his chest that he was hard-pressed to contain.

Finally Gregory grew silent and looked about with a raised brow. "But I thought you had learned your manners, Danny. No tea and biscuits for your dear cousin?" Before Daniel could think to apologize, the other man gave him a pitying look. "Well, no worries. I'm certain you'll master the social niceties. Eventually."

As Daniel stared mutely at him, Gregory stood with a fluidity and grace that would have had Daniel envious even at his most hale and hearty. "But I'd best be on my way. I've a mind to see this quaint little town while I'm here. Don't get up on my account," he continued when Daniel made to rise. Again, that pitying look. "I wouldn't want you to hurt that leg of yours, after all."

As Gregory headed for the drawing room door, whistling jauntily, Daniel finally managed to speak up. "Will we be seeing you again?"

His cousin paused and looked back at Daniel with unbridled humor, letting loose a gay laugh. "Oh, you are a funny one, Danny. As if I would come all this way for a single visit, and without even a drop of refreshments." He grinned, almost a feral baring of teeth, all the pleasantness seeming to have been leached from it. "I've already taken a nice little room at the Master-at-Arms Inn, and so yes, Cousin, you can be certain you'll be seeing more of me. Who knows, mayhap I'll be able to assist you in preparing for London and seeing Erica again, eh?" And with that he was gone.

Daniel sat dumbly for a moment, staring at the open door, listening as his cousin exited the house in that boisterous, cheerful way of his that never failed to grate on Daniel's nerves. The man's parting words filled him with a hollow dread, as well as a remembrance that it was all too possible he might see Erica in London. Although there was little chance she would be out much in public, being so close to her confinement, a vivid image nevertheless popped into his mind then, of meeting

Erica face-to-face, of seeing with his own eyes her swollen stomach, her contentment with Thrushton—and perhaps a vague pity and disgust in her eyes, as well as a deep relief that she had escaped having to make a life with Daniel.

To his shock, however, that possibility did not have the power it used to. Instead, it was quickly replaced by another: Margery, glorious and glowing, and heavy with *his* child. And his heart ached for that.

He recoiled as if burned. He saw now that the love he'd had for Erica was pale in comparison to what he was beginning to feel for Margery.

Erica had been beautiful, and graceful, and at ease with everyone. Everything that Daniel had not been. She'd dazzled him, like a star. But he had only known her by her social persona; he hadn't known who she truly was beneath the glittering exterior. His affection for her had been unformed, a mere bit of clay.

But with Margery, he was beginning to know her heart. His affections for her were being formed like a vase on a potter's wheel, growing more complete with every conversation, every shared laugh, every glance. Every kiss. And he wanted so much more of that with her.

In the next moment he cursed himself for being the biggest fool alive. He had done the one thing he had vowed never to do, had put his guard down and let his emotions guide him. If he wanted to keep Gregory from eventually getting his hands on the dukedom, he had to secure a bride, and an heir. And by falling in love with Margery, who had proclaimed she would never marry, who was so against marrying again that she would hire herself out to him to find him a bride, though she was willing to take him to her bed, he would essentially be shooting himself in the foot.

He blanched then. Love Margery? Surely he didn't. Theirs was a temporary affair. They had agreed on just that. And hadn't he determined that he would never put himself in the position of loving another? Hadn't he promised himself, with his broken heart and shattered dreams, that he would never grow close to another person again?

A numbness spread over him and seeped down to his very bones. His days of idyllic happiness were over. London or no London, he could not allow himself to continue falling in love with Margery. It was time to choose a wife, to marry. And to leave Synne—and Margery—behind for good.

* * *

Anticipation filled Margery as the carriage approached Seacliff. She had been gone the better part of the day, visiting Swallowhill and offering what help she could with Clara and the babe. But though she'd been kept happily busy, though she'd enjoyed the time spent with her family, the hours had dragged. She couldn't stop thinking of Daniel.

And as the carriage rocked to a halt and she descended to the drive and entered the house, she felt quite honestly as if she were coming home.

Which shouldn't surprise her. She had been a resident at Seacliff since Lenora and Peter's marriage, after all, and before that had come to stay with her grandmother more times than she could count. But there was something different in the feeling just then, a warmth deep in her chest, a certainty that she had finally found her place.

She rushed into the house, up the stairs, down the upper hallway to her room, eager to change out of her clothes and join the rest of the household for dinner. She certainly didn't expect to see Daniel's door ajar. Nor did she expect to see him within.

He stood at the window, his back to her, seemingly focused on the garden below. Smiling to herself, mischief rearing up like a naughty child whispering in her ear, she crept up behind him. So engrossed was he in the view he didn't hear her approach. When she reached him she snaked her arms about his waist, felt his start of surprise as she rested her cheek on his broad back.

"Hello. Did you miss me?" she murmured.

"Mrs. Kitteridge."

The laugh that bubbled up in her throat at what she thought was teasing on his part in reverting to her formal name died a swift death as he extracted himself from her embrace and turned to face her. There was no humor in his expression. Rather, his eyes were somber, his scars standing out in harsh relief against the unnaturally pale cast to his skin.

"Daniel, what's wrong?"

"Nothing at all." But his eyes slid from hers as he said it. Clearing his throat, he made his way to the full-length mirror on the far side of the room and stared intently at himself. "I'm actually glad you've come. It seems we've lost track of the days, you and I. And the time for me to travel to London grows dangerously near."

A chill began to creep through her. She clasped her

hands tight before her to stave off the sudden shaking in them.

"I think it's best if we put our focus once more on our original agreement," he continued. His voice sounded distant, neutral. And like knives to her heart. He smoothed the front of his jacket, large, rough hands drifting over the impeccable material. "And I believe I've made a decision on whom I should court."

Dragging in a deep breath, he looked her way. She felt as if she were watching him through a tunnel, the great roaring in her ears nearly blocking out what he was saying.

"I do think Miss Pickering will do just fine," he said. "She seems a sensible girl, and would be more than happy, I think, to have a marriage of convenience. And I can provide her the space and privacy she no doubt requires for her studies."

"Miss Pickering," Margery repeated dazedly.

He nodded. "Really, I don't know why I didn't see her as an ideal choice from the start. There won't be any demands for a deeper connection from her. And, as you've known from the beginning, I'm not looking for a romantic attachment. Quite the opposite, really." He paused. Then, his gaze sliding to his cuff as he made some adjustment, he said, "No, friendship and love are the last things I want or need."

Margery's head spun. She thought she might be sick.

"This will, of course, mean an end to our affair."

"Of course," she managed through stiff lips.

He raised his eyes to hers. She felt as if she'd been slapped. There was nothing there, none of the warmth she'd come to recognize, no emotion. It was as if she were looking at a painting. No, less than a painting, for even an amateur artist could elicit emotion in art. And there was not a hint of emotion, either warm or cold, in his flat gaze.

"We had always meant it to be temporary, just that one night. It went on longer than we had planned."

"Yes."

He regarded her for a long moment. Then something shifted, emotion peeking through the veneer. His voice, when he spoke, was a mere rasp of sound. "I will never forget our time together."

Which only made this worse. Self-preservation and pride and fury at herself for letting it get so far brought her shoulders back, forced the bright smile to her lips. "Certainly. And I shan't forget it, either." She let loose a laugh. "Goodness, but this is a relief. I had come here to suggest the very same thing. But I'll send a note to the Pickerings immediately, shall I? Though I'm quite certain there won't be any difficulty in securing something with them right away."

Before he could answer she spun about, rushing from the room. Only when she was safe behind her own closed door did she allow herself to breathe. But there was no relief in it. Her chest felt tight, air barely wheezing through her suddenly dry lips.

Had she been so starved for physical affection that she would put aside everything she held dear once she finally tasted it again? She went to twist her wedding ring— and her heart dropped into her stomach to find her finger bare. It took her some seconds to remember she had removed it that first night she'd lain with Daniel.

Stupid, stupid woman, she berated herself as she hurried to her desk. All the care, all the caution, and still she had come to care for Daniel. She yanked open the drawer, retrieved the ring. Pushing it onto her finger, forcing it over her knuckle, she let it settle back where it had rested for so long. The coldness of the metal seemed to seep down into her very bones. And then, as a further reminder, she lifted out the miniature of Aaron she'd hidden alongside it. She traced her gaze over his features, the faint roundness still present in his cheeks, the unruly curl that never would lay flat no matter how he tried.

But, to her dismay, the connection she usually felt when gazing at his beloved features—the one and only painting she had of him—was just out of reach. She tried to remember the day the miniature had been painted. He'd been so embarrassed to sit for it; his family had never been well-off, and having a portrait done of oneself was the height of vanity and excess to them. But with kisses and pretty begging she had finally gotten him to agree to sit for Lenora, however reluctantly. They'd been newly married at the time, just learning the physical joys of one another, beginning to set up a home together in London. Though he'd tried to hold himself in what he deemed was a properly sober fashion for his forced portrait, he still hadn't been able to keep his eyes from Margery as she'd sat beside Lenora. They'd drifted her way time and time again, the promise of love in his eyes. And Lenora, with her incredible talent, had captured the moment perfectly, the slight flush to his cheeks, the small smile on his lips, the affection in his gaze. One of the happiest moments of Margery's life.

But though the memory was there, it wasn't as clear as it typically was. She focused harder, but it was like trying to peer through a thick fog.

Suddenly frightened that she might be losing even the memory of him, she hugged the small framed portrait to her chest. Then, dragging in a shaky breath, she placed the miniature on the desk and ran her finger along the edge before, setting her jaw, she made her way from the room. Daniel had been right; time was quickly flying by, much more quickly than she'd realized. The blackmail money was due in less than a fortnight, and she didn't have room for any more dalliances, any more distractions. It was time to get Daniel married.

Chapter 17

"Your Grace, are you certain my Bronwyn cannot get you another scone?"

Daniel started, tearing his eyes away from Margery. Where they'd been for a disturbing amount of time all that hellish afternoon. Before he had a chance to answer Mrs. Pickering, however, the woman turned to her daughter, who was at that moment using a small item secured on a chain about her neck to peer at something on the ground.

"Bronwyn, dear, fetch His Grace a scone. Hurry up now."

The girl let out a huff and stretched out inelegantly across the blanket to dig in the basket nearby, quickly removing the requested pastry. He thought for a moment she would chuck the thing at his head. Instead she reached across the blanket and, sliding a hooded glance her mother's way, handed it to him with a smile.

Though to call it a smile was being much too generous. It was more a baring of teeth; together with the reflection of the sun on her spectacles, it gave her features a frightening cast. *London*, he told himself brutally. *Think of London, and not having to search for a bride while there. And keeping the dukedom out of Gregory's hands.*

And yet, though those two things had been his driving force for so long, he could not dredge up the sense of urgency needed to begin courting the odd, slightly resentful Miss Pickering.

But that did not make it any less imperative that he forge forward. He tried to recall all the reasons he'd thought her the ideal candidate for a wife during those horrible hours after Gregory had left Seacliff the day before: She was serious, and focused, and used to looking at disturbing creatures all day long. And she did not appear to have a sentimental bone in her body. All of the Gadfeld girls were sweet things, and one or two seemed perhaps to be receptive. But they all had stars in their eyes, and he did not want a sentimental wife who would hope one day for more than a business arrangement. Miss Denby made his head spin with her fast talking. Miss Peacham had shown in small ways she would have no patience for him distancing himself, and as well seemed disinclined to move on from the Beakhead Tea Room or her life here. And Miss Athwart of the Quayside Circulating Library—and her bird—frightened him nearly witless. No, Miss Pickering was the perfect candidate.

Why, then, could he not summon the necessary enthusiasm for courting her?

An easy enough question to answer, he thought despondently as his gaze once more slid to Margery, seated close to Mr. Pickering. She was valiantly joining the man in a lively discussion—on Mr. Pickering's side, at least—on the benefits of sailing, as the man had recently purchased himself a small skiff.

But his infatuation with her was not doing him a bit of good where Miss Pickering was concerned. He looked to the girl, who was once more using the small item on the chain about her neck—a delicate magnifying glass, he saw now—to peer at something on the sand beside her. Clearing his throat, he shifted his leg into a more comfortable position—no easy thing, reclining as he was on this blasted blanket in the sand—and leaned closer to her.

"Are you finding any interesting insects today?"

She blinked owlishly at him before looking down to the scone still in his hand. "You have not eaten your scone."

"Ah, er, no. My apologies." With that he took a large bite. Which perhaps had not been the wisest course of action, as he now had a mouthful of dry crumbs to contend with. Valiantly chewing, he finally managed to get the thing down. All the while she watched him, her eyes huge behind her spectacles. Much like those insects she was so fond of.

"You don't care for it," she said when he'd finished and washed it down with a generous gulp of lemonade.

"No, it's very good," he lied.

She pursed her lips. "I did tell Mother it wasn't wise to have me bake. We have a perfectly good cook, after all, who could have done a much better job at it. But she was under the assumption you would appreciate the effort."

Ah, God. She had baked them, had she? He was

suddenly deliriously happy that any wife of his would not have to cook. Ever.

"I do appreciate the effort," he assured her.

Mrs. Pickering spoke up then. "Ah, yes, our sweet Bronwyn is quite the homemaker. I daresay, Your Grace, she would make any man a fine wife."

As comments went, it was about as transparent as glass what the woman was attempting to convey. How lucky for her, Daniel thought grimly, that he was already of a mind to court her daughter.

"You are so very right, my dear Mrs. Pickering," her husband declared, his conversation with Margery apparently at an end. "I daresay it will break my heart to see her marry and leave our home. She is so accommodating, so generous, always thinking of others."

The girl in question appeared not to hear her loquacious father, as she was already immersed in sketching out the long, spindly legs of some creature in her notebook. But from the way her mouth tightened at the corners he rather thought she was far more affected by the man's heaping of praise on her head than she let on—though not at all in a positive way.

Perhaps, Daniel mused, that might work in his favor where the girl was concerned.

"Miss Pickering," he said. "Might I tempt you in a walk down the beach?"

Once more those overlarge eyes landed on him, though this time a healthy dose of annoyance was present in them. Before he could react, she sighed mightily and placed her sketchbook aside. "Very well," she said with little grace, rising with impressive quickness.

He, unfortunately, was not so quick. But he finally

managed to get to his feet and, offering his arm to the girl, they started down the beach together. Though he didn't know what he should be prouder of: his ability to rise with little embarrassment in front of a prospective bride, the fact that she looked at him with a lack of disgust—though there was a decided lack of interest as well—or that he had not looked Margery's way as he carefully guided Miss Pickering away from the small group. No matter how much he wanted to.

* * *

Margery determinedly kept her gaze from straying to Daniel and Miss Pickering as they strolled down the beach arm in arm. This was a good thing, she told herself bracingly. The wheel had been set in motion. The young lady, while not particularly exuberant—or even remotely thrilled—about the potential of a duke courting her, seemed nevertheless receptive in a reluctant kind of way. Margery rather thought Daniel would have no trouble getting Miss Pickering to accept him once he finally got up the nerve to propose. It was a huge relief; with the clock ticking relentlessly toward the blackmailer's deadline, she should be able to breathe a bit easier, now that Daniel had made his choice and was one step closer to securing the hand of his duchess.

And the relief was there, easing the band about her chest. Why, then, did she also feel like crying?

"They make a fine couple, don't they?" Mrs. Pickering gushed. She clasped her hands to her ample bosom, staring after her offspring with glowing eyes that could not fail to hide the greedy gleam in them. "Oh, Mr.

Pickering, look at how well our daughter looks on the duke's arm."

"She does, my dear. She does." Spearing a square of cheese with his knife, he brought it to his mouth and chewed on it thoughtfully for a moment while giving Margery a considering look. "What think you, Mrs. Kitteridge?"

She knew what he was asking: Were the duke's attentions serious? Was this the signal they had waited for to tell them they had landed him, and that their daughter was to be a duchess? It was the perfect opening she needed to help guide this whole endeavor to a satisfying conclusion.

Yet the words stuck in her throat. Why? She didn't want him for herself.

She didn't.

She dredged up a bright smile. "You're quite right that Miss Pickering looks lovely on his arm. They make an attractive couple."

As she expected, the words had an instantaneous effect on Mr. Pickering. "Splendid, splendid," he said in such a tone that Margery would not have been surprised if he had begun to rub his hands together in glee.

Suddenly he turned to his wife and muttered an aside that nevertheless carried to Margery on the breeze: "Well, our Bronwyn is not plain at any rate. But with such a catch as a duke, beggars cannot be choosers."

Mrs. Pickering tittered.

Margery froze. "I'm sorry, what was that?"

The man had the decency to look abashed, though only slightly. "Well, you must admit, my dear Mrs. Kitteridge, the man's scars can be a bit unsettling."

Outrage rose up in Margery like tidewater. She sat up straighter and leveled a glare on the man. "There is nothing at all unsettling about His Grace's appearance."

"Your loyalty is commendable, Mrs. Kitteridge," Mrs. Pickering said with a small smile that spoke of some secret understanding between them. "But even you in your boundless kindness cannot deny that His Grace's scars can be difficult to look upon."

Margery gaped at her. Then, vision turning red, she said, "One wonders how you could entertain the idea of him as a son-in-law if you view him in such a way."

Again that titter, this time making Margery clench her back teeth until she thought they'd shatter. "One can entertain a good many things if the man in question is a duke," the other woman quipped. "Isn't that so, Mr. Pickering?"

The two laughed uproariously, wholly unaware of Margery's growing fury. Unable to remain in their presence a moment longer, she stood. The couple started, their laughter dying away as they gaped up at her.

"I do hope you'll forgive me," she bit out in a tone that belied her pleasant words, "but I just recalled His Grace and I are expected back at Seacliff. I'm afraid I'll have to cut our afternoon short. If you'll excuse us?"

Without waiting for them to reply—if they did, they would most likely say something offensive, and Margery could not be responsible for her actions if they did—she stalked down the beach after Daniel and Miss Pickering. They had not gone far; the sand made it difficult for Daniel to maneuver with any speed. But the girl was more animated than Margery had ever seen her. As she approached, she heard Miss Pickering going on about thoraxes and mandibles—whatever in the world those were—in an energetic way.

But in that moment, with fury pounding through her, Margery wasn't in a mood to appreciate the fact that Daniel had somehow managed to open the girl up, as so few had. Not that Margery would ever appreciate something of that manner, she reflected sourly.

"Your Grace," she said with a falsely bright smile, "I just recalled that we're expected back at Seacliff. Miss Pickering, if you're agreeable, His Grace and I can escort you back to your parents."

Then, with all the skill of a sheepdog, she herded the two back to the blanket. In no time they had said their hasty farewells and were heading back to their carriage.

Daniel remained quiet through the whole thing. It was only when they were settled within the open carriage, however, that he finally spoke in a low voice.

"What the devil was that about?"

Margery glanced at him before returning her gaze back to the beach. "Nothing at all," she mumbled.

"It did not seem like nothing," he replied.

Margery pressed her lips tighter. The carriage started off then, heading down The Promenade toward Seacliff. She focused on the rhythmic sounds of the horses' hooves on the cobbles, the wheels against the road, the hush of the waves beneath it all. But nothing, it seemed, could take away the fury simmering in her veins.

"Margery—"

"It was nothing."

He let out an aggravated breath. "I was finally making headway with the young lady. Which was the point of the whole thing. Wasn't it?"

Still, she refused to look at him. "Perhaps she's the wrong young lady."

"She may be a bit odd—"

"It's not that."

"What then?"

It was the frustration in his voice that finally broke her resolve to remain silent on the matter. Heartbreak and pain and anger all coalescing into a perfect storm, she turned to face him. "You don't deserve to be talked about in such a way by your future bride's family."

Understanding lit his eyes. He let out a weary laugh. "Ah, I see the way of it. Mr. and Mrs. Pickering were open about their feelings on my appearance, were they?"

"Yes," she managed.

He merely shrugged, his expression proclaiming he was not the least surprised.

She gaped at him. "How can you not be enraged by it?"

"I am not enraged," he said with infinite patience, as if dealing with a recalcitrant toddler, "because it is expected."

"Expected!"

"Yes."

She shook her head. "How can you be so untouched by something so heinous?"

"Oh, I'm not completely untouched." His lips twisted. "But I have seen firsthand for four years now what my appearance does to people. I assure you, after all that time one does begin to grow numb."

She gripped the cushion beneath her. "It's not right," she cried.

Again he shrugged. "Perhaps. But it's the way of the world, I'm afraid. And anyway, what would you have me do, turn away every woman who I might take as a wife because someone in her family is troubled by my appearance?"

"Perhaps," she replied mutinously in the face of his faint reprimand.

He let loose a sharp laugh, yanking off his hat and running a hand through his hair. "I won't have any candidates if that's the rubric I use to find a bride."

"But—"

"No." He cut her off, raising a hand. "No buts. It doesn't matter to me in the least what the elder Pickerings say, I assure you. Put it from your mind."

She threw her hands up in the air. How could he be so blasé about this? "And so I'm just supposed to sit quietly by while someone bashes your appearance?"

"Yes."

She gaped at him. "Well, I can't."

Finally anger reared up, flooding his face with heat, making his scars stand out in violent relief. "You must," he bit out. "We had a deal, you and I. I'm to become engaged by the end of the month, a date you yourself decided on and that is fast approaching. I'm to pay you one hundred pounds to see it happen. Do you still require the funds? Or should we part ways on this?"

She felt the blood leave her face. The funds. The blackmail.

But though she knew how dire the situation was, how imperative it was to secure the funds, it suddenly seemed equally important that Daniel not sacrifice his future happiness by marrying a woman he would never love.

Margery had seen firsthand how affectionate Daniel could be. He was caring and considerate. He felt things deeply. And the idea of him entering into a cold, color-less union with a woman who only wanted him for the title and money he could provide her, all the while being disgusted by his appearance, made her want to weep.

But that was not for her to concern herself with, she told herself brutally. Her fingers reached for her wedding band and she twisted it viciously, as if to remind herself of why she was embroiled in this to begin with. Aaron's honor was at stake. But the words rang hollow.

He watched her the whole while. His eyes snagged on her hands, narrowing for a moment, before return-ing to her face. "Is our agreement still valid?" he asked her quietly.

She looked back at him, aware of a faint cracking in her chest. "Yes," she whispered.

Chapter 18

Daniel, still reeling from the devastation of the afternoon's fight with Margery, could not comprehend how Gregory had gotten himself invited to dinner that night at Seacliff.

But there he was, seated across the table. Next to Margery. Daniel pressed his lips tight, forcing his eyes away from the pair of them. They looked very well together, indeed.

As was typical with his cousin, he had been all that was charming the moment he'd entered the house, ingratiating himself with the older women, flirting with the younger. But Gregory was not fond of dogs, especially large ones, and the presence of Mouse kept him far from Miss Denby. And so Margery had received the majority of his attentions. Daniel had been unable to discern her thoughts on his cousin. She was pleasant enough when talking to him. But then, she was pleasant with just about everyone. Thus far she seemed immune—one of the few people of any gender—to Gregory's excess of charm. What did she think of the man? Not that it should matter.

But damn it, it did.

As soup was served, his cousin sent Lady Tesh his most charming smile, something that had been perfected over the years to melt the heart of even the most irascible matron. Which Lady Tesh certainly was.

"My lady, I cannot thank you enough for having me to your table this evening. It is an honor."

"You are most welcome, Mr. Hayle," the dowager viscountess said. She shot Daniel a perturbed glance. "Though why His Grace failed to make mention of your presence on Synne is a mystery to me. Why, if you had not left a message for your aunt that you had been by, I daresay we would not have known at all."

Gregory laughed merrily. "Ah, that is Danny for you. Horribly forgetful. Though," he continued, sending Margery a melting grin, "I can see why it might have slipped his mind, with such enchanting company."

Daniel, in the process of cringing at the use of his boyhood name in front of everyone, squeezed his hands into fists at the blatant flirtation. Margery merely nodded her thanks.

It should not have been a relief that she didn't seem to notice the man beyond polite acknowledgment. She was not for Daniel, after all. He had one duty, and one duty only: to secure a wife so he might continue the family line, and without marrying someone who affected his emotions in such a frighteningly intense way. He would not risk his heart again, especially as it seemed that, should things turn sour, he would be hurt even more desperately than he had been before. For, as Gregory had been inferring since he was a boy, and as had been proven with Erica's betrayal, who could possibly love a clumsy beast such as himself?

And yet he could not help the small exhale of relief as she purposely turned back to her soup.

Which, of course, did not discourage Gregory one bit. He was nothing if not tenacious.

"My dear Mrs. Kitteridge," he said, his eyes heavy with interest though she was not looking his way to see it, "you are a saint for dragging my poor cousin about. It could not have been easy."

"There was no difficulty in it, I assure you," she said. Was it Daniel's imagination, or was there a slight tightness to her tone?

Gregory chuckled. "Come now, madam. I'm certain you've gotten to know him well enough these past weeks."

Margery, in the process of taking a sip of her soup, lowered the spoon back into her bowl and looked fully at him. "I don't know what you mean."

"Oh now, there's no need for prevarication. I assure you, Danny here is all too aware of his shortcomings, and so it will not surprise him one bit. Isn't that right, Cousin?"

Daniel, drawing upon years of practice in subduing any desire for retaliation against his cousin, pressed his back teeth tightly together. Margery, however, was not so reticent.

"I assure you, Mr. Hayle, if there are any shortcomings you might be conscious of, they are all in your head. His Grace has been a delightful companion."

"Goodness, Danny," Gregory drawled, eyeing Margery with new interest, "what a champion you have."

"I am no one's champion," she said, turning away from Gregory, yet frustratingly keeping her eyes well away from Daniel as well. "I merely state the truth."

Daniel's mother, no doubt hoping to smooth things over, as she always had in an attempt to keep peace in her home, spoke up then. "How long are you visiting Synne for, Gregory?"

"That depends entirely on you and my cousin, dear Aunt Helen," he said with a syrupy sweet smile. "I've a mind to join you in London after your visit here is done, and so why not wait for your own departure? My equipage is sadly out of date, after all, and may not make the trip back to town. I've been of a mind to sell the blasted thing off and purchase a new one. And so why not relieve myself of it while I'm here, and purchase something shiny and new once we reach London? Surely you have enough room for me in your carriage."

"No."

The word exploded from Daniel on an exhale quite without him meaning for it to. But the very thought of being trapped for days on end with his cousin was making him faintly ill. "That is," he said, flushing as every eye swung his way, "sell off your carriage if you like, but surely you would be much more comfortable in your own equipage; I would be happy to pay for the rental of a post chaise for you."

But the man, as ever, did not get the hint that he wasn't wanted. "Oh, you've no need to worry about taking up too much space with that lame leg of yours, Danny. I'm slender enough that I won't mind the lack of room a bit."

Daniel, his appetite gone at not only his cousin's

subtle jab but also at the thought of being forced into company with him in the close confines of a carriage with no means of escape, pushed his untouched bowl away. Mayhap he could postpone the trip to London and still escape Gregory's company. If things went as planned, he would soon be taking a wife, after all. And so there was no reason whatsoever to allow the man to affect him in such a way.

But as his gaze strayed to Margery, who was still resolutely staring at her soup, he found that the idea of taking Miss Pickering as his wife did not give him a modicum of comfort. Any path that did not have Margery beside him on it was no path he wanted to tread.

Breaking into Daniel's shocking thoughts—for hadn't he been doing his best to nip any affection he might have for Margery in the proverbial bud?—Gregory spoke up again.

"Besides," he said, "Danny here will need as many allies as he can in London. Not only is the man horribly awkward, but there is a certain lady in residence there who he will not wish to run into."

Daniel sucked in a sharp breath. "I'm sure I'll be fine," he managed.

Gregory tsked. "You've never been to London, Cousin. You could not know just how small the circle is for polite society. Though," he continued, giving Daniel a pitying look, "seeing as she's in a delicate way, you may be able to avoid her." He turned to Margery, who was gaping at him. "When he was younger our Danny here was lucky enough to engage himself to a stunning creature, Lady Erica. She had been a neighbor of ours at Brackley Manor, and we'd known her since we were children. Danny had pined over her for years, though she didn't pay him the least mind. Their engagement was a shock to me, let me tell you, for you never knew two people so different. But she sadly broke things off with him after he returned." He winced and motioned to his cheek. "Though now she's quite happily married to Viscount Thrushton."

If fire had shot out of Margery's eyes to smite Gregory on the spot, Daniel would not have been surprised. "Mr. Hayle, do you enjoy torturing your cousin?"

The room went still. Gregory, for his part, barked out a laugh. "Why, Mrs. Kitteridge, I don't know what you mean."

"If you had any regard for the duke you would not talk to him or of him in such a way. Though," she continued, her eyes narrowing as she took him in, "I daresay you are fully aware of what you're up to."

"Mrs. Kitteridge," Gregory said, his persona still in place though a surprising amount of uncertainty was present in his eyes—and no wonder, for no one had ever dared stand up to him before, "you've got me all wrong."

"No," she murmured, "I don't think I do. And I find your attempts to undermine your cousin despicable."

"Margery," Lady Tesh said, all agog with shock. "What's come over you?"

"I'm sorry, Gran," her granddaughter said, fairly shaking with rage, "but I cannot sit here and listen to a charlatan denounce someone I—" She cut herself off, and Daniel found himself holding his breath, both eager and dreading what might come next.

In the end she threw her napkin on the table and stood abruptly. The chair gave a grating scrape on the floor.

"Please forgive me," she said to no one in particular—and most certainly not to Daniel, who she hadn't looked at once since their return from the picnic with the Pickerings earlier that day. "I believe I have a headache. I'll take my dinner in my room." With that she stormed out into the hall.

A thick silence followed. Suddenly Gregory's voice sounded. "Goodness, wasn't that an overreaction to a bit of ribbing?"

Unable to take even a second more of his cousin's company, Daniel pushed to his feet and grabbed his cane. "If you'll all excuse me?" Before anyone could reply he limped out the door.

Margery was pacing the floor in her bedroom when he pushed inside. Myriad emotions had swirled through him on the long trek upstairs, but one stood out from the rest: frustration. Both at himself and at her.

He closed the door with more force than warranted. She continued to pace, her gaze focused on the rug beneath her, her skirts snapping as her feet ate up the space. He thought for a moment she had not heard him enter, so completely did she ignore him. But as the seconds ticked on and the clock on the mantel kept time with her agitated footsteps, the bright flush of anger on her cheeks spread down over her neck, proof that she was not as unaffected by his presence as she appeared.

Finally, when it became glaringly apparent that she would wear a track in the floor rather than acknowledge him, he spoke. "You need to stop defending me, Margery."

She stopped abruptly and glared at him. "*I* need to stop defending you? You need to start defending *yourself* from that—that—" She let out a little growl and stomped her foot, looking for all the world like an enraged kitten. He might have laughed if the subject didn't pain him so damn much.

Suddenly achingly tired, he let out a sigh. "What will it accomplish if I fight back?" he demanded wearily.

She gaped at him. "So you would have him run roughshod over you? You would allow him to demean you in such a way?"

"You don't understand," he muttered.

"So enlighten me."

He blew out a harsh breath. "I know the man is a pompous arse who doesn't know when to leave something alone. But he's had a hard history. I grew up with him, Margery. He's had much to overcome."

"That does not give him any right to treat you as he does. And I'm willing to bet he's part of the reason why you are determined to settle for a cold, loveless marriage."

He gritted his teeth together with such force he thought they might shatter. "I told you why I don't want affection in my marriage."

"Because of Erica?"

He sucked in a sharp breath at that name falling from her lips. "Don't bring her up."

She scoffed. "And why not? Your cousin was certainly willing to, in his efforts to get under your skin." Suddenly her voice dropped, the tone of it so raw it fractured something in him. "And it worked, didn't it? You're more closed off than you ever were. But you cannot sit huddled behind the barricade you've built up around your heart forever, Daniel."

"It's a way to survive."

"But no way to live, forever in the past."

Anger boiled up in him, so swift that he said the first thing that came to mind. "As you live, forever mourning Aaron?"

The color left her face. And Daniel had never felt so low in his life.

"Ah, God," he said, running a hand over his face, aching to go to her and pull her in his arms but knowing he never could, not if he wished to keep the distance between them that he so desperately needed to keep his heart intact. Or, as intact as it could be, considering she'd already undermined his careful defenses. "I'm sorry, Margery," he rasped. "That was inexcusable of me. And I know it's not the same for you. You know your husband loved you. He didn't leave you willingly."

"Didn't he?"

The words appeared to shock Margery as much as they shocked him. She pressed a hand to her mouth, her eyes wide in her pale face. But she recovered quickly enough. Though still alarmingly pale, she straightened and looked him full in the face. "But this is not about me. This is about you and your need to marry."

He frowned, his frustration back. "I have decided who to marry. And if you had not cut our afternoon short owing to some meaningless words that such a man would spew about my appearance, I would be a good deal further along in that endeavor."

She bristled. "They were not meaningless words."

"To me they are," he lied.

She threw her hands up in the air. "And so what then? You would willingly marry into a family that does not respect you? Though seeing how your own cousin treats you, I can see how you're used to such things."

"Margery, you go too far," he growled.

"I don't go far enough," she declared. Suddenly her expression shifted; she appeared infinitely sad as she approached him, her mournful eyes focused on his face.

In that moment, with her beautiful, soulful eyes on him, Daniel felt more exposed than he ever had in his life. He tensed, fighting the urge to run and never look back.

"I can see you think you deserve people treating you in such a way," she said, her eyes scouring his face with such intensity he was hard-pressed not to cover his scars with his hand. "But you deserve so much more than to marry someone who merely tolerates you. You deserve—"

"Love?" he burst out, desperate to cut her off, instilling as much coldness into his voice as he could dredge up. "I assure you, being that vulnerable has only brought me pain. And besides, hasn't it occurred to you that, if I give up on my plans to find a woman to marry in a little over a sennight, you will not get your money?"

As he'd expected, the mention of her required fee completely distracted her from the subject of his marrying for love. But as much as he'd wanted to redirect the conversation, he didn't expect such a reaction from her. She appeared for a horrifying moment as if she might collapse on the spot.

He reached out for her arm when she swayed. "Margery. Are you well? Margery!"

She started, looking up at him with eyes that had gone glassy with—what? Fear?

It was quickly doused. Or, if not doused, covered up

so he could no longer see it. "I'm fine," she said through stiff lips.

"Fine," he muttered. Taking her arm, he guided her to the closest chair, the one at her desk. She sat heavily.

Then, though it physically pained him to do it, he sank to the floor before her, the better to look at her face. Her eyes were dull, her skin pale, the angry flush having fled her cheeks. "Margery, what is it?"

"Nothing at all," she managed. But she would not look him in the eye.

He blew out a frustrated breath. Taking up one of her hands in both of his, he was shocked at how cold it was. "What do you need the money for?"

"I hardly think that is any of your business," she replied. But her words lacked heat. Instead there was a kind of weary defeat in them.

"No, you're right in that," he said gently. "It is no business of mine. But I would help if I could." When she merely pressed her lips tighter together, he continued. "Margery, are you in some kind of trouble?"

That flash of fear again, there and gone so quickly he would have missed it had he not been watching her so intently.

"Margery," he tried again, squeezing her fingers, "I'll help you if I can. What is it?"

So many things went to battle on her beautiful face, thoughts and emotions all warring with one another, one indiscernible from the next. Finally she dragged in a shaky breath and looked at him. And the hopelessness in her gaze nearly undid him. "Tell me," she said, her voice so low he almost couldn't hear her, "what would you do if the memory of someone you loved was threatened?"

He had expected all manner of things, from in-laws extorting her to mismanagement of funds to even gambling debt. But that question, spoken with such heartbreak, told of something so much deeper and more troubling.

"Whose memory is being threatened?" he asked.

She pressed her lips tight, as if she regretted saying as much. But when she pulled her hand from his grasp and started a frantic twisting of her wedding band, he knew.

"Aaron."

She blanched. It was all the proof he needed that he was right.

But why would she need one hundred pounds, an incredible sum of money, to protect her husband's memory? And why not ask her family for the funds? Why hire herself out in secret, unless—

"You don't want your family to know what your husband did."

The fury in her eyes was swift and all-encompassing. "Aaron didn't do anything wrong. He was a good man. A brave man. He would have never—"

Again she cut herself off. But he had heard enough. One word stood out from them all: *brave*. A horrible premonition was rising up in him.

Before he could fully grasp it, however, she reached for something on the desk, held it in her lap. He glanced down to see what her fingers cradled so tenderly—

And froze. Staring back at him was that boy that had haunted his nightmares, both waking and sleeping, for the past four years.

A whistle started up in his ears, like round shots

falling from the sky. He felt, for a horrible moment, as if he were floating up out of his body. He grabbed the desk, gripping tight to keep himself from falling over. Had he been thrown back into his nightmares? Was this some horrible hallucination that he would soon wake from?

But the seconds passed, and he did not wake. His heartbeat pounded in his temples, and he felt he might be sick.

"Margery," he rasped through a throat tight with panic. "Who is that?"

"This is Aaron."

He shook his head almost frantically. "No. No, that can't be your husband."

"It is." She frowned. "Daniel, what's wrong?" And then realization flared. "You recognize him." Her voice was tight with disbelief.

He nodded, beyond words as he looked back to that familiar face. But whereas the boy peering up at him from this frame was young and vibrant, that same face had been contorted in pain and fear, covered in mud and blood and sweat, when Daniel had known him. And pale beneath it all as death took over him.

When he looked back up at Margery, hope and fear all swirled in the beautiful brown depths of her eyes. And he wanted to howl at the unfairness, the cruelty, of life.

"That's the boy from my dreams," he said, the words like knives in his throat. "The boy I shot. The boy I killed."

Chapter 19

A horrible, violent ringing echoed in Margery's head. "No." Daniel could not have killed Aaron. It must be a mistake. A horrible, devastating, disgusting mistake.

But his eyes, those amazing slate-blue eyes that she had gazed into on so many occasions over the past weeks, first as secret associates, then as friends, then as lovers, were full of anguish. "I'm so sorry."

"I don't understand." The words barely emerged from the parched desert her mouth had become. She swallowed hard, but there was no relief. His whispered words from two nights ago came to her then, as clear as if he had spoken them again.

I took aim, pulled the trigger...suddenly this boy was there, in front of me...He was running from the battle...when the smoke cleared he was gripping his chest...blood was bubbling from his lips...

"No," she said again, even as pain sliced through her. "You have to be mistaken. You cannot have killed Aaron."

But he only looked at her with a kind of fatalistic

dread. In desperation her mind spun, searching for something, anything, that could disprove him. If he was telling the truth, it would not only mean that Daniel had killed her Aaron, but also that the blackmailer had been right all along, that Aaron had deserted his fellow soldiers, had betrayed his country.

Finally she latched onto something. "You said he called out for his sweetheart. Surely he didn't say my name. He didn't say Margery."

"No." The word was said slowly, an almost hopeful spark igniting. "No, he didn't say Margery."

Relief washed through her, leaving her nearly limp. Until he spoke again.

"He called out for Pearl."

She closed her eyes as grief scorched her from the inside. "I'm Pearl," she rasped.

A beat of silence. And then, "What do you mean?"

"It's the name he gave me when we were children. *Margery* means 'pearl.' He always said I was his Pearl, as rare and as beautiful—"

Her throat closed off. Ah, God. How was this possible? What cruel joke was Fate playing on her, that she would cross paths with Daniel, that she would want him.

That she would love him.

Because she knew in that devastating moment, with her world once more crashing down on her head, that she did love Daniel. So very much.

She wanted to laugh. She wanted to weep. Instead she closed her eyes tighter, trying to block out the image he had put in her head two nights ago, of that boy he had shot, then cradled as he died. Only now Aaron's face was there, covered in blood and mud. How much pain did he feel? How much fear that he was about to die? He had called out for her, and she hadn't been there...

She bit her lip so hard she tasted blood.

A tentative hand on her arm. "Margery—"

"I need you to leave." She didn't know where she got the strength to say the words. Not when all she wanted was to curl up in his arms and cry. Something she could not ever do. Most especially not with this man, who had ended Aaron's life, no matter how accidentally it might have been. And who had proved that every horrible thing the blackmailer had claimed was true.

She waited, hardly breathing. Finally he exhaled, a mournful, hopeless sound she felt down to her soul. He rose, made his slow way from the room, stopping when he reached the door.

"I'm so sorry, Margery," he whispered. And then he was gone.

* * *

There was one thing abundantly clear to Daniel even as he lay awake that whole horrible night: for Margery's sake, he had to leave Synne.

And so, before the sun could so much as peek over the horizon, he was up and packing. Was he a coward for leaving? Perhaps. But he didn't give a damn. The only thing he could think of in that moment was the look on Margery's face when he'd revealed to her the truth about his part in Aaron's death, and that he could never, ever, cause her that pain again. He would not forget it for as long as he lived, the stunned disbelief quickly transforming into a dawning horror and bone-deep grief. He had done that, had put those devastating emotions in her heart. And he would never forgive himself.

By the time Wilkins arrived Daniel was ready to depart Synne for good.

The valet stopped in the doorway, taking in Daniel's hastily patched outfit and the leather satchel on the mussed bed, confusion and uncertainty evident on his narrow face. "Your Grace, you're leaving?"

He gave the man a quick glance before limping his way to retrieve his hairbrush from the washstand. "I'm sorry to spring this on you, Wilkins. But something has come up overnight that has made it imperative that I depart for London with all haste. I'll be leaving immediately; I've already called for a carriage. If you would be so good as to stay behind to collect the rest of our things? You can meet me in the capital later. My mother will stay behind with Lady Tesh. I'll visit with her before I leave, to apprise her of the change in plans."

All the while as he babbled he moved about the room, grabbing things at random, tossing them into the open satchel. Suddenly Wilkins was there in front of him.

"What did he do?"

The man's face was florid with his daring. But he stood planted in place, his small frame fairly quivering with anger.

Daniel, his quest to escape Seacliff as soon as humanly possible forgotten in the face of the man's fury, gaped at him. "Who?"

"Mr. Hayle."

The name escaped on a snarl that had Daniel blinking in shock. "He's done nothing."

The valet scoffed. "Please, Your Grace. There can be

no coincidence that the man showed up last night for dinner and now you're fleeing Synne."

But Daniel's shock was quickly transforming into anger of his own. Though whether it was directed to Wilkins or to himself was debatable. "You overstep yourself."

"I have not overstepped enough," the man spat, snatching the pair of gloves from Daniel's hand and storming to the satchel to drop them in. "Perhaps if I had, you would not now be fleeing to London before dawn like a dog with its tail between its legs."

Before Daniel could so much as react to that Wilkins stopped and let out a defeated sigh, his thin shoulders drooping. "I'm sorry, Your Grace. That was inexcusable of me. But I've stood by for so many years, while Mr. Hayle made your brother's life hell. I cannot see the same thing happen to you."

Daniel's breath left him. "Nathaniel? What do you mean?" When Wilkins merely bit his lip, Daniel swept an arm out, indicating the chairs before the hearth. "Sit and tell me. Please."

Releasing a shaky breath, the man did as he was bid. He perched on the edge of his seat, as if about to take flight, a look of acute discomfort on his face that had nothing at all to do with the conversation they were about to have. Daniel only recognized it because it mirrored the discomfort in himself. This was a foreign thing, facing one another like this with such familiarity. He had fought against the man's efforts to befriend him for so long, had tried so hard to keep the line in the sand between them, that he felt himself instinctively rebelling now. But a stiff breeze had come in, obliterating that line. And he was too weary, too heartsick, to redraw it.

It took some minutes for Wilkins to begin, and when he finally did his voice was reed thin.

"You knew, of course, of your brother's inability to hold his liquor."

Daniel nodded, pressing his lips tight as pain flashed through him. It hadn't been a well-known fact; Nathaniel had bluffed enough over the years that most people, even his closest friends, didn't realize just how sick he became when drinking.

He shook off the flare of grief that was always there when he thought about his brother. Damnation, but he missed him, now more than ever. "But what does my cousin have to do with this?" he demanded.

Wilkins gave him a mournful look that chilled him to the bone. "You know your brother loved you and wanted to protect you. Just as you wanted to protect him. He knew you tried to hide Mr. Hayle's harsher abuses. But what you may not know was that he was hiding things from you as well."

Wilkins dragged in a shaky breath and ran trembling hands through his straw-colored hair. "Mr. Hayle taunted your brother in private for years about his inability to drink. And His Grace ignored it as best he could. But when they were in London together, Mr. Hayle's taunting became public, and more than your brother could bear. He felt he needed to defend his honor, to prove himself. I begged him to ignore Mr. Hayle and the others. But your cousin, being the devil he is, had worked his evil. His Grace was so ill when he returned to the London townhouse that last night, and hardly able to stand, much less make it to his room—"

The man's voice cut off. Daniel gaped at him. "Are

you telling me Nathaniel had been drinking when he fell down those stairs?" At Wilkins's nod Daniel slumped down in his seat. "I had no clue," he said through stiff lips. "Why didn't he tell me what Gregory was doing to him?"

Wilkins gave him a sad smile. "He loved you, and didn't wish for you to worry." Suddenly his expression shifted, anger taking over his thin features once more. "Mr. Hayle is as bad as they come. And while he didn't directly cause your brother's death and did not force the bottle to your brother's lips, he was certainly indirectly responsible for bringing it about."

Tears burned Daniel's eyes. Damnation, he hadn't known.

But Wilkins was looking at him with uncertainty. And no wonder, for Daniel had never allowed the man to cross into familiarity before.

Suddenly he frowned. "But why didn't you say something at the time? We never knew Nathaniel was intoxicated. We believed it was just a horrible accident."

Pain flashed in the valet's eyes. "I couldn't bear to see anyone thinking badly of him. He was a good man, your brother. I couldn't see his memory tarnished."

Overcome at this man's unswerving loyalty, Daniel leaned forward and held out his hand. Wilkins looked at it uncomprehendingly for a moment before, with tears in his eyes, he clasped it with his own.

"Thank you," Daniel managed. "Thank you for protecting my brother, and for telling me the truth."

Wilkins nodded, swallowing hard. Then, dragging in a deep breath, he stood.

"But we should prepare to leave. You'll no doubt wish

to tell your mother in person of the change in plans. I'll have the rest of your things packed in a trice and we can leave for London straightaway."

Daniel blinked. "You're going with me?"

"Of course," Wilkins said. "As if I would allow you to travel to London alone." He gave Daniel a bracing smile and, spinning about, started his work.

Daniel, with nothing left to do—and surprisingly relieved to have an ally—made his way to the large oak desk in the corner. Once there he sat heavily, looking at the neat stacks of papers, the lead crystal inkwell, the spotless blotter. He knew what he had to do. But what to say? And how to say it. Finally, knowing he was only delaying the inevitable, he took up a creamy piece of foolscap and, dipping a pen in the ink, began to write.

It wasn't a long note. The words he longed to say to Margery could never be said, could never be written. And so the letter was straight to the point. And much colder than he would have liked. Then, tucking the bank draft inside and folding it up, he secured it in his pocket and made his way from the room. Wilkins was right in that he had to speak with his mother. Though he only hoped she would not question what he was about to suggest.

She was sitting up in bed when he arrived at her room. He expected surprise at his early appearance. Instead she gave him a sad smile, as if she had expected him.

"Leaving, are you?"

He stood by the door, feeling as awkward as if he were a ten-year-old boy being called to the carpet. "Yes."

"Was it Gregory?" she asked sadly.

"No."

"Was it Mrs. Kitteridge?"

He sucked in a sharp breath. There was entirely too much knowing in her eyes.

She nodded, as if his silence gave all the answers she needed. "Come here, Daniel," she said softly, patting the bed beside her.

He did as he was bid, making his slow way to her side, sinking gingerly to the feather mattress.

"Now," she said softly, "why don't you tell me everything?"

He let out a humorless laugh at the knowing look in her mild eyes. "I expect, madam, that you've understood my heart better than I myself have these past weeks."

"Are you admitting it then?"

"What, that I love Margery?" He sighed heavily, running a hand over his face, his fingers tracing the puckered scars. "Yes, I love her. Which is why I have to leave."

She bit her lip. "And is there nothing I can say to change your mind?"

"No." The word was quick, and certain. She thought this was a mere matter of him refusing his heart. When in reality it was so much more devastating, so much messier. And so unfixable as to be laughable.

"I want you to stay here on Synne, with Lady Tesh," he continued, looking down at the coverlet so he didn't have to look her in the eyes. "You've healed so much in spirit since we've arrived. I don't want you to lose whatever ground you've gained by going to the London house. I don't want you to revisit that grief. I want—no, I *need*—you to get well."

She was quiet so long he thought she might not answer. Finally she spoke. "If that's what you wish."

"Yes," he lied. Of course it wasn't what he wished. But it was what needed to be done.

"Before I leave, however," he continued, reaching into his coat pocket and retrieving the letter, "could you promise to give this to Margery for me?"

"Of course, darling," she whispered, taking the letter and holding it gently.

That done, he nodded grimly and rose to standing. Before he could turn away, however, she reached out and grabbed his hand, squeezing it.

"Please take care of yourself, Daniel."

"I will," he said with a smile that felt so stiff he thought his cheeks would fracture. Then, bending to kiss her, he was off, down the hall to his room. Trying not to notice how his steps faltered as he passed by Margery's door.

All too soon he and Wilkins were off. The carriage rattled down Seacliff's drive, and Daniel kept his gaze out to the horizon, refusing to look back at the manor house. He didn't know what would be worse: seeing her there, watching him leave, or not seeing her at all.

He sat in silence for a time as the carriage rattled down the gradual incline from the cliff-top house, feeling his loss like a leaden cloak about his shoulders. Memories swirled: Margery that first night when she'd asked him to hire her; her smile when they'd attended the Assembly Rooms concert; that first kiss at the tide pool; the determination in her eyes when she'd suggested they conduct an affair. And then, so vibrant it stole the breath from his lungs, making love to her, feeling her come alive in his arms, even as she'd broken down the barriers that he'd so carefully built up about his heart.

But soon the memories were supplanted by other

harsher memories: their fight after she'd defended him from Mr. Pickering; her seated beside Gregory; the anguish in her eyes when he'd revealed his part in Aaron's death. He ran a hand over his face, trying to erase the memories. But he knew, deep in his heart, he'd never be free of them.

Impotence reared up in him, that he could never repair the pain of the past, could never fix what had been broken.

Suddenly he straightened, determination racing through his veins, an electrical current. He might not be able to turn back time. But he'd be damned if he would go forward without rectifying some of the past wrongs.

He reached up and knocked on the roof. Wilkins gave him a curious look but said nothing as the coachman slowed the carriage and opened the trap door.

"Your Grace?"

"Please make a stop at the Master-at-Arms Inn before we leave."

"Yes, Your Grace."

As Daniel settled back against the squabs, he caught Wilkins's gaze again. A quiet pride shone from his eyes, satisfaction fairly oozing from him. Though humor was the last thing he was feeling just then, Daniel's lips quirked. "You approve?"

"I do," the man said with a small smile.

In no time they had pulled up to the inn. "I'll be back momentarily," he said to the coachman before making his way inside, Wilkins behind him. Gregory's room was easy enough to find out from the harried innkeeper. It seemed his cousin had not made any friends in his short time on Synne. Soon Daniel was making his way up the narrow stairs, the key he had paid to obtain clasped tightly in his fist. A swift turn in the lock, and he sent the door crashing against the wall.

Gregory, sprawled amid the rumpled sheets, a naked woman curled against his side, startled awake. Arms and legs flailing, he lurched to sitting, pointedly ignoring the shrieking woman as she tried to drag the sheets over her body. "What the hell…? Danny?"

Daniel glared down at him. "I am Carlisle to you. Or Duke. Or Your Grace. But never refer to me by that name again."

His cousin scowled, rubbing sleep from his eyes. "Damnation, what the devil is wrong with you, man?"

"I'm waking up, finally, to the person you are. And that you won't change." Limping to the bed, he reached down to the floor and took up a blanket that had been thrown there. "Miss?" he said, offering his hand to the woman, who was looking at him in shock. When the woman continued to stare, he gently placed the blanket about her shoulders and, taking her arm, helped her to stand.

"Wilkins," he said over his shoulder, "please retrieve the lady's clothes, and provide her with coin to get home safely."

"Yes, Your Grace."

"I say," Gregory scowled, lurching after the girl. "You can't come in here and take my whore from me. I paid for her time, and it's not yet up."

Daniel took his cane and pressed it against Gregory's chest, sending him falling back among the sheets. "You will not refer to the lady as such in my presence, is that understood? Your time is done; she is free to go."

Gregory merely stared in outrage, his handsome face flushed bright pink. Behind Daniel he heard Wilkins talking in a low voice to the woman as he helped her dress, the clink of coins as he passed them over to her, her hasty thanks. And then the door closed, leaving him alone with his cousin.

"I came here to tell you I'm leaving for London. Also, I do not want to ever see your face darken my door again, is that clear?"

Gregory's mouth dropped open. "You're cutting me off?"

"You're very perceptive."

"But...I'm like a brother to you!"

A snarl curled Daniel's upper lip. He felt it tighten his scars, but for once he relished what it might do to his features, at the danger it might lend him. "You were never like a brother to me. You took my only brother from me. You've been a devil in our midst this whole while. And, God help me, I didn't see it until it was too late."

For the first time in the exchange, the hint of uncertainty was finally seeping into his cousin's eyes. He gaped at Daniel like a fish. "What the ever-loving—I don't know who the hell you think you are—"

"I'm the duke. You'd best remember that." Daniel looked Gregory in the face. His hands shook, but for the first time in his dealings with this man, he felt certain. He stepped closer, pressing his cane to his cousin's neck. Gregory's eyes flared wide with fear. But, stubborn man that he was, he stuck his chin out and glared at Daniel.

"What are you going to do, kill me?"

Daniel let loose a harsh laugh. "I won't deny that you would deserve it. Especially after what you drove

Nathaniel to." A cold satisfaction filled him as the blood drained from his cousin's face. "But no, I won't kill you. Death is too kind for the likes of you. I'm cutting you off without a penny, Gregory. You'll be destitute. And if you ever seek out myself or my mother or any other member of our family again, you will rue the day."

With that promise hanging in the air, he turned away. Behind him he heard Gregory scrabble to his feet, heard the faint wheezing as he caught his breath. Just as Daniel reached the door his cousin spoke.

"Do you forget what your father made you promise?" he called out in desperation, his voice a croak. "That you would always look after me? Would you break your promise to your father?"

Daniel turned back to him. Rage was flaring up, hot and swift, unlike anything he had felt before. "You took advantage of my father's generosity," he spat. "You threw our love back in our faces. You were given everything."

"And what was I given?" Gregory snarled. He stood in the middle of the room, naked, pure hatred sparking from his eyes. "My father was dead, my mother off with the bastard who killed him. And then to be taken in like some pathetic orphan, to be pitied. I hated you all for it."

"I'm sorry you felt that way," Daniel said softly. "But I can rest easy knowing we did our best by you. We tried, every one of us, to show you that you were wanted. I pity you, that you've had so much anger and hatred in your heart that you have never been able to see how dearly we loved you. But I can no longer ignore the mischief and pain and destruction you've caused. Goodbye, Gregory."

His cousin's face, stricken pale and staring with mute shock, was the last thing he saw as he turned and left.

Chapter 20

*L*enora was in her studio when Margery arrived. A large canvas was propped on an easel, angled to take advantage of the early-afternoon sun. Lenora, apron in place and a determined gleam in her eyes, peered closely at the painting as she added some small detail.

Margery waited patiently in the doorway for her friend to notice her, not wanting to disturb her concentration. And, truth be told, to gather her thoughts—and her courage.

The past hours had been something of a haze. She'd not slept after Daniel had left her the evening before, instead sitting at her desk until the small morning hours, staring dry-eyed at Aaron's portrait. And so she'd heard the commotion in the hall around dawn, had heard the low murmur of voices, Daniel's telltale uneven gait. She'd known in her heart what was happening, that he was leaving. But though her heart cried out for her to stop him, the bone-deep exhaustion of grief from the revelation of the night before had kept her from doing so. There was no way a relationship would have ever worked out between them, seeing where they each stood on the subjects of marriage and love. That fact was doubly true now, knowing the part he'd had in Aaron's death. And though she recalled with painful clarity how that one act had weighed on him all these years, though she knew deep inside that he was not truly to blame and it had all been a horrible accident, she could not now look at him in the same way. She would forever see him as the man who had ended Aaron's life. And the man who had forever doused the hope in her that the blackmailer had been wrong, and her husband had not turned his back on his fellow soldiers.

Just then Lenora started, wide green eyes blinking owlishly at her. "Oh! Dearest, I didn't see you there. What a lovely surprise."

Margery moved forward to kiss her friend on the cheek. "I don't mean to intrude."

"You could never," Lenora declared with a wide smile that quickly fell away as she scanned Margery's face. "What's happened?"

Instinct had her ready to declare that nothing was amiss. It was what she would have normally done, after all.

But she was through with prevaricating, through with hiding. She had come here with a purpose. And she would see it done.

She sighed. "Do you by chance have time for me? I'm afraid it won't be pleasant."

"I always have time for you, pleasant or otherwise," Lenora declared without hesitation. She turned about, presenting her back to Margery. "Help me remove this apron, will you? And then we can have a nice chat."

Margery had expected such a reaction. She had known Lenora for most of her life, after all, and they were closer than sisters. But that certainty did not stop the tears from burning her eyes as she undid the tapes and helped her friend tidy up her paint things. Soon they were settled cozily on the overstuffed plush sofa in the corner.

"Now," Lenora stated bracingly, "you may talk to your heart's content."

Margery's lips twisted as she looked down to her lap. "It's not pretty."

"The important things rarely are," her friend murmured kindly.

Margery nodded. Then, taking a deep breath, she opened her mouth to begin.

But the words would not come. Where to start? There was so much she had been keeping secret, so much that needed to be said.

Lenora seemed to understand. She placed a comforting hand over Margery's. "Just start at the beginning."

"Of course." Another trembling breath. And then, setting her shoulders, she did just that.

"Nearly a month ago, I received a blackmail letter."

There was a beat of silence. "Well," Lenora said, her voice faint, "I certainly didn't expect that."

"I assure you," Margery said with a humorless smile, "I didn't either."

Still, Lenora seemed at a loss. She rubbed a hand over her forehead, as if to jar the information into an order that made sense. "But I don't understand. Who in the world would be blackmailing you? And *why?*"

And here it was. The moment of truth, revealing that thing she had fought so hard to keep secret. All these weeks of working at finding a wife for Daniel in order to pay the blackmailer, all the while slowly but surely falling in love with him.

But if she looked at her friend and witnessed the horror and pity in her gaze she would break apart. And so she closed her eyes tight and forged on.

"The note claimed Aaron was a deserter, and that he died while betraying his battalion at Waterloo." She swallowed hard. "This person claims to have witnessed it himself."

"No. I don't believe it; they're lying." There was no delay in the words, only utter conviction. Margery recognized that conviction; it had lived in her for weeks with what she thought was the sturdy foundation of her love for him. As the days passed, however, it had slowly grown weaker, eroded by a gradual doubt that had been all the more devastating for how silently it had undermined everything she'd believed. Until it had broken apart entirely last night in a moment of utter devastation.

"I thought so, too. At first." Finally she looked at Lenora. Confusion and outrage twisted her friend's beloved features, and Margery's heart swelled with emotion at this proof of her devotion. For a split second she considered not telling the rest. Maybe, just maybe, with Lenora's fierce certainty, she might forget last night ever happened and could return to those days of being blind to the truth.

But no, that door could never be closed again.

"I have since learned unequivocally that the letter was stating fact." Like a floodgate breaking apart it all poured out of her then: her fear, how she'd hired herself out to Daniel to pay the funds to the blackmailer, how they'd quickly realized an attraction for one another. She told about the affair, the growing affection, the heartache of ending things. And then, heart in her throat, she told of Daniel's recognition of Aaron's portrait and his confession.

Through it all, Lenora sat silent. Her face, however, betrayed every emotion coursing through her, from horror to grief to fury to disbelief. Finally Margery, exhausted, fell silent. It was one thing to have it all bottled up in her head. Putting it out into the world made it all too real.

But she also realized, while it had brought the facts into unequivocal focus, sharing it had also eased some of the burden of it from her shoulders. And she knew in that moment she had been a fool to fear her loved ones might view Aaron differently, might love him less. Because the truth of the matter was, she didn't feel different about him. She still loved him as much as she ever had. And that would never change.

Which also led to the realization that, though she had fallen in love with Daniel, there was room in her heart for both men.

It stunned her, that realization. She had thought that by falling in love again, she would be betraying Aaron's memory. But the present and the future—whatever it might hold—did not change the past, and did not detract from the importance of her time with Aaron, or how deeply she loved him.

Lenora's voice broke through the shock of that revelation. "My goodness," she said, her voice faint. She slumped against the back of the couch. "And so you love His Grace."

Margery, stunned, could only manage a weary laugh. "That's what you took away from all that?"

"It does seem the most pertinent bit of information," her friend murmured.

"And what of Aaron's defection? What of the black-mailer?"

To Margery's shock, her friend waved her hand in dismissal. "Not important."

Margery gaped at her. "Not important?" she demanded.

Lenora's head, which had been resting against the back of the couch, rolled to the side so she could spear her friend with an arch look. "Does it change your feelings for Aaron?"

An apt question, as she'd just been asking it of herself. But of course her friend would get to the heart of the matter, and so much quicker than Margery had. She deflated into the cushions. "No."

Lenora grabbed her hand and squeezed it. "And there you are," she said with a gentle smile. "I knew Aaron, and the only thing important to him was that he stayed true to himself. You know as well as I that he didn't care for what others thought of him. He stood up to your father, gladly brought the censure of his village down on him for daring to marry up, and turned down Gran's generous—and safer—offer to buy him a commission to do what he truly wanted. No matter what one terrifying moment might have pushed him to do, it does not change who he was. Or the fact that he loved you."

Margery fought back tears. "And the blackmailer?"

Lenora pursed her lips. "That person is a fool to think Peter and Quincy and your grandmother won't fight this matter to the teeth. And besides," she continued with a wry smile, "I think this family has experienced its fair share of scandals, including a blackmail attempt or two. Should you wish to pay, we have the funds to help you. Should you wish to fight it, we shall lead the charge. And should you choose to weather the scandal, we'll be at your side for that as well."

The tears Margery had been holding at bay spilled over. Right away Lenora was there, wrapping her arms about her, smoothing a hand over her back.

Margery sank into her embrace, the fears of the past weeks finally easing. "I've been so afraid," she whispered into Lenora's shoulder.

"You silly thing," her friend murmured, her voice thick. "You should have come to us immediately."

"I didn't want you to hate Aaron."

"We could never," she declared with a certainty that prompted more tears, though these were borne of relief. "We will always love him the same as we always have, not only for the good man he was, but also for how deeply he loved you and wanted you to be happy."

But suddenly Lenora pulled back and looked her friend in the eye. "That, of course, does not answer the most important question: What will you do about His Grace?"

Margery extracted a handkerchief from the pocket in her gown and wiped her eyes. "There is nothing to do about Daniel."

"Isn't there?"

"No," Margery said, slow and precise lest her friend read something into it that wasn't there.

Lenora pressed her lips tight, a mulish expression that said they weren't quite done with the subject. But, blessedly, she did not push. Instead she asked quietly, "When is the blackmail money due?"

Margery exhaled, reality crashing down on her once more. "In a little over a sennight."

"What will you do? For I'm sure you comprehend that, if you pay this person what they demand, they will come back for more."

"I know." She sighed. "I've been doing my best to focus on one step, one day at a time. But I've always known deep inside that this would only be the beginning." She gave Lenora a sad smile. "And so you see, even if I was of a mind to be with Daniel—if he would even have me— this right here would be reason enough to stay as far away from him as possible. I would not want him to be polluted by this scandal should it one day come out."

"I have a feeling," Lenora murmured with an affectionate look, "that he would not mind any more than us, especially if he loves you as much as I believe he must." When Margery opened her mouth to denounce such an idea—never mind the surge of joy it brought her— Lenora held up a hand in surrender. "But I promise not to say another word about it," she declared. "First and foremost, we shall see about securing you the necessary funds should you need them. There will be time in the next few days to decide what path you wish to take."

As Lenora made to rise, however, Margery stopped her. "But I already have the funds."

Lenora blinked, sinking back into the worn cushions of the couch. "I don't understand. Your deal with His Grace was not completed. How did you get the money?"

In answer, Margery pulled a letter from her pocket and handed it over.

The confusion on Lenora's face was quickly replaced with understanding as she opened the already-worn missive and read it over. Margery didn't need to look over her friend's shoulder; she had read it so many times that morning that she had it memorized.

My dearest Margery,

I cannot begin to make amends for the great wrong I've done. If I could go back in time and give my life up for Aaron's I would. I will never forgive myself for his death, or for the hardships and pain I've caused you.

By now you know I've left for London. No matter my aversion to that place, no matter we were nearing the end to our agreement, I cannot stay on Synne knowing I might cause you pain. Though I know you might not wish for anything from me, please accept our agreed-upon sum, which I've enclosed. And please know that if you require anything at all, no matter what that might be, I'm at your disposal. I only want you happy.

Yrs,
Daniel

"Oh, Margery," Lenora whispered. She hastily swiped at her cheeks. "He cares for you a great deal."

"Lenora," Margery warned, even as she fought tears herself.

"Well, what did you expect?" Lenora demanded. "I cannot keep my promise to not mention the possibility of something between you when I'm faced with his obvious devotion to you."

"Devotion," Margery scoffed softly, taking the letter back. Despite her dismissive word, however, she scanned the missive with hungry eyes. Lenora had read that in those carefully penned words? She saw that within the bold, inked script?

"And so you have the funds you require?" Lenora asked cautiously.

"Yes." She frowned. "No."

Lenora blinked. "I don't understand."

Truthfully Margery didn't either. All she knew was she couldn't take Daniel's money, couldn't use it to pay off that evil person who would ruin Aaron's good name.

And though she knew such a sum was small in comparison to Daniel's fortune, she knew deep down he had paid enough for that horrible, tragic accident. She wanted him to heal, to put it behind him. To forgive himself and come to terms with the past.

She looked down at Daniel's letter, her fingers tracing the sweeping lines of her name on the paper. She should hate him for all he had taken from her. She *wanted* to hate him. Instead all she felt was a bone-deep weariness and sadness. She knew, despite everything, she still loved him.

She very nearly laughed, though it would have been a mad, manic sound. She had thought loving again would be a betrayal to Aaron's memory. But the idea of that paled in comparison to this travesty, in loving the man who had ended her husband's life. Had she lost sight of what she and Aaron had shared? Had she forgotten all he'd been to her?

She wouldn't allow that to happen.

"I have to return home," she said, the words escaping her before they had fully taken form in her mind.

Lenora blinked. "Home? You mean to the townhouse in London? But I thought you gave up the lease?"

"No, not to London." She drew in a deep breath. "To Dewbury."

There was no need to give her reason for returning. Not with Lenora. Understanding and sadness flared in her eyes. No, Lenora would know that returning to Dewbury, the little hamlet close to Epping Manor and the seat of the Viscounts Tesh for generations, did not mean Margery was returning to see her father.

She had seen her father once since he'd turned her out of the house, when he'd visited her in London just after they'd learned of Aaron's death. He had decreed in his brusque way that she was to return to his home and care for her stepmother.

Margery had told him in no uncertain terms that she would never do that, and had not had contact with him since. And she had no intention of changing that now.

Aaron's family home, on the other hand, where he had grown up, where she had been welcomed as a child, where she and Aaron had stayed for several days as a newly married couple shortly after their elopement before heading to London...

She bit her lip. Perhaps in going back there she might feel close to him again, and remember what they had been to one another.

And maybe, if God was kind, she might stop loving the one man she shouldn't.

Chapter 21

argery left for Dewbury within the hour. A necessity, she knew, for the more time she thought about returning to Aaron's childhood home the more chance she had of reversing her course. The ferry trip and carriage ride there, five hours on a good day, would do enough damage to her resolve.

Something that was proven as the carriage approached the turn into the small hamlet.

Dewbury, just outside of Ampleforth, was something out of a fairy tale. Small stone cottages with trim little gardens, a wide main avenue, ancient trees that shaded a neat green. The sun had just dipped below the horizon, the light of day quickly fading, yet there was still life about, men and women returning home from a day of work, small children running at their mothers' calls, eager for their dinners.

Margery's heart lurched in her chest at the sight of it. It was all so very dear to her, so very familiar. She had spent much of her childhood on Synne with her grandmother. But the majority of those halcyon days had been spent at Epping Manor, or running wild here in Dewbury. Here was where she had met and struck up a friendship with the blacksmith's son, where they had played. Where they had fallen in love.

She bit her lip to keep from crying. She had not been back here since leaving with Aaron, beginning what she had thought was to be a long and happy life together.

How very wrong she had been.

The carriage pulled up before the small inn. Before she could compose herself, Gran's groom opened the door and held out a hand for her. Swallowing hard, Margery descended to the street and entered the building.

She had known this visit would be difficult. But seeing Mrs. Manning behind the desk, so very familiar, made her realize just how difficult it would be.

The woman's eyes widened as large as saucers from behind her spectacles when she spied Margery. "As I live and breathe. Miss Ladbrook, is that you? Ah," she said, pity saturating her features. "I mean Mrs. Kitteridge. I was so very sorry to hear of Aaron's death, my dear. He was such a good boy. All of us in Dewbury miss him terribly."

It wasn't the pity that struck Margery so forcefully. It was the sugary words of affection for a man the village had reviled in his final days here. Margery had been the local nobleman's daughter, who had married so far beneath her that her own father had cast her out. The scandal had been well known in Dewbury. And suddenly Margery remembered the ridicule that Aaron had dealt with in marrying her. While she had been pitied for marrying down, Aaron had been despised for daring to marry so far above his station. It had pained him, she knew, having these people who he had grown up around turn their backs on him.

And now that he was gone, they would think of him fondly?

Without a word, unable to speak for the grief and anger closing her throat, Margery spun about and stormed out of the inn. And ran right into a large male with arms the size of tree trunks.

"My God," the man exclaimed in awe. "Margery? Could it truly be you?"

At the sight of Aaron's father, still strong and broad though decidedly older, his tanned face made ruddy and lined from a thousand fires—as well as the grief of losing his only son—Margery's hold on her composure slipped completely. The fury of moments ago vanished, leaving only a bone-deep grief in its place. Hot tears spilled over then, tracking in rivers down her cheek, and she could do naught but stare at this man who held remnants of Aaron in his gentle eyes.

"Ah, my girl," he murmured. Placing a burly arm about her shoulders, he guided her down the street. "Come along, and we'll get you a bracing cup of tea. No worries, my good man," he continued, presumably to Gran's groom. "I'm the lady's father-in-law; I'll make certain she's safe."

Their walk to his house was a haze for Margery. The only things she was aware of were the comfort of his arm about her, and his soothing, rough baritone murmuring in her ear. Soon they were tucked in his small kitchen, Margery gently pressed into a sturdy wooden chair. He worked slowly as he boiled water, and Margery, her shock receding at this comforting familiarity, saw what she had missed before: shoulders still broad but stooped now, hands stiffer than they had been, the knuckles knotted. He winced and fumbled as he grabbed the wooden handle of the kettle.

Margery was on her feet in an instant. "Let me get that for you," she said with a gentle smile.

An embarrassed flush stained his cheeks but he nodded his thanks and sat at the table with a weary sigh. "These hands aren't what they used to be, I'm afraid," he said, his voice gruff.

Margery cast him a worried look as she filled a pair of plain stoneware cups and carried them to the table. "Are you able to work?"

"Haven't for a year now. My youngest daughter's husband has taken over the business." His chest, still wide, puffed up, a light returning to his eyes. "He's got a talent, that one. My Joan was lucky to snap Bill up. And they have a wee one now, too. They're out for the time being but should be back soon. They'll be so very happy to see you."

Margery smiled, remembering Aaron's sister, a dark-haired imp who had followed them about, causing chaos with her high spirits and mischievous ways. Fetching the milk and sugar, she placed them on the table before taking a seat herself across from Aaron's father. And so Joan had wed Bill? It was hard to imagine the girl married, and a mother. It made Margery realize just how much time had passed since she'd left.

Her smile slipped then. She wrapped her hands about the sturdy, lovingly cared-for cup, willing the warmth of it into her suddenly chilled fingers. "I'm sorry I haven't written much since Aaron died. There's no excuse for it."

"Ah, no worries, my girl," he said, patting her arm. "It couldn't have been easy on you. I'm just thankful you had your family to get you through it all." He paused then, taking a slow sip, eyeing her carefully over the rim. "Did you come to see your father?"

She frowned, looking into the opaque depths of her tea. "Nothing has changed between us. I came to see you, and you alone."

Mr. Kitteridge let out a sad sigh. "I'm sorry to hear it, my girl. Not that you've come to see me, of course," he clarified when she glanced up at him in hurt. "Goodness, but it does my heart good to see you. I've missed you something terrible, and having you back makes me feel I've got a bit of my boy back with you."

Tears burned Margery's eyes again at the admission. But the man's expression resumed its serious mien as he continued to gaze at her.

"I do wish you could put your hurt behind you. There's no room for bad blood between a parent and child. And if you only knew what he's suffered since."

Margery gaped at him. "You cannot mean to tell me you pity him. After all he's done? How unworthy he made Aaron feel?"

But there was no nod of agreement. Instead he only seemed to grow more pained, more frustrated. As if something inside him ached to be let loose. Just as she was about to question him on it, however, there was a commotion at the front door. And suddenly Joan burst into the room.

The girl—ah, no, she was a girl no longer, but a woman grown now—was, as ever, a whirlwind of energy as she dropped her packages in the corner and swung off her cloak to hang up on a peg. "Papa," she said as she grabbed her apron and began to busily secure the back, "I've bought that handsome fabric you were admiring in town the other day, and shall make you a fine new suit with it—"

Her voice cut off abruptly as she turned and spied Margery sitting at the table with her father. Her jaw dropped, her eyes widening.

Margery smiled wanly. "Hello, Joan."

The squeal that burst from Aaron's younger sister was deafening. She rushed forward, throwing her arms about Margery. "We never knew you were coming. Oh goodness, how wonderful to see you. Bill!" she called out, her voice echoing in the small space. "You must come quick, and bring the baby. Oh, Margery," she said, "we've missed you so. Why have you not come before now? But never mind, for you're here now. Oh! But here is my handsome husband," she said with a grin as Bill entered the room with a dark-haired baby cradled in his arms. "I went and snatched him up, as you can see. Not that he had a chance of refusing once I set my sights on him. Bill, darling, you remember Margery, Aaron's wife? Oh, and you've never met Wesley. But what do you think of my son? Isn't he as handsome as his father?"

Margery couldn't help but laugh. Joan had always been boisterous, almost larger than life, and Margery had forgotten how exhausting it could be—and how much she'd missed it.

"Bill," she said with a smile, stepping forward to take his free hand, as the other was busy cradling the baby. "How good it is to see you again. Congratulations on your son. He's beautiful."

Bill beamed, his teeth flashing in his dark face as he passed Wesley over to Margery. "Thank you. But don't let his calm demeanor fool you; he's as spirited as his mother."

"And how lucky you are," Joan quipped, sending her husband an arch look. "But sit while I prepare dinner. I've some mutton stew I need only reheat, and so I won't miss a minute of anything."

The familiarity of the scene tugged at her heart. Granted, Joan and Bill were married now, and with a baby. Mr. Kitteridge was more frail and had stepped back to allow his son-in-law to take over his business.

But that same camaraderie that had called to her when she'd been a young child visiting her dear friend's home was still there. The same welcome and acceptance was still present that she'd found solace in when newly married and cast from her father's life. And so she hugged Wesley closer to her and sat again at the table.

The child gazed back at her with wide, curious eyes. She smiled down at him. "Do you love to torment your poor papa?" she teased. "I daresay he has enough to deal with in your mama."

The baby gurgled merrily, flailing his fists in the air.

Joan, from her place at the stove, laughed. "He does like you, Margery. Not that I had any doubt he would. You love your Aunt Margery, don't you, my darling?"

Aunt Margery. The title struck her mute. Not that she was unused to being an aunt, especially with Lenora and Clara recently adding to that particular blessing. But knowing she was still connected to the Kitteridge family, that she would always belong no matter where life took her, touched something deep in her, something she thought she'd lost.

The rest of the evening passed with a swiftness that stunned her. How lovely it was to be reminded of Aaron in these warm, welcoming people. How wonderful to forget for a time her pain over the revelation about her husband and to remember who he had been.

And so when supper was over, and she finished helping Joan clear the dishes and clean up the kitchen, she didn't even consider refusing when they insisted she stay the night.

"I'll locate your carriage and fetch your things," Bill said. Then, kissing his wife and smoothing his son's dark hair, he was off.

"Papa," Joan said, rocking a sleepy Wesley in her arms, "I'll put the baby down. Why don't you get Margery settled?"

Margery followed Mr. Kitteridge up the narrow flight of stairs. It wasn't until they reached a familiar door, however, that she realized just where she would be sleeping.

The breath left her as the door swung wide. Aaron's room was just as it had been all those years ago. There was the narrow bed they had shared in the early days of their marriage before leaving for London, the dark blue quilt his late mother had made for him when he was a child still smoothed over the top. She spied the small wooden box that contained his battalion of lead soldiers, the framed watercolor of Margery that Lenora had painted, the collection of shells she had brought back for him after each of her summers spent on Synne.

Mr. Kitteridge cleared his throat. "I haven't changed a thing," he said gruffly. "Couldn't bring myself to. I hope you don't mind spending the night in this room."

"Of course not," Margery managed, though it was the furthest thing from the truth. She had come here with the hope of remembering Aaron and all they'd had. But would it break her, staying in this place where she had loved Aaron? Would it destroy her, being surrounded by reminders of him?

Especially knowing what she now knew.

"Well, then. We'll bring up your bag when Bill returns with it." He gave her a pained smile. "Good night, my girl."

He turned to go. "Wait," Margery called out.

When he turned back to face her there were tears in his eyes. She swallowed down her own.

"Thank you."

She meant it as so much more than having her to dinner, inviting her to stay the night. She meant it also for welcoming her in, as they always had, for making her feel connected again to Aaron, for helping her to remember the good times before he'd gone off to war, before Waterloo, before the desertion.

He nodded, beyond words, closing the door softly behind him.

Margery stood numb in the middle of the room for a moment, feeling lost. Memories were flashing through her mind, faster than she could react to them, each one centered around Aaron, until she couldn't breathe.

With a gasp she made her way to the bed, curled up on the quilt, dragged the pillow to her chest. Only then did the tears come. And they were a torrent.

She felt as if she were being emptied out, all the grief, all the pain of the past years without him. When she thought there could be nothing left and she must surely be wrung dry, however, the tears started up again. Only this time they had the flavor of anger to them. And not anger at herself for falling in love with another. No, this anger was focused on Aaron alone.

Her entire being shied away from such a devastating emotion. She had done everything she could to honor Aaron, to protect his memory. But she realized in that moment she had forgotten things in the process, like how much she'd hurt when he'd insisted on going off to war, how she'd felt abandoned when he'd left her though she'd known from the beginning that it was what he'd always wanted.

And then the newer anger at being blackmailed, and the betrayal of learning what the blackmailer had claimed was true. She let it all come, washing over her like a waterfall. Finally accepting that she was not without blame. She had put her late husband up on a pedestal, refusing to think badly of him, determined that no one else should, either. But she was human. And Aaron had been human as well, with all the messiness that came with it. And she realized in that moment that no matter what might have happened at Waterloo, it didn't define Aaron. She knew who her husband had been.

Just as she knew who she was. She was no longer that fierce girl with stars in her eyes. She was a fierce woman who had seen her share of pain and had come out the other end of it stronger; who had loved a good man and lost him, and who now loved another good man who continued to suffer for a horrible, random tragedy. And, despite coming to Dewbury with the purpose of remembering Aaron and what he had been to her, and in the process burying her love for Daniel, she saw now that would never happen. Just as she would love Aaron all her days, she would love Daniel as well, and the loving of one did not diminish the love for the other.

But she would not think of Daniel just then. She couldn't. There was still too much to resolve in her heart for that, too many things to fight before she could think of any possible future.

She prayed, by this time tomorrow, she might know what to do about it.

Chapter 22

The faint bustle of a busy household starting its day woke Margery just before dawn: the muted sound of laughter, a baby's demands for breakfast, the clatter of dishes. She stretched, wincing at the soreness in her back and neck, and looked down at herself. She was still clothed, though her shoes were off, a blanket she didn't recognize tucked about her. A quick scan of the room in the dim predawn light and she saw her shoes placed neatly beside her bag near the door. Joan must have come in last night after she'd cried herself to sleep. She should perhaps feel embarrassed that she'd needed caring for in such a manner. Instead she felt a spark of warmth in her battered heart. Life went on, didn't it? The proof was in the changes here in Aaron's old home. It was as if she had, quite literally, weathered a frightening storm the night before and opened her eyes to clear skies.

Mr. Kitteridge was the first to see her as she entered the kitchen. "Good morning, my girl," he said with a wide smile. The sadness of the night before was no longer clouding his eyes, a new vigor in his step as he made his way to her and kissed her on the cheek. "And did you sleep well?"

"I did, thank you. But goodness, Joan, that smells divine. Can I help you?"

Joan grinned at Margery over her shoulder. "Not a bit. Have a seat. The bread is already toasted, and these eggs are almost done."

Margery greeted Bill, who was trying to steal a triangle of toast—and a kiss—from his blushing wife. Then, greeting a bright-eyed Wesley, who was happily gnawing on a wooden horse on a blanket in the corner, she sat across from Mr. Kitteridge. Once again Margery felt fairly enveloped in love and goodwill.

Only now she felt as if she were missing something precious. Daniel's face floated into her thoughts. How she would love to share such a scene with him, seeing his happy face in the morning, stealing kisses, doting upon their children—

She frowned. How could she have come here determined to forget about him and only find herself more certain of her love for him? But she could not think of him now, not while she was in this place, with these people. So she laughed and ate, reminiscing gently about the past. And felt a certain melancholy—yet healing—farewell in it.

When breakfast was over and done, Bill rose and kissed his wife and son.

"As much as I wish to stay, I must be off." He turned to Margery. "I hope we'll see you again, and soon?"

Margery smiled. "If that's an invitation to return, you may depend upon it. You just might grow sick of me."

"Highly doubtful," he said with a grin, kissing her cheek and shaking his father-in-law's hand before heading out the door.

Margery, rising from the table, was about to help Joan clear the dishes and clean the kitchen when Mr. Kitteridge spoke.

"Will you give me a minute of your time, my girl?"

Margery blinked, surprised, as she sank back down. "Of course."

He ran a hand through his graying hair and blew out a breath. The frustration in him was palpable. And she suddenly remembered the same reaction from him the night before, how she'd been about to question him on it when the others had arrived.

She leaned closer to him. "What's preying on your mind?"

He gave her a tortured glance. "I promised I wouldn't mention it. But it's killing me to remain quiet."

She frowned. "Promised what?"

But he seemed not to hear her. He caught Joan's eye. She gave an imperceptible nod before turning back to her work. It seemed to bolster something in Mr. Kitteridge. His expression shifted, a determined gleam entering his eyes. "Though that promise was only that I wouldn't write to you of it, not that I wouldn't tell you outright."

Margery was growing alarmed. Had the man received a blackmail letter as well? She had not even considered it, but wasn't it possible? "Mr. Kitteridge?"

He took her hand and pressed it between his. "My girl, your father is not the villain you believe him to be."

She blinked. Well, she certainly hadn't expected that.

Though she was relieved that the man wasn't aware of his son's desertion—and she prayed he might never find out, for it would destroy him—she didn't know what to make of this new subject. "I don't understand."

"I've come to know your father over the past years since my Aaron died. He's visited me often, has offered help, has made it so we could keep our heads afloat while grief ate at us. And I can say, with absolute certainty, that there is not a man alive who feels his guilt more keenly."

Margery, stunned, could only shake her head in disbelief. Her father was a proud man, a stern man. Picturing him befriending Mr. Kitteridge, confiding in him, was as foreign to Margery as picturing him skipping down Dewbury's main street wearing a flowered hat.

"And now I've said my piece," Mr. Kitteridge said.

"I—I don't know what to do with this," she admitted.

He patted her hand and nodded in understanding. "I know he's hurt you. But I do hope you can forgive him and move on, if only for your own sake. Won't you visit with him before you leave?"

Margery stared at him, stunned. "I—I can't," she whispered.

He nodded sadly, sitting back in his seat with a heavy sigh. Margery, confused, needing something to do, rose and gathered up dishes with shaking hands. Mr. Kitteridge should despise Lord Tesh. The man had outright refused Aaron's suit for Margery's hand, had made him feel unworthy. And here he was, pleading his case?

So immersed was she in her troubled thoughts, she didn't immediately realize that Joan had become uncommonly quiet. Nor did she realize there had been a knock at the front door until Mr. Kitteridge rose from his place at the table and spoke.

"I'll get it," he murmured. Then, casting Margery a hooded glance, he made his slow way from the kitchen. In short order he was back. But now he was accompanied by someone who was painfully familiar.

Margery gaped at the newcomer, unable to believe her eyes. "Papa?"

Viscount Tesh, looking as out of place as any one person could, standing in the doorway of this simple kitchen in his fine, expensive clothes, stood ramrod straight and gazed at her with uncertainty. It was an expression she had never seen on his face before.

He cleared his throat. "Hello, Margery."

She shook her head, still unable to comprehend that he was here in Mr. Kitteridge's humble home. "What are you doing here?" she asked.

He motioned to the kitchen table. It was only then she realized Mr. Kitteridge and Joan and baby Wesley were nowhere to be seen. In a daze she stumbled to the table and sat down heavily.

Her father sat across from her. "I didn't think you would ever return to Dewbury," he said.

"I didn't do it for your benefit."

The words escaped before she quite meant them to. But they opened something up in her, the anger of years coalescing into something sharp and painful. Here was a man who should have supported her in everything, loved her through everything. And she had never doubted his love for her. Until she'd needed it most. It was then he'd turned his back on her.

His eyes fell from hers, as if he could hear the shouts

of condemnation ringing through her head. "I under-stand," he rasped. "And if you never want to speak to me again, I understand that as well. But I am sorry. I'm more sorry than I can ever say."

She gaped at him. This was not like him. Lord Tesh never apologized, never begged for forgiveness. She re-membered Mr. Kitteridge's confession shortly before her father's arrival then, his claims that the viscount had been giving the Kitteridge family help, that he'd been visiting. She narrowed her eyes. "What are you playing at?"

"Nothing—"

"No, you are." Her body fairly vibrated with her anger and confusion. She clenched her hands tight beneath the table. She longed to rise, to run from the room. But she feared in that moment her legs would not hold her.

"You don't do anything but for your benefit," she continued. "And I've never known you to suffer from a moment's guilt in your life." An idea struck her then. "Is it to save face with the villagers? Or did my stepmother put you up to it? Is that why you've had a change of heart with the Kitteridges?"

"You have no excuse to think any better of me, I know," he managed, looking more miserable than she had ever seen him. "And perhaps if I had better handled things with you after Aaron died, perhaps if I had been able to look past my pride to do what was right, we would not now be where we are. But I know now I was wrong, Meg, to refuse your marriage to someone you loved, and to cut you out of my life. And I'm so very sorry. Can you forgive me?"

It was not that he begged—something she had never seen him do—that brought the sob rising up in her throat. Nor was it the use of his childhood name for her, something she had not heard from him in nearly two decades. No, it was him calling Aaron by his name that finally made her see that he was sincere. Before this moment he had always been "Kitteridge" to her father, first said with unconcerned boredom, then with disdain, and finally with barely suppressed anger. But saying "Aaron" in that anguished way, a tone that spoke of regret, fairly broke her heart.

He must have seen how deeply she was affected, for he suddenly leaned forward. "Meg," he said, his voice broken, "I can never undo the damage I've caused. But please, can we move forward? Can we try to rebuild what we've lost?"

She stared at him, torn between the anger that had burned bright inside her for so many years and the quieter part of her that remembered how much she had loved this man. Even now, after all he'd done, he was still her father.

She dragged in a deep breath, seeing him with new eyes. "Have you truly helped Mr. Kitteridge and his family?"

His gaze dropped from hers as a faint blush stained his cheeks. "He wasn't to tell you that."

A warmth started up in her chest, a healing of a wound that had long festered. She smiled, a small thing, and murmured, "I do believe the promise was to never write of it."

He blinked, his gaze flying back to her. Then, an uncertain smile. "I suppose I should have expected the man to find a loophole. He's a clever one."

She leaned forward. "Tell me about it."

He did, haltingly at first, how he'd known from nearly the moment she'd left with Aaron that he'd made a mistake. But pride had kept him stewing in his outrage. Until news of Aaron's death had reached him. He had meant the trip to London to see her and tell her to return home as a kind of reconciliation, to let her know all was forgiven and he wanted her back. Another mistake, he soon realized.

When he'd learned of Mr. Kitteridge's troubles he'd decided to step in, to help. He'd thought himself a great benefactor, forgiving and kind. But he soon learned with their weekly visits that the man had far more to give him, far more to provide and teach.

They could be just words, the more stubborn part of her brain argued. He had hurt her too much to allow her to trust him so quickly, so completely, no matter that the young girl she had been, and that was still somewhere deep inside her, wished to do so.

When Joan reappeared some hour or so later to check on them, however, with Wesley in tow, and Margery's father held the child on his lap with an eagerness and ease that told of many such scenes, she began to believe that what he had told her, all he had claimed, was true. And so, a short while later when her father rose to leave, and he hesitatingly went to hug her, she stepped into his arms willingly.

He started in surprise. Then, heaving a deep sigh, he held her tighter. Their relationship was not fully healed; she wasn't sure it could ever return to what it had been before her marriage. But it was a hopeful beginning, and for that she could only be grateful.

She stood at the door after he'd gone, watching

his carriage as it made its way down Dewbury's main thoroughfare. Suddenly a comforting presence stepped up behind her.

"Do you forgive me?"

She turned to face Mr. Kitteridge. "For inviting him here despite my declaration that I wouldn't see him? For explicitly going against my wishes?" she asked archly, before ruining her stern affect by smiling. "I don't like being manipulated in such a way. But I forgive you for it, as I know you had my best interests in mind."

She sighed then, looking up at the sky. The sun was climbing toward its zenith, and the day was fast progressing. She'd best get going if she was to return to Seacliff by nightfall. She had a decision to make regarding a certain blackmail demand. And a certain duke who still inexplicably held her heart though she had tried her best to pry him from it.

He seemed to understand. "Time to leave then?"

"I'm afraid so," she said, taking his arm as they made their way back inside the small house.

In short order Mr. Kitteridge fetched the carriage while she and Joan packed up what few things she had brought with her. Goodbyes were said, tears shed. And by the time the coach pulled up before the house she was ready—finally—to let go.

Joan and baby Wesley blew kisses from the door before heading back inside, leaving her alone with Mr. Kitteridge.

"I'm glad you came," he said.

"I am as well," she agreed quietly. "But I'll return soon, and promise to write often."

"And you'll be welcome anytime," he pronounced.

Then he frowned. "But you can't be worrying about the likes of me. You need to look to yourself now, start a family of your own." At her stricken look he smiled. "You think I didn't notice your half-mourning? Or that ring still tight on your finger? But you need to live your life now, my girl."

"I am living my life," she said through stiff lips, though even to her ears the words lacked conviction.

He raised an eyebrow, an expression that said she was fooling herself but couldn't fool him. It was an expression she had often seen on Aaron's face, and it made her heart lurch in her chest.

"You've got one of the biggest, kindest hearts I know," he said. "And I can see there's a sadness to you that has nothing to do with my boy being gone. But Aaron wouldn't have wanted you to waste your life away. Go and be happy, my girl." He patted her hand. Then, letting her go, he stepped back.

For a moment Margery felt unmoored, lost. But then she looked at Mr. Kitteridge's smiling face, at the certainty that shined from his eyes, and knew in a moment she wasn't lost. Rather, she had been set free.

Chapter 23

*H*ot air. Acrid smoke. Suffocating him, burning his eyes and nose. Filling his mouth. The roar of cannons, constant crack of musket rounds, screams and shouts. And the humming beneath it all, like a million angry hornets.

The mud sucked at his boots, dragged at his legs. His thighs burned. He took sight down his rifle, aimed, fired. Before his adversary finished falling he was reaching back into his cartridge box. Then, so quick but never quick enough, like an automaton: tear the paper with his teeth, half-cock, pour gunpowder in the pan, close, spin upright. Gunpowder down the barrel, cartridge follows. Ramrod out, tamp it all down tight. Make ready. Full cock. Present. Tight against shoulder…

Only this time, when he would have fired, a body slammed into him. Spinning, a face in his vision, for the briefest of seconds. One of their own. Fleeing the battle. He hardly had time to understand it before he was in the mud. Not just mud. Water, too, a puddle, churned up into a thick sludge beneath a thousand marching feet. It filled his mouth, a foul refuse he spit out.

On his feet again in an instant. No time to waste. If he delayed he would be trampled or shot. Pull the gun up again, take aim, pull the trigger.

Another of theirs stumbled in the way. Too late to stop. In horror he waited for the telltale spark of the flint.

But no spark, only smoke in his eyes again. From his gun or another's? He hadn't shot the boy. Relief. When the smoke cleared, however...

A pale face, hand at his chest, stumbling toward him. He caught the boy as he fell. Blood foamed from his lips.

"Pearl..."

Daniel awoke with a gasp. No battlefield, no death and pain and fear. Well, perhaps fear. He ran a shaking hand over his face, looked up at the ceiling in the dim early-morning light. Rough plaster, nothing he recognized. Confused, he tried to throw off the damp sheets. But they were twined about his legs. There was a horrible moment of panic as he fought against them. Finally free, he lurched to his feet.

Pain tore through his thigh. Gasping, he fell back to the bed. His fingers dug into the twisted flesh, the burn in the muscle dulling to a sharp ache just as the realization of where he was came to him. An inn. On his way to London.

Away from Margery.

No. He shook his head fiercely. He could not go down that path, or he would go mad.

A light knock at the door. And then Wilkins was entering, a freshly brushed jacket slung over his arm. His eyes flared wide when he spied Daniel, and he put the jacket aside, hurrying forward.

"Your Grace, are you well?"

"I'm fine," Daniel muttered, then immediately regretted his dismissive tone. He and the valet had made such progress lately. And he found, after their sudden bond over the situation with Gregory, over their shared grief over Nathaniel—and after having experienced a closeness with Margery—he had missed having someone to lean on. And he no longer wanted to keep the man at arm's length.

But no matter his curt words, Wilkins, it seemed, was through being cowed. He dropped to his haunches and brushed Daniel's hands away, as if they were mere flies. "I've done a fair amount of research on wounds of this sort," he said as he pulled Daniel's nightshirt up to reveal the puckered wound on his leg. Before Daniel had time to react the valet's fingers were pressing into it.

Pain, though this time a good kind of pain. Daniel hissed as the man found a particularly tight area.

"I received a recipe for a liniment from the physician back home. Once we get to London I'll have the housekeeper at the townhouse assist me in mixing it up. In the meantime, we'll massage and stretch your leg twice daily, and apply ice when we're able. And no more long stretches of road; we're to take breaks and often, to make certain you're able to exercise it to prevent it from stiffening."

Despite himself Daniel smiled. "Thank you, Wilkins," he said gruffly.

"Of course, Your Grace."

The man worked for a time in silence, alternating massaging and stretching the abused muscle. Just when Daniel was about to close his eyes from exhaustion, however, the man spoke up again, this time with the same hesitation that used to highlight their time together.

"You were having a nightmare, Your Grace?"

Daniel paused. And then, "Yes."

"You haven't had one for some time."

Daniel blinked in surprise. "You knew about the nightmares?"

Wilkins gave him an apologetic look that nevertheless conveyed what Daniel should have guessed all along: servants quite often knew much more about a household than those living in it. No doubt the man had been aware of the nightmares from the moment Daniel began having them upon his return.

"Do you know what might have brought them on again?" Wilkins queried.

Something tugged at his memory then, that same sense of recognition and anxiety as that day on the beach with Margery when they'd met with her veteran friends. Though a face flashed in his mind now from that day at Waterloo, that boy who'd pushed past him just before he'd shot Aaron. Before he could make sense of it, however, panic reared, and his mind closed off against it, an instinctual defense.

Wilkins had seen something in his eyes, however, that gave him pause. "What is it?"

"Nothing," Daniel muttered. He let loose a sigh, frowning in frustration. "I met some veterans of the Waterloo conflict on Synne recently. I suppose it brought it all back again."

"Ah. I'm sorry, Your Grace."

Daniel nodded his thanks. But his thoughts were already drifting back to that elusive memory that had tried to surface before his defenses had snuffed it out. He frowned. What was it about those men that had affected him so? It was not as if he had not met with veterans before. He had even met with other men who had fought in that devastating battle. And not a one of them had affected him as Aaron's three friends had. Anxious to know so he might understand, he prodded it carefully. But it wouldn't budge. Dragging in a deep breath, he tried again. Once more, however, it eluded him. He let out a frustrated burst of air.

Wilkins paused. "What is it, Your Grace?"

Daniel shook his head. "Just a memory. But it isn't clear. The moment I think I've captured it, it slips right through my fingers again."

"Brought on by these three men?"

"Perhaps." But at the mention of them the memory surged again. Daniel, determined to hold on to it this time, grasped at it. But once more it vanished, like a puff of smoke.

Like the brief burst from the end of a musket as it fired . . .

Waterloo . . .

Suddenly it took form, brilliant and devastating and horrible. And he saw what he couldn't before: not a faceless boy, but Mr. Newton's frightened face as he pushed past Daniel, knocking him off his feet, sending him to the muddy ground.

Daniel gasped and reared back. Alarmed, Wilkins reached out to steady him.

"He was there," Daniel said. "He was the one to push past me, who sent me sprawling."

Wilkins, confused and more than a touch concerned, stood and clasped his hands in worry. "Perhaps we'd best stay here another night, Your Grace. I worry that you're exhausting yourself."

"You don't understand." Frustrated, Daniel surged to his feet. He was no doubt undoing whatever good Wilkins had managed to do in working on his leg, but in that moment he didn't care. Everything was falling into place, rearranging into a new and stark reality. And all he could think of just then was getting back to Synne.

Back to Margery.

No, he told himself brutally. Back to Synne. To confront Newton.

"He was there," he said, slowly and distinctly, as if making Wilkins understand was paramount in understanding it himself. "One of those men from the beach, Mr. Newton. He was running away from the fight. And Margery's husband was not deserting. He was running after Newton, his friend."

If anything, Wilkins appeared more confused. "Margery? You mean Mrs. Kitteridge?"

But Daniel hardly heard him. Faster and faster pieces were clicking into place: Margery needing money, frightened. Her voice, so low and tortured: *What would you do if the memory of someone you loved was threatened?* And then, *Aaron didn't do anything wrong. He was a good man. A brave man. He would have never—*

Ah, God. She thought her husband was a deserter. When all along he had been trying to prevent his friend from deserting.

Which, of course, didn't lessen Daniel's own guilt in shooting the man, no matter how accidental. But he couldn't allow her to think for even a minute more that Aaron had done something wrong.

But why would she think such a thing? Who had made her think it? Newton's face flashed again. He frowned. No, the man had been Aaron's friend. What reason could he have for making Margery believe such a heinous thing?

The answer was instantaneous: *money*. Money would make a person do all manner of horrible things.

Desperate now, he turned back to face Wilkins. "We have to return to Synne."

* * *

It didn't take Daniel long to locate Mr. Newton's residence. For all that Synne was a sprawling island, the town center was not, and the areas where the veterans resided even smaller.

Though the man wasn't at home, it wasn't hard to learn just where he spent the majority of his days. And so, just as the sun was beginning to dip beneath the horizon, Daniel found Newton on that very same rock he and Margery had been resting on that fateful day when they'd first seen the man. He didn't look up as Daniel approached and sat beside him. But Daniel could see he was aware of him all the same in the tight press of his lips and the deepening lines about his eyes.

"I was wondering when you'd show up," the man murmured. "Only I didn't expect you to take so blasted long figuring it all out."

"So it's true then." Daniel turned to face Newton more fully. "You're blackmailing Mrs. Kitteridge."

Newton heaved a heavy sigh, closing his eyes, as if in acute pain. "I didn't mean to hurt her. But I was desperate. I got in too deep, owed too much." A rough bark of laughter escaped him. "I began drinking, began gambling, to distract myself from my memories of war. But it proved just as much of a curse, if not more so."

Daniel shook his head, clenching his hands on his thighs, fury and disgust and pity all warring in his chest. "But Aaron was your friend. And you accused him of deserting."

Newton dropped his head into his hands. "I was desperate," he rasped.

But Daniel hardly heard him for the roaring that started up in his ears. "You destroyed Margery's memories of her husband. It's all she had left of him, those memories. And now she thinks her husband betrayed his country, that he's a deserter." He turned to fully face the man, fighting against the urge to grab him by the shirtfront and shake him until his teeth rattled. "When all along, *you* were the one deserting. *You* were the one turning your back on your battalion, on your country."

A sob escaped Newton, quickly stifled as he bit his lip. "Are you going to tell the authorities?"

"Worried about your own skin?" Daniel snarled. Unable to sit close to Newton a moment longer, he lurched to his feet and looked out over the waves. Down the beach a couple strolled in the cool evening air, and several young girls laughed as they packed up their game of battledore and shuttlecock. But Daniel felt a world away from those happy scenes.

Breathing deep of the briny sea air, he closed his eyes and said, his voice rough, "In regard to your desertion, I was at that battle; I recall the chaos, the fear, the stench and noise. And so, while I despise you for your cowardice, there's little point in seeking justice now."

He turned to face Newton. "But your despicable act of tormenting Margery is another matter entirely."

The man swallowed hard. "It was but a hundred quid," he said, his voice dropping to a whine that made Daniel clench his back teeth so hard he thought they'd shatter. "She's related to two bloody dukes, is daughter of a viscount. That sum is a mere drop in a bucket to one such as her."

Daniel's control snapped. "You bastard," he snarled, lurching forward to loom over the man. "You bloody sniveling coward. If you were as close to Aaron as she seems to think you were, you would know that her father cut her off without a cent."

Newton's eyes widened in fear, his gaze snagging on Daniel's cheek. His scar must be standing out in frightening relief. But for once Daniel was glad of it, was glad that it was terrifying to behold.

"B-but surely," the other man stuttered, "she receives support from the others. They could not have all left her out to dry with no financial help. She practically lives at Seacliff, after all."

"You obviously know nothing about her. Margery has pride. She would never go running to another for funds. And she would protect Aaron's memory with her life."

Once more he recalled the desolation on her face when she'd believed Aaron to have deserted his battalion. She'd held out hope that her husband had been innocent. Until Daniel had gone and made her believe such a heinous thing was true.

How she must be suffering. And he refused to allow her to believe such a thing for even a second longer.

Reaching down, Daniel grabbed Newton's shirtfront

and hauled him to his feet. The man gasped, flinching. If Daniel had looked down to find the man had wet himself, he would not have been surprised.

"What are you going to do to me?" Newton cried.

"I'm going to haul you before Margery, so you might tell her the truth of your deceit yourself. She'll be your judge and jury." He bared his teeth in a grin, felt the pull of tight scar tissue as he allowed his features to take on a terrifying cast. And was rewarded as Newton paled and blanched at the sight of it.

"If you're a praying man," he bit out, "I'd start praying now."

* * *

Margery should have expected her grandmother to question her disappearance. She'd given her no real excuse, after all, merely leaving a note stating that she would be gone to Dewbury for the night and would return the following afternoon.

She should have expected it. Yet she had not.

Margery threw open the door to her room and strode inside, not realizing she wasn't alone until her grandmother spoke.

"Finally back, are you?"

Gasping, Margery placed a hand over her racing heart. She searched the room, spying the older woman seated near the window.

"Gran, what in the world are you doing here?"

"I think," her grandmother said in a tone that brooked no argument, "that you and I are due for a talk."

Margery, still emotionally drained from her time in

Dewbury—facing her grief over Aaron, the unexpected anger she'd been carrying, reconciling with her father, and realizing that she still loved Daniel no matter what he had done—was in no mood to sit and talk with her grandmother in what she was certain would be a stressful conversation. But she also knew that, if she asked the woman to leave, she would be courting a much bigger problem than just having an unpleasant conversation. Namely, Lady Tesh's effrontery, which could be frightening, indeed. And so, sighing heavily, she trudged to the chair facing her grandmother and sat.

Gran pursed her lips as she regarded Margery. Freya, seated in her mistress's lap, eyed her with equal intensity, and Margery felt, inexplicably, as if she were being judged and condemned by the pair of them.

"You went to Dewbury, did you?" her grandmother drawled.

Just keeping herself from rolling her eyes, Margery said in the pleasant, singsong voice she usually adopted with the older woman when she was in a snit, "I did. As you well know, seeing as I left you a note telling you just that."

Gran's eyes narrowed, proof that she had heard the little jab. "You did. But what you failed to tell me in your frighteningly succinct letter"—here she raised one eyebrow imperiously—"was *why* you went to Dewbury. A place, I might add, that you have not been to in some years."

Frustration reared up, that her grandmother would be angry over such a thing, or even question her on her decision to go back there. She very nearly lost her patience—until she saw the tight press of her grandmother's lips, the flare of concern quickly suppressed in her sharp brown eyes.

Gran was worried about her.

Affection for this woman, who had helped raise her, who had been there for her through so many horrible instances of her life, who had never wavered in her support of her, filled Margery to the brim. Her frustration gone in an instant, she leaned forward and placed her hand over her grandmother's gnarled one. "I'm fine. Truly."

Finally a crack in the ever-present tough veneer. Gran swallowed hard, her chin wobbling ever so slightly. "You're certain?"

"I am."

The woman seemed to deflate with relief. "I'm glad of it." She let out a deep breath. But soon her gaze was back on Margery, the worry returned. "Why did you go? Did you—did you visit your father?"

Once more Margery's chest swelled. Gran had not wavered in her determination to support Margery and Aaron all those years ago, taking their side against her own son in the process. And yet, though she never complained about it, Margery knew it pained the woman. She might have appeared unfazed by anything, but the woman loved her family fiercely.

"I didn't mean to," Margery admitted. "But it seems Mr. Kitteridge knew better than I in what I needed and made certain a meeting took place, whether I wished it or not." She gave her grandmother a sly look. "He sounds like someone else I know."

Her grandmother's eyes opened wide in feigned innocence. "I don't know what you're talking about."

"Don't you?" Margery pursed her lips in humor. But

it was short-lived. She smiled sadly at her grandmother. "I'm sorry things didn't work out with the duke and me as you must have wished."

She fully expected Gran to deny any intention to match the duke with anyone, much less Margery, who had declared loudly and determinedly since Aaron's death that she would never marry again. But the woman gave her a sheepish shrug. "You can't blame me for trying, can you?"

Margery chuckled. "No, I suppose not."

Suddenly her grandmother looked frighteningly shrewd. "Although, it isn't too late, is it?"

Margery gaped at her. "But the man has left; he's gone to London. And I can assure you, he would not have me even if he were here."

Too late she realized she had revealed too much to her incredibly cunning grandmother. The woman looked positively victorious.

"The stubborn ones are always the most satisfying to pair up," she declared with glee.

"We are not paired up!" Margery cried. "And we never shall be."

"But you wish to," Gran crowed.

"No—"

"Don't deny it, girl. I see it in your eyes. You think your grandmother is stupid, but I'm not so old I can't see you've formed a tendre for him."

Margery groaned and dropped her face into her hands. There was nothing more dangerous—or maddening—than her grandmother when she sensed a victory could be close at hand. No matter how untrue it might be. "What does it matter?" she muttered.

"It matters a great deal." There was a pause. And then, her grandmother's voice incredibly gentle, "You deserve to live a happy life, child. Don't let it slip through your fingers if you find yourself lucky enough to have the chance again."

It was so close to what Mr. Kitteridge had said to her that Margery's breath caught in her throat.

But even if she were to go against everything she had held on to for four years, determined to honor Aaron's memory and never take another husband— goodness knew she had already decimated the other half of her promise to herself by falling in love again— could she reconcile herself to loving Daniel and making a life with him knowing what she did about his part in Aaron's death?

Daniel's face floated in her mind, and the myriad emotions that had crossed it: tenderly smiling; filled with desire; tight with despair. He was a good man, an honorable man. She knew that deep down in her soul. Fate had been cruel when it had put Aaron in the path of Daniel's bullet. But it was not Daniel's fault. Could Fate have brought the two of them together on purpose, a kind of apology for the devastation that one moment had caused? A way for them to find healing, in each other?

Gran, seeming to have seen something telling in her face, lowered Freya to the floor and stood. "I'll leave you to your thoughts then," she said. "And, maybe, to pack for a trip to London?"

Her tone, infinitely smug, should have rankled Margery to no end. Instead she found herself smiling as she rose. "Thank you, Gran," she said, kissing the woman on the cheek.

Gran, her eyes suspiciously moist, patted her cheek before making her way from the room. Leaving Margery alone with her thoughts.

She loved Daniel. So very much. She had already seen that her love for him did not lessen her love for Aaron. Could Daniel love her as deeply as she loved him? And could that love perhaps be just the thing that both of them needed?

She was hurrying to her small bag, still packed from her trip to Dewbury, before she knew what she was about. Excitement strummed through her. She didn't know if what she was doing was wise. It could be quite possibly the worst thing she had ever considered, hying off to London after Daniel, and beginning her journey just after nightfall, no less. He might turn her away, might proclaim he didn't care for her in that way. Or it might lead to more heartache than they were currently suffering.

But if there was a chance at happiness for them, wasn't it worth fighting for? Wasn't *Daniel* worth fighting for?

Yes.

She hurried to her armoire, digging through the gowns that hung there. And suddenly she didn't want to bring her half-mourning gowns with her. She wanted color, hope, joy again. Once more she searched out that chest hidden within the depths, the same one that she had pulled the pink ribbon from. Only this time she didn't limit her search to the top layer. Instead she removed the fan and dance card and myriad mementos of her life before, and lifted out the tissue-wrapped parcels in its depths.

With shaking hands she unwrapped them. Her breath

stalled in her chest as the gauziest greens and palest pinks and softest blues were revealed. The gowns of a girl full of hope.

She set her jaw and shook out the pink muslin. The folds of it lay over her lap, like an old friend. Small white blossoms and twining vines circling the hem, embroidery she had worked into the delicate material with her own hands. She may no longer be that naïve girl. But she was still full of hope, still full of that same stubborn determination. Scrabbling to her feet, she moved to her dressing room. It was time to embrace that side of herself again, to throw caution to the wind and jump into life with both feet.

Some minutes later, with the pink gown hugging her curves a bit tighter than it had before—goodness, she'd have to get some new ones made up—and her bag repacked, Margery turned for the door. But at the last minute she paused. Then, with determined steps, she made her way to her desk. With fingers that shook only slightly, she removed her ring for the last time. No matter what might happen with Daniel, she would never wear it again. Gran and Mr. Kitteridge were right; Aaron would not have wanted this for her. It was time to move on, to live her life.

Placing the ring on the top of the desk, she lifted up Aaron's portrait and gazed down on his beloved face. "I'll always love you, my darling," she whispered, giving it a gentle kiss before placing it back down and turning again for the door.

This time she didn't stop, hurrying down the stairs and through the front hall. She could very well falter in her determination in the four days it would take to reach

London. But damned if this wasn't the most exciting, frightening thing she'd done in years. Her whole future had been opened up before her, a vast, unmapped horizon. Only God knew what she would find at the end of her journey. It could be more heartache, of course. But wasn't that the chance one took for the possibility of happiness? No matter what Aaron's death had brought, she would not have given up her time with him, however short, for anything. And the same was true for a chance at a future with Daniel. She would fight for him, for whatever chance they might have of being together, with everything in her. Stifling a manic giggle as anticipation pounded through her, she reached the front door and threw it open—

And stopped cold.

"Daniel." She caught her breath. What was he doing here? Hope bloomed in her chest; had he come back for her?

But no, her muddled brain told her, men in love didn't look at the object of their affections like that, with such grim determination. Nor, she thought, even more confused as she took in the man at his side, did they bring the woman's late husband's friend along with them.

"Margery," Daniel said then, dragging her attention back to him, "may we have a moment of your time?"

Her heart sank. No, it didn't just sink, it dropped like the heaviest anchor into her stomach. Whatever this was, it was no social call.

Schooling her features into a calm she didn't feel, she dropped her bag beside the front door and stepped back. "Of course," she murmured through numb lips. And as they entered and she closed the door behind them, the echoing sound of it held the finality of a death knell.

Chapter 24

Margery, her legs trembling beneath her, led the men to the drawing room, where a fire was already burning merrily in the hearth. As they settled themselves, she creased the delicate folds of her gown with nervous fingers, casting anxious glances between the two. Mr. Newton had seated himself as far as possible from Daniel, and appeared positively green, as if he would cast up his accounts then and there.

Daniel, on the other hand, looked like an avenging angel. His features were stark, his scars standing out in sharp relief, a muscle ticking in his jaw. What, she wondered wildly, was going on?

But still they sat there, not speaking. Finally, unable to stand it a moment longer, she burst out, "What are you two gentlemen doing here?"

She'd meant it to sound easy and unconcerned, as if this were a mere social visit. Trying to hold on to the niceties as long as possible, a kind of lifeline for her.

Instead it came out in a jumble of words, rushing over one another in their attempt to break free.

Daniel cleared his throat, casting a dark glance at the other man. "Newton has something he needs to tell you."

Margery blinked. Which should not have surprised her, she supposed. Why else would the man be here, after all?

And yet it shocked her just the same. What in the world would Mr. Newton have to say to her that had him so terrified, that had Daniel so furious? A wild, horrible idea flitted on the outskirts of her mind, but she hastily pushed it away before it could find purchase. Schooling her features as best she could, she looked at the man. "What was it you needed to tell me, Mr. Newton?"

If anything, Newton's face turned greener. He looked to Daniel with wild, pleading eyes.

Daniel's expression turned furious, and what seemed to be a threat appeared in the stormy depths of his eyes. But still the other man sat in mute fear.

Letting out a low curse that made Mr. Newton flinch, Daniel finally turned to face her. And the breath was sucked from her body at the raw emotions in his steady gaze.

In the next moment he said the very last thing she expected.

"Your husband was not a deserter."

She actually felt the blood leave her face. "Wh-what?"

"Aaron did not desert his battalion."

Still, she could not comprehend what he had said. How had he known about Aaron's desertion? She had never told him. A high-pitched whining sounded in her ears, her vision turning black at the edges. She did not realize she had begun to list to the side, however, until Daniel's hand was there on her arm, steadying her.

Jolted back to her senses, she was shocked to see him kneeling before her. In the back of her mind came the realization that he must have lurched forward to get to her, that his leg must be in horrible pain from the swiftness of his actions; the proof of it was there in the tightness at the corners of his eyes, in his pallor.

And yet, though she ached to comfort him, his words from seconds ago came back to her, quickly drowning out every other thought.

"Aaron wasn't a deserter?"

Her voice was a mere agonized rasp, hope rising up in her. His eyes gentled, his hand rubbing her arm.

"No," he murmured.

But another memory surfaced, of him telling her of Aaron's death, before either of them had known the identity of that doomed boy. "But—" She stopped, nearly gasping from the pain of the recollection, before taking herself firmly in hand and forging on. "You said he was running away from the battle. You witnessed it."

He looked as if he was in physical pain, a pain that had nothing to do with his leg. "I was mistaken. And I'm so sorry for making you think it was true."

She swallowed hard, closing her eyes tight. "But you're not the only one. There is another who claims it's true as well."

"The blackmailer."

She blanched, an instinctual fear ripping through her as her eyes flew open to meet his. "You know about the blackmailer?"

"I do," he said, his voice low and tight with fury though his eyes were gentle on her. "Moreover, I know who the blackmailer is."

And then he looked to Newton.

"Oh, God." The man moaned.

"You're a bit late for those prayers, man," Daniel growled.

Margery looked back and forth between the two of them, that same horrible idea from before rising up again. "I don't understand," she managed through stiff lips. Though deep inside she feared she did.

"Tell her," Daniel snarled when the man looked at him with pleading in his eyes.

"Mr. Newton?" His name came from her in an agonized whisper, practically begging him to denounce what Daniel was implying. The man could not be the blackmailer.

"I'm sorry," he said, tears springing to his eyes as he stared at her in misery. "I'm so sorry, Mrs. Kitteridge."

"It was *you*?" She shook her head, her whole being shying away from the truth of it. "You blackmailed me? You made me believe Aaron deserted his battalion?"

"I'm sorry," the man repeated hoarsely.

Understanding was finally beginning to dawn on her. No, not to dawn, for dawn implied hope and renewal. This was a falling, like the darkest night. "But you were his friend." Fury boiled up in her. She lurched to her feet, her hands balling to fists at her sides. "You were his friend, and you would tell such despicable lies about him? Lies that I refused to believe but that started to poison my mind—" A sob cut off the rest of her words. She pressed a fist to her lips, tasting the metallic tinge of blood as her teeth cut into the tender skin of her mouth.

Suddenly Daniel was beside her, his deep voice in her ear. "Margery?"

His comforting presence rallied her. She looked at him, and drawing in a shaking breath, she nodded firmly. "I'm fine, Daniel."

Mr. Newton, however, seemed to think that was the end of it. He rose, began inching for the door. "I'm glad that's behind us," he babbled, as if the faster he talked, the quicker he moved, the better chance he had for escape.

Which only angered Margery the more. "We're not even close to putting this behind us," she raged, the fury behind her words sending Mr. Newton back to his seat. She glared down at him, disgust for this man who had claimed to be Aaron's friend nearly choking her. "You defiled his memory, and for what? Money?"

"You don't understand," Newton said, his voice a pitiful whine. "My debts—"

"I don't care," she snapped. "I don't care why you did it. Nothing you can say will ever be reason enough for doing what you did. Had you come to me in need of funds I would have found a way to get them to you, and gladly. You were a friend to my husband; he valued you. I would have done anything in my power to assist you."

Mr. Newton turned as white as a sheet. "Surely not now."

"Of course, not now," she bit out. "You blackmailed me, Mr. Newton. And for an abhorrent untruth."

"Yes." Then he did the thing Margery least expected. He looked at Daniel, agony clear in his gaze. "And for my part in Aaron's death, which His Grace will surely tell you. He was witness to it, after all."

* * *

Daniel froze, his insides turning to ice. Such a reaction was surely ridiculous; the man must be referring solely to his own desertion, which Aaron had been attempting to prevent, thus leading to his being shot by Daniel.

But he sensed there was more, much more, behind the man's words.

Margery wrapped her arms about herself, her expression stricken. She didn't once look Daniel's way, and he ached to look in her eyes to see her reaction to Newton's words. But she kept her gaze fixed to Newton and said, her voice a mere breath of sound, "I would hear it from your own lips. Explain yourself."

Newton cast Daniel another glance, as if pleading with him to step in. His every nerve suddenly alive, Daniel merely indicated with a raised brow that he should continue. He would not have been able to speak if his life depended on it just then.

The man, seeing he was not going to get an ounce of assistance, dropped his head in his hands. "You have to understand," he cried into his lap. "I was so frightened. There was so much noise, so much blood. I didn't want to die—" He bit his lip as a sob bubbled up.

Margery seemed to sense something life-altering was coming as well. She stumbled back to her seat and dropped heavily onto the cushion, her fingers gripped like claws about the arm of the sofa, her gaze frozen on Newton in fatalistic horror.

Finally, when Daniel thought he'd scream with the waiting, Newton spoke again. "I was just one soldier. I certainly wouldn't affect the outcome. Surely I could slip away, hide until the battle was done. Only Aaron saw me, tried to stop me—" Another sob, this one seeming to have been dredged up from the depths of his soul. "The French soldier came out of nowhere. He shot Aaron in the chest, right in front of my eyes. And I ran. I didn't stop to help him. I ran..."

Daniel felt as if he were floating up out of his body. And suddenly he was there in that field once more. Only now it was all in slow motion: Newton pushing past him, sending him sprawling into the mud and water; Daniel lifting the musket out from beneath him; sighting down the barrel, pulling the trigger. And Aaron, stumbling in front of him. No flash of flint. He'd thought it had been a misfire. But the smoke was in his eyes. And when it had cleared, Aaron again, his hand at his chest. But had he already been shot? Had his hand already been at his chest? Had he been stumbling after his friend for help?

A wild hope flared to life. Was Daniel innocent in the man's death after all?

As he looked at Margery, however, he knew that his own guilt or lack thereof was the least of his concerns. She looked as if she might faint.

He hurried to her side, sank down next to her once more. His thigh screamed in pain again, but as before he didn't give a damn. His entire focus was on Margery and her well-being. Her hand was like ice when he gripped it between his own. "Margery?"

"I'm well," she managed, the weakness in her voice

belying her words. But her eyes when they met his were brimming with emotion.

Before he could comprehend her expression, however, she straightened away from him and turned to look at Newton. The man was still hunched over, his hands now tangled in his hair.

"Your cowardice led to Aaron's death," she said, her voice flat. "And then you abandoned him."

"I did." He moaned. "God help me, I did."

He peered up at Margery then, as miserable as any person Daniel had ever seen. Despite the pain and heartache this man had caused, Daniel felt sorry for him. To live with such a thing for so long could tear a person up inside. He knew firsthand. And though Newton hadn't pulled the trigger that had caused Aaron's death, his actions had caused it just the same.

"Will you tell the authorities what I've done?" Newton asked Margery then, his voice pitifully small. "About my desertion? About the blackmail?"

Margery was silent so long Daniel thought she might not answer. Then, her voice a mere whisper, "I should. *I want* to see you pay for what you did to Aaron, for the torment you've caused me."

She turned to look at Daniel then, and her eyes were brimming again with emotion. This time, however, he could see that, mingled with the grief, was something that gave him hope like never before.

"But no, I won't," she continued, the strength returning to her voice as she looked again at Newton. "Despite the devastation you've caused, Aaron wouldn't want it. He would instead want you to get help. He was a good man, my husband. And much better than you ever deserved as a friend. I'll see you get the help you require to get back on your feet, in his honor. But after that, I don't ever want your face darkening my door again."

The man broke down in sobs. After much groveling and thanks he left. Leaving Daniel and Margery alone.

He watched her closely, desperate to give her what she needed, but not knowing what that might be. Her profile was unchanging, her gaze steady on the open door of the sitting room. She seemed utterly unaware that he was even beside her.

Mayhap she needed time alone. It could not be easy for her, learning the truth, finding out that a man who had claimed to be her husband's friend had not only kept the truth of his death from her all these years, but had also blackmailed her with horrible lies about her husband. And so, though his heart ached to stay beside her, he reached for his cane where it lay on the ground and struggled to standing.

Before he reached the sitting room door, however, she spoke.

"You didn't kill Aaron."

Her voice was stark and raw in the quiet of the room. He stopped, facing the door. "It appears not," he managed.

Once more that loud quiet, going on so long he thought he might split apart from needing to know what was going through her head. And then, "You were there for him when he was dying. You held him, comforted him. He wasn't alone because of you—"

Her voice broke off, an agonizing sound. Without a word he closed the door and turned to hurry back to her side. But she was already on her feet and rushing to him. Her arms came about him, her face pressing into his chest.

"You were there for him," she repeated. "He wasn't alone."

He guided her to the sofa and sank down onto it with her, his arms still about her, his hands rubbing over her back. "I'm sorry, sweetheart," he murmured into her hair. "I'm so sorry."

He knew her tears would come, and that they would be terrible, that they would rip him in two. He did not expect, however, the violence of them. They wracked her body, the sobs raw and painful to listen to, the agony and grief of weeks' worth of fear bursting from her. The fire in the hearth receded, the room falling into gloom, and still she cried. And through it all he held her.

Finally, after what felt like hours, her tears subsided and she fell into an exhausted silence. The only indication that she had not fallen asleep were her fingers, gently rubbing over the sleeve of his jacket. He should go now, he knew. He had told her what she needed to know, after all, which was the only reason he had returned to Synne. But he couldn't bear the thought of leaving her just then. He would see her to her bed, he promised himself. He would see her safe. And then he would leave her for good.

"Come along then," he murmured, gently extricating himself from her embrace and helping her to her feet, securing an arm about her shoulders lest she fall. What he wouldn't give, he thought, to sweep her in his arms and carry her up the stairs. But the bitterness didn't come as it typically did. Instead a soft sadness took its place. The truth was, no matter what he was or was not physically capable of, if he could be by Margery's side he would be happy.

She followed along quietly as he led her through the house, not making a sound when he stopped to ask a footman to inform Lady Tesh that her granddaughter was safe and was not to be disturbed. Her head listed on his shoulder, and once or twice he feared they might topple over—he was not the most balanced fellow, after all.

But they finally made it to her rooms. He guided her to the bed, assisted her in removing her clothes— how was he just noticing the pink dress, and what did it mean?—with infinite care and gentleness until she wore nothing but her chemise. She remained still and silent through his ministrations, not saying a word as he pulled the pins from her hair, one by one, letting the curling locks, thick and silky against his fingers, fall loose down her back. Too soon—he could have played ladies' maid to her forever—he guided her back against the pillows and tucked a blanket about her. He took one last moment to gaze down at her. Her eyes were closed, her lashes thick and curling against the paleness of her cheeks. He hoped—prayed—that he had given her a modicum of peace.

As he turned to go, however, her voice, small and frail, called to him from the shadows.

"Stay with me."

He dragged in a ragged breath. "You need your rest."

"I need you."

The same ragged breath left him in a burst. Surely she was delirious and fragile, and simply didn't want to be alone. She would have asked it of any of her family as well if they had brought her to her bed in such a state.

Why, then, did his heart leap with joy?

Even so, though everything in him cried out to remain, he might have been able to refuse her. Had she not spoken one devastating word.

"Please."

As if drawn to her on a string he closed the door and went to her. In silence he sat on the bed, removed his jacket, managed to pull off his boots. And then he was stretched out beside her. She came to him immediately, curling against his side, warm and soft and her body fitting against his with an aching perfection. As if she belonged there.

And as he held her close and listened as her body grew relaxed and her breathing slowed in sleep, he thought for one mad moment that maybe, just maybe, she did.

Chapter 25

*T*he room was dark as pitch when Margery woke. And yet there was not a single moment of confusion. She knew exactly where she was. And who she was with.

She smiled, tightening her arm about Daniel's middle. His breathing had the deep and even cadence of sleep, his heart beating strong under her ear. He smelled of soap and fresh air and warm man. It was exactly where she wanted to be.

She lay like that for a time, listening to his breath as it joined in chorus with the faint sound of the waves outside her window, feeling the heavy weight of his arm about her shoulder as he held her to him even in sleep. The events of the previous day played over in her mind. What gifts she had been given. To be free of the black-mailer, to learn that Daniel had not had a part in Aaron's death, to know that Aaron had not been alone when he'd died, were all like balms to her soul. And now Daniel was back in her arms. And she'd be damned if she would let him go again.

She felt it the moment he awoke. His breathing changed, his body stirring against hers, his hair scraping the pillow. And then his utter stillness as he realized where he was. She tightened her arm about him, not about to let him pull away.

"Margery?"

His voice was deep and rough with sleep. And so dear it brought tears to her eyes.

"Yes, Daniel?"

"You—are you well?"

She smiled into his chest. Sweet man, to think of her before he had full command of his faculties. "Better than well," she murmured.

"I didn't mean to fall asleep," he mumbled. She could hear the fight in his voice to wake fully. And then a sigh. "I should leave."

"I wish you wouldn't."

His body shuddered beneath hers, as if her words brought him actual pain. "You're making this harder than it has to be."

She smiled into his chest. He had yet to remove his arm from around her. If anything, his grip had unconsciously tightened. He didn't want to part, either. Though, stubborn man that he was, he wouldn't admit it.

She had wondered all those weeks ago who might heal his heart. But the answer had been there in front of her all along: *she* would.

"On the contrary," she answered him. "I am about to make this extremely simple." She rolled from him and rose from the bed, then moved about the room lighting lamps. At one point he made to get up and she gave him a warning look.

"Don't move from that bed," she said.

He could have easily left, regardless of her command. Despite his leg, he was still incredibly strong, and there would be nothing she could have done to stop him had he truly wanted to go.

Instead he obediently settled back against the pillows. She smiled and continued, not stopping until the room was as bright as day. She was through with him hiding away in the shadows.

Finally she turned back to him. He was watching her silently, still settled against the pillows, an air of uncertainty and sadness wrapped about him like a cloak. Well, she was about to do her damnedest to take as much of that sadness and uncertainty away as she could.

"I don't want you to go to London."

He blinked. "I assure you, I don't, either. But I do think it's for the best."

"Best for whom?"

That seemed to trip him up. His brow furrowed. She smiled and returned to the bed, sliding across the mattress until they were close enough to touch. Which she did. Her fingers trailed along his damaged cheek, feather light, tracing his scars. He sucked in his breath and grabbed her hand, trapping it in place. In his eyes were confusion and longing and fear. She smiled, tears burning her eyes.

"I can understand you wanting to leave when you thought you might have had a part in Aaron's death. But you can have no reason now. Especially as I believe I have finally found the perfect woman for you to take as a wife."

His frown deepened. "You needn't make certain our

deal is completed. It was foolish to go into it, considering our—attraction to one another."

"Oh, I don't know," she replied. "I think it was the most brilliant thing I've ever done. It made me face something important."

She waited, to see if he would take the bait. He very nearly didn't. She could see in his eyes that he was fighting his curiosity with everything in him. But eventually—finally—curiosity won out.

"And what was that?"

Her smile grew. "That I needn't spend my life alone any longer. That it's not dishonoring Aaron to move on. That I can love again."

She should probably be nervous just then. She was all but admitting she loved him. He might not reciprocate her feelings. He might reject her. Hadn't he told her that he didn't want to enter into a marriage with someone he could love? His whole purpose in hiring her, after all, was to find a wife who did not want to share with him any of the softer emotions.

But in that moment, with her heart so full she thought it would burst out of her chest, as she watched the spark of something almost like hope ignite in his eyes, she felt only joy and a certainty that what she was doing was right.

Her hand was still trapped against his scarred cheek. She brought her other up to cradle his face. "I love you, Daniel," she said.

He swallowed hard, his eyes gazing into hers, the fear in them nearly extinguishing the joy. "You needn't say that, you know," he said gruffly, even as his hands came behind her back to draw her closer. "I know you must be emotional over learning the truth of Waterloo, must be feeling relief, gratitude even—"

"You silly, stubborn, wonderful man," she said, rubbing her thumb over his cheek. He shuddered under her touch.

"While those particular events have given me the greatest relief and happiness," she continued gently, "my love for you didn't spring from that moment. Rather, it has been building, steadily and surely, over the past weeks. And if you are still in doubt," she said, smiling, "you may return to the front hall. Beside the door should still be the bag I had packed for the express purpose of hying off to London after you. Which I would have done had you not stopped me in my mad dash to secure a carriage."

His jaw dropped. "You were coming after me?"

"Of course." She leaned forward, brushing her lips against his own. "I could not have you marrying another, after all."

Still, he gaped at her. "You wish to marry me?"

"I do." When he continued to stare at her in incomprehension, she brushed an unruly lock of hair back from his forehead and smiled tenderly. "I know you've been hurt, Daniel. I know your trust has been damaged, and that you had no wish to marry a person who you might be able to care for. But I swear to you, I won't hurt you. I love you." And then, her heart in her throat: "Marry me."

* * *

Daniel wanted to say yes. With everything in him he wanted to say yes. Margery loved him? Never in his dreams had he dared to hope that a woman such as she could love him.

And he loved her, so much it hurt.

Why, then, did he pause? Because Erica had broken his heart? Because a woman had looked in horror at his leg? Because his despicable cousin had made him feel unlovable for so many years? And in an instant he saw it so clearly: he was an absolute idiot.

Margery was his whole heart. And he would be a fool to not grab tight at the chance of a life with her.

The breath left him in a rush and he gazed into her eyes, not caring that his heart was in his own. "I love you."

Joy filled her beloved features, and he found himself grinning, though tears sprang to his eyes. He turned his head and kissed her palm. "God, I love you," he murmured. "So very much."

"Daniel," she said, his name exploding from her, suffused with the very essence of her heart.

"I love your smile and your laugh," he continued, the words tumbling from him now that they'd been loosened. "I love your kindness and your strength, your stubbornness and your fierceness." He shook his head in amazement as his gaze scoured her face. "I don't deserve you."

"You deserve every happiness in life, Daniel," she said, certainty imbuing her voice with a brilliance that touched his very soul. Then, her tone dropping to a mere whisper, "Do I—could I—make you happy, Daniel?"

"God, yes." He groaned, pulling her to him. He claimed her lips with his, imbuing his kiss with every bit of love he had for her. She gasped into his mouth, her arms going around his neck, her body pressed to his. He ached to lose himself in her.

But there was still one small bit of him that held on to fear.

He pulled away, just enough to leave a hairbreadth of space between their lips. "Margery, you still haven't seen—you might not wish to after—"

She placed a finger over his lips, a soft smile lighting her eyes. "Why don't you let me prove to you that your worries are for nothing," she murmured. Her fingers trailed down to his cravat, loosened it. She pulled the silk free, worked at his waistcoat, pushing it off his shoulders, made short work of the buttons on his shirt.

All the while he watched her, the tension in him growing, both desire and fear churning together. Ah, God, he loved her so damn much. But their entire future together could hinge on what she thought of him when she saw his body. He wanted her. But if she turned away from him, it would destroy him.

She pulled his shirt from his breeches. He waited, breath stuck in his chest, for her to pull the material up. Then...

Nothing.

She looked up at him, her heart in her eyes. "Daniel, do you want me to stop?"

Did he? Could he stand making love to her for the rest of his life in the dark? Never seeing the glory of her body, the look of passion in her eyes when she came undone in his arms?

Could he live the rest of his life having her think that he didn't trust her fully? Because he knew in that moment he did. He trusted her with everything in him.

She watched him, her teeth worrying her delicious

full bottom lip, ready to stop then and there if he wished it. In answer, he rolled from the bed, stood on unsteady legs, reached for the bottom of his shirt, and pulled it up and over his head. And then, before he could think better of it, he unfastened his breeches and, taking a deep breath, pushed them down his legs, his smalls quickly following, and kicked them off.

In for a penny, he thought a bit madly.

"Oh." The word escaped her on a breath, and he flinched. His mind, prepared for flight, screamed at him to turn around, to cover himself. But his heart, full of love for her and the hope that she could love him as he was, kept him in place. He raised his chin and looked at her.

And his legs nearly gave out at the love and desire illuminating her face.

"Daniel," she whispered, her eyes roving his body with hunger. Stunned, he could only watch mutely as she moved across the bed and stood before him. The one sane bit of his brain still working told him he should be feeling shame, should be feeling horribly vulnerable and exposed. He was naked, after all, with every flaw laid out for her to see. He had never wanted to be put in this position ever again, to be in someone else's hands, to invite rejection and disgust.

But as Margery looked up at him, her eyes clear and full of love, a small smile curving her lips, he could only feel an overwhelming trust in her.

She licked her lips as her gaze returned to his body. "Can I touch you?" Her voice was achingly gentle.

"God, yes," he managed.

Drawing in a shaky breath, she reached for him.

Her fingers trailed over his chest, tracing each scar with reverence, down over his abdomen, to his leg.

She paused again, looked up at him with a question in her eyes. But his fear was gone. Taking her hand, he guided it to his scar.

Her fingers were light, just barely tracing the mangled flesh. "Does this hurt you?"

"No," he managed, his breath hitching in his chest.

Then, to his shock, she dropped to her knees before him—and pressed her lips to his scar.

"Margery." Tears clogged his throat, burned his eyes. He pulled her to her feet, wrapped his arms about her, pressed his face into her neck.

"I love you," she whispered, her hands trailing over his bare back. "I love you."

And then her mouth was under his.

He didn't know who began the kiss. It didn't matter. What mattered was the glowing in his heart that had burned away the last remaining bit of distrust and fear and anger. What mattered was this woman in his arms, who was the most important thing in this world to him.

His fingers fumbled on her chemise, dragging it up and over her head. He longed to lose himself in her. He *ached*, with everything in him, to join with her.

But he wouldn't. Not yet, not until he'd seen his fill of her.

Which, he realized as he stepped back from her, he might never do.

She was glorious. He swallowed hard as his gaze skimmed down her body. Every inch of her was soft and luscious: full breasts, a rounded stomach, the flare of wide hips.

"God, you're beautiful," he rasped. "The most beautiful thing I've ever seen in my life."

And he would burst into flames if he didn't hold her in his arms that very second.

She seemed to be of the same mind. Stepping back into his arms, her hands were everywhere at once, roaming over his body with a desperation that he felt was mirrored deep in his soul. Their kisses were frantic now, and they fell back on the bed in an inelegant heap, arms and legs tangled.

"I love you," he murmured as his lips trailed down, over her breasts, needing to say it, needing her to understand how deeply he felt it.

"I love you," he repeated as he kissed down over the glorious, trembling fullness of her belly.

"I love you," he whispered as his mouth found the thatch of curls between her legs.

She gasped, her hands finding his hair as he loved her there. She tasted of the sweetest drink, the most heady wine. He drank of her until she was writhing beneath him, until her cries filled the air and her thighs trembled on either side of his face. Only then did he rise above her and slide with a groan into her welcoming heat.

There was no need for words. Every kiss, every caress was full of their love for one another. Their breaths mingled, their sighs becoming one. And when they found their completion, they found it together.

* * *

"I never did answer your question."

Daniel's voice, thick with sleep, pulled Margery from

the call of slumber. She smiled, snuggling farther into his embrace, breathing in the warmth of him. "Mmm, and what question would that be?"

"Never tell me, madam," he said in mock outrage, "that you have forgotten your proposal of marriage."

"Oh, did I propose?" she queried innocently. "Must have slipped my mind."

"Minx," he growled, shifting them so she lay on top of him.

She giggled, then moaned as he pulled her down for a kiss.

"Haven't changed your mind, I hope," he murmured against her lips.

She very nearly laughed and considered teasingly asking him to persuade her a bit more. But she was through with waiting to start her life with this man. "No." She breathed deeply, brushing his mouth with hers, trailing her lips over to his cheek, raining soft kisses over his scar with each sentence she spoke. "I haven't changed my mind. If anything, I want you more. I want to bear your children and grow old with you. I want to spend the rest of my days making you happy. I love you, Daniel."

He shuddered under her touch. Then, groaning, he dove his hands into her unbound hair and brought her lips back to his for a soul-shattering kiss. "You're my life, Margery."

The emotion in his voice had tears springing to her eyes. How was it possible to be so blessed? "Is that a yes then?" she asked, her voice husky.

"Yes." The word exploded from him on a joyous breath. The first of many more, with her at his side.

Epilogue

The wedding was supposed to have been a small affair. Margery had declared to Daniel that, since it was her second marriage, it seemed silly to have a large, ostentatious event. And besides, she only wanted to marry him as quickly as possible and start their life together.

Lady Tesh, however, had refused any such thing. Her beloved granddaughter had eloped the first time around; she'd be damned if she'd do the same this time, especially when marrying a duke. She'd insisted on the banns being posted, on invitations being sent out, on having everyone who was anyone there for the blessed event, managing it in an impressively short amount of time.

And they had come, in droves.

Daniel looked out over Danesford's wide back lawn in trepidation. He'd been glad for the woman's interference. At first. He'd not wanted some shabby, hastily-put-together affair for Margery. She deserved everything and more.

Now, however...

He took a deep draught of his champagne. The stuff had been flowing like water since the ceremony several hours before, and he'd taken advantage of that fact. Already his brain was properly fuzzy. Unfortunately, his slightly inebriated state had done nothing to decrease his unease. No, it was surely more than mere unease. After all, it appeared as if all of London had made the trek to Synne for the wedding. Ironic, that, he thought with a wry smile, as he had fought so blasted hard to stay away from that illustrious city; now his marriage to Margery had brought that city to him. The guests, nearly all of them unknown to him, dressed in all their elegant finery, congregated in an undulating mass across the smooth green expanse of lawn now, talking and laughing and making merry. One group in particular caught his eye: Lord and Lady Tesh stood conversing in an animated fashion with Mr. Kitteridge and his family. Margery was in the midst of them, one arm tucked in her father's, her face glowing with happiness as he laughed at something she said.

She stood out like a beacon to him, a veritable ray of sunshine. But it wasn't owing to her pale-yellow gown, nor the mass of white rosebuds that festooned the thick, loose mane of her hair. No, it was her, and her alone. The essence of her. He let loose a sigh of happiness as he watched her. How was it possible that such a glorious creature could be his?

As if she heard him, she turned, her gaze finding his. She smiled, in her eyes all the love she had for him, and the promise of their future.

His unease was gone in a moment. Placing his glass

down on a stone balustrade, he grabbed up his cane and started off toward her.

Just then, however, two heavy hands landed on his shoulders. Startled, he stopped and glanced back into the faces of the Dukes of Dane and Reigate—ah, no, he reminded himself. They had asked to be called Peter and Quincy. Though, he thought with some trepidation as he saw their stern expressions, perhaps their friendly overtures toward the newest member of their family were at an end.

"Walk with us, won't you?" Quincy smiled, which should have put Daniel at ease. Instead his bared teeth, an expression that could only be called *predatory*, made alarm bells peal in Daniel's head.

But he couldn't very well refuse them. These men were family now, after all. Besides that, they were incredibly dear to Margery. And so, sighing, he allowed himself to be guided down the steps and into the side garden.

Immediately the sounds of merriment and revelry faded, the thick foliage dulling it to a muted rumble. Most of the guests were gathered across the rolling back lawn, beneath billowing white tents, surrounded by elegant tables topped with all manner of silver and fine china and delicious delicacies. But here, along the meandering path that butted up to the house, there was not a soul to be seen.

Which perhaps should have given him warning that this was not going to be the most pleasant conversation. Yet he was still wholly surprised when the two men turned down a side path and guided him to a small fountain...which was conveniently positioned behind a hedge, making it almost frighteningly private.

Daniel eyed them with trepidation. The two men were beasts, each as tall as Daniel was. One light and rough, the other dark and debonair, they were, quite literally, as different as night and day. Yet both wore identical expressions of furious judgment. Like two avenging angels about to wreak havoc.

Daniel cleared his throat, feeling instinctively—for reasons unknown—they wished to intimidate him but refusing to be cowed. "Is there something I can help you gentlemen with?"

"I don't know," Quincy drawled, his nearly black eyes scanning Daniel from head to shoe. "What do you think, Peter? Is there something he can help us with?"

"Oh, I've no doubt there is," Peter said, the sound of it more a low rumble of thunder than the voice of a man. He crossed his massive arms over his chest; the muscles strained against the fine material, bunching with a threatening flex, even as he widened his stance. Like a sailor on board a ship. Or a pugilist ready to throw a punch. From the deadly look in his eye, Daniel rather thought it was the latter.

"But perhaps he doesn't understand just how precious this person is that he's taking from us," the blond Viking of a duke continued.

"Hmmm, mayhap you're right," Quincy said. "I suppose there's only one thing to do." He grinned with wicked intent, his gaze never leaving Daniel. "We must make him understand, fully and completely, just how important she is to us. And that we will see he pays should he cause even a single tear of sadness to fall from her eyes."

"But how to do that?" Peter continued. Stepping closer

to Daniel, his cool blue eyes narrowed dangerously, a muscle ticking in his jaw beneath his closely trimmed golden beard. "How do we make him understand that Margery's happiness is paramount to our own. She is my dear cousin, after all, and Lenora's best friend in the world."

"Not to mention my Clara's cousin. As well as my own close friend. Why, I do believe, Peter, that Margery is one of the most important people in the world to us," he said, his voice dipping to a deep rumble as he stepped closer as well. They boxed Daniel in on both sides so that escape could only be had by falling back in the fountain—something Daniel was not opposed to doing in that unnerving moment. The cold stone Poseidon at its center looked a sight more welcoming than the two men standing before him, after all.

"I do hope Margery's husband, lucky bastard that he is, understands just how important she is to us," Peter replied, talking about Daniel as if he were not even present, though his gaze had not wavered. "And that we would do anything to make certain she does not have a day of unhappiness as his wife."

The men fell silent then, glaring at Daniel. And Daniel, quickly taking stock of the situation, realized this could go one of several ways. He could lash out in anger, which could let the men know he was not to be underestimated; though in doing so he could possibly drive a permanent wedge between him and them. He could stammer and quake in the wake of their combined fury, cementing the idea that he was weak and could be easily manipulated. He could laugh it off and leave them to stew in their outrage. Or…

Or, he thought with a smile, he could let them know just how much Margery meant to him.

He looked them full in the face, one after the other, and said, his voice deep and calm and certain, "I love Margery with everything in me. She is my entire world. I promise, here and now, that for whatever time we're blessed with, for however long I have with her, whether it's a single day or a hundred years, I will never stop working to make her happy. I will do everything in my power to show her, in word and deed, how much I adore her."

For a moment there was silence, the two men staring hard at him. Daniel merely raised his chin, his gaze unwavering, the certainty in his love for Margery, and hers for him, making his heart feel as if it were fairly glowing from within him.

Then, in the blink of an eye, the dukes relaxed, grins breaking over their faces.

"Splendid," Quincy said, holding out a hand and shaking Daniel's heartily. "Glad to hear it."

"You understand," Peter said, clapping him on the shoulder in a friendly manner, "we had to make sure you knew that Margery is protected. She's very dear to us."

"Of course," Daniel murmured. "And I'm glad to know that she has such fierce protectors should I ever fail. Which, I can assure you, I won't," he finished, with just enough steel in his voice to let the men know his place at Margery's side was not to be trifled with.

"Oh, he'll do," Quincy murmured with a grin for his friend.

"Very well, indeed," Peter agreed, satisfaction fairly oozing from him.

The words were so reminiscent of those that Lady Tesh had spoken to Daniel's mother when they'd first arrived on Synne that he was momentarily struck mute. An idea formed, mad and unbelievable: Was it possible the two older women had meant for this very thing to happen? Could they have been working toward pairing him with Margery from the very beginning?

Before he could think how to react to such an idea, or to even comprehend such a thing, Margery's voice suddenly rang through the air. "I thought I saw you two great lumbering beasts steal my husband away," she said with mock sternness. "And just what do you think you're about?"

Daniel's heart leapt at the sound of her voice. He looked over the dukes' shoulders and spied her approaching them, the delicate folds of her pale-yellow gown dancing with each sway of her hips, the curling tendrils of her hair bouncing about her shoulders. She gazed with wry affection on the two massive dukes before looking to him. And the transformation in her was total, her gaze softening, her love for him clear in the gentle brown of her eyes.

"Margery." He caught his breath, quite unable to help it after her name escaped his lips like a benediction.

"Oh, he has it bad," Peter murmured as Margery brushed them aside as if they were mere insects and made her way to Daniel's side, intertwining her fingers with his.

"Bad, indeed," Quincy agreed. Suddenly his tone turned sly and he grinned that wicked grin of his, a harbinger of mischief. "Almost as bad as you had it for Lenora," he quipped.

"I'll have you know," Peter said in loud, officious tones, staring his friend down, "that I still have it bad for Lenora. Just as you have it bad for Clara, you arse."

"I do," Quincy agreed readily, almost proudly. "And speaking of my wife, when last I checked, our little Frederick was happily sleeping in the nursery. I've a notion to seek my wife out and let her know just how *badly* I have it for her."

"That's my cousin you're talking about," Peter growled as together they turned and meandered away.

"Who I have made *very* happy," Quincy drawled.

"Arse," Peter said again, though with little heat.

"It takes one..." Quincy shot back, his voice fading as they walked out of view.

Daniel and Margery stared after them for a bit, before, glancing at each other, they burst into laughter.

"I would ask you if they're always like that," he said as he pulled her into his arms. "But I've seen plenty of proof that they are."

Margery, laughing, twined her arms about Daniel's neck. Her eyes dropped to his mouth. Before Daniel could oblige her in a kiss, however—something he was more than willing to do—another voice sounded. This time, however, it wasn't necessarily a welcome one. At least, not in the present situation, when all he wanted to do was to lose himself in his wife's welcoming arms.

"Katrina, rein in that beast of yours before I do."

Lady Tesh's voice rampaged through Daniel's blissful moment of peace with his bride like the proverbial bull elephant. And then it was as if a real bull elephant came tearing around the corner of the hedge. Mouse galloped into view, then just as quickly stumbled to a stunned halt when he spied them. No doubt he'd expected this portion of the garden to be empty. But his surprise was short-lived. Instead a kind of delight took over his canine features as he spied one of his favorite distractions in the form of Daniel and his...nether regions. The beast grinned, an almost humanlike expression, his tongue rolling out like a great pink carpet. And then, with one massive bark of joy, he bounded toward them with flailing legs and flopping ears. A black-and-white devil bearing down on them, intent on wreaking havoc.

Miss Denby, having just rounded the hedge, looked positively horrified. But in that split second, with Margery still cradled in his arms and utter chaos in the form of a very large dog racing full-tilt toward them, Daniel knew with grim certainty that the young lady would not reach them in time to keep disaster from striking— namely in Margery and him taking a very thorough dunking in the fountain just behind them.

Calling upon all of his training, he looked the beast square in the eye and said in a booming voice that brooked no argument, "Mouse, sit."

The dog stopped, mere inches from them, his bottom hitting the path with a thud that reverberated through Daniel's shoes. His tail wagged furiously, swiping with deadly precision every leaf and twig in its path. He gazed in adoration at Daniel.

"Goodness," Miss Denby said, reaching her pet and securing both hands around its collar. "I am so very sorry. He was being such a dear thing, and looked so forlorn when I checked in on him earlier. I thought for certain he wouldn't cause any mischief. I didn't think it would hurt, to let him out for a bit of the festivities. He's usually such a dear, docile thing."

How Daniel didn't laugh outright he didn't know. Margery seemed to be of the same mind. She gazed up at Daniel, mirth dancing in her eyes even as she bit her lip to keep her laughter from spilling over.

Blessedly they were saved from possibly hurting Miss Denby's feelings as Lady Tesh and his mother rounded the corner, Freya prancing regally in front of them.

"Katrina," Margery's grandmother scolded, her tone acidic, "I told you to keep that beast of yours shut up inside. Why I allowed you to bring it to Danesford at all is beyond me."

As the young woman, spouting effusive apologies, dragged her dog away, Daniel's mother turned to the viscountess. "Oh, Olivia," she said, even as she grinned. "Don't be too hard on the girl. She means well."

"If by *means well*, you're referring to her determination to send me off to Bedlam, I absolutely agree," Lady Tesh grumbled.

"Oh, I'm sure you won't have to worry about that for long," Margery murmured, grinning at her grandmother. "You no doubt have another matchmaking scheme brewing. And, going by your level of success, she'll no doubt be happily paired within the year."

"You think it will take me a year?" Lady Tesh asked archly. "I think I've proven I can work much quicker than that, especially when I have the assistance of someone like my dear Helen here."

Daniel gaped at them. "So you *did* intend this trip as a way to match Margery and me?"

Which sent the three women into gales of laughter. Even Freya seemed mildly amused.

"My sweet son," his mother said fondly, shaking her head and grinning.

Lady Tesh, wiping at her eyes, moved forward to kiss them both on the cheeks. "Welcome to the family, m'boy," she murmured to him. Then linking arms with Daniel's mother, the two women—and the dog, of course—made their way back toward the party, laughing merrily.

Daniel stared after them for a moment before looking down at Margery. Her eyes were shining with humor.

He growled playfully, catching her up against him. "Minx. You mean to tell me you knew about their matchmaking? And you never warned me?"

"In my defense," she murmured, twining her arms about his neck, "once I realized what they were about I thought it must be quite obvious. Though I didn't think for a single moment it would work. Mayhap," she continued, her voice turning husky, her gaze dropping to his mouth, "I should suggest they take on the open position of *conjugality coordinator*. I was rubbish at it, after all. As I wound up marrying my one and only client."

"God help the world if your grandmother and my mother decide to take on that particular job," he managed, even as his body went hot all over at the heated look in her eyes. "Though I daresay the world would be a much happier place."

She chuckled, the sound going straight to his heart. "Does that mean that my family has not managed to frighten you away? After showing their true colors this past half hour, I mean?"

He smiled, not caring that his heart was in his eyes.

"Does this answer your question?" he murmured before lowering his head to hers.

"Just as well they didn't frighten you off," she whispered when later—much later—he raised his head again. "For I'm afraid you're quite stuck with me."

"As to that, my duchess," he murmured as he bent his head to hers again, "I can only say, I'm a lucky man, indeed."

Don't miss Lenora
and Peter's story in

A Good Duke Is
Hard to Find,

the first book in the Isle
of Synne series!

About the Author

Christina Britton developed a passion for writing romance novels shortly after buying her first at the tender age of thirteen and spent much of her teenage years scribbling on whatever piece of paper she could find. Though for several years she put brush instead of pen to paper, she has returned to her first love and is now writing full-time. She spends her days dreaming of corsets and cravats and noblemen with tortured souls.

She lives with her husband and two children in the San Francisco Bay Area.

You can learn more at:
ChristinaBritton.com
Twitter @CBrittonAuthor
Facebook.com/ChristinaBrittonAuthor

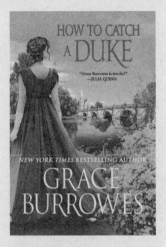
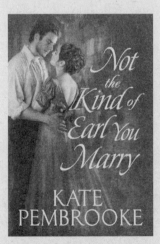

Follow @ReadForeverPub on Twitter and join the conversation using #ReadForever

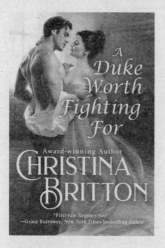

A DUKE WORTH FIGHTING FOR
by Christina Britton

Margery Kitteridge has been mourning her husband for years, and while she's not ready to consider marriage again, she does miss intimacy with a partner. When Daniel asks for help navigating the Isle of Synne's social scene and they accidentally kiss, she realizes he's the perfect person with whom to have an affair. As they begin to confide in each other, Daniel discovers that he's unexpectedly connected to Margery's late husband, and she will have to decide if she can let her old love go for the promise of a new one.

SOMEDAY MY DUKE WILL COME
by Christina Britton

Quincy Nesbitt reluctantly accepted the dukedom after his brother's death, but he'll be damned if he accepts his brother's fiancée as well. The only polite way to decline is to become engaged to someone else—quickly. Lady Clara has the right connections and happens to need him as much as he needs her. But he soon discovers she's also witty and selfless—and if he's not careful, he just might lose his heart.

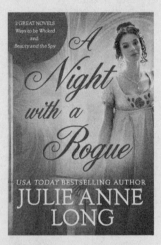
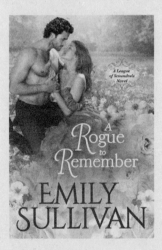

Find more great reads on Instagram with @ReadForeverPub

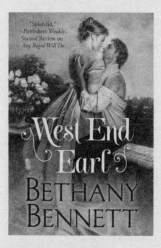

WEST END EARL
by Bethany Bennett

While most young ladies attend balls and hunt for husbands, Ophelia Hardwick has spent the past ten years masquerading as a man. As the land steward for the Earl of Carlyle, she's found safety from the uncle determined to kill her and the freedoms of which a lady could only dream. Ophelia's situation would be perfect—if she wasn't hopelessly attracted to her employer...

HOW TO SURVIVE
A SCANDAL
by Samara Parish

Benedict Asterly never dreamed that saving Lady Amelia's life would lead to him being forced to wed the hoity society miss. He was taught to distrust the aristocracy at a young age, so when news of his marriage endangers a business deal, Benedict is wary of Amelia's offer to help. But his quick-witted, elegant bride defies all his expectations...and if he's not careful, she'll break down the walls around his guarded heart.

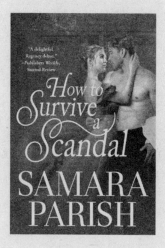